"This refreshing new series by James is a tender excursion into the lives of an uptight billionaire and a company employee. Although not as spicy as her usual fare, James's latest still conveys the depth of emotion and sexual fire between Brady and Lennox. She draws family and their interactions perfectly."
—*RT Book Reviews*

"Fun, sweet, and sexy. Lorelei James captures the angst and anticipation of a slow-burn family-run-office romance with engaging characters . . . a promising start to a new series."
—Harlequin Junkie

"The characters are perfect; the romance is perfect and takes things step by step. Not too rushed, not too slow. . . . This is a series I'll be looking forward to seeing more of soon!"
—Under the Covers

"Lorelei has blown me away with a beautiful romance that is sexy and sweet, and I loved every second of it!"
—Guilty Pleasures Book Reviews

PRAISE FOR THE OTHER NOVELS OF LORELEI JAMES

"Filled with unforgettable characters, fiery passions, and an all-encompassing love story, it's a must read."
—*New York Times* bestselling author Tara Sue Me

continued . . .

Just What I Needed

THE NEED YOU SERIES

LORELEI JAMES

WITHDRAWN

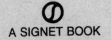

A SIGNET BOOK

SIGNET
Published by New American Library,
an imprint of Penguin Random House LLC
375 Hudson Street, New York, New York 10014

This book is an original publication of New American Library.

First Printing, August 2016

For more information about Penguin Random House, visit penguin.com.

ISBN 9780451477569

Printed in the United States of America
10 9 8 7 6 5 4 3 2 1

Designed by Kelly Lipovich.

Penguin
Random
House

One

TRINITY

"Happy Hour" always perked me up.

I loved the two-for-the-price-of-one drink specials.

I loved the camaraderie in celebrating the end of the workday with other working stiffs.

I even loved hearing the cheesy, but hopeful pickup lines.

Except none of it was making me happy today.

I sat alone in a booth at the back of the bar, nursing my second crappy margarita. Even my friend Genevieve had abandoned me—not that I blamed her. If the hot rugby player from Ireland would've hit on me instead of her, I wouldn't be here still wallowing in my shitshow of a day.

As much as I wanted to forget today, my brain insisted on recapping the events that had led to an unhappy Happy Hour.

First, I lost an art commission: a lucrative deal that would've kept me busy for months and kept me from subsisting on ramen noodles. At the prospective client's insistence,

I'd completed detailed sketches of the piece—a rarity for me since my muse preferred to carve her own path rather than follow someone else's map. Consequently, for that extra effort, I'd expected to collect a check this morning; losing the project hadn't been on my radar since the couple were proven patrons of the arts. But evidently the wife had decided my art design was too edgy.

I scowled at my half-empty glass. *Too edgy, my ass.* The proposed mixed-media wall hanging fit perfectly within the realm of contemporary art. Not that it mattered now; I didn't have the luxury of finishing the piece on principle. I had to swallow my pride and find a paying gig immediately. I'd applied for a set painting job for the production of *Into the Woods* at a local community theater. And unless Eugene Lee—Broadway set designing legend—had applied for the same job, I was pretty much a shoo-in.

If that hadn't been bad enough, I'd been dealt a second blow when my stepmonster, Laura, called to inform me that my younger half sister, Kathryn, had gotten engaged. The knocked-low feeling hadn't come from not being invited to the surprise engagement party, but from the fact that my father had given Grandma Minnie's pearls to Kathryn to wear on her wedding day. As the oldest daughter, those pearls—and the right to wear them first—belonged to me. When I mentioned it, Laura coldly informed me that it wasn't fair to deny Kathryn when it was unlikely I'd ever make the trek down the aisle. After ending the call, I wondered if everyone saw the "unlovable" mark on my soul. Today I felt as if it'd been stamped across my forehead.

Morose much, Trinity?

Hey. I was entitled to a pity party once in a while. Especially when I figured nothing else could make the day any bleaker.

Of course, that's when karma laughed in my face.

I glanced up just as my ex-boyfriend Milo walked into the back room with his new girlfriend clinging to his side like a barnacle.

This chick sported at least a D cup and was polished from her trendy asymmetrical haircut to the tips of her silver stilettos.

My gaze caught on the hemline—if it had more material it might actually qualify as a cocktail dress. But the scant coverage showcased the bombshell's killer body. She could probably crack open walnuts with those muscled quads. But that meant she'd have to close her legs and I doubted that happened very often.

Not nice, Trin.

But I snickered anyway. Since the toothpick and my ex had been caught going at it on a weight bench at the gym where she worked as a personal trainer—while we'd still been dating—she'd brought the snarky comments on herself.

When I'd relayed the breakup story to my friend Ramon, he hadn't offered the sympathy I'd been looking for. Instead, he'd chastised me. "*Chica*, why do you punish yourself by dating loser men like Milo? You're past due for an upgrade."

I'd gone through phases in my dating life. I'd started out with the all-American types—jocks and smart nerds. Then I moved on to bad boys—until I realized unpredictable macho dudes made better boyfriends on paper than in real life. In college I decided only other artists would understand me, so I chose intellectual men who were proud to admit they'd embraced their softer sides. That phase had lasted until I recognized the similarities between myself and a door-mat. How hadn't I noticed the supposed sensitive types were often bigger assholes than the self-centered, self-destructive bad boys?

After learning that lesson, I'd opted to date suits—white-collar nine-to-fivers. Polite guys who picked up the dinner check and drove cars that didn't break down. Men who were invested in their careers and their futures.

That's when my subconscious piped in with . . . *You mean, men like your father?*

With that disconcerting thought planted in my head, I'd done the mature thing and moved on to blue-collar guys—men nothing like good old Dad. Men who worked hard and played harder. Men more interested in literally climbing the ladder rather than just metaphorically. Solid men who didn't wear their hearts on their sleeves or their causes on their T-shirts. They just humped along, year after year, working for the man, living paycheck to paycheck.

Milo, the electrician and my recent ex-boyfriend, had checked all the right boxes. He'd never dated a woman who "made real good money drawing pictures and shit." I guess I'd been lonely enough to find his interest in me refreshing. He'd had some odd ideas about what constituted fun, and physically he was as reserved when we were naked as when we were clothed. So I'd truly been shocked to find out he'd gotten down and dirty in a public area equipped with a se-curity camera. Heck, he'd never even left the lights on the few times we'd had sex.

That thought gave me a complex. Well, another one at any rate.

Although, watching him exhibit over-the-top PDA with the toothpick, I wondered if I'd mistakenly placed my ex-pectations—he's stable so he'll stabilize me—on him when that hadn't ever been any part of who he was. Heaven knew I wasn't the uninhibited artist living a bohemian lifestyle that he'd envisioned. Had he gleaned that impression of me . . . *from* me? Sometimes in social situations my nervousness overtook my common sense and I'd blurt out ridiculous random things . . . and then have zero recollection of what I'd said.

So yeah, men got to deal with "social anxiety blackouts" as a benefit of dating me.

Milo must've sensed me staring at him. I didn't duck fast enough before he saw me.

Please ignore me swilling cheap tequila as I lament the sad state of my life.

He seductively caressed the toothpick's arm and murmured in her ear.

Her blond hair swung in a perfect arc as she turned her head to look at me.

I offered a smile and tiny wave—dismissive enough that I hoped it would keep them away from my little corner of doom.

No such luck. They started toward me.

Dammit. I should've worn Spanx. And combat boots. And boxing gloves.

I kept my smile in place as a string of lies formed in my head about why I was sitting alone in a dark corner.

Milo stopped a solid two feet away from me. "I thought it was you back here."

"You caught me trying to have a quiet moment before my date arrives." And there was a perfect example of random words spewing from my mouth.

"I wouldn't think this was your kind of place," Milo said.

Ooh, *snap*. In retrospect, it was shocking how little we knew each other.

The toothpick chirped out, "Hi. I'm Penelope," as if I didn't know exactly who she was.

Milo looked uncomfortable. "Well, I just wanted to come by and say—"

"Good-bye as you two crazy kids head out the door?" I supplied.

"Oh, we're not leaving yet," Penelope said. "This is our Tuesday tradition. Right, My-love?"

My-love instead of Milo? Eww. Didn't this dim bulb realize it took a while before something became a tradition? But I played along. "Have you had this tradition long?"

When she said, "A little over three months," I felt steam curling from my ears.

It'd been only two months since I'd told Milo's cheating ass we were done.

Before I could ask Milo if his anal rash had cleared up, he was dragging Penelope away.

I scooted out of the booth and snagged my watered-down drink. As I maneuvered through the crowd, it didn't escape my notice that several admiring looks were aimed my way, which buoyed my spirits. I spied an empty table close to the front door. Keeping my back to the room meant I got first dibs on any attractive single guys who walked in.

The bouncy waitress from the back section had followed me up front. "I was hoping you hadn't disappeared since I let you run a tab."

"I'm not wired to drink and dash." I removed a credit card from my wallet and handed it over. "I'll take another margarita."

"You've got it."

When you give off the vibe that you're waiting for someone? Men always pick *that* time to hit on you.

Two guys, at least five years younger than me, approached. The one with the military buzz cut spoke first. "Hey. Weren't you in the back room earlier with a redhead?"

"Yeah. Good memory."

"Is she coming back?"

Ah. I saw where this was headed. Two of us; two of them. "No. She had a date."

"That's a shame she left you alone. But her loss is our gain, huh, Tommy?"

Tommy nodded.

"I'm Vance," Buzz Cut said. "What's your name?"

"Amelia." It just slipped out. In college I'd given an altered name (and fake phone number) to guys I met in a bar that I had no interest in. Seemed that reflex still worked.

"Well, Amelia, do you mind if we join you?"

I gave them a regretful smile. "I'm sorry. My boyfriend is coming when he gets off work. He wouldn't be happy seeing me making new male friends."

"I wouldn't like it either if you were my girl," Vance said. "Seems it's our night to strike out."

"Did you see the ladies playing pool in the back room? A blonde and a brunette?"

"No. Don't know how we missed them." Vance grinned and saluted. "Thanks for the tip, Amelia."

After that I was left alone. As I sipped my drink, I wished I'd remembered to grab my new phone. Then I could kill time and send hate texts to Genevieve for ditching me in my hour of need. But since I hadn't shared the details of my monumentally craptastic day with her, she'd be mad that I'd let her leave in the first place.

Two men walked in. Neither was my type. A trio of guys showed up next and joined the people at a table somewhere behind me. Much back-slapping ensued. Then a couple, surrounded by half a dozen dudes, blocked the entryway as they argued whether to come in and have a drink or just go to another bar.

When the crowd cleared, he stood alone off to the side, his right hand on his hip as he scanned the room.

Good lord. There was no way to miss *him* with that massively tall body. And check out that gorgeous beard; as the light changed it seemed to range from golden blond to a creamy white. He angled his head, giving me a killer view of his strong jawline and high cheekbones. Then I caught a glimpse of his longish blond hair messily fastened at the base of his skull. Oh, hell yeah. That was some serious sexy right there—a guy confident enough to pull off a man bun.

He raised his left hand to his jaw and scratched his cheek. No wedding ring. He wasn't acting as if he was meeting someone; he acted like he was looking for a place to sit.

How fortunate that I had a cozy table for two.

I slid out of my chair and right into his line of vision.

Immediately his focus homed in on me. Interest flared in his eyes.

Then something stronger than awareness flowed through me. An electric charge that gave me a sense of urgency. A magnetic need that pulled me. I floated to him practically in slow motion, my heart racing as I erased the distance between us. I said, "You're finally here." Then I stood on tiptoe, slipped my arms around his neck and pressed my mouth to his.

His warm, woodsy scent hit me like a drug. The softness of his lips and the brush of his beard against my chin had me parting my lips, letting my tongue trace the seam of his mouth.

His hands had been idle at his sides. But the instant our breath mingled and our tongues touched, he moved one hand to the back of my head and curled the other one around my hip.

The teasing thrust and retreat of our tongues seemed familiar, as if we'd been mouth-to-mouth a hundred times before. Yet this restrained passion was so damn hot I might combust on the spot. Every cell in my body screamed for more.

When I pressed my body closer to his, he released the deepest, sexiest groan before he retreated.

His eyes, an icy Nordic blue, locked to mine. He appeared to be as breathless and confused as I was. "Was that kiss part of a bachelorette party game?"

"No."

"A dare?"

"No."

"Then why did you kiss me like that?"

"I saw you and I couldn't resist."

"Or maybe because you thought you knew me?"

"Why would I know you? Are you famous or something?" He definitely could be on the TV show *Vikings*.

His gaze turned more skeptical. "Why are you dodging the question?"

"It's because—ah . . . I'm a little hazy on why the urge to kiss you overwhelmed me."

"Hazy from too many shots of tequila?" he said sharply.

"No. I can't even blame it on that since I've had two drinks over the past two hours."

He gave me a slow, sexy blink and then he smiled.

Heaven help me. His dimples were deep enough his beard couldn't mask them. His perfect teeth gleamed in a stunning smile. His lips retained that full, pouty look even with his wide grin.

He brushed his mouth across mine and whispered, "Guess it's my lucky day."

My lips parted to say, "Mine too," but no sound came out.

"How about we have a drink and you can tell me the real reason you used your tongue to introduce yourself instead of a handshake?"

That broke the spell. I lowered my arms and stepped back. "I'm sitting over here." I turned and headed to the table.

Perky Waitress showed up immediately after we took our seats. "What can I get you?" she asked him.

"Grain Belt, if you've got it on tap."

"Coming right up."

As soon as she was gone, he set his elbows on the table and invaded my space. "As much as I'd like to call you Hot Lips"—he grinned—"what's your name?"

Just then Vance and Tommy walked by—each with an arm draped over one of the women from the back room. Vance said, "See ya 'round, Amelia."

Crap. Of course karma, that vicious bitch, had ensured that I had to start this conversation with my new hot crush with the fact that I'd lied to those guys about my name. That'd go over well. Then he'd wonder what else I lied about and this would be over before it began.

"So . . . Amelia," he said, sounding pleased he'd overheard my name.

Surely at some point I could explain and we'd have a great laugh about it, right? So I went with it. "Yes?"

"What's your last name?"

"Carlson. And you are . . . ?"

"Walker Lund." His gaze roamed over my face. "Seems we're both of Scandinavian descent."

"You seem surprised. Because I'm not a six-foot-tall, rail-thin blonde with cheekbones that could cut glass and piercing blue eyes?"

He lifted a brow. "You got something against tall blonds with blue eyes?"

Then I realized how snappish my retort had come across. "Sorry. No. I find tall, blue-eyed blonds incredibly attractive." I flashed him a quick smile. "Especially the bearded variety. I've been overlooked and occasionally dumped because I'm not a blonde temptress, so it's a knee-jerk reaction."

"You're plenty tempting, trust me. And don't pretend you aren't aware that any guy in this bar would change places with me in a heartbeat."

"Because I marched up to you and kissed you like it was my right?"

"I ain't gonna lie—that was one hot 'Hello, baby. I wanna eat you alive' kind of kiss. It's especially sexy when you've got wide-eyed innocence. Yet that mouth of yours . . ." His gaze dropped to my lips. "It's the stuff fantasies are made of. Plus, you've got great hair and a fantastic ass."

"When were you looking at my ass?"

"As soon as your back was turned. I really wished your table had been farther away."

Oddly flattering.

"So, sweetheart, why don't you come clean about why you really kissed me?"

"You want the long version?"

He shook his head. "I don't care just as long as it's the no-bullshit version."

The words tumbled out of me in a rush. "My friend dragged me here and within an hour she'd hooked the interest of a really hot rugby player and left with him. As I lamented my crappy day and the sad state of my life lately, my ex-boyfriend showed up with his new girlfriend. And through a very awkward conversation, I learned that he'd been with her *before* we broke up. So in trying to not look pathetic because I was sitting alone, I lied and said I was waiting for a date."

Walker assessed me with scary detachment for several long moments before he spoke. "So that knockout kiss was all for show to make your dickhead ex jealous?"

"No." I glanced down at my hands. "I mean, yes, I had a plan of sorts, but when you walked in—"

"When I walked in . . . what?" he said testily.

"My plan vanished. I wasn't thinking about my jerk of an ex at all because I was entirely focused on you." As embarrassing as that was to admit, I met his gaze again.

"Is your ex still here, watching us now?"

"I have no idea."

He frowned as if he didn't believe me.

"Look. I didn't come up with the date idea to make him jealous. It was a spur-of-the-moment decision to make sure he knew that I'd moved on. I moved on the day I found out he was cheating on me. And to hear that he'd been cheating on me longer than I'd been aware of? I considered kneeing him in the nuts and using her fake boobs as speed punching bags. But then I figured even a dive bar like this would frown on that behavior. And the person I'd call to bail me out of jail was on a date with a rugby player." Somehow I managed to stop the blast of words and took a breath.

Walker let loose a robust laugh that was as charming as it was sexy.

The waitress returned with his beer.

He tried to pay but I waved him off and sent our server on her way. He held his mug up for a toast. "To giving in to overwhelming urges. You made this crap day a hundred times better."

"Back atcha." I touched my half-empty glass to his and drank.

After he set his beer down, he leaned back and crossed his arms over his chest. "So tell me what you do when you're not randomly kissing strangers in a bar."

I played coy. "Why don't you *guess* how I make my living?"

"What do I win if I guess right?"

Ah. So he was the "What's in it for me?" type. "What do you want?"

"Your phone number."

"Okay."

He pulled out his phone and looked at me.

"Oh. You want it *now*?" I rattled off the number without thought, watching his thick fingers type the digits in, wondering what he did for a living to earn calluses like that.

After he slipped his phone into his front pocket, he studied my face before his gaze dipped to the lace camisole stretched across my cleavage. "You're a teacher cutting loose during summer vacation. Your recent ex was also a teacher and you caught him banging more than the erasers with his new student teacher."

I laughed. "I'll give you points for creativity, but I'm afraid I'll just deduct those points when I tell you that you're wrong."

He affected an expression of shock. "I'm wrong? Damn. I'm never wrong. But I get another chance, right?"

"I don't remember agreeing to those parameters."

"Aha. That answer gave you away."

"How so?"

"Only lawyers or cops phrase things that way."

"Strike two." I sipped my margarita and eyed him over the salted rim. "You confident your third guess is a charm? Or are you about to strike out?"

He ran his hand over his beard. "You sound like my brothers with the sport references."

"Which is totally out of character for me since I don't follow any sports."

That surprised him. "None?"

"Nope. I don't get men's fascination with all things ball related." Right after the words left my mouth, Walker grinned.

"I could try to explain it to you, but I don't know if a conversation about my balls is appropriate since we just met."

I nudged his knee with mine beneath the table. "Quit stalling. What's my occupation?"

"You're a hostage negotiator with the FBI."

I made a buzzer sound.

Walker leaned forward. "I give in. Tell me."

Part of me wanted to lie and tell him I was a flight attendant—that had been a favorite fake occupation of Amelia's during college. But I liked this guy. He seemed to appreciate my quirky sense of humor, instead of acting like he wanted to run for the door. "I'm an artist."

"Really? That's cool. What medium do you work in?"

"All of them. I couldn't decide on a specific discipline because I couldn't see myself doing the same thing over and over like Thomas Kinkade does." I always used him as a reference because everyone seemed to know his name.

"But he's mega-rich," he pointed out.

"Good for him that he's above the poverty line as a working artist," I said dryly. "But making money with my art hasn't been my priority. I'm not saying that from an elitist attitude. The art I create just usually doesn't fit any kind of commercial mold."

"Such as?"

"The commission I lost today—which was one thing that contributed to my crap day—was for a textile piece. A mixed-media wall hanging that Missus Art Patron deemed too . . . modern and edgy."

Walker frowned and reached for his beer. "Isn't the definition of mixed media . . . modern?"

"Apparently she didn't get the memo regarding the parameters of newfangled artistic mediums. So rather than working with me to find a compromise, Mister Art Patron canceled the entire project. Now I'll have to find a part-time gig to cover that chunk of lost income."

"That sucks. You said that was one thing. What's the other crappy thing that happened today?"

The situation with my family seemed too personal to share. I stirred my watered-down drink, trying to come up with something else.

Walker took my hand and swept his thumb across my knuckles. "Might make you feel better to talk about it."

My belly did a little flip from his touch. I glanced up at him. He appeared genuinely interested, so I let fly. "My grandma left me her pearls after she passed on. I was too young to take 'proper' care of them, according to my stepmonster, so she put them away until I was older. Every time I've asked about them, I've been assured the necklace is in a safe place and I can have it once I'm settled. Except now, since my half sister has gotten herself engaged, there was an engagement party I wasn't invited to and she's getting the pearls to wear on her wedding day. I hate to sound like a petulant child, but that's not fair. My grandma did not put a stipulation on them that the first granddaughter to tie the knot gets the pearls. But I have no recourse. It was just so typical of my stepmonster to make me feel like even if 'first wed' had been a determining factor in who gets the pearls, everyone knows it wouldn't have been me anyway."

"Babe. I'm sorry. That *isn't* fair." He set his forearms on the table. "Maybe we oughta plan a heist."

I couldn't help but grin. "Can't you see the headline? 'The Case of the Purloined Pink Pearls.'"

He laughed.

"While I appreciate the offer, should I be worried that you're a professional cat burglar?"

"Nah. I'm more of a dog guy."

"Funny. But speaking of . . . what does Walker Lund do to fill up his weekday hours?"

He smirked and those damn dimples winked at me. "Guess."

"I should've seen that coming."

"Yep."

"You dress up like a Viking warrior and reenact famous battle scenes at the Shakopee Scandinavian Culture Center. You wear skintight leather breeches and a fur vest over your bare, glistening chest. Oh, and you have a big . . . sword and kick-ass shield that you use to beat back all the wenches who stand in line to be pillaged by you."

"Nice try. Points for vivid imagery and the use of the word 'glistening' with a straight face. But no."

"Shoot. I so thought I'd nailed you." *Dammit, Trin. What is wrong with you?*

"And extra points for sexual innuendo."

"Unintentional," I retorted.

"Still counts. Quit stalling and guess."

He'd set his hand back on the table by his beer glass. I reached over and ran the tips of my fingers across his rough-skinned knuckles. "Workingman hands," I murmured. "Maybe you're a Viking longboat builder?" When I looked up at him, the heat in his eyes set my stomach into free fall.

"That. Right there," he said on a low growl.

Confused, I said, "What?"

"That innocent look in your big green eyes. Makes a man think about all sorts of things that aren't even close to in-nocent."

I blushed and felt like a complete dork. Wasn't I supposed to be past this at my age? "With that smooth line, you've got to be a salesman of some kind."

"Me? Smooth?" He laughed. Hard.

I half expected him to start slapping his knee.

Then he picked up my hand. "I'm not some smooth-talking bar rat. In fact, according to my mother and my sister, I'm more than a little rough around the edges."

"It looks good on you." I paused, resisting the urge to lift my hand high enough to stroke his beard. "What does a rough-around-the-edges man do for a living?"

"I'm in construction."

"Any specific area? You build roads or hospitals?"

"No. Mostly we renovate."

"Like historical renovations? You make sure that when houses and buildings are updated the elements indicative of their period remain intact?"

"Yes, in some instances. My business is eighty percent renovation, ten percent restoration and ten percent falls into an 'other' category. Right now we're in the middle of two major restorations and three renovations. Summer is our busiest time since the season is so short. I hit a couple of snags today—the client demanding changes that a third party suggested. I had a late meeting with the building owner on one of the properties. And that conversation went so well I immediately needed a drink."

"No girlfriend waiting to soothe you with a cold brew after a hard day's work?"

"Sweetheart, I wouldn't have let you kiss me like that if I was in a relationship and I sure as hell wouldn't have kissed you back the way I did."

I fought another blush. "That makes my behavior really irresponsible . . . not even considering you might be involved with someone." I shook my head. "It was like I was in a lust-trance."

"Lose the guilt. There were two pairs of lips working that kiss." He swigged his beer. "And I don't cheat."

"Is that a rule you've always abided by?"

His left eyebrow winged up. "You think I made that decision out of guilt after cheating?"

"I just wondered if we have that hard learning curve in common. It sucks that I have to make a mistake—sometimes a big mistake—as a catalyst to change my ways."

The intent way his eyes searched mine indicated I'd ventured too far into personal territory. This was the point where the guy usually retreats. In a preemptive response, I'd smile and say something noncommittal as I dug my car keys out of my purse. But for some reason this time . . . I froze.

Evidently my deer-in-the-headlights look amused him.

"You have any idea how hard I'm digging on you right now?"

"Digging on me," I repeated. "Is that a construction worker's come-on?"

He laughed. "No. But I wish I'd made that connection. What I'm trying to say is, I want to see you again. Is that a possibility?"

"Walker . . . can I be blunt?"

"I don't know—you've been so vague in your answers prior to this," he said dryly.

"That candor gets me in trouble more often than not. So here goes. You're hot. Like hard-core hot. I honestly can't imagine why I thought you'd be single. And guys like you don't take an interest in women like me." I held up my hand to keep him from interrupting. "That isn't me fishing for compliments. So I have to know: Are you asking me out because you're assuming that I'm okay with a hookup?" I had some pride. I didn't want to be the weird chick he'd thrown a bone. I really didn't want to be the tagline to his "This one time a woman kissed me in a bar and I ended up banging her next to the Dumpster" drinking tales shared around the construction site.

Walker angled forward. "Were you trying to be insulting with that question?"

"No! It's a legitimate question, given that I threw myself at you and said hello with my tongue. It's not a stretch for you to be hopeful that I'd up the ante to saying hello on my knees if we went on an actual date."

The ferocity in his eyes and in the hard set of his jaw made him look even more like a Viking about to wage battle. "If I thought you were just looking for a hookup, I wouldn't be sitting here. I've had a better conversation with you in the last half hour than I did the entire time I was with my last two girlfriends."

He paused and looked at me—really looked at me. The way I'd always wanted a man to look at me, and it knocked the breath from me.

"From the moment I saw you, I felt that same unexplainable pull."

"You did? Seriously?"

"Yeah. So let's see where this goes. Say you'll go out with me."

Maybe it was crazy to say yes, but I did anyway.

His phone in his pocket started to buzz. He didn't ignore it—I was on the fence whether that was a good or bad thing.

He answered with, "Hey. What's up?" He frowned. "Are you okay?" He briefly closed his eyes and ran his hand over his beard. "Where? Yeah. I know that area—I don't know what the hell *you're* doing there. Just stay put. I'll be there in fifteen. Is the tow truck already there? Okay, good. When it gets there, do *not* get in with the driver." He held the phone away from his ear for a moment as the woman on the other end yelled at him. "Dallas. Knock it off! Jesus. You do *not* get to bite my head off when you're calling for *my* help. I hear any more insulting shit and you can call your mom and dad for a ride." Walker looked at me and covered the mouthpiece. "I knew that'd shut her up."

I snickered.

"I'm leaving now. Stay put. Call me if you get freaked out." He pocketed his phone. "My youngest cousin is having car trouble and I won the lottery to go fetch her."

"You're a good cousin."

He stood and said, "I'm a sucker," without any real malice in his voice. Grabbing a handful of my hair, he tilted my head back and kissed me.

Holy hell, did he kiss me. The kiss was short, but there was nothing sweet about it.

After ending his onslaught, he eased back slightly so he could gaze into my eyes. "That was in case your douchebag ex is still watching."

"Uh. Okay." *Eloquent, Trinity.*

Walker lowered his lips to mine again for a slower kiss. A deeper kiss. A kiss packed with raw hunger that sent me spiraling. I had to clutch his shirt to ground myself and keep from getting dizzy.

When he pulled back, my dazed look brought out his satisfied male grin.

"What was that one for?" I managed.

"That one was just for me."

Swoon.

"I have your number so expect a call from me soon. Real soon, because I cannot wait to see you again." Then he was striding out the door.

As I tried to unscramble my brain, I was aware of a few things:

The man took kissing to a whole new plane.

I couldn't wait to hear that gravelly voice on the other end of the line when he called me *soon*. *Real soon* because he couldn't wait to see me again.

My euphoria faded fast.

Not only had I given him a fake name, I'd given him my old phone number. There was no way he could get in touch with me.

So I left the bar in the same type of crappy mood I'd arrived in.

Happy Hour. What a freakin' lie. Happy Hour could suck it.

Two

———

WALKER

After washing off the dirt from another lousy day on the Smith Brothers' job site, I slipped on board shorts and a tank top. A swim in my pool would erase the remnants of this shitty week and I could start the weekend with a better attitude. I snagged a beer out of the fridge and barely had a chance to enjoy that first frosty sip when the doorbell rang.

Tempting to ignore it since I suspected a family member lurked on the other side wanting something from me. Again. I didn't bother to check the security camera before I disengaged the locks and opened the door.

My older brother, Brady, stood on the threshold, one hand on his hip, the other holding a cell phone at eye level. Right in front of my face.

I heard the click as he snapped my picture. "What the hell, Brady?"

"I'm texting Mom proof that you're alive."

"She's sending you to do her dirty work these days?"

He lifted a brow. "*These* days? As the oldest it's always fallen on my shoulders to make sure none of you stray too far from the flock." He slipped his phone into the inner pocket of his suit jacket. "So you gonna let me in or what?"

"As long as you're not here to preach the doctrine of love."

"I'll endeavor to not wax poetic about Lennox for at least fifteen minutes," Brady said dryly.

"Smart-ass." I stood aside to let him in.

He headed straight to the kitchen.

I followed him and wondered how he wasn't roasting in this heat and humidity in that suit. But then again, Brady had damn near been born in a suit, tie and wing tips. Our clothing choices were only one of the many differences between us.

Brady rummaged in my fridge until he found a Grain Belt beer. He twisted off the cap, took a long drink and leaned back against the counter.

I mirrored his pose across from him. "Mom really sent you over here?"

"Dad did." He lifted the bottle for another sip. "Which we both know means Mom put him up to it. I planned to give you another week before I showed up to grill you."

"Considerate of you."

"I thought so. Anyway, why are you avoiding the family, little bro?"

Little bro. Right. I topped him by two inches and thirty pounds. It'd be easy to slip into the bullshit banter we normally did, but the concern on his face gave me pause. "I've been busy. I deal with people all damn day, so on the weekends I want to chill at home. Alone. Mom doesn't get that. She wants . . ." I'd been scarce because I didn't want to explain this to any of them. Especially not to Brady. I swigged my beer. "Never mind."

His eyes narrowed. "Never mind Mom wants . . . what? You to remodel the guest bathroom again and you're avoiding her?"

"Hilarious. But that's not it."

"Then what?"

"Look. Can we just drop it? You can report you were successful and I've promised to be at the next Lund family weenie roast." I reached down and yanked a loose thread from the waistband of my shorts. I crossed to the garbage can to throw it away.

"Walker," Brady said sharply.

I slowly turned around. "What?"

"It's me." He threw out his arm not clutching the beer. "We don't do this polite dancing-around-the-subject crap. Quit being a dick and talk to me."

"*I'm* being a dick?" I repeated.

"Yeah. This Mr. Nice Guy 'I'm all right' attitude is passive-aggressive. So quit throwing me softballs. Step up to the plate and let fly."

Asshole knew a sports analogy would incite me. But he asked for it. "Okay, Mr. Oblivious. Ever since you and Lennox started proving to everyone how disgustingly happy you are, at every opportunity, Mom has been a hard-core pain in my ass about finding the right woman and settling down because, as usual, she wants me to be exactly like you." I held up my hand to stop his automatic protest. "You'd think she'd learn, after all these years, to stop trying to make me into a blond, blue-collar version of you. But no. She's redoubled her efforts. *Every* conversation I've had with her in the past three months has been focused on who she plans on pairing me up with if I don't find a woman on my own. I'm tired of it. So I stopped putting myself in those situations."

Brady didn't say anything for several long moments. Then

he sighed and raked his hand through his hair. "Mom just wants you to be happy."

"Then she should just let me be. I do things on my own time frame."

"How well I know that." He set his beer on the counter behind him. "How are things at work?"

It surprised me he'd asked; I couldn't remember the last time we'd talked about anything going on in my life. I shrugged. "One job is chugging along slower than everyone would like. I tried to tell them that restoration of this building would take twice as long as new construction, since every exterior structural change has to be approved by the histori- cal preservation committee. Come to find out that's not the problem. My crew has been able to finish exactly one interior room. Even that was a struggle."

"Why?"

"The interior designer they hired is a nutjob. She wanted the walls to have *flair*. I told her the walls need to be structur- ally sound. She actually asked if I could keep three random sections of the lath-and-plaster wall intact and 'open' so her designs could pay homage to the 'bones' of the building's past." I shook my head, still in total disbelief about that idi- otic idea. "Yeah. No problem. There's no reason to fix the water-damaged sections of the walls and ceilings because cracked plaster looks so freakin' cool covered in shimmery blue paint as it's falling down on top of you."

Brady laughed. "You could totally mess with Mom and tell her you've got your eye on a feisty interior decorator, but neither of you wants to pursue a relationship outside of work- ing hours until the job is done. That'd buy you . . . what, another year?"

"You are one devious bastard. No wonder no one screws with you at Lund Industries."

He flashed me a sharklike smile. "Only one person I want screwing with me."

I smirked back at him. "How is the lovely Lennox?"

"Amazing."

"Annika was singing her praises the other night when I went over and fixed her broken closet door."

"She loves working in Annika's department. I love the fact she's kept PR's office budget in line for the first time in two years."

"You two totally geek out together about numbers, don't you?"

"Yes. I finally found a woman who understands that talking about a balanced P&L and above-average quarterly projections makes me hot. One of these days you'll find a woman who'll gaze at you adoringly while you yammer on about the benefits of using your big tool to hammer on hard wood."

"Wow. I'm disappointed you didn't work 'nailing her' into that sentence." I drained the last of my beer. "In all seriousness, I *am* happy for you, Brady. I don't want you to think I resent you."

He raised both eyebrows. "Wait. You don't blame me for Mom's recent matchmaking threats?"

"Oh, I totally blame you. I just wanted to clarify that I don't resent you."

"Good to know."

I shrugged.

"So let *me* clarify something. You're not involved with anyone right now purely to spite Mom? No offense, but that's some fucked-up logic."

"Mom doesn't have that much control over my life—my job does. I've been busting ass since this spring trying to keep my various projects running on schedule. At the end of a long workweek, I'm too freakin' tired to hit the bars. After the other night, when I did meet a woman I might be interested in? She gave me a fake name and number. That just drove home the point I suck at the whole dating thing." Heaven knew I had plenty of bad experiences to back up that statement.

Brady cocked his head. "Wait—run that by me again."

There was no way to spin it so I didn't look like a loser who needed my mother's matchmaking skills, so I didn't bother. "What's hard to understand? I. Suck. At. Dating."

"Bullshit."

"Yeah? That's why you guys call me a magnet for crazy?"

"That's better than Nolan insisting you only date women who need fixing," Brady reminded me. "But still . . . you haven't brought a woman to any family thing since before I met Lennox."

"Exactly. I'm out of practice for this dating shit since I'm team captain of 'Hit It and Quit It.'"

"I've seen you in action. Chicks fall all over themselves for a chance to run their fingers through your long golden locks or to stroke your beard."

"Piss. Off."

"I'm serious. The last family brunch you attended at the club? Lennox kept pointing out the women who were checking you out in all your lumbersexual glory."

I repeated, "Piss. Off."

He held up his hands. "Don't snap at me because you're so busy trying to avoid Mom's attempts to fix you up that you're missing other opportunities."

"Yeah, Mr. Love Connection? So why did my most recent opportunity give me a fake name and number?"

"I don't know. Tell me what happened."

Like I wanted to relive that. "Forget it."

"No can do. Talk."

"Fine. I had an early-evening appointment with Bob Higgins at his office downtown. He was a total douche and I needed a drink to wash away the bad taste I'd gotten from the meeting, so I walked into the first bar I saw. I'm scouting the joint for a place to sit and I'm there . . . maybe a minute when this sexy brunette marches up, twines herself around me and lays a big wet kiss on me. My first thought was that it was a 'Kiss a Stranger' bachelorette party dare."

"Was it?"

I shook my head. "Her friend had ditched her and then her ex and his new squeeze showed up in the bar. She wanted to save face . . . by sucking mine, evidently." Just thinking about that kiss was enough to get me riled up again because it was good. Damn good. And she knew it was too.

"Dude. That stuff never happened to me when I was single."

"It doesn't happen to me either. We started talking and I found out her name is Amelia Carlson. We shared a brief rundown of our crappy days. Things were going really well. She wasn't looking over my shoulder to see if the ex was paying attention to us. She was invested in the conversation—so was I. I made sure she knew I wasn't playing her, looking for a quick hookup. Sounds freakin' lame, but we connected and she agreed to go out with me. But before I could pin her down for a day and time, Dallas called in a panic."

"Did her damn car die again?" Brady demanded.

"Yes. So when I got there, I told the tow truck driver to drop it off at my mechanic's place. I don't know why she's so dead set against buying a new car. It's not like she doesn't have the money." Then something occurred to me. "Maybe it's a college thing. She wants to struggle like her friends who have shitty cars and no cash?"

"Who knows with Dallas? Maybe she should've been looking for the 'check engine' light instead of looking at the sky for an astrological sign. Back to the story about fake-name-and-number chick."

"I called her around noon the next day. The number was out of service. I tried off and on to get ahold of her. So, like a chump, I went back to the bar, thinking maybe she's a regular. I sat at the same table watching the door. Two hours passed and no sign of her. I was getting ready to leave and I recognized our cocktail waitress from the night before. She remembered me, so I asked her if Amelia—the woman I was with—is a regular at the bar. She looked confused and then she said the woman I was with wasn't named Amelia. At my look of surprise, she said she noticed the woman's name when she signed the credit card receipt, because it was un-usual, some sci-fi name like Tris or Trillion. But definitely not Amelia." I scratched my beard. "That's when I knew she'd been dicking with me from the start."

Brady was quiet for a moment. Then he said, "I don't know what to say except that sucks."

"So the 'Amelia Carlson' I thought I'd made a connection with doesn't exist. It burns my ass. It was a harsh reminder to stick with hookups from here on out."

"For real?"

"Yeah. Why?"

"While the situation sounds fishy, your 'Screw her' reac-tion doesn't ring true, Walker."

I scowled at him. "How so?"

"Sounds like you're giving up."

"How am I supposed to track her down when I don't know her name? And besides, even if Carlson is her last name, do you *know* how many thousands of Carlsons there are in the Twin Cities?"

"Did she tell you what she does for a living?"

"She's an artist." I paused. "That part wasn't a lie because her fingers were discolored by paints."

"See? Now you're thinking. What else did she tell you? Anything about the ex-boyfriend so you could track her through him?"

I stared at Brady. Hard.

"What?"

"Why are you pushing me on this?"

He stared back. "Because I don't see you doing a damn thing except standing around whining and wringing your hands like a jilted Victorian maiden."

My jaw dropped. "Victorian maiden? Who are you and what the ever lovin' fuck did you do with my brother?"

He laughed. "I'm serious, bro. Track her down if for no other reason than to let her know it wasn't all that hard to track her—her fake name and number didn't give her anonymity. Be proactive instead of reactive."

That skated close to stalking behavior. But if I didn't come up with a plan, Brady would; he was loyal, and as a Lund corporate executive he'd use every resource available to him to find information. While I appreciated that he had my back, I had to handle it my way—which was to forget it'd ever happened.

Yeah. And how well is that going for you so far?

"Walker?" he prompted.

I looked at him. "Just because I work with my hands doesn't mean I don't know how to use Google."

Annoyance crossed Brady's face. "No need to take a shot at me, especially when I've never implied you didn't have the skills to do it yourself. I'm just trying to help."

Then I felt like an ass. "Shit. Sorry. I just . . ." I sighed. "I'm dragging my feet because maybe I don't want to know who she is. Maybe finding out the truth is worse than speculating."

"I get that. But I could point out that you're a believer in signs. You know I thought it was a bunch of crap until you, Ash and Nolan staged the intervention on me last year. Seeing Lennox at Maxie's that night and then again the next morning when we were both community volunteers for different organizations . . . I became a believer. That stuff isn't random. There's a reason you and this woman crossed paths. It might be your cosmic responsibility to track her down."

I kept a straight face when my just-the-facts brother said the words "cosmic responsibility" without a sarcastic sneer.

"And speaking of responsibilities . . . since you're not answering Mom's calls, I'm supposed to remind you that your volunteer stint with LCCO starts tomorrow."

"I know. I already talked to the assistant director this week. He's got everything I requested."

"Good. Look. I don't want to tell you what to do"—I snorted at that; he'd been bossing me around my entire life— "but just call Mom. Be blunt with her about why you've been avoiding family stuff. She'll stop because she misses you."

I did miss the crazy, sweet hilarity that was our mother. "I'll call her tonight."

"Great. Now that I've done my duty, I've got a hot date with my woman."

"Oh yeah? Where are you guys going?"

"Flurry."

How things had changed. This time last year Brady worked practically twenty-four/seven and I was the one out on Friday and Saturday nights. Now he and Lennox were hitting the clubs on the weekend and I fell into bed alone.

I followed Brady to the front door. "Have fun."

"We plan on it. And we'll see you next Sunday for brunch?"

"Yeah."

"Bring gear. Jaxson will be in town and Jens challenged them to a rematch."

Our Lund cousins Jaxson, Ash and Nolan had shown us up the last time we'd played basketball and our super-competitive younger brother hated losing.

After Brady left, I grilled myself a steak, threw a handful of "super greens" into a salad bowl and pulled a potato out of the microwave. Although it was still humid, I sat on the patio by the pool. One of the things I loved about this house was the enormous outdoor space. These lots didn't exist in the city anymore. The trend for people of means was to buy an old house for the location, then turn around and rip the house down and build a McMansion with all the amenities older homes lacked.

I'd been picking away at updating this house for six years, since around the same time I'd gone into partnership with Jase Flint. I saw the irony—living in an undone house and I was a partner in a renovation and restoration business.

After I returned from apprenticing with my grandfather in Sweden, I'd taken a job with one of the big construction firms. At twenty-three I'd had no problem starting at the bottom—setting forms for concrete. Within a month I was "promoted" to the demolition crew. A month later, I filled in on the framing crew and was permanently reassigned there. Once my boss saw my skills were wasted with framing, he switched me to finish carpentry. I lasted a month before the old-guard carpenters complained I rushed through projects—which wasn't true; I refused to milk the clock like they did. When I found myself back on the concrete forms crew, I quit. There was a difference between paying my dues and being penalized for having a strong work ethic none of the other guys my age had.

Through the grapevine I'd heard that Flint-Co, a subcontractor, was circling the drain. Jase Flint's foreman had bailed out, leaving Jase with contracts to fulfill and no one to run the projects. I approached Jase for the project manager position. He was up front with me that he needed a partner to replenish his capital, not just a manager.

As one of the eight heirs to the Lund family fortune, I had several trust funds, enabling me to buy in to Flint-Co with a substantial amount of cash. Partnering with Jase was the smartest move I'd ever made. From day one he'd treated me as an equal, renaming the business Flint & Lund.

I worked my ass off. I was proud of helping take Flint & Lund to the next level. Jase respected me. He trusted my judgment. But it'd taken a solid year for our crew to reach those conclusions. I'd neither hidden nor bragged about my family connections, but several guys assumed I'd get tired of "playing" the working stiff and I'd return to my cushy job at Lund Industries.

I'd never had any desire to work at Lund Industries—aka LI—the family-run corporation worth billions. I sat on the LI Board of Directors because it was the one family obligation that gave me the freedom to *not* have to work for LI. Brady and Annika loved their jobs with the company. As did my cousins Ash and Nolan. My younger brother, Jensen, played football with the Vikings, so he wasn't on the company payroll. Neither was my oldest cousin, Jaxson, who played hockey with the Chicago Blackhawks. Dallas, the cherished baby of our Lund family tree, was still in college, but I knew she planned on taking LI by storm once she had her degree. I'll admit some days it bugged me to be the only Lund heir without a college degree, so I'd jokingly started calling myself the black sheep of the family. Yet the joke was on me; the only person who denied that moniker was my dad.

Speaking of . . . I'd stalled long enough. Time to make the call.

I shoved my plate back and picked up my phone. Scrolling through my recent calls, I counted the number of times my mother had called.

Twenty-seven times in the last thirty days.

Had it really been a month since I'd seen her?

I was such a tool for not calling her back. I hit Dial.

She answered on the fourth ring. "Is this a trick? Or is it really my beautiful boy reaching out to his mother?"

"Hey, Mom. It's me. Sorry I—" I closed my eyes. "I'm a terrible son, all right?"

"No, you are wonderful son with terrible manners. Big difference."

"Thanks for the clarification."

"It's what I do. Point out truths. So, I've missed you."

"I've missed you too."

"I hear that 'but' in your tone."

"But I need to talk to you about something."

"Of course. You can speak of anything."

I didn't sugarcoat it. "Please back off on your constant pressure for me to find a woman and settle down."

A pause followed. Then, "I know not what you mean."

"Yes, you do. I haven't been around lately because you

harp that it's not good for me to be alone; then you point to Brady with his perfect match, Lennox, expecting me to follow his same path. I'm not him, Mom."

She sighed. "I know this. But you are mistaken about who you're avoiding at family time. It is not me you're avoiding. It is Brady."

"How'd you come up with that?"

"Walker, a mother sees these things. You are a green-eyed alien around Brady and Lennox. You've always expected to find your life partner long before Brady. That's why you've auditioned *so very many* ladies for the part, no?"

I said nothing, even though it wasn't a rhetorical question.

"My part is to encourage you to look for her. That's all I have done. Not because Brady found his, but because you've been ready to meet the right woman for a long time."

Her image immediately popped into my head. Hair the color of rich mahogany that framed her heart-shaped face. Large green eyes fringed with sooty lashes. Her lush pink lips curled into a secret smile. The sassy tilt of her head. And that body, all soft, plush curves I wanted to sink into, taste thoroughly and worship with my hands and mouth.

"Walker, my sweet boy, are you still there?"

"Yeah."

"Your silence makes me wonder if you're thinking of one woman in particular?"

Maybe I'd been too hasty in telling Brady I didn't want to track her down. Because I hadn't been able to stop thinking about her for more than an hour since I'd left her at the bar three days ago.

Bottom line was I needed to know if the spark between us had been real, or if I'd been a chump. I'd call Brady on Monday to ask for his help since he'd offered it.

"I'm thinking of only you, Mom."

She snorted.

"What's new with you? Annika said you were bugging her about a heritage thing."

"Ann-i-ka. Don't get me started on her."

But that's exactly what happened. She went off on a tangent and I was off the hook.

For now.

Three

TRINITY

I hadn't painted sets since college. But I'd dabbled in every discipline within the fine arts curriculum, so I wasn't worried that the set designs would be out of the realm of my experience. I just hoped Nate wasn't expecting museum-quality artwork. He'd been impressed by my portfolio, if confused why an artist with my background would be applying for a set-painting job at a small community theater for minimal pay.

My spin on it wasn't a lie . . . exactly. I wasn't doing it only for the money. I did enjoy interacting with other creative types and used that energy to create a fresh perspective in my own work. When I got stuck in a rut, the only thing that kept me from spiraling into a massive depression was working on a project completely different from what I'd just done.

I'd learned—the hard way—that after finishing a project, be it a mixed-media piece, a sculpture, a painting, glassware, metalwork or textiles, I couldn't do the next logical thing: stick with that medium and build on the (modest) success of it. No, I had to upend my creative process entirely. Every time.

I'd been told by more successful artist friends to focus and control the chaos instead of allowing it to lead me astray. I pretended to soak in their words of wisdom, all the while knowing they didn't understand. My brain, my process just didn't work that way. So I'd stopped trying to explain. I'd also stopped listening to advice—especially unsolicited advice.

My phone rang and I glanced at the caller ID.

Speaking of unsolicited advice . . . in that moment I wondered if I should've given the caller my new phone number. I took a deep breath and put a smile in my voice. "Hey, Ramon. What's up?"

"*Chica*. Please tell me you're up early because you're in your studio working on that textile commission."

"Nope. The client opted not to follow through with it." *Please don't say I told you so.*

Silence.

Judgy silence.

"I am sorry. I love you . . . but I could've told you—"

"That you win some, you lose some. That's how it goes, Ramon. Being a working artist is a fickle business."

"As I well know, since I'm supplementing my art career by running a food truck," he retorted.

Ramon had chosen to use his Mexican heritage in both his art and his cuisine. His food truck business was doing remarkably well, and instead of embracing that success, he was obsessed with taking his art to the next level. Somehow I'd become his sounding board, even though I rarely reciprocated. Except in a moment of self-doubt the week before,

I'd shown him the sketches for the Stephens project. And in typical fashion, he'd pointed out several things I'd done wrong.

"Hey, I'm not immune to needing to pay the mortgage either. That's why I'm sitting in the parking lot of the Seventh Street Community Center, about to head in so I can start painting sets for the production of *Into the Woods*."

More silence.

Great. "What?"

"How did you even find out they were looking for a set painter?"

"I saw an ad in the *Twin Cities Reader*. Why does that matter?"

Ramon sighed. "Did you ever consider if you're selling your skills to the lowest bidder then that's a reflection on what your art is worth? Maybe that's why you didn't get the textile commission."

I refused to get suckered into an argument with him about artistic integrity when he had a separate stream of income that allowed him to make that choice.

"I'll admit I am happy knowing that you didn't hear about this job from Randy. You don't need to do another freebie."

Ramon hadn't liked my ex-boyfriend—the ex before my last ex, Milo—at all. "*I* took the job painting the mural in his sister's coffee shop even though it wasn't for much money. It turned out great and was a lot of fun. I could've said no, but I'm glad I didn't."

"You should've said no. You shouldn't be wasting your time painting common murals, Trinity. If you would've focused your energy on—"

Not this again. "Look. I've gotta go in. I'll talk to you later." I hung up.

I snagged my messenger bag from the cargo area of my

SUV and draped the long strap over my shoulder. I garnered a few curious looks as I passed by groups standing around smoking, because I didn't fit the "actor" mold in my white painter pants and *Star Trek* T-shirt.

Nate was the first person I ran into.

"Trinity! Great to have you on board. I'll show you what's been done so far."

I followed him into a conference room. Plastic tarps were stacked on the counter and long rolls of paper were bundled together alongside a table filled with dozens of brushes. Another conference table held cans of paint and an industrial-sized airbrushing machine.

"Wow. This is a pretty sweet setup."

"LCCO is amazingly generous with their funding." He paused. "I should probably tell you that when some of the sets are constructed and painted, you will have high school–age volunteers helping you assemble them."

He laughed at my look of horror.

"The kids are great. Only the students with an interest in art and theater will be assisting."

"Okay, that makes a difference."

Nate pointed to the wide strip of tape down the center of the floor. "Half of this space is yours. The other half is for the set builder. He'll mark pieces once they're ready for paint and you can move them into your work area."

"Is there a particular order? Or do I just finish them as they're brought to me?"

"I'll get you a list. We need to have everything finalized two weeks prior to the first performance." He skirted a stack of plywood and led me to a desk in the corner. "I know you were a late addition to the crew and we appreciate you step-ping in on such short notice. I've drawn everything out, adding color so you can see exactly the look and style I'm going for. I made blank duplicates of the basic design, so if a concept doesn't look right onstage, we can change it here first before tackling the paint."

"Sounds like you've thought of everything."

He smiled. "We're a community theater group, but we don't want to look like amateurs."

"I get that. Trust me."

"Good. I have to get back since I'm also Chris's AD, but I'll let you familiarize yourself with everything. Our builder set up his machinery outside so you won't have to hear saws and hammers. He'll have at least two pieces ready to go after lunch." He cut back through the piles and disappeared.

I wandered through the space, gauging the materials. Then I sat at the desk and flipped through the schematics. Nate had been very thorough. But in order for me to get a feel for his designs, I'd need to start fresh. I pulled out my sketchbook and colored pencils and got to work.

Sometimes I listened to music while I worked. But today, with the door between the spaces open, I let the sounds of being backstage inspire me. Snippets of music. Laughter from the cast. Chris and Nate barking instructions and encouragement.

Every once in a while I'd hear the back door open and footsteps shuffle across the tile into the conference room, but I couldn't see anything from my corner hiding spot. I'd finished re-creating half of the sketches when a sharp pain reminded me it'd been a few hours since I'd moved.

I stood and stretched until the tendon in my neck popped back into place. My left foot had fallen asleep, and when I took a step, I lost my balance and my hip connected with the rolls of paper, sending them crashing to the floor.

"Awesome."

Just as I bent over to grab one, I heard a deep male voice say, "Let me help you with that."

"Thanks." I moved the closest roll back up and froze when I saw who had helped me: Walker, the sexy blue-eyed Viking I'd been dreaming about all damn week.

He stared at me.

Ha! More like he *glared* at me.

He bit off, "You," as if too angry to say anything else.

My mouth opened to explain when Nate sailed into the room. "Trinity, I need some—" He stopped and his gaze winged between us. "Oh, good. I see you two have met."

"Not exactly," the bearded wonder muttered low enough for only me to hear.

Outside the room, someone hollered, "Nate, Chris needs you."

"It never fails." Nate grabbed a roll of masking tape off the table and breezed out the door.

"So who are you pretending to be today? Amelia *Earhart*? Because you're not Amelia Carlson."

I took a step backward. "What are you doing here? Are you stalking me or something?"

"I'd have to know your name to stalk you, sweetheart, and we both know you lied to me about that. So I'll ask again. Who are you?" He tipped his head toward the door. "Unless you want me to go out there and ask Nate, in front of everybody, who you really are?"

"Just chill for a sec. It's not what you think."

"Babe, I'm so chill I'm fucking *frosty*. Who. Are. You?"

"Stop crowding me."

"Have it your way." He spun around.

"Walker. Wait." I set my hand on his upper arm to stop him. The feel of his bulky biceps caused a strange tickle in my belly. This guy was solid muscle. He could break me in two if he wanted. And he seemed mad enough to do it.

Do you blame him?

He got right in my face. "I'm surprised you remembered my name. For the last time. Who. Are. You?"

"Trinity Carlson."

He muttered about a weird *T* name and then demanded, "Why lie about it?"

"I didn't lie."

"Bull. Shit. Did you or did you not tell me your name was Amelia?"

I'd had enough of him looming over me. "No, I did *not* specifically tell you my name was Amelia. You overheard someone call me by that name and assumed it was mine."

That literally knocked him back a step.

See? Not the only one at fault here, big guy.

Then he rallied with, "But you didn't correct that assumption either."

"No, but I didn't lie to *you*, Walker."

I saw the moment when it clicked. "You lied to those other guys? Why?"

"There were two of them, one of me. I was in a strange bar without my wingwoman or my cell phone—so yeah, do the math." I paused. "Look, the name thing wasn't a blatant lie, but more like a . . . half-truth. And I felt bad about doing it."

"Half-truth?" He made a sound of disbelief. "You do realize that's the same as a lie?"

He sort of had me there. "Let's not delve into an 'Is the glass half full or partially empty?' argument," I said breezily. "My full name is Trinity Amelia Carlson. Professionally I go by Trinity Amelia."

"But everyone calls you Amelia?"

I shook my head. "Just my family." My stepmonster

started calling me that because Trinity sounded too hippie-ish. Heaven knew a man of my father's stature didn't want the general public to be reminded of his out-of-wedlock dalliance. "I go by Trinity. And I never told you to call me Amelia. In fact, I think you said my name once."

"Fine. *Trinity*. Maybe your name was a half-truth, but don't deny the number you gave me was completely fake—and that, sweetheart, was a total dick move."

My mouth dropped open. "What? It was not fake! Which means it was *not* a dick move! That was my old cell phone number."

"Old, like from years past? Because even if you change cell phone providers, you can keep your 'old' number."

"Unless the reason you change it is because of harassment," I retorted. "Last month I got twenty-four thousand unknown calls. Twenty-four thousand. Do you have any idea what it's like for your phone to ring every two minutes? Day and night? My provider threw out an excuse about autobot issues and refused to do anything. I'd just switched providers and got a new phone number the day we met. So when you asked for my number, the one I gave you was a reflex, okay? I had that number for four years and the new one for four hours." I inhaled a deep breath. "Besides, you didn't give me *your* number. And you did leave the bar in one helluva hurry. Maybe I took that to mean you only wanted to contact me on your terms. So I'm mostly at fault here, but not completely, and *you* know it."

He stared at me for several long moments—as if his oversight hadn't occurred to him.

"Yeah, well . . ." He jammed his hand through his thick blond hair. "Whatever." He turned and walked off.

"Where are you going?"

"To beat the shit out of something."

When he was out of earshot, I said to the empty room, "I seem to inspire that reaction in a lot of people."

I returned to my safe little corner and for the rest of the morning I did what I did best: lost myself in a two-dimensional world where things were simpler and mistakes were easily fixed—by either erasing or starting over on a blank canvas.

Somehow I doubted I'd get a clean slate with Walker Lund. And that made me more than a little sad.

After lunch, which I ate alone in my car, I started on the first set, a forest scene. It wasn't a happy bright blue sky, but an ominous gray. The pine trees were dark, angry slashes of green. I began to add layers, smaller trees, bushes and a rock-strewn path. These layers were softer, with feathery-looking pine needles, and a faint hint of light glowed beneath the lowest boughs.

I stepped back to gauge the image as a whole. It needed more distinct branches in the trees in the middle. Add a few dabs of yellow-green to balance the gray shadows and then this one was done. I snatched my bottle of water off the table and drained it.

"I hate to admit it, but you are one amazingly talented artist."

Startled by the deep voice, I dropped the bottle on the floor and whirled around. "God. Don't sneak up on me like that."

Walker had his hands in the pockets of his well-worn jeans. "Sneak up on you? I've been right here watching you for the last half hour." He paused. "You didn't know I was here?"

I shook my head. "People have said bombs could go off around me when I'm working and I wouldn't notice."

"I don't know if I've ever experienced that level of concentration—to say nothing of harnessing it repeatedly on cue to create something like that."

Usually I let compliments—and criticisms—roll off me. Yet his praise struck a chord since it wasn't about the finished product, but his appreciation of the process. "Thank you." Feeling self-conscious, I grabbed a smaller round brush and returned to painting.

I twisted the brush as I moved down the image. After the third pass, when I still felt him watching me, I said, "I'm sorry."

"For?" he said behind me, closer than he'd been a few minutes ago.

"For not correcting your assumption my name was Amelia."

During his silence, I fought the urge to fill the conversational void.

Finally he sighed. "I've spent the last four days pissed off, directing my anger outward because I knew exactly where the blame belonged."

On you.

"Evidently my ego couldn't handle the fact *I* might've screwed up, so it conveniently blocked that part out."

I snickered.

"What's funny?"

"That typical male response. You admit you have an ego but act like it's a separate appendage you have no control over. Kind of like when guys claim the little head is always at war with the big head for who's in control."

He laughed.

God. He had such an awesome laugh.

"Can you stop painting happy little trees for a moment and look at me?"

I whirled around. "Did you seriously just make a Bob Ross reference?"

"Why? Do you hate him or something?"

"No! I love him. In fact, he's a large part of why I became an artist. He was so positive and encouraging, which was so not the norm in my childhood. And it's not the norm in the art world either. He took such joy in creating. I loved how he made it look so effortless, even when I kind of resented him for that too, because it's *not* easy. Some of the happiest times in my childhood were spent in front of an easel, just me and Bob Ross on the TV in the background, painting happy little trees."

Walker was studying me.

"What? Do I have paint on my face or something?"

He shook his head. I swear his mouth twitched as if he was trying not to laugh.

Then I realized I'd gone off on a tangent again. Annoyed with myself, I said, "Stop staring at me."

"But I really like your face. And I thought I wouldn't see it again, sweetheart, so I'm gonna look my fill."

I had no idea how to respond to that.

"Can I ask you something?" He paused in speaking but kept inching forward. "Did you consider getting in touch with me?"

"I considered it."

"And?"

"And I concluded chances were slim you'd lay a big wet kiss on me if you saw *me* again after you discovered you had the wrong name and number for me *from* me, so I let it go."

"You didn't think about me at all?"

I hedged, pointing the paintbrush at him to stop his advancement. "I have to finish this. So if you want to continue talking, you'll be talking to my back."

As soon as I turned around, I heard, "Then you can't complain if I'm staring at your ass."

Shivers danced down my spine from the sexy, growly way he'd said that.

I switched brushes and colors.

"You were wrong to assume that I wouldn't want contact with you," he continued. "My brother offered to track you down with the little information I had. But I told him I just wanted to forget the whole thing." He laughed softly. "Of course, you're here—the last place I expected to run into you."

Using the wooden end of the paintbrush, I dragged lines through the paint, adding another facet to the branches. "So what now?"

"You tell me."

"Tell you what?"

"That Tuesday night was a fluke."

His denial surprised me. Or was he baiting me? "I should admit I'd had too many drinks and that was the only reason I kissed you?"

"Was it?"

"No. But I think you know that."

He exhaled loudly. "I do. I mean I did and then I didn't, and now I'm really freakin' glad I didn't imagine this."

My hand stopped midair. "But you said you wanted to forget the whole thing."

"That was then." Walker had moved in close enough that his breath drifted across the nape of my neck. "This is now. As far as I'm concerned, we haven't even started."

"You are confusing me."

"Welcome to the club, sweetheart."

"Do I get to choose a welcome gift for becoming a new member of this club?"

He laughed. "You have a bizarre sense of humor."

"So I've heard. Sorry."

"Don't be. I like it."

"Really? Most people don't get it. Most people don't get me."

"Their loss. Because I get you."

I almost demanded he prove it because I didn't want to get my hopes up about this guy.

The soft bristles of his beard grazed my cheek. "Trinity."

Gooseflesh rippled down my arm from his mouth being so close to my skin. "What?"

"Can you look at me?"

I turned around. This man was just so . . . manly. Big athletic body, toned muscles, and I couldn't help but wonder if the hair on his chest was as thick as his beard.

Warm, rough-skinned fingers rested beneath my chin when he angled my head up to peer into my face. And those eyes of his. *Sigh.* Cerulean blue on the outer ring, a smoky gray by his pupil. Beautifully expressive and laser focused with intensity on me right now.

"There are millions of people in the Twin Cities. There are hundreds of bars, theaters and volunteer organizations. The chances of us randomly running into each other twice in one week are miniscule. But we did." His thumb brushed over the divot in my chin. "I'm considering it a sign."

Chills danced down my spine. I was glad he'd said it first. Part of me wanted to point out this connection could be a bad sign just as easily as a good one, but the hope—and, yes, forgiveness—on his face had the rebuttal drying on my tongue.

"Let's start over."

"You want to pretend that kiss never happened?"

"No. I want to pretend you gave me your real phone number and real name so I can spend time with the real you."

"That was the real me in the bar, Walker."

He smiled. "Good. Because I liked you."

"Past tense?"

"So literal for an artist," he murmured. "The past is past. But I want the future tense to belong to me."

Okay. His confidence? Completely sexy.

"Come out with me tonight. You owe me that much since you did agree to a date."

His insistence didn't surprise me. But I'd had an exhausting week. All I wanted was to slip between my sheets, try to shut down for a solid eight hours. "Thank you for the offer. But I'll be worthless company tonight."

"I doubt that." He touched my cheek. "Just dinner, then. You have to eat."

"Do I look like I miss many meals?"

Walker's eyes turned stormy. "Don't."

"Don't what?"

"Say shit like that about yourself. I like what I see when I look at you, Trinity."

"Oh." That was really sweet. "I like what I see when I look at you too."

"But that's not a point in my favor right now, is it? You're still turning me down for dinner."

I set my hand on his chest. As hard and muscular as I remembered. "Yes. Just for tonight, though."

"How about lunch tomorrow? A long lunch."

He smiled—*oh, hello, sexy dimples.* I wanted to press my lips to the deep divots and feel his beard tickling my lips. Next time I kissed him, I'd take it slow and explore.

"So is that a yes?" he pressed.

My focus snapped back to his eyes. "It depends on where you're taking me. I'm not a fan of bar food—chicken wings, nachos, all that fried crap."

"Got it. Any other things to avoid?"

"I spend so much time inside that I'd like to enjoy the fresh air—as long as it's not a hundred degrees in the shade." I could see the ideas churning in his head and then one clicked.

"You're all right with it just being us tomorrow? Not in a restaurant or a bar or surrounded by people?"

I appreciated that he'd asked and hadn't assumed. "Sounds good. Where are we meeting?" I knew he probably expected to pick me up, but I needed the option of being able to leave whenever I wanted.

"I'll text you around ten and let you know. I have to check on a couple of things before I decide exactly where we're going." His eyes roamed my face. "Bring a hat and sunscreen."

"Anything else I should bring?"

"Just your beautiful self."

"You are smooth." I slid my hand up and curled it around his neck, intending to pull his mouth down to mine. But something stopped me.

"I have no problem with you taking the lead," he murmured. "Kiss me anytime you get the overwhelming urge again. But this time, it's my turn."

I groaned when our lips met and he swallowed the sound in a hot and hungry kiss. I hadn't embellished this passion between us. And he seemed determined to remind me of that with every teasing flick of his tongue, with every soft growl, with every angle he moved my head so he could delve deeper into the kiss.

When he broke the seal of our mouths, my lips tingled and my head buzzed. I'd melted against him and was having a hard time remembering why I couldn't stay right there forever.

Oh yeah. I'd opted to give up more of this to go home

alone to my quiet house and my neurotic, cranky cat who hated me.

Sometimes I'm a complete idiot.

Stepping back, he said, "Got that new number memorized yet?" and pulled out his phone.

I'd given the number out enough times in the past few days I could rattle it off without writing the digits on my wrist every morning.

Ten seconds later my phone buzzed in my purse.

He smirked at me. "Just checking."

"I'm glad you see the humor in it."

"I do now. But at the start of my day . . . let's just say being pissed off isn't always hell on productivity. I finished twice as many set cutouts as I'd planned."

"I'm taking credit for that."

"See you tomorrow, Trinity."

Four

WALKER

With energy to spare the next morning, I added two miles to my run. During my cooldown in the kitchen, I made the call.

My cousin Nolan demanded, "Why in the name of all that's holy would you call me this early on a Sunday morning?"

Because I miss you, asshole. "Because you're a dog and I was providing you with an excuse to shoo the chick in your bed out the door." I lowered my voice to mimic his. "'Babe, I've gotta help my cousin or he wouldn't have called so early. Do you mind taking off? But it was great. I'll call you.'"

"I don't sound like that," Nolan retorted. "And FYI: I was sleeping in because no lovely woman warmed my bed last night or this morning."

"No wonder you're snapping at me."

"Whatever. Where were you last night?"

"Building sets for my Lund Cares Community Outreach

volunteer project. It went later than I planned. What did you do that kept you from banging the headboard?"

"I worked until midnight."

I laughed. "Right."

"I'm serious."

"You were working at LI?"

"Did you hit yourself in the head with a hammer or something? Of course I was at LI. Where else would I be?"

"Doing what?" As far as I knew, Nolan didn't have the same level of responsibilities that Brady did as CFO, or our cousin Ash did as COO.

"Ash asked me to look into a few things that are usually under Brady's purview since he's busy with the Duarte Foods acquisition. And before you ask, yes, Brady is aware of what's going on. It's time-consuming."

"It'd have to be if you're burning the midnight oil on the weekend."

Nolan sighed. "That's why I'm hoping if you called so blasted early it's because you have big plans for us today. Something with hot half-naked chicks and cold beer."

"Sorry to disappoint, but my plans with a hot half-naked chick and cold beer don't include you. I called to tell you I'm taking 'Devil's Plaything' out for the afternoon. First-come basis with notification. That was our deal." I wiped my face and chest with a towel. "But if you had plans—"

"I don't. I might actually stay in bed all day and watch ESPN. The Twins are playing today."

I considered myself a sports guy—I loved watching football, hockey, basketball, boxing, soccer and MMA. I played soccer and basketball in high school. I was good enough to be a starter, but not good enough to consider pursuing either one on a higher level after high school. I made it to the slopes to ski and snowboard at least half a dozen times in the winter. But the appeal of baseball eluded me.

"Why else did you call?" Nolan asked.

I hated asking for help. Hated it. "So this woman I'm taking to the lake . . . I want to . . ." *Just spit it out.* "Her ex was a real tool. I'd like to set myself apart from him. What would be a good way to do that?" I held my breath for Nolan's snarky response, but he didn't give me one.

"Taking her out on the boat is a great idea. It's casual, yet intimate. What are you doing for food?"

I groaned. "I hadn't thought of that."

"You can't schlep a cooler of beer and a bag of sunflower seeds if you're gonna be outside all afternoon. But you need to do something classier than a bucket of fried chicken." He paused. "You tapping that yet?"

"No. Why?"

"If you're banging her, then food won't matter because neither of you will be thinking about anything but banging again."

True.

"You have to impress her enough so she knows you put in extra effort picking the food—but skip eats like caviar, champagne and chocolate-covered strawberries. Totally clichéd douchebag move."

"Not really my style. But maybe I should stick with sub sandwiches and chips."

"Boring. Stop at Surdyk's. They have an awesome deli and they'll furnish utensils. Because, dude, there's a fine line between showing up with classy grub and showing up toting a wicker picnic basket totally kitted out with a tablecloth, wineglasses and matching plates."

"No doubt. Thanks, man."

"No problem. So do I know this chick?"

"Nope. Just met her last week."

"Where?"

"Why does that matter?" I said sharply.

"Because you pick women like you pick building projects. You always go for the 'unique fixer-uppers.'"

"Not true."

"Keep telling yourself that. And when you figure out her walls are impossible to break down—or, worse, if her foundation crumbles—"

"I get it, okay?" While I appreciated that my cousin went to bat for me no matter what, I wasn't blameless in any of my failed relationships. I'd always been drawn to women a little left of center.

"Have you told the posse about her yet?"

Posse. I bit back a snort. But the term did fit my family. "Just Brady."

"Ah. He's loosened up since Lennox came into the picture. Last night the manager of Flurry texted me a pic of your brother and his woman getting their dirty groove on."

"Brady's got a life outside LI, which is what we were aiming for with the intervention last year."

"I don't begrudge him a second of happiness. I just wish it wasn't giving the Lund matriarchs matchmaking ideas."

"Aunt Edie is trying to set you up with someone?"

"Yeah. Since Jax has brought forth the lone grandchild, he's not a target. I am. But it won't work. I'm completely committed to having no commitment."

I laughed. "Bet you don't say that to her face."

"I don't have a death wish. I'll bet you're skirting the issue with Aunt Selka too."

"That'd be a sucker bet, cuz. Think Ash is getting the same pressure from Aunt Priscilla?"

"He mentioned she's dropped suggestions like he needs to 'get over Veronica' and move on."

Glad to hear I wasn't the only one being singled out for not being coupled up. I'd pulled back from Lund family gossip for longer than anyone had noticed, so I was out of the loop. "Thanks for the advice, man. I've gotta hit the shower."

"No problem."

I waited for Nolan to say, "Let's grab a beer after work one night next week," like he used to. But he didn't.

I wasn't surprised; I'd gotten used to it.

I texted Trinity the directions to our meeting place at Christmas Lake. Then I dressed in board shorts and a T-shirt—I'd be ready to swim even if she opted out.

The female college student who helped me at Surdyk's had a romantic streak and made tons of suggestions for picnic fare—all of which I was only too happy to follow.

At the marina, I loaded the cooler onto the boat, then readied the boat for takeoff. I tried not to pace in the parking lot when thirty minutes had passed and she hadn't shown up.

I checked my phone. No text messages or voice mail.

Then she finally pulled in and parked her Toyota 4Runner five spaces down from my truck.

I played it cool, waiting until she'd exited the vehicle before I approached her. I couldn't withhold my grin upon seeing her with her hair pulled back and wearing knee-length denim capris and a loose-fitting gauzy white blouse.

"Hey, pretty lady." I bent down and kissed her cheek. "You look beautiful and summery."

"Thanks. Sorry I'm late. I had trouble finding it." She wrinkled her nose. "It's a big lake. How could I have missed it?"

"No worries. I'm not on a schedule. Are you?"

She shook her head and slung a large canvas tote bag over her shoulder. She seemed tense. Had she changed her mind about being here? Or being with me?

Don't overthink this.

"If you've got everything you need, the boat is ready."

"Lead the way, Captain."

I snagged her hand and led her across the asphalt parking lot. We passed a few people I knew as we traversed the floating dock and we exchanged the typical comments about the weather. When we reached the dock space, I stepped over the railing first, then held my hand out to help her aboard.

"This is your boat?"

"Not entirely mine. My cousin and I own it together. Why?"

Trinity laughed and her entire demeanor changed.

"What?"

"I thought you'd have a fast jet boat or one of those fancy boats that are used for wakeboarding and competition skiing. So I'd prepared myself to spend the day trying to shout over the loud engine noises and white-knuckling my life vest as we zipped around the lake at high speeds. But this—?" She pointed to the pontoon. "Is so much better."

"I'm glad you approve. Hand me your bag." I wasn't prepared for the weight of it. "What do you have in here, woman? Rocks?"

"My purse, a life vest, a sun hat, a beach towel, sunscreen, my water bottle, my sketch pad and pencils." She hopped down but kept ahold of my hand.

I slid my hand up her arm and curled my fingers around the ball of her shoulder. Her skin was soft and she smelled like apples. "Thanks for coming today, Trinity."

"Thanks for asking me. I had no idea what you meant by 'water fun,' so I've been a little anxious."

I couldn't see her eyes beneath her sunglasses to gauge her level of anxiety. "What was your worst-case scenario?"

Her lips curled. "A waterslide park."

"Not a fan?"

"Of screaming kids, yelling parents and getting sunburned while eating overpriced food? Not to mention the fear someone will steal your stuff while water jets are shooting into places on your body that only your waxer, gynecologist or significant other should ever see."

I laughed and lowered my head to kiss her quickly. "You're funny."

She placed her hand on my cheek and smoothed the tips of her fingers over my beard. "No one ever says that to me. Thank you."

For that sweet show of affection, I kissed her again. "I thought we could do a leisurely jaunt around the lake, then pick a place to drop anchor and have lunch."

"That sounds fantastic." She stepped back. "Where do you want me to sit?"

"Across from me. Once we decide where to stop, you move around." While she got settled, I unhooked the boat from the dock and backed out of the space. As soon as the boat exited the no-wake zone, I increased the speed.

The breeze eddied around me and I inhaled deeply. Being on the lake in the summer was my slice of paradise.

There weren't a ton of boaters out, but prime time was around three in the afternoon when the sun was high and the air temp stifling. I cruised closer to the shoreline and waved at people out on the docks. Two towheaded boys around ten jumped up and down when they saw the boat. I slowed and the lanky kid clutched the fishing poles while his shorter, stockier buddy held up a stringer with a few smallish fish. I gave them a thumbs-up and watched as they high-fived.

"Friends of yours?" Trinity asked after we pulled away.

"I don't know their names, but they've been out on that dock every time I've been here this year. They remind me how crazy my cousin and I were for fishing at that age."

"The same cousin who owns part of this pontoon?"

"Yep."

"So this is a fishing boat?"

"Sort of." I looked straight ahead instead of at her since swimmers on tubes were hard to see until I came right up on them. "We just like to cruise around on the lake, kick back in the sun, drink beer and—"

"Pick up hot women in bikinis?" she supplied.

I shook my head. "It's a guy thing. We load the cooler with beer and the bucket with bait. Then we cast off and kick back and wait for something to bite. No one else in our family is into fishing—they never were when we were kids either. I'm not sure anyone knows we have the boat. And they'd have a hard time believing my fashion-focused cousin would go out in public without showering, shaving, styling his hair, wearing ratty-ass clothes and flip-flops."

"I get it. The lumbersexual and metrosexual have secret identities where they revert to preteen boys and indulge in spitting contests, dunking each other in the lake, eating sunflower seeds, telling fart jokes, talking about how stupid girls are and being happily oblivious that they stink to high heaven."

I looked at her sternly. "Were you once a preteen boy? Because that's all listed in the boy handbook."

She snickered. "No, but it seemed to be my half brother's goal to see how long he could go without showering or changing his clothes. His mother threatened to take him to the car wash."

I started to ask about her family but stopped.

After a bit, Trinity tapped me on the arm. "Tell me about

these houses ringing the lake, since you're a restoration expert."

"Such as?"

"Such as . . . which ones have been revamped? Which ones are new construction? Which ones are still old-fashioned family lake houses? Which ones are year-round residences?" She poked my leg. "I'll bet you pay attention to all that stuff. Not because it's your job but because it interests you—but that, in turn, makes you *better* at your job."

My chest puffed up at her assessment. In the past, women I dated preferred the fun-loving side of me, not the work-obsessed side. I couldn't remember the last time a date asked about my company or the work I do. "I'll show you a few of my favorites. I doubt you want a three-hour tour."

"Sail on, captain of the SS *Minnow.*"

I tilted my head to look at her. "She gets the *Gilligan's Island* reference and tosses one right back at me. Nice."

She laughed. "I'm impressed you got it. Our age group uses *Saved by the Bell* or *90210* for pop culture references, not classic TV shows."

"If you start quoting *Quantum Leap*, I'll probably have to marry you."

"*Theorizing that one could time travel within his own lifetime, Dr. Sam Beckett stepped into the Quantum Leap accelerator . . . and vanished.*" Trinity smirked at me. "What? You expected I'd be a *Matrix* expert?" She blew a raspberry. "Too obvious. But maybe we oughta revisit the plan to steal Grandma Minnie's pearls, since you and me are getting hitched."

I was so freakin' crazy about this woman. Every little thing I discovered about her made me want to know every-thing. "Heist planning later. Let's hit the high points of Christmas Lake architecture."

After I pointed out the new McMansions, I showed her my favorite, a smaller single-story home heavily influenced by Frank Lloyd Wright's Prairie-style design.

"I love that one. I can imagine several generations of a family coming here every year and vowing to keep it in the family. When I was poring over real estate ads, nothing like that was ever listed. I'll bet there's a realty company that deals with unique high-end properties that the unwashed masses aren't allowed to drool over."

I had used that kind of company to find my house. "You mentioned living in different places. Buying a house usually means you plan on staying around. So why did you choose Minneapolis?"

She laughed.

Talk about sexy. Her soft, husky laughter did it for me in a bad way. "What's funny about that?"

"If I tell you, you'll think I'm a free-spirited bohemian artist with no practical business plan."

"Doubtful. So hit me with it."

"One year I did the state fair circuit and sold a bunch of pieces at the Minnesota State Fair. The work was odds and ends, quirky experiments I'd tried to sell in a traditional gallery or gift shop. But Midwesterners love a bargain, especially if they believe it's one of a kind. During that two-week stint, I realized I could make a living here creating that type of art."

I slowed the boat and put it in neutral. "What about dropping anchor here?"

"Looks good."

After killing the engine, I hopped up and pushed the anchor off the back end of the platform. "Sorry, didn't mean to interrupt. You said you realized you could make a living here selling a certain kind of art."

"Yes. By here I meant in the entire state of Minnesota, along with North Dakota, Wisconsin and Iowa. My smaller, funkier pieces are spread across the upper Midwest. Anyway, since I was born in the North Woods"—she smirked at me—"I know how cold the winters are. And with crappy weather eight months out of the year, I could hole up in my studio and work on larger pieces and commissions and finish projects that interest me."

"Trinity, that sounds like a solid business plan."

"Thank you. But the length of the winter was a shock to my system. For the first year I wondered why I'd tortured myself."

"Then you got used to it."

"Somewhat. I'd still rather be inside when it's cold."

"You just haven't found a winter activity you like."

She peered at me over the top of her sunglasses. "I happen to *like* sitting inside wrapped in a blanket sipping hot chocolate, watching classic TV. That counts as an activity."

"Not in my family." I opened the cooler and snagged a bottle of water, then held it out to her. "Want one?"

"Yes. Thank you."

After grabbing another bottle, I moved the chairs into the sun. For a brief moment I let myself bask in the heat. Some guys I worked with spent their nonworking hours inside, claiming they had enough of the great outdoors during the workweek. Not me. I preferred to be outside—and not just in the summer.

"Your family expects you to participate in outdoor . . . stuff in the winter?"

"Mmm-hmm."

"What's your favorite activity? Ice fishing?"

"Nope. That's one I'll skip. Being on a frozen lake freaks me out even now. So downhill skiing is first choice. Then hockey. Snowshoeing. Last is cross-country skiing." I looked at her. "Talking about snow activities when I'm baking in the sun seems wrong."

"You don't seem to have the type of skin that gets fried."

"I don't. I just get tan. Speaking of . . . don't you wanna sit out here with me?"

"I'm not wearing a swimsuit."

I lifted an eyebrow. "Naked is fine by me."

"Nude sunbathing is never gonna happen with me because I'd look like a boiled lobster."

It was hard to bite back my comment about how much I loved lobster. "You can sit out here fully clothed. Or I'm a pro at applying sunscreen."

Trinity pushed to her feet. "If I fry, it's on you."

"Grab your sunscreen and I'll get you slicked up." When she bent over to dig through her bag—she wasn't wiggling that ass in my face on purpose, was she?—I had to swallow a groan.

"Stop staring at my butt, Walker."

"But it's right here, Trinity. I thought I was being gentle-manly by not smacking it."

She stood and slowly turned around. "Well, it *is* huge so it's sort of hard to miss."

I leaned forward and slipped my arms around her waist, dragging her closer, forcing her to straddle my lap.

"What are you doing?" She wiggled to get free but I held firm.

"I warned you I wouldn't put up with you saying that kind of mean shit about yourself."

"Walker—"

"So let's work on some positive reinforcement." I slid my hands down her hips and latched onto her butt. Then I repositioned her, forcing her to brace her palms on my chest. I kissed the tip of her chin as I squeezed her cheeks.

"Comfy?" she said testily.

"Getting there." I trailed my lips down her throat, not licking, not sucking, just pressing gentle kisses on her soft skin.

"You didn't ask me if *I'm* comfy," she retorted.

"Because I already know you're not. But it doesn't have a damn thing to do with how you're sitting on my lap." My mouth followed her collarbone from the hollow of her throat to her shoulder and back.

She shivered. She tried to hide it, but I caught it.

I caressed her backside and my mouth sought out all the sweet spots on her neck. "I really like your body. Even now when I've got my hands on it, all I can think of is . . . *more*." I nuzzled the section of skin where her neck curved into her shoulder. "Repeat after me. Walker thinks I'm sexy."

"Walker . . . I—"

I lightly tapped her butt. "Huh-uh. Repeat what I said, nothing else." I nipped her neck. "Or don't, because we can stay like this all day as far as I'm concerned."

"You're pushy, you know that?"

"Says the woman who put me in a lip-lock the first time we met."

She moaned huskily as my tongue flickered over the pulse point in her neck. "Okay. I'll say it. Walker thinks I'm sexy."

"Now say, 'Walker thinks I'm sexy and he wants to have me for lunch instead of the picnic he packed.'"

Trinity pushed herself upright with one hand and shoved her sunglasses on top of her head with the other. "You packed a picnic for us?"

"I didn't make the food, but yeah, there's picnic stuff."

Then she pushed my sunglasses on top of my head and stared into my eyes. Whatever she saw there caused her to smile. "Walker thinks I'm sexy and he wants to have me for lunch instead of the picnic he packed." She drifted closer, her focus on my lips. "But Trinity admits she needs an appetizer to tide her over."

Our mouths connected in an explosion of sweet fire.

I loved that she didn't hold back and wait for me to make a move. I really loved the greedy way she touched me and the sexy noises she made when I touched her.

All too soon, she tried to end the kiss. I made a growling sound and held on to her tighter.

She poked my belly until I started laughing and released her. Then she planted herself in front of me, a challenge quirking her well-kissed lips. "You volunteered to apply sunscreen?"

"Yes ma'am."

Keeping her gaze on mine, she slowly unbuttoned her blouse, shrugged out of it and draped it over the back of a chair.

Trinity had worn a swimsuit—at least the top portion—in a retro 1940s pinup girl style, with wide black straps that circled her neck to form a halter top. Made me a letch to leer at those beautifully full breasts, creamy white against the shiny black material, but I couldn't look away.

"Walker?"

"Give a man a minute to admire the outstanding view." I finally looked up at her face. "Did you say something about topless sunbathing?"

"Since I've never sunbathed topless, I can't imagine how fiery red that lily white skin would burn the first time." She held up her hand to stall my immediate comment. "While your forthcoming offer of kissing my sunburned skin is appreciated"—I laughed that she'd homed in on that because that's *exactly* what I'd been thinking—"how about you focus on keeping my back and shoulders from frying?"

"With absolute pleasure and utter dedication."

She rolled her eyes. "Focus on putting *sunscreen* on those areas, not your mouth."

"I'll try, babe, but no guarantees."

I moved in behind her and started applying lotion at the nape of her neck. Even the heat from the sun couldn't keep her from breaking out in gooseflesh as my hands molded and shaped her strong arms and shoulders. Made me a little crazy to see how much my touch affected her this way. As much as I wanted to drag this out, discover all of her hot spots inch by inch, there was no way to mask a hard-on in board shorts.

"I suppose you're too macho to wear sunscreen," she said.

"Nope. I'll let you coat my back when I'm done because I'm sweating through this shirt so much it's gotta come off."

She muttered something I couldn't make out.

"Done." I stepped back and yanked my T-shirt over my head. "My turn."

Trinity hadn't bothered to put her sunglasses back on, so I saw those green eyes widen. Then her gaze roamed over my chest and belly with frank admiration. "Of course you're built like that."

I liked the way she was eyeing me. So did another part of my body and I willed the damn thing to stand down.

Then she muttered, "Of course you have a blond happy trail."

I quickly skirted her and dropped into the chair. Maybe if I leaned far enough forward I could hide my body's reaction.

And what happens when she puts her hands on you?

I was screwed.

The bottle of sunscreen made an obscene noise and cool droplets landed on my shoulders. At first her touch was tentative. Exploratory. And that was pure torture.

"Trinity—"

"I want to sketch you," she said huskily. "The way your muscles bunch together here"—she traced my triceps and the upper bulge of my biceps—"you have exquisite form. I'd like to try to capture the power of them even in rest."

"Sweetheart, you can do whatever you want."

She squirted more sunscreen in the middle of my back, rubbing it in with slow, sensual strokes. "Anything? What about doing a nude?"

I chuckled. "Anything but that."

"But this would be strictly for my personal collection."

"So I'd just be one of many male forms in your private portfolio?" Why did that bother me? As an artist she'd probably drawn hundreds of nudes over the years.

"No." Her lips grazed my ear and I shivered. "You'd be the first one."

I turned my head until my cheek connected with hers. "Then I'm yours anytime you want me."

"I'll take you up on that later, when there's more shadow to highlight the contrasts."

When she kissed the hollow beneath my ear, my blood turned molten.

"Now that I'm protected, I'm ready to soak up the sun." She moved to the seat beside me and stretched her legs out. Lowering her shades over her eyes, she aimed her face skyward and exhaled. "This is the perfect way to spend an afternoon. Thank you. I needed this."

We didn't talk for the longest time. The lapping of the waves against the side of the boat, the drone of other motors and the occasional high-pitched shrieks of happy kids lulled me into the peaceful state I only ever found here. Which is one of the reasons I usually came to the lake by myself. Bringing other people meant a rowdier time, loud tunes, free-flowing booze, requests to go tubing or wakeboarding. Sometimes I wanted that, but it was rare. Mostly I wanted this peaceful feeling.

After a bit I heard her shift in her seat.

I cracked an eye open and watched her settle a floppy orange hat on her head that put her face entirely in shadow.

Without looking at me, she said, "The hat is hideous, isn't it?"

"It's . . . colorful."

"Artfully dodged," she said dryly. "My stepmonster gave it to me. She said I wear entirely too much black and it depressed her." She snorted. "It depressed *me* that she thought this 'pop of color' was what my wardrobe lacked."

"Why'd you keep it?"

She shrugged. "A perverse sense of pride? It *is* actual proof she doesn't know me at all."

"That reminds me . . . Yesterday you said your family calls you Amelia. Why? What's wrong with the name Trinity?"

Her body tensed. "Short version of my early life. My mom and dad met when he started an internship after law school clerking for the judge she worked for as a paralegal. They dated; she got pregnant. Mom refused to marry him, but she didn't deny him or his family access to me. By the time I was three, he'd married the stepmonster. I saw him maybe twice a year. His mother—my grandma Minnie—I saw every couple of weeks because she adored me even when he didn't. Anyway, when I was nine, my mom died in a—" She paused. "She died suddenly. Since she didn't have family, and Grandma couldn't take me because of her health issues, Grandma guilted her son into bringing me to live with him."

"Guilted him into it," I repeated. "He was your father. Taking care of you should've been his joy, not a damn burden." I reached for her hand.

She twined her fingers through mine. "In a perfect world? Yes. But in my world I was his burden. By that time, he and the stepmonster had two other kids, so I just . . . assimilated. But that meant having a normal name like their kids, instead of a 'hippie' name. I went from Trinity to Amelia."

"That's just wrong."

"Freshman year in college I refused to respond to them unless they called me Trinity."

And it made perfect sense to me why she'd use Amelia to ward off potentially unwanted attention—it was her way of taking ownership of that name.

"I never knew what to sign on my finished art, so I went with Trinity Amelia. Being called Amelia growing up did affect me on a creative level, both positively and negatively, and yet it formed me as a person so I wanted to acknowledge it."

"Professionally, you ditched your last name entirely?"

"Yes. It's not like there's family pride in what I do for a living."

I brought her hand to my mouth and kissed her knuckles. "Healthy attitude, Trinity Amelia Carlson."

She tilted her head toward me. "It's so sexy when you say my name like that."

"Ditch the hat, sweetheart. I hate that it masks your face."

Trinity tossed it aside. "Probably the stepmonster's intent."

Probably because the woman was jealous. Trinity had the fresh-faced girl-next-door look that was both sexy and sweet. I took that expressive face in my hands and kissed her.

We were both breathing hard when I pulled away.

"What was that for?"

I lifted an eyebrow. "I gotta have a reason to kiss you?"

"When you kiss me like that? Yeah."

"It just struck me how happy I am that you're here with me."

Trinity turned her head and kissed the center of my palm. "Despite your protests to the contrary, you are smooth."

"That didn't sound like a compliment."

"It was. A big compliment. I like that you're honest rather than trying to play it cool. Mixed signals suck." She pecked me on the mouth. "Unpack the picnic, Walker. You need to satisfy one of my appetites today."

"Only one?"

"One at a time."

The spread from Surdyk's impressed her. Fussy food tended to piss me off, but the roast beef, arugula, roasted red pepper and lemon aioli sandwich managed to be light and filling. Trinity raved about the beet, goat cheese and pepita salad, as well as the bourbon and salted caramel brownie we shared. I'd chosen hard cider instead of beer and it rounded out the meal perfectly. Yeah, I was a freakin' natural at this romantic meal stuff.

In my head Nolan took a bow and I flipped him off.

After we cleaned up, I returned to the chair in the sun and closed my eyes. I must've been more tired than I thought because I awoke with a start when a jet boat motor blew past us. I scrubbed my hands over my beard. Had I really fallen asleep on my date?

"Don't move," Trinity warned.

I squinted and saw her sitting in the shade beneath the canopy, her knees drawn up, a sketch pad on her lap, a pencil in her hand and one clamped between her teeth. "How long was I asleep?"

"Long enough for me to get a basic sketch. Now go back to the way you were."

"Asleep?"

"At least when you were sleeping you weren't moving," she said with saccharine sweetness.

"You weren't this bossy about the sets yesterday."

"Apples and oranges, Walker. When I work for someone else, it's on their terms. When I'm creating something for myself, I call all the shots."

"Was my head positioned like this?"

"Perfect. Don't move until I tell you."

I grinned. "You being bossy is kinda hot."

"Stop smiling! Sheesh. How am I supposed to concentrate when all I can see are your dimples?"

Like I could stop smiling after that comment? No. Way.

I really tried not to move. But when the tiny bit of breeze died entirely and I became sticky with sweat, staying still was impossible. My nose itched. So did my beard. The back of my left thigh was stuck to the chair. A fly buzzed around my ear.

Enough.

I jumped up, climbed on the ledge of the boat and dove into the water.

The cold shocked my system. When my momentum stopped, I tilted my head and looked up at the spot of light above me and propelled myself toward it. I broke the surface and saw Trinity leaning over the edge.

"Was it something I said?"

I laughed. "No. I was burning up. Who knew modeling is such hard work?"

"It is hot in the boat."

"Jump in."

"I only have the top half of my suit on."

"So? It's not like your pants won't dry."

Trinity seemed to consider it before she shook her head. "I've had a great time today, but I'm ready to go."

Although I was disappointed, the traffic on the lake had quadrupled in the last hour. "No problem. We can head back." I climbed up the swim ladder onto the swim deck. My hair had come undone during my plunge, so I shook it out.

Trinity watched me closely. "You have better hair than I do."

"Not true. Feel it. It's tangled like seaweed."

Right after she reached out, I snaked my arm around her waist and hauled her against me.

"Eww, you're all wet with lake water! Let go!"

"Just trying to cool you off since you said you were hot." I tilted her face up to meet my gaze. "But I don't think there's a cure for your hotness, sweetheart." I started the kiss out slow and teasing.

Trinity grabbed a handful of my hair and one of my ass. She whispered, "Fair's fair," against my lips and kicked the kiss up to the "I want you naked" level I was trying to avoid.

Fuck it. I went with it.

Through the fog of lust, I heard a motor gunning close to us—too close. I managed to end the kiss and spun her around, caging her body beneath mine as I latched onto the railing with both hands.

A huge wave hit us. The boat pitched and swayed, but we stayed upright.

Trinity turned and twined her arms around my neck.

"Thanks for the quick thinking, Captain. You probably saved us a broken tooth or a broken bone."

I planted a chaste kiss on her lips. "Aye, these be mighty rough waters, lassie."

She laughed. "You are so funny."

"Does that mean you'll go out with me again?"

"Absolutely."

"Good. I'd make you walk the plank if you said no."

She laughed again.

I could become addicted to that sound.

After pulling anchor, I headed straight back to the marina.

She stayed around while I secured the boat and did all the last-minute checks.

I picked up the cooler. "Let me drop this off first and then I'll walk you to your car."

Trinity followed me across the floating dock. I carried the cooler to the back of my truck, hoisting it over the side. When I turned around, her hungry gaze progressed up my arm, across my chest and down my other arm.

"Everything okay?" I asked.

"You developed all those big muscles from hard labor, not hard hours at the gym, didn't you?"

I shrugged and reached for her hand. "Be careful crossing the parking lot. The asphalt is squishy."

She squared off against me. "You can give my entire body a look so hot that the backs of my knees were sweating, but I can't do the same? Not fair, Walker."

I pivoted and pressed her against me, one hand braced in the small of her back, the other curled around the back of her neck. "No offense, sweetheart, but you're acting as if you've never seen a man's biceps before."

"I've never seen ones like *yours*," she retorted.

"You had your hands on them about an hour ago." I affixed

my gaze to hers. "And weren't you telling me you wanted to sketch my arms?"

"Yes."

"So didn't you get an eyeful of them then?"

"No. I became so focused on re-creating the flawless angles of your face that I forgot about your arms. Seeing them flexed and bulgy when you walked in front of me reminded me of their utter perfection." She nipped my chin. "Buck up and take the compliment."

"Fine. But I want to see that sketch."

She glanced away. "When it's finished." She ducked under my arm and started for her car, walking backward so she could leer at me. "I'll text you later, hot pipes."

"Hot pipes? Seriously, Trinity?"

She smirked. "It'd be funnier if you were a plumber."

Christ. I was falling for this woman so fast.

"Thanks for a great time today."

"No good-bye kiss?"

"I specialize in hello kisses. Good-bye kisses are your deal. So next time . . . I expect one that'll blow my hair back."

Five

TRINITY

After my date with Walker, I headed to my studio.

I began my sessions in the same way every time, wandering through my work area to take stock of the status of my various projects. Upon seeing the easel with the unfinished painting I'd been stuck on for months, I wondered when I'd have the guts to admit that it wasn't salvageable. I'd tossed away hundreds of projects that weren't working, so ditching a concept and starting over normally didn't bother me.

But something about this fragmentary piece haunted me. I suspected I'd regret dumping it instead of fixing it. Since it was a large canvas, I could see the false starts and the sections where I'd attempted to mask my errors. It taunted me in all its ugly, undefined glory.

Just take it off the stand and face it against the wall. Move on.

I sidestepped it and the lower left corner caught my eye. The dark colors, black, gray and shades of purple, looked angry—like a newly formed bruise. With the raindrop technique I'd used, the bruises appeared finger shaped. As if I was seeing a section of a body that'd been beaten down.

So if that was the result . . . what was the cause? In an inspired moment, I flipped the canvas, putting the image in the upper right corner. The ugliness of the murky image hadn't changed, but it had definability.

It had a name.

Broken.

That's when I knew why this hadn't worked. In the opposite corner I'd tried to disguise the anger by surrounding the black slashes with brightness. In the center I'd used neutral tones, trying to downplay the darkness.

But this piece needed darkness—demanded it.

And I knew exactly how to fix it.

Immediately I grabbed my paints and brushes and got to work.

I've been lost in creative chaos too many times to count. It's a fugue state where I am merely a conduit between what could be and what is. I'm pretty good about self-censoring my emotions so as not to affect the tone of a piece—too good sometimes. Whatever blockage I'd erected crumbled with the first stroke of my brush.

The downside of existing in that creative rush is the shock of the passage of time when you come out of it. When I finally deemed the painting done, I glanced over at the window to see the yard light had come on.

On automatic, I cleaned up my mess. I welcomed chaos in my work, but not in my workplace. I even had a shower installed so I could leave the studio as paint-free as when I'd arrived. A cleansing of sorts before I rejoined the real world.

I checked my phone. A flirty text from Walker was in my messages dated six hours ago.

Hope you had a great day. I'm around if you want
to grab dinner after you're done working. If not, I'll
see you tomorrow night at the community center.
Just wanted you to know that I'm thinking about you.
A lot. ☺

I felt a little guilty that I hadn't thought about him after I fell into a painting fury.

I texted back:

Thanks for the offer. As usual I lost track of time once I
was in my studio and just finished. I look forward to
seeing you tomorrow night. Sleep well.

I hit send and then immediately regretted it because I worried I sounded lame. And aloof.

I reread it.

Yep. Totally nailed both lame and aloof. Yay me.

Not to mention I'd texted him at one o'clock in the morning.

Ugh.

I pressed my forehead into the table. I wondered if there was a book *Sending Sexy, Flirty Texts for Dummies.*

If anyone knew the answer to that, it'd be Genevieve. So I fired off a quick text to her.

Only after I crawled in bed did my cat, Buttons, deign to acknowledge me.

WALKER

The offices of Flint & Lund were housed in an old fourplex that had been a single-family home at one time. We bought the property—and the vacant lot behind it—six years ago when I'd become a partner in the company. Gutting the brick building and renovating it to suit our needs nearly ended the partnership before it began.

But that's why Jase Flint and I made good business partners. I was happier to get my hands dirty on the job site, letting him sit in the office writing bids and drawing up building plans.

So I wasn't in the office long in the mornings. Jase and I kept each other updated throughout the workday, but meeting face-to-face over coffee every day had kept everything running smoothly.

It also helped that we'd hired a top-notch office manager. Jase and I joked that the only way we'd ever let Betsy quit was if she ran for president. If anyone could inspire parties with opposing political views to cooperate for the overall greater good . . . it'd be our scarily efficient Betsy.

As usual, Betsy was already in her office when I arrived. Without glancing away from her computer screen, she said, "Good morning, Walker. Tell Jase I'll be right in after I type up these notes. There's coffee in the break room."

"Who made it?" I asked warily. Jase's coffee looked like sludge and tasted worse. Megan, our receptionist and Betsy's tyrant in training, made it so weak it tasted like water.

"I did."

"Thank you."

She waved me off.

After I filled my insulated mug with coffee, I scaled the stairs to the conference room.

Jase sat at the end of the table muttering to himself, his glasses sliding halfway down his nose.

"Morning," I said and slipped into the chair to his right.

He glanced up and pushed his glasses back in place. "Please tell me you brought donuts or bagels or something not healthy."

I stared at him. "Dude. In the six years we've been partners, have I *ever* bought donuts for the office?"

"No. But there's always a first time." Jase removed his glasses and rubbed his eyes.

He looked tired and sloppily dressed—at seven thirty in the morning? Not like him at all. "What's going on?"

"Tiffany has me on a damn diet."

"Why? You're in good shape for an old guy." Jase had hit forty last month and I still owed him payback for the surprise thirtieth birthday party he'd thrown for me last year . . . at a senior citizens center.

"Bite me, asshole. It's not that kind of a diet."

"Tiffany on a vegetarian diet kick or something?" His wife, Tiffany, was a doll. Sweet, utterly devoted to him, even if she went a bit overboard sometimes. I attributed her enthusiasm to her age since she was fifteen years younger than Jase. But as far as I knew, they were ridiculously happy together—a happiness that'd been long overdue for my partner, who'd lost his first wife to cancer two years before I'd met him.

"No. It's a 'reproduction' diet. She claims certain foods will build my sperm count because we're trying to get pregnant."

I held my hand up. "Say no more. Seriously. My brain shut off after you said *sperm*."

"Walker, I have no one else to talk to about this. My

friends already have kids, and none of our office staff is married or in a relationship, so suck it up and listen, will ya?"

"Fine. How long have you been trying?"

"Five months. First she started making me wear boxers. Then she took away my nightly soak in the hot tub. Last month we only had sex when she was ovulating. Now I'm on this no-sugar, high-protein diet." His eyes met mine. "I'm freakin' sick of steak. There, I said it. I don't give a damn if my man card is revoked. If I have to eat another fillet I might go vegan."

It was hard not to laugh. "How long is she enforcing this diet?"

"Her doctor said since Tiff is young and healthy, we should try 'naturally' for a year before looking into medical options."

"So basically in order to get laid all the time, you've gotta quit eating stuff that's bad for you for seven more months?"

"Yeah."

"You're getting no sympathy from me, pal. A hot woman, cooking you a hot meal, who is constantly hot to get you in bed? Yeah, your life sucks. A big bowl of ice cream is definitely worth giving all that up."

Jase blinked slowly, like he was coming out of a fog. "God. You're right."

"Say that one more time? No, wait until Betsy gets here so she can record it. Then I'll have proof."

"Do I need to brush the dust off the Dictaphone?" Betsy said as she breezed in, holding a bagel in one hand and a coffee mug in the other.

"You've heard of a Dictaphone?" I asked.

"Only in the historical context. It was outdated when I started school." She set the bagel, smeared with pink cream cheese, on the table. For a moment I thought Jase would lunge for it. Then Betsy moved it out of his reach and pointed at him. "This is not on your diet."

"Tiffany told you that she put me on a diet?"

"Of course. I'm supposed to let her know if I see you eating foods not on the list."

"You'd tattle on me to my wife?"

"In a heartbeat. Because I, for one, cannot wait until there's a baby around here to spoil."

"As much as I'd love to talk about baby bootees and cravings for carbs," I inserted, "I have a job site to get to. So give us the rundown on last week, Bets."

Betsy studied me. "You *still* grumpy about whatever happened to you last week that you refused to talk about?"

"Good question," Jase said. "Betsy and I tell you about the things in our lives that make us pissy. Maybe you'd be less pissy if you talked it out with us."

I groaned. "I'll pass."

"We're a team. Or so you're always telling me," Betsy retorted. "You were an ass last week, Walker. And not just here. Did you really chew out the driver from the lumber warehouse?"

"Yes, he needs his damn driver's license revoked. He ran over a freakin' tree when he was backing in. The tires also ripped the shit out of the yard. So I told him I'd be forwarding the landscaping repair bill to his supervisor and he could explain how he managed to take out a tree and a rock garden on a drop-and-go delivery."

Silence.

The outburst was out of character for me and I waited for either one of my coworkers to rail on me about it.

"So your weekend was good?" Betsy said to me. "Ask me about mine. I heard a great new band at the Cabooze. And . . . I might've banged the bass guitarist of said band."

My gaze flicked to Jase. But he didn't seem concerned by Betsy's abrupt topic switch.

"I don't think he's seeing the parallels," Jase said to her.

"Parallels to what?" I demanded.

"Your erratic behavior. Snappy, then defensive, and then back to your pleasant self. We weren't sure which guy would show up this morning."

"Is something going on with your family?" Betsy asked.

"No!" I forced myself to keep my temper in check. "You want me to share? Fine. It started last Tuesday night after my meeting with Dick . . ."

When I'd finished spilling my guts—without telling them Trinity's name; I deserved some damn privacy—Jase's mouth hung open and Betsy wore a smirk.

"What?"

"Walker's got a girlfriend," she said in a singsongy tone.

Jesus.

"And I know why you didn't complain to *me* about the mystery woman," Betsy added. "Because you know I would've dug in until I tracked her down for you. I live for that kind of *Alias* stuff."

I rolled my eyes. But I knew she was right.

"When do we get to meet this chick who led you on a merry chase?" Jase asked. "I know—invite her to dinner tomorrow night. I'll buy. Pasta."

"Too soon," Betsy said. "He hasn't told his family about her. If the Almighty Lunds hear that we met this woman before they did?" She shuddered. "I, for one, do not want to deal with a pissed-off Selka Lund."

"My mom isn't *that* scary."

Both Jase and Betsy laughed.

"Besides, you're on night duty this week as the painters finish up the McHenry project," Betsy reminded me.

That blew. After tonight I couldn't make plans with Trinity until the weekend. I checked the time on my phone. I had a meeting in forty-five minutes. "Now that we've bonded over Jase's low sperm count, your new status as a rock band groupie and my week of lost and found, can we get back to business?"

TRINITY

My best friend, Genevieve, was a morning person.

I was not.

We compromised. She could come over after eight a.m. . . . I could call her up until midnight. The texting rules weren't clear.

So when my doorbell rang at eight oh one, I was somewhat prepared. I'd put the coffee on, but I was still wearing my pajamas. I opened the door and covered a yawn as she brushed past me. "Coffee?"

"I've already had four cups, so one more won't hurt."

Genevieve plopped down at the dining room table. I heard a thump when her gigantic purse hit the floor.

I poured two cups of coffee and set them on the antique serving tray she'd given me as a housewarming gift. I'd intended to use it for special occasions, but Genevieve pointed out I'd never take it out of the cupboard. So I used it every time she came over.

She poured a slug of cream in her cup and stirred. "Now tell me about the Viking. Don't leave out any details."

I laid out all my thoughts, fears and weirdly happy moments with him, but for some reason didn't tell her his name. "So what do you think?"

Genevieve took her time responding. "He sounds too good to be true—or too practiced."

I stared at her with total surprise.

"What?"

"That's what you gleaned from everything I told you?"

"Do I think it's some kind of cosmic sign you two were predestined to be together? No. It's me, Trin. I don't believe in that crap." She pointed at me. "And normally you don't either. You've had one date with him."

"But it was a great date. The best I've had"—well, ever, but Genevieve didn't want to hear that so I said—"since I moved here and I want to see where this goes. I like him." Walker seemed to get me and I could count on one hand the number of people in my life I could say that about.

"Then why do you care what I think? It sounds like you've already made up your mind."

I blinked at her. "I guess I have."

She smiled slyly. "That's what I wanted to hear. You go, girl."

"And your reasoning for playing devil's advocate was . . . ?"

"I wasn't playing devil's advocate, *chica*. I was channeling Ramon. You're too easily swayed by his opinion—which is only offered when he wants to act superior."

"Not true. He's—"

"A condescending ass to you, Trin. I know you don't see it, and I hate hate *hate* that I have seen it from the start." She paused and poured more coffee. "You and me? We're best pals. Everyone knows this. And yet, in the last year, Ramon hasn't invited me to a single bash he's thrown. I can tell you exactly when I got put on the blacklist. That night of his Gatsby-themed party. We were knocking back Jäger bombs and he got snippy because the drinks weren't 'period appropriate.'"

"I'd forgotten about that." Some of the details were fuzzy,

courtesy of said Jäger bombs, but I remembered dissolving into a fit of giggles over something stupid that Genevieve had said. It was one of those times when you can't stop laughing, and the harder you try to stop, the harder you laugh. Ramon got pissed off about my behavior and told me to grow up; I was embarrassing him and myself. Gen got in his face and lit into him like I'd never seen. So Ramon wasn't a big Genevieve fan. But she'd said nothing to him that had been cruel or untrue—unlike Ramon, who snidely called her "your fat friend."

"I'm sorry I didn't connect the dots."

"You haven't been hanging out with him as much the last year. That makes me happy because I think he's toxic. Plus, he's stoned more often than not. Besides, I know where I stand on the friendship scale. I don't see him as competition for the other half of your BFF keychain."

She'd never let me live that down. When we'd exchanged house keys, the way friends do, I'd bought a heart-shaped BFF double key ring set and given her one half of the heart and kept the other. She'd called me a sweet, sentimental dork and hugged me. So when she brought it up, it wasn't in a mean-spirited way, because that wasn't her way. And that was why she was the one person in the world I could count on no matter what. I bumped her knee under the table and broke into a chorus of "Piece of My Heart."

"Girl, I love you like crazy but you are a horrible singer."

Just then Buttons's loud yowl confirmed it.

"Enough about me. What's new with you?" I eyed her uniform. "Did your shift get changed with your new promotion?"

"No. There's a mandatory supervisors meeting at ten. The new head of zoning wants to discuss 'critical issues.'"

"Regarding snow removal? It's August!" Genevieve worked

in dispatch for the Department of Transportation. Summers were her slow time.

"Oh, he wants to buy new equipment. But we all have to sign on before it gets pushed to the next level and no way will the dudes running the other ten zones agree to it. I swear, they throw a fit like we're yanking away a little boy's favorite Tonka truck. They get so attached to their machines."

I wondered if Walker dealt with heavy machinery. I imagined him in the cab of a backhoe, finessing the controls like a lover as he made the earth move.

"What were you just thinking about?" Genevieve demanded.

"Walker's big equipment," I said distractedly.

She choked on her coffee. "You already know the size of his—"

"No! I literally meant the equipment he uses in his construction job."

"Oh. So, knowing that, I won't demand specifics on the sketches you did of him yesterday."

"Mind out of the gutter." I got up and grabbed the canvas tote I'd left in the entryway. I pulled out my sketch pad and flipped it to the page I'd been working on.

Her eyes widened. "Holy Valhalla—Viking dude is hot."

"Told ya."

She squinted at the picture.

"What?"

"Just checking to see if you at least outlined his junk."

"Genevieve!"

She laughed. "Too easy." She pushed pack from the table and stood. "I've gotta jet."

"But we didn't talk about sexting. Or how to send flirty texts."

Genevieve clamped her hands around my upper arms and

gave me her stern face. "Trinity. I say this with love in my heart for you as a sister, okay?"

"Okay."

"You're thirty-one. The fact you think you need help texting a man . . . it's all kinds of paranoid, babe."

"I don't want to screw this up."

"*One* date, Trin. Remember that. You've had *one* date with him. And prior to that one date, you lied to him about your name, you gave him the wrong phone number . . . and he's still interested. So I don't think he'll give a damn if you're not cutesy emoji girl when texting."

Just like that, my paranoia fled. "Thank you."

"You're welcome. Is that all of what's dogging you?"

In the past I would've lowered my eyes in shame and mumbled something about being fine. But I'd gone beyond that with Gen. She knew I struggled with the highs and lows of creative chaos. She didn't laugh it off as drama. She didn't judge me. She didn't tell me to snap out of it when that cloud of depression enveloped me completely. She just thrust her hand deep into the darkness, allowing me something to grab onto if I needed it. I hadn't needed it often, but it was a relief to know it was there.

I smiled at her. "Sensors haven't picked up signs of stormy weather ahead. You're on first alert if anything changes."

"Good. Losing that commission last week . . . ?"

"Took a bite out of me financially, but not emotionally. I'm making calls this morning about a couple of pieces I finished last night."

"All right. Call me this week—any night but Thursday. Got a date with hot Irish rugby boy."

"Break him in gently."

"Where's the fun in that?"

After she left, I ditched my pajamas and put on real

clothes. I'd just finished my short beauty routine (teeth brushed, hair combed) when the doorbell rang. I checked the peephole. What was she doing here?

I opened the door. "Mrs. Stephens?"

She smiled. "Surprised to see me?"

"Yes. I don't give clients my home address." Or encourage them to drop by. I paused. "But since your husband declined to commission my piece last week, you don't fall into the client realm."

"I don't blame you for being bitter. But there's a method to my madness that I'd like to explain. Do you have time to hear me out?"

"I was just about to head to my studio. It's around back." I slipped on my flip-flops and stepped onto the porch, closing the door behind me.

When we reached the studio, I punched in my code and the door opened. I led her to the small enclosed courtyard where I'd set up a fire pit (against city code) and a lounging area.

"This is lovely."

"Thank you. Now, Mrs. Stephens—"

"Please call me Esther."

"All right, Esther. Give me your spiel."

She drummed her fingers on the arm of the chair and stared into the cold fire pit.

Her unease increased mine.

Finally she spoke. "Michael's dismissal of your proposed project last week was my doing. I'd made him think that your work was too left of center for my taste and I asked him to cancel the commission." She looked at me. "I'm not a good liar, but I'm afraid I pulled it off too well with him. See, I'm a huge fan of your work. I picked up a piece in Santa Fe, probably seven years ago, at the Shifting Sands Gallery."

Somehow I hid my shock and managed to say, "A watercolor?"

"And charcoal. I believe the piece is titled *Desert and*—"

"*Darkness*," I finished. "I always loved that piece."

"It just struck me, the complete separation of night and day. With the inky darkness at the top and the vivid colors of a reflective sun at the bottom. But, looking at it, you can't tell if night is ending as morning approaches or if the day is fading into night."

"There's no right or wrong answer—that was the point."

She nodded. "Stunning imagery. Anyway, Michael knew I liked your work and he recognized your name after seeing the *Honor and Lies* piece in the Federal Reserve building."

I'd created that mixed-media piece after being bombarded with images of memorials for victims of violent crime and the news headlines about combat-related deaths. Images from soldiers' military funerals—distorted to protect their identities—were juxtaposed with flyers, pictures and notes left at the site where a violent crime had occurred on an enormous canvas I'd textured like cement. In the corners, I'd splattered red paint to resemble blood. I'd added shell casings, broken handcuffs, frayed sections of a discarded American flag, soles from worn-out combat boots, candles and teddy bears and love notes with lipstick kisses, handwritten prayers and camo material. The 3-D effect is startling. As your eyes search out specific images, trying to separate them into neat categories, the images overlap and it's impossible to discern between domestic violent crimes and the results of international terrorism. That'd been one of the rare works I'd created out of my own frustration and anger. I hadn't been trying to make a political statement; I'd been searching for answers.

The only reason that work had made it out of my studio was my friend and fellow artist Nicolai's insistence I enter it in a cattle call—an invitation for artists to display their projects for a limited time. Then businesses and gallery owners could browse and buy. I'd lived in the Cities for only nine months and was a complete unknown, both with my art and in the Minneapolis art community. So it shocked everyone when my piece was the only one that'd sold. The Federal Reserve purchased it for its local-artists wing. It'd been the single biggest paycheck of my career. I'd immediately put the money into updating my studio and purchasing supplies.

Esther had stopped speaking while I'd been lost in thought, so I motioned for her to continue.

"He contacted you to commission a piece for our upcoming anniversary. I planned to torpedo *anything* you showed us."

"Why?"

"My husband is a wealthy man. He wants something, he buys it. So he's impossible to surprise. I saw my chance to pull off the mother of all surprises. See, I want to hire you to do that mixed-media commission, not for our anniversary but for his birthday next month."

"Same design?"

"No. Different. You can keep some of the elements he loved. There are certain textiles I want included, but the rest of it—" She smiled. "Get as edgy as you want. Just nothing lewd."

"Well, there goes my plan to stick a 3-D image of Michael's head on a life-sized plaster cast of Michelangelo's *David*."

Esther laughed. "It wouldn't be anatomically correct."

Don't blush. Don't speak. Just nod your head.

"I understand this will be a rush job, and I'll make sure you're well compensated."

"Define 'well compensated.'"

She gave me a number that made my jaw drop.

"I can work with that."

"I thought you might." She stuck her hand in her pocket and pulled out a folded piece of paper and handed it over. "Forty percent down, thirty percent after design approval and thirty percent upon completion, correct?"

"You did your homework, Esther." The check was inside the paper, which turned out to be a copy of my rough draft for the piece rejected the week before.

"You're the artist. I won't tell you how to do your job, but I kept this as a template, mostly so you know what the textiles are that I'll be giving you."

I stood. "There's better working space in the studio if you want to go over some of this now. Then I can have a mock-up to you by . . . Wednesday? And we'll reconvene on Friday for the last draft?" I wouldn't mention that even what she saw on Friday might not be completely what she ended up with. The best art wasn't perfectly planned out.

"Perfect."

Inside my studio, I unrolled a large sheet of paper and settled it on my drafting table. "All right, you start talking and I'll scribble."

"Talk about what?"

"Michael. How you met, what made you fall in love with him, where you lived, your kids, how you've been able to stick it out for almost fifty years, anything that will be useful to evoke strong feelings in him when he first sees this."

"I met Michael when I was nineteen and he was twenty-four."

"That's basic, Esther—give me more intimate stuff. Like, he had the nicest buns, greatest smile, cheesiest pickup line . . ."

"It wasn't love at first sight for me. We were at a frat party and he copped a feel. Not me, but my best friend, Liddie. She was easily flustered so I knew she wouldn't tell him to get his hand off her butt. So I moved in behind him and pulled his hand away. When he turned around, I punched him in the stomach."

I laughed. "Is that a story you've told your kids?" Right after I said it, I wondered how something like that would play out in my life. *Yes, honey, the instant I saw your dad in that dive bar I was compelled to attach my lips to his and give him the hottest, wettest kiss of his life . . . before I'd even introduced myself.*

My hand froze above the drawing. What the hell? Walker and I had been on one date and the next day I was crafting "how we met" stories for our kids?

Repeat after me, Trin. You've had one *date with him.* One.

"Trinity? Are you all right?"

I managed not to jump when Esther interrupted my "one date" mantra. "Yes. I'm fine. I should warn you that I'm often sidetracked by the images in my head."

She smiled. "I'm honestly thrilled to be here seeing your artistic process firsthand."

"It's more . . . controlled chaos than a legitimate process."

"Controlled chaos *is* a legitimate process if it works for you."

How sweet that she was trying to reassure me. "Chaos is a fickle mistress, so let's crack the whip on her while I have her full attention." I'd need every bit of focus this week to hit Esther's deadlines.

At the door, she said, "There is one more thing I forgot to mention. Dagmar Kierkegaard is a friend of ours. He'll be at the party."

Dagmar Kierkegaard was a freelance art curator who had
ly acquired pieces for the Walker Art Center's perma-
'lection but also acquired for four galleries in Chi-

cago, the Milwaukee Art Museum and galleries in New York and Washington, D.C.

"Okay. And you're telling me this why?"

"Because this one time he'll be your captive audience since yours is the only art he'll see. Make it shine, Trinity."

No pressure.

Six

—

WALKER

Right after I'd knocked off for the day, my cell rang. The caller ID popped up on my navigation screen and I poked answer. "Hey, baby sis. What's up?"

"I'm going to murder some family members and I need to borrow your backhoe thingy to bury the bodies."

"Am I on the hit list?"

"Not unless you volunteered me for babysitting duty for dumb hockey players who don't speak English."

"Who did that?"

"Nolan."

"Annika, here's where I point out you're an adult and no one can make you do anything you don't want to."

"Oh, really? If you could be doing anything else tonight, you still would've chosen to volunteer at the community theater?"

"Yes." I might've answered differently last week, but knowing I'd get to see Trinity changed things.

"You're not there at Mom's command? Bull."

"We're all at LCCO's command. And we do get to choose." Better this gig than the bachelor auction. No way would I strut around in a leopard-print loincloth, regardless of whether the money earned went to a good cause.

"I have no problem giving time to LCCO, but this doesn't have anything to do with community involvement. And I *did* tell Nolan no. The jerk went behind my back and enlisted Mom's help. She told Nolan I'd be 'happy in a clamshell' to translate."

"Translate?" I asked.

"From Swedish to English for hockey player number one. Nolan assumes I'm fluent."

"Uh, you *are* fluent."

"So are you, Mr. I-lived-in-Sweden," she reminded me. "And Nolan didn't call *you* to translate."

"Nolan hardly ever calls me for anything anymore. You work with him, so it makes sense he asked you."

"Except I'm not fluent in Russian, which is the only language hockey player number two speaks."

"You're babysitting more than one?" I whistled. "That is asking a lot. Who are these guys?"

"Friends of Jaxson's. One of them is named Igor—probably the Russian. The Blackhawks traded him to the Wild. I don't know the Swede's name—probably something unpronounceable with twenty consonants—and he's a recent trade to the Wild too." She sighed. "And I shouldn't know any of this news since I don't give a puck about hockey, so will you *please* blow off your volunteer duties for one night and come to dinner?"

"I can't. I have to be two steps ahead of the artist, and

we're running night shifts on the McHenry job the rest of this week, so this is my only free night."

"Fine. Be upstanding."

"I don't know any other way to be."

"Boring."

I laughed. "You done nagging me?"

"Almost. Brady said I'm supposed to ask if you had any luck finding what you were looking for—whatever that means."

"Why are you asking me instead of Brady asking me himself?"

"Because he and Lennox took off on vacation Sunday afternoon. I hate that you guys have secrets."

"And you and Dallas don't?"

She paused. "Dallas! Of course. I'll ask her to be the fourth wheel at the babysitter's club dinner."

"Good luck."

"I'll call you later."

"Don't. Seriously. I'll be busy."

TRINITY

Normally on a job like this I didn't bother wearing makeup or fixing my hair. I put on my white painter's pants, an old shirt, tossed my hair into a messy bun and I was good to go.

But today I'd decided an upgrade from my usual sloppy look was in order. It made me hot all over whenever Walker's lusty looks expressed his appreciation for my overly curvy body and I couldn't wait to see it again.

The actors were sitting in a circle onstage while the director paced around them outside of the circle. Nate gave me a chin dip in greeting and I cut through the auditorium to the backstage area.

The door to my room had been propped open. I flipped on the lights and saw the specific paint colors I'd asked for lined against the wall. Canvas tarps had been spread out and the next pieces I needed to work on were stacked against the wall.

Wow. That was a big stack. Walker had accomplished a lot.

You're slacking. Is that the impression you want him to have of you?

My thought processes were skewed to the negative side. A trait I'd had since childhood. My stepmother chirped at me incessantly to think "happy thoughts," as if that would alter my mood or fix me. I hated that they believed I was in need of fixing. I really hated they believed I'd succumbed to the brooding-artist stereotype. They never once considered I might've had a serious issue with depression. We didn't talk about it after the one time I'd brought it up and my father lost his shit. He listed all the things I should be *grateful* for. He snapped that there was no reason on earth why I should be depressed.

When I struck out on my own, I finally understood that my artistic gift had manic bursts of creativity followed by episodes where I couldn't create at all. There was no magical formula to change that, so instead I'd accepted it'd always be a struggle to find the balance points between highs and lows.

Gen was the only one I'd ever shared this with because it was intensely personal and to some extent it still felt like a flaw. I'd managed to mask that aspect of my personality during the few intimate relationships I'd allowed to last more than one night. I didn't let lovers get too close—and the sobering part of that was that none of them had seemed to notice I wasn't giving my all.

"You've been staring at that piece a long time," Walker said behind me. "Is there something wrong with it?"

"No. I was just lost in thought." I turned around. He stood back, his hands in the pockets of his jeans, a hopeful smile on his lips and wariness in his eyes. His hair was loose and it looked like he'd been running his hands through it all day. Oh, such lucky, lucky hands.

"That happens to me too. Then I wonder where the hour—or sometimes half a day—went."

"I only lost around ten minutes this time." I tried really hard not to stare. But the man's presence just filled a room in a way I'd never encountered before.

"Are we really gonna do this, Trinity?"

"Do what?" I asked. I wasn't clear on what he meant.

"Stand here and look at each other awkwardly? I don't know what you want me to do."

"Maybe the real question is, what do *you* want to do, Walker?"

He eliminated the ten feet between us in three quick steps. Then his hands cradled my face and his mouth crashed down on mine.

His kiss was electric. Hungry. Relieved. Sweet.

After he ended the kiss, he crushed me to his chest. "That's what I want to do every time I see you."

"Well, speaking from experience, that *is* a great way to say hello."

He chuckled.

I tipped my face back and nearly lost my head again as I gazed into his intensely beautiful blue eyes. "Thank you."

"For?"

"Making the first move. Even when we've kissed, and gone out on a date, I wasn't sure if we're together."

"Yes, babe, we are."

"Then I will accept your class ring on a necklace as proof that we are going steady and are officially a couple."

Walker gave me the dimpled grin that made my knees weak. "Or I could give you a hickey."

"That actually sounds like more fun."

Soft, warm lips landed on the side of my neck. He brushed his mouth up and down in an erotic arc. "I could spend hours kissing you right here," he murmured against my skin, "trying to choose the perfect spot to leave my mark."

Yes. Let's start now.

"Hey, Walker, is Trinity in here?" Nate yelled from the doorway.

Walker raised his head and said, "Do you want to keep on the down low here? Or do we admit we're coupling?"

Two voices warred inside my head:

Keep it under wraps; who knows how long it'll last?

Screw that. Let the entire world know that this hot man is hot for you.

Keeping one hand on Walker's chest, I stepped to the side.

Nate looked confused for a moment. "Oh, uh . . . hi, Trinity. I didn't, uh . . . see you there."

"Walker casts a pretty big shadow. What did you need?"

"The director wants to know if you can paint the section with the flowers next. We'll be doing the blocking for that scene first thing on Thursday."

"No problem."

Walker faced Nate and draped his arm over my shoulder. "The schedule is done?"

"Yes." Nate pulled out a piece of paper and handed it over.

"The other thing I'm supposed to ask Trinity: Would it be easier if someone else primed the sets?"

"That would be great."

"I'll let the director know. If either of you can think of anything you need, don't hesitate to ask."

"I do have a question," Walker said. "Would it be possible to get a key so I can come in late when no one is here? I have insomnia some nights and I might as well be productive."

It shocked me that Walker had admitted that to a stranger. But there were more important things to address. "I imagine the answer will be no since I also imagine there'd be issues with liability insurance, especially since you'd be here alone running power tools. From a commonsense standpoint that's not safe. What if something happened? You couldn't call for help. And if you could, emergency services would have to break down a door to gain entrance. And no offense, but how can they be sure if something *did* happen that you wouldn't sue them?"

Walker made a noise like he was choking down a laugh. "I can promise I'd never file a lawsuit. But I understand your concerns, *Nate*—" he said to me since I'd just jumped on in. "Why don't you call LCCO, ask for Priscilla in the main office, explain the situation and my request for a key. I suspect she'll give you an immediate answer."

"Sure. It's worth a shot. I'll let you know. Later." Nate hustled out the door.

I shook my head at Walker.

"What?"

"It's dangerous to be here alone."

"I'm not an amateur, babe. I'd probably stick with finish work, which requires minimal power tools." He bent closer and kissed me on the nose. "It's sweet that you're worried."

"I *was* worried. Now I'm just annoyed because you're

acting as if a big, macho tool expert such as yourself couldn't possibly have an accident." I poked him in the chest. "FYI: They're called *accidents* for a reason."

He curled his hands around my hips and squeezed. "Then in that case maybe you'll have to meet me down here. That way, if I break a nail you can patch me up."

"Funny." I slid my hands up his chest and smoothed my fingertips down his beard. "Do you really have insomnia?"

"Yes, unfortunately." He sighed. "And it's worse when I have to work nights—I get home and I can't wind down. I figured I'd use that time to my best advantage since I'm not sleeping."

"Maybe, after we've been going steady for more than a couple of days, we can come up with a better way to kill time together in the wee small hours of the night," I said, adding a *rowr*.

"Jesus, Trinity." His sexy growl rolled over me as potent as a caress. "Lock the door so we can try out a few of those late-night fantasies right now."

His phone buzzed in his back pocket.

I stepped away to let him answer it, because I knew he would.

"I thought I told you not to call." Pause. "Like I'd know the Swedish phrase for that? You wanna call him a scum-sucking douchebag, do it in English! He'll get the gist."

But I didn't bother to pretend I wasn't listening.

"No," he said adamantly. "Because you'll end up in jail and I am *not* bailing you out. Oh yeah? Call Mom and tell her what your plans are. Or maybe *I* should tattle on you like you used to do on me?" He laughed. "Anatomically impossible. And just for that—no way. You need help, call Jens. Fine. Ash is in town. Or call Nolan—he's probably still at the office. It's only Monday. He hasn't picked his skank-of-the-week yet. I'm hanging up now." He held his phone in front of him. "Fuck."

"Is everything all right?"

Walker whirled around as if he'd forgotten about me. "My sister is way the hell pissed off about the favor she was railroaded into doing for our cousin. But instead of railing on him, I get to deal with her in Godzilla mode."

"Same cousin that had car trouble last week?"

"No."

"Swedish curse words, skank-of-the-week, possibility of jail time . . . sounds entertaining."

He snorted. "Don't get me started on the craziness that is my family."

I recognized he'd said that with no real malice. Not like my family—who really meant it when they said *the craziness that is Amelia*.

"Come find me if you get done early," he said distractedly and walked out.

I found the pieces needed for the scenes this week and primed the boards. One coat took thirty minutes to dry, so as I waited I went over my sketches again. This backdrop would be the only spot of color in the otherwise dreary background, so color was more important than fine detailing. I cracked open the paint cans and stirred the paint. I needed a shade between dark burgundy and scarlet. I dumped some of each color into an empty quart can, added white and kept mixing until I was satisfied.

Once I fell into that working groove, everything around me blurred. I kept at it until I'd filled the board.

I tossed my paintbrush onto the plastic tray and noticed the mess I'd created. Some painters could go all day without getting even a single drop of paint on their clothing. I was usually covered. It didn't matter what medium I worked in—

even with textiles I'd be coated in fabric fuzz and metal shavings.

"I love to watch you work."

I glanced over my shoulder at him. "How long have you been there?"

"Long enough to see the last two flowers take shape." He offered me his hand and helped me up.

"They were trickier to get right than I'd allotted time for." I gave him a once-over. He was sawdust-free. "You're already done?"

"Already? It's been three hours."

No wonder my neck hurt. I moved my head from side to side, trying to work the kinks out. "Is everyone gone?"

"Nate's still here."

"Waiting on me to finish."

Walker grinned. "Another logical reason for me to have a key. He could've already gone home and I could lock up."

"Since Nate is here . . . you don't have to stay."

"I want to stay."

"I'm about to delve into the suckiest part of being an artist. Cleaning up."

I expected him to leave. But he just said, "What needs done first?"

"The paper I used as drop cloths can be picked up and thrown away. Unless you'd rather clean brushes and the airbrush machine?"

His face fell. "You airbrushed something? I wanted to see you do that." Then he headed toward the section of sky and clouds I'd propped beneath the chalkboard. "This is it." He crouched to get a better look and studied it for several long moments. "You nailed it."

"It's a simple cloud formation. I hope I nailed it."

"No, it's not simple. That's what you see at first glance on one of those gloomy winter days when you gaze up at the sky and wonder if everything will always be colorless and bland. But then you notice the shadows and highlights of different shades of gray in the clouds and the hidden textures. It amazes me you can capture this on Styrofoam." He moved and stopped in front of me. "Am I wrong? Did I not see it the way you'd intended?"

"I'm thinking you see too much," I murmured.

"That scares you."

Not a question, so I wasn't compelled to answer.

The silence stretched as we considered each other.

Finally, he said, "Why does it scare you?"

"I'm not exactly normal, Walker."

"Can you explain that, sweetheart?"

"Have you ever been involved with a woman who creates something out of nothing? Who spends a lot of time alone staring at a blank canvas or a blank computer screen or block of clay? And I'm not talking about women who draw for fun, or write for fun, or sculpt for fun. I'm talking about women who make their living solely from their creativity."

He shook his head.

"Creative people . . . our brains work differently. Not better, not worse, just not like yours. There has to be a certain amount of ego involved to believe that strangers are willing to pay you for what you create. But the balance to that ego is loads and loads of self-doubt. At least it is for me. Add in income highs and lows to the creative highs and lows . . ."

"And?"

"And that doesn't make you reach for your hat as you're booking it out the closest door?"

"Are you trying to stop this before it starts?" he said softly.

"No. But being involved with me won't always be easy."

"Nothing worthwhile ever is." He gave me a wistful smile.

"I like that you're warning me up front that you're going to be a lot of work."

"You are?"

"Yep. It'll give me a chance to prove my awesome work ethic."

Oh yeah. He was so smooth even I believed him. "Don't say I didn't warn you."

"Duly noted."

We were stuck in that awkward "Who talks first?" silence.

"Trinity," he finally said. His gaze roamed from my forehead to my chin, across my cheeks and lingered on my mouth. "I need to tell you something."

My stomach clenched at the seriousness of his tone. "What?"

"There's paint all over your face. Speckled white spots on green streaks. And a big purple dot on your chin. Reminds me of that Dr. Seuss book my mom read to me as a kid."

"Why didn't you tell me I resemble a freakin' Dr. Seuss character before now?"

He grinned. "Because you look adorable."

I flapped my hand at him, trying to shoo him away.

"Where were you using purple paint?"

"I mixed it with white to get the shade of gray I needed. Why?"

"You really got into the grays, didn't you?"

"What?"

"Your ponytail. It's streaked with gray. Is using your hair as a brush some fancy technique you learned in college?"

I curbed the urge to smack my forehead—or his. "Don't you have paper to pick up?"

After he started his task, I grabbed the rubber mallet and hammered the lids on the paint cans. Then I lined them along the back wall in order from darkest to lightest and did the same with the spray cans. I made sure the cans of primer were in plain sight so people wouldn't rummage through my organized paint stash. I gathered all the brushes into a large plastic container and took them to the big sink in the kitchen.

Walker crossed the tile floor behind me. He pressed his front to my back and kissed the side of my neck. "I'm done. Need help?"

"No. I'm finished with everything except removing the polka dots from my face."

"That I can help with."

The next thing I knew, I was sitting on the counter with Walker's hips pressing the inside of my thighs. He gripped my jaw with one hand and dabbed at my face with a damp strip of cloth.

"You don't have to do that. If I'm a serious mess it'd be best if I clean up at home."

"Just sit there and look pretty. It's not as bad as I made it out to be."

"Why would you tell me that?"

"Because I wanted an excuse to touch you."

"Oh. Well. Okay, then."

Being this close to him, I could study him without it being weird. The man truly was a work of art. From his bold bone structure to his vivid blue eyes, his facial features were stunning. There were his thick eyebrows, his long sweep of dark eyelashes, his regal nose and the pouty bow of his lips. His facial hair was a mix of tawny browns and muted golds, with white blond strands and wisps the color of dark chocolate.

"You're staring at me," he grumbled.

"Because you are a feast for the eyes."

His lips curled. "Glad you think so."

"Would you let me sculpt you?"

"Depends."

"On?"

"If I have to sit still for hours on end."

Funny that was his biggest concern. "No. But I'll need to touch you a lot."

Walker's powerful gaze locked on to mine. "I'd only agree to that if I got equal time touching you."

The nearness of him—his scent, his body heat, the sensual way he performed something so basic as removing paint from my skin—had me tossing caution to the wind. "That'd only be fair."

His mouth crashed down on mine.

The kiss was a shot of rocket fuel.

When I arched into him, he responded intuitively, rolling his hips until we were perfectly aligned where I ached and he was hard. I wrapped my arms around his neck, frantically freeing his hair so I could sift it through my fingers.

He groaned when I got a little rough and pulled.

I groaned when I felt his hand on my breast, his thumb sweeping inward to connect with my nipple.

Then Walker ended the kiss as abruptly as he'd started it. He buried his face in the side of my neck and exhaled slowly; the air drifted across my damp skin, sending goose bumps spreading outward.

He straightened upright and ran both his hands through his hair. "Sorry."

"Sorry? Really?"

"No, not really. I just don't normally act like a horny teen. That's what it was starting to feel like."

I lowered my head and glanced at my hands resting on my lap. I still had paint ringing two fingers. I doubted Walker had gotten the gunk off my face since water smeared color rather than cleaned it.

Rough fingertips slipped beneath my chin, forcing my head up. "Bad timing on my part."

"Probably. I still liked it, though."

He dropped his hand from my face. "Let's get out of here. We need to talk."

That didn't sound good. "About?"

"The rest of this week. Namely my schedule, which in-cludes night supervision on the last stages of a project."

"Does that happen often?"

"A few times a year. My partner and I switch off, so it's my turn. From past experience I know we won't get done before midnight." His eyes latched onto mine. "Which means I'm screwed for getting to see you the rest of the week."

Might make me a jerk, but I was happy he was unhappy about that.

"I didn't want you to think I'm blowing you off."

I set my hand on his chest. "It didn't occur to me. But the truth is, that actually works out really well for me."

"Why?"

"Remember the commission I lost last week? The woman who deemed the art too edgy? She showed up today and hired me to do a rush commission."

Walker's smile lit up his eyes. "Trinity. That's great."

"I thought so, especially since I can pay my mortgage *and* buy groceries this month. With this supertight deadline I'll be swamped with work until Friday. So even if you weren't working nights, I would be."

"You'll keep in touch with me this week."

Not a question—a demand. "I will try my very hardest." I poked him in the chest. "But what if I forget? Sometimes I lose track of—"

"Then I'll be forced to use positive reinforcements on you. It worked last time."

I smirked. "Maybe I'll forget on purpose."

After a hectic week, I groaned when the alarm went off at seven thirty a.m. When I remembered I'd see Walker at the community center today, I bounded out of bed.

As I pulled into the parking lot, my phone rang. At the sight of Ramon's name on the caller ID, I had a sense of déjà vu since I had spoken to him this time last week. Part of me wanted to ignore the call, but a bigger part of me wanted to point out he'd been wrong about the reason I'd lost the Stephens commission.

Pride won out. I answered, "Good morning, Ramon."

"Someone is in a good mood this morning."

"I am. It's a gorgeous day. The sun is shining, the birds are chirping . . . all that jazz. So what's up?"

"Just checking up on you. How was your week?"

"Great! I got a second chance to work on the textile project."

"You did? How'd that come about?"

"I can't say—it's a little hush-hush because of the surprise factor for the client. And as a bonus, I learned that Dagmar Kierkegaard is on the guest list for this shindig where the piece is being unveiled! Can you believe that?"

Silence.

I grinned because it was so rare that I stunned Ramon into silence. Dagmar Kierkegaard defined elusive. We'd heard rumors that he wore disguises when he appeared in public so he could attend random art openings at smaller venues without anyone recognizing him.

"Your luck is unbelievable. You are getting extra party invites to hand out to your friends, right?"

I managed a neutral, "I'll ask closer to the event."

"Excellent! And I'm sure you'll do fine with all the extra pressure to really make your textile piece stand out."

"I'm up to the challenge."

"I assume you're working on it this morning? Need me to come by and help?"

"No, I just pulled into the community center. These sets won't paint themselves."

"I thought you decided your talents are wasted there."

I bristled up. "No, Ramon, *you* decided that."

"But you agreed with me!"

"I did not. We've been friends for three years so I know it's pointless to argue when you've made up your mind. I let it go." The way I'd been letting a lot of things go with him.

He expelled a string of Spanish words—curses mostly.

After he finished blustering, I said, "Do you feel better?"

"No. I'd feel better if you were here to witness my hand gestures while I pace like a madman. My frustration loses impact over the phone lines, *chica*." I heard him snap his fingers. "Next time I'll use FaceTime."

"Cool. That'll give me time to perfect my resting bitch face."

"Anyway, we can talk about this in more detail when I see you tonight."

I frowned. "Did I forget we had plans?"

"No. Davina has decided to throw a dinner party. It'll be our usual group, so say you'll come." When I didn't say yes right away, he said, "I'm making *migas*."

Ramon knew that would tempt me—I loved his *migas* and it had been ages since I'd had them. "All right. What time and what am I bringing?"

"Show up after seven; we'll eat at eight. Bring beer. You and Esteban are the only ones who drink it."

I fought a groan. I did not want to deal with Esteban.

"Esteban is looking forward to seeing you again."

"When are you going to stop pushing your brother at me?"

"When you agree to try one date with him," Ramon said sweetly. "If you give it a chance, you'll see that you two are a good fit."

My mind jumped to Walker. His dimpled smile. His compelling blue eyes. The easy banter between us. The way our mouths—and bodies—had fit together perfectly.

Dammit. I'd been so eager to brag about my good fortune that I hadn't considered that Walker might want to do something with me tonight.

"Davina is yelling for me. Adios."

I stared at my phone. Being prideful always turned around and bit me.

I hoped that wasn't a precursor of how the rest of my day would go.

As promised, I had help from high school volunteers. They were eager and followed directions well, but I still had to direct them.

It would've been easier and faster to do everything myself. I had to keep reminding myself this was what the word "community" meant: multiple people working toward a common goal.

But with five volunteers, we ran out of things to do right after noon. I hadn't seen Walker all day, although I'd heard the saws going. I wondered if he'd been saddled with volunteers.

As soon as I stepped outside, a blast of heat hit me like a glory hole furnace in a glassworking studio. I noticed a long extension cord ran to the only shaded area at the back of the lot. Big pieces of plywood rested against a tree.

Walker stood between two sawhorses manning a jigsaw. He wore goggles and ear protection. Wood shavings covered his chest and dusted his hair. Even in the heat he wore jeans and a long-sleeved shirt. He looked so ruggedly delicious in work mode I just stopped and watched him.

He must've sensed me because he glanced up after he shut the saw off and set it aside.

Oh, that smile. Seeing it was like standing in a beam of sunshine that was just for me.

As I meandered toward him, he tossed his gloves on the ground and brushed himself off. I wouldn't have cared if he'd been covered in mud. I still would've wrapped myself around him.

Walker kissed the top of my head. "Hey, beautiful. I'm glad to see you. I did wander into the set-painting room after I first arrived, but I saw you had a crew to supervise, so I didn't bug you."

"Did you have volunteers?"

"Nope. Guess teens and power tools aren't a good idea."

I laughed. "Probably not. But teens are excellent with paint-brushes. We are completely caught up."

Walker groaned. "I'm going as fast as I can."

"I figured that. But until you get more sets done . . . there's no reason for me to be here."

He sighed. "So you're headed home?"

"I have projects to work on there."

"Not all night, I hope. Because I wanted to take you out to dinner." He nuzzled my ear. "Someplace secluded and romantic where we can get to know each other better."

I managed to keep from asking . . . *In the biblical sense?* "That sounds good . . . but . . ."

He leaned back to look at me. "But what?"

"I already have dinner plans."

Walker's eyes immediately narrowed.

"And I want you to come with me. My friend Ramon is having a dinner party."

When he smiled, I wanted to stand on tiptoe and feel it on my lips. "What?"

"You're introducing me to your friends?"

"Are you okay with that?"

"Very okay. What time should I pick you up?"

I read the challenge in his eyes. He thought I'd argue and insist on meeting him. But I wanted to prove to him I considered us a couple. "Seven thirty. Ramon said we were eating at eight, but he runs an hour behind. Casual dress. I'll have to stop and get some beer on the way."

"No problem. Where do you live?" Walker pulled out his phone and paused to look at me. "I don't have to worry that you'll give me the wrong address?"

"We're past that," I said softly.

"Good."

After he plugged in the address, I wreathed my arms around his neck. "I missed you the last couple of days."

"I wondered when you'd get around to kissing me hello," he said gruffly.

"This one will have to serve as hello and good-bye," I murmured, rubbing my cheek along his jawline. I kissed him slowly, a tease of the wet glide of my lips and little nibbles with my teeth rather than a deep kiss.

As I took several small steps back, he kept ahold of my hand and my eyes until I broke our connection and walked away.

Seven

———

WALKER

I parked on the street in front of Trinity's house.

The place wasn't what I'd expected. A single-level ranch with a decent-sized front porch. Cottonwood trees towered over the top of the structure, putting it in shadow. A sidewalk disappeared around the side of the house. The lawn wasn't neglected or pristinely manicured. Juniper bushes had gone wild around the entire perimeter, but they'd been pruned to below the lowest window level. Given the style of siding, stone and the location, I guessed the house had been built in the 1930s.

It wasn't until I reached the top porch step that I realized Trinity was sitting in one of the wicker chairs on the porch.

She smiled and granted me a very slow, very heated once-over from the tips of my boots to the top of my forehead. "You clean up well."

I bowed, hoping to hear that irresistible laugh again. "Thank you."

"Would you like a beer? I made a mad dash to the store when I realized I'd run out of soap for the dishwasher, so we don't have to stop on the way to Ramon's."

I noticed she had a bottle of Bud Light Lime sitting on the table beside her. "I'll pass, but I'll sit with you while you finish yours." I settled into the chair next to hers. We faced the street. "This is a great area. How long have you lived here?"

"About two and a half years. It's affordable, even in those months when my artistic endeavors don't quite make the mortgage payment."

"I'm restoring my house and it's slow going. I get done working and the last thing I want to do is spend more time ripping out walls and sanding floors."

"I hear you. Painting walls is nothing like creating paintings. But the plaster could've been falling from the ceiling and I still would've bought this place."

"Why?"

"Because of the enormous garage around back. It's been perfect for my studio." She drained her beer. "I had it updated before doing anything to the house."

"Can't say as I blame you. I'd like to see it sometime."

"Sorry. My studio is my sanctuary. I can't handle anyone judging my half-finished projects."

Before I could respond, Trinity laughed.

"I couldn't even say that with a straight face." She squeezed my knee, a sexy half-smile on her lips. "I'd love to show you my etchings sometime."

I liked this playful side of her.

She stood and tugged on my hand.

All the blood left my head and traveled south when I saw

Trinity's outfit. When she was sitting, the dress had looked nondescript. When she was standing, the emerald green fabric clung to every curve, showcasing her gorgeous feminine form, from the tease of cleavage to the narrow expanse of her ribs to the roundness of her hips and ass. The long dress ended just above her ankles, giving a peek at her feet in rhinestone flip-flops. Her toenails were painted a sunny yellow and on the center of each nail was a tiny bright orange flower.

"Walker? You all right?"

My gaze snapped to hers. "Just admiring the full picture. You look amazing."

"Thank you. And I should warn you . . . you'll probably get some . . . ah . . . admiring looks tonight since a lot of our friends are gay men." She paused and studied my face. "Will that be a problem for you?"

"Problem, meaning . . . am I a homophobe?" I shook my head. "Do I have an issue with them checking out my appearance? No. Just as long as no one starts giving me clothing and hairstyling tips. My buddy Reggie constantly laments my 'hipster meets Grizzly Adams' clothes. Now it's sweet payback to point out I was fashion forward—years ahead of the lumbersexual craze."

Trinity touched my face. "The beard, long hair and man bun thing aren't new either?"

"No." I watched her eyes as she stroked my beard—her tentative touch sent a jolt of heat through my body. As much as I wanted more, now wasn't the time. I turned my head to kiss the inside of her wrist, breaking the connection. "We should go."

"You aren't like any of the guys I usually date."

Hard not to bristle up at that.

Then she twined her arms around my neck, pressing her

lips to mine briefly. "I meant that in a good way, so lose the scowl."

"I'm not scowling, Trinity."

"Prove it. Kiss me."

Tempting, to dive in and kiss her until we were both panting as our bodies were plastered together, seeking to sate this growing ache. But making out and grinding on her in the front yard . . . we were a little too old for that. I softly kissed the right side of her mouth, then the left. "We'll pick this up later, okay?"

"Okay." She ducked under my arm and walked to the pickup.

Once we were on our way, I said, "Tell me about your friends. How you met, all that jazz."

"Ramon and I met at an artists' co-op after I first moved here. He also runs a food truck business. When he had last-minute problems airbrushing the graphic designs on his truck, he asked for my help."

"He didn't know how to do it?"

She adjusted the seat belt and straightened her dress. "Ramon's got a Master's in Fine Arts, so he's one of those guys who thinks 'How hard can it be?' and discovers it's way harder than it looks."

"I deal with that mind-set all the time in the construction business."

"I'll bet. I'm fairly adept at airbrushing, so I finished it. Ramon was so grateful he threw a party and introduced me to a bunch of people in the art community, which was nice because I'd only been in town six months."

"But you're a Minnesota native, right?"

Trinity nodded. "When I was eleven my dad got a job on the East Coast. I lived there until I went to college. After graduation from art school, I traveled all over the country, trying to find my niche in the art world." She sent me a sideways glance. "I'm still looking a dozen years later."

"Do your parents still live on the East Coast?"

"No. My dad and stepmonster"—she flashed me a sheepish look—"stepmother returned to our hometown. And before you ask, I don't see them. They weren't on board with my decision to make my living as an artist."

"That sucks. Even when I opted not to join the family business, my family was pretty supportive."

"You've mentioned your family a lot. I take it you're close to them?"

"Very. Not just my brothers and sister but my cousins too. Growing up, we lived close to each other. Now we still hang out when we have time." So far Trinity hadn't asked questions about what business my family was in. The Lund name was well known in the Twin Cities—I couldn't remember the last time I'd gone out with a woman who didn't have a clue about my family's wealth or connections. I wished I could keep it under wraps a little longer; I liked that Trinity was getting to know me, not a guy with a fat bank account.

"You're lucky. I've always wanted that connection. Maybe even to the point I've tried to force it with friends, believing the 'You choose your own family' saying."

I shot her a sideways glance. "So these friends I'm meeting tonight? They're like your family?"

"I guess."

"You . . . guess?"

"It's complicated." She sighed. "There's a rift between Ramon and Genevieve and I'm caught in the middle. I know about the cyclical nature of friendships in theory, except in reality it's hard to say, *See ya—this isn't working for me anymore.*"

"You don't get that option with family. For better or for worse, you're stuck with them."

"That's equally scary." At the stop sign she said, "Take the next left. It's the last condo on the right."

This community defined bland suburb. Each cookie-cutter structure had some variation of maintenance-free siding in a shade of tan or gray. Narrow sidewalks separated artfully kept lawns. If someone blindfolded me and dropped me in the middle of the street, I'd be hard-pressed to pinpoint my location since this area was identical to a dozen residential areas across the city.

I parallel parked behind a Prius. "I'll get the cooler."

As we stood on the sidewalk facing the condo, I said, "Which one?"

"They own both units. They live in one side and Ramon uses the other side for his studio and runs his food truck business from there. The party is on the patio out back."

I was so busy watching the soft sway of her ass that I almost clipped a solar light at the edge of the sidewalk. That'd be my luck—to face-plant and embarrass myself and Trinity first thing.

She opened the gate. "Just set it down anywhere back there. One of Ramon's server minions will take care of it."

I lowered the cooler to the grass. When I turned around, I expected Trinity's focus would be on her friends across the yard. But her gaze was on me. "What?"

Almost absentmindedly, she traced my biceps from the ball of my shoulder to the outside of my elbow. "I'm fascinated by the way your muscles flex and flow in your back and arms. I'd love to try to capture the movement on paper."

I slid one hand around her hip to the small of her back, pulling her closer as I brushed my mouth across her ear. "You keep saying that, yet you've never officially asked me to take off my shirt and flex for you."

"Clichéd. I'm more original than that."

When Trinity stared at me another long moment, I murmured, "What's going on in that creative head of yours?"

"Don't tell my friends about the kiss and the wrong name and number thing when we first met, okay? It'll just be another thing they'll tease me about endlessly."

"I wouldn't do that." I'd started to get a bad vibe about these friends of hers before I even met them. I leaned in to nibble on that lip she was biting when someone behind us shouted her name.

Startled, she stepped back and spun around.

A stocky Hispanic man hustled over. He wore a black chef's jacket and pants. I guessed his age to be around forty—even though his 1980s Erik Estrada hairstyle suggested otherwise. He kissed both of Trinity's cheeks. "Hiya, sugar lump. Are you arriving fashionably late now?"

"No. I just had a busy day."

"Apparently too busy to call and let me know you were bringing a guest," Ramon said, ignoring me completely.

"You always say the more the merrier, so I knew you wouldn't mind." Her smile looked strained. "Besides, he's not just any guest. He's my boyfriend. Ramon, meet Walker."

"Boyfriend?" he repeated. That's when he scrutinized me.

I kept my left hand pressed in the small of her back as I offered him my right. "Pleased to meet you, Ramon."

He shook my hand without comment and addressed Trinity. "Davina will just have to deal with an uneven number of dinner guests at the table."

"If seating is a problem, I can always sit on Walker's lap," she retorted.

I chuckled. "I'm good with that."

"I'll just bet you are. But I am not."

Wow. No animosity there.

Ramon leaned in and peered at Trinity's face. His gaze

dropped to her cleavage. "Please tell me you didn't take your last lamebrained boyfriend's advice and start fake baking in a tanning bed?"

My eyes narrowed. This guy was supposed to be her friend and he said shit like that to her?

"It's a real tan. Walker took me to the lake last weekend."

"Must be nice not to be so swamped with work that you can't take a day off," he said with a sniff. "I spent all day and most of Sunday night in the studio fine-tuning a piece for the Chanhassen art show next month." He cocked his head. "What are you entering?"

"Nothing. Between the new commission piece and finishing the sets at the community center—"

"Excuses. If you fill all your hours with things"—he spared me a dark look—"that aren't worthy of your time, you're settling for less than you deserve."

This dude deserved a bloody lip for that superior remark.

Trinity placed her hand on my chest. "Would you grab us a beer?"

"Sure."

I meandered across the yard and opened the cooler. I took out two bottles of Corona Light and glanced over at Trinity. She was in Ramon's face and gesturing wildly. Ramon didn't appear cowed. But he wasn't participating in the conversation either.

"She's really pissed off at him this time," a voice said behind me.

"Do they do this a lot?"

"No. Usually Trinity backs down. She hates conflict."

That made sense from what I'd seen of her.

"I'm glad to see her pushing back. This has been building for a while." A Hispanic man, roughly the same age as Ramon, moved in front of me. "I'm Miguel. Ramon's partner in the food truck business."

I shook his hand. "I'm Walker."

"Fair warning—if Trinity doesn't get Ramon to back off, you're in for a bumpy night." Miguel handed me a bottle opener. "Keep it close by. You'll need it."

A tall, thin woman wearing an ugly plaid golfing skirt and a screaming yellow polo shirt stomped outside. She skidded to a stop next to Ramon and screeched, "The peppers are burning!"

Ramon turned and raced into the house.

I crossed the lawn, reaching Trinity before the screecher did. "You all right?"

She shrugged. "We'll see."

"This'll help." I popped the cap off the beer and handed it to her.

"Thanks."

The plaid-clad woman stopped in front of Trinity and did the air-kiss-on-both-cheeks thing. "Darling. I'm so glad you could make it. I was about to ask what you'd done to upset Ramon"—she sent me a pointed glance—"but now it's perfectly obvious." Smiling, she offered her hand. "I'm Davina. Ramon's more civilized half."

"Walker."

"Well, Walker. Your presence has caused quite a stir."

Did she expect me to apologize? Or Trinity to apologize?

Trinity rolled her eyes. "It's good to mix things up once in a while."

"Right you are." Davina's gaze winged between us. "Let's head to the patio so you can introduce your date to the rest of the guests."

Davina disappeared around an eight-foot-tall hedge.

Trinity moved closer when I placed my palm in the small of her back.

"Sorry. We should've gone out just the two of us, like you suggested. You shouldn't have to deal with this."

"I'm a big boy. I can fight my own battles. I won't fight yours, but neither will I stand back and watch Ramon—or anyone else—be an ass to you."

"You'll protect my honor?"

"Damn straight."

We stepped onto a brick-paved path that led to a covered patio.

A long table, decorated with brightly colored dishware, had been centered beneath a string of Japanese paper lanterns. A bar took up the opposite corner. Someone had already placed the beer we'd brought in a metal tub filled with ice. Soft jazz drifted from someplace.

Several people—men mostly—lounged in oversized furniture.

Trinity muttered, "Great."

"What?"

Before she could answer, Davina clapped her hands.

All eyes swiveled to her.

"Everyone, this is Walker, Trinity's *date* for this evening. Feel free to mingle. The food will be done in ten . . . or longer if the chef isn't finished with his temper tantrum." She flounced off.

Only one person from the group rose to greet us. After he gave Trinity an overly familiar hug, I wished he would've stayed put.

"Trinity. You look as beautiful as ever."

"Thank you, Esteban."

"Ramon said I'd have you all to myself tonight so we could catch up." He tried to intimidate me with a narrow-eyed glare.

"Esteban, is it?" I said with a "Back the fuck off" stare as I thrust out my hand. "I'm Walker."

"Interesting name," he said while squeezing my hand with excessive force. "You any relation to them?"

"Them who?"

He rolled his eyes. "The Walker family—namesake of the Walker Art Center?" He paused. "Please tell me you've at least heard of it."

Was this guy for real? "I've heard of it."

"I've been there dozens of times. I know Trinity has too." He offered her a sly smile. "But it wasn't until you and I went to that exhibit last fall that I grasped the subtleties in style that only an artist can explain with knowledge and passion. I never considered an artist's temperament played no part in the creative process. How much you have to get outside yourself and push boundaries."

Trinity slipped her arm around my waist. "Speaking of temperament . . . maybe you should check on Ramon."

"Davina can handle him. I did my time in Ramon's kitchen."

"Are you in the food truck business with him?" I asked.

He looked aghast, as if I'd said something idiotic. "God no. I went to college specifically to escape life in the food service industry."

The smug little prick wanted me to ask him what he did for a living. So I didn't. "Good for you."

"We'll catch up with you later," Trinity said and nudged me away. She didn't stop moving until we were at the bar and she positioned herself in front of me.

"Want to tell me what's going on?"

Placing her hand on my cheek, she stroked my jawline with her thumb. "Esteban is Ramon's brother. Ramon has been trying to set us up for a while."

"Esteban seems on board with that."

"I'm not on board with it, Walker. I never have been."

A thought occurred to me. "Is that why you dragged me along tonight? Because he would be here? Am I being used as a shit-stirrer to 'mix things up'?"

She shook her head.

"Am I just a buffer between you and Esteban?"

"No!"

"You sure?"

"Yes, I'm sure." She rifled her fingers through my beard, gathered a small section between her thumb and forefinger, and tugged on it. Hard.

Fuck. That hurt.

"No games between us, Walker. Yes, I knew Esteban would be here, but I didn't bring you to antagonize him."

"Did you bring me to antagonize Ramon?"

"No."

"Then why did you bring me, Trinity?"

"Because I wanted to spend time with you . . . but I didn't want to assume we'd do something tonight since we hadn't spoken much this week. So when Ramon invited me to the dinner party, I said yes without thinking."

"Babe. It's safe to assume if I haven't seen or talked to you all week that doing something with you is a priority."

That seemed to surprise her. "Okay." She sighed. "Now I wish I would've backed out of this stupid dinner party. This isn't the group I thought would be here tonight."

"All the more reason for us to dine and dash." I slid my hand up her forearm, circling my fingers around her wrist, pulling her hand away from my face. I lowered my mouth so our lips nearly touched. "If you don't want me to kiss the hell out of you, say so now."

"Like I could say no to that."

The instant our mouths connected, I felt that spark of heat between us ignite.

She made a soft moan and swayed against me.

And we were so caught up in the hunger that kept expanding, neither of us was aware we had an audience until Ramon yelled, "Do I need to get out the garden hose and spray you two off? Are you in high school or what?"

Laughter behind us broke the moment.

I rested my forehead to hers. "Sorry."

She rubbed her cheek against my beard. "The only thing to be sorry about is that you had to stop. Let's get this dinner over with."

"Deal."

Ramon stepped in front of us and addressed Trinity haughtily. "Will it be a problem if I keep the original seating arrangement?"

"Yeah, it'll be a problem if she and I aren't sitting together since we are here together," I answered.

He harrumphed. I thought he might snap, *Deal with it*, but he spun away, announced dinner and told his guests to find their places at the table.

I was placed at the end of the table. I doubted Ramon put me there because I'm a big guy and need extra room—he intended to put me on the spot where everyone could see me.

Ramon and Davina directed the servers on where to set the food on the table. Then they shooed them away.

"Turn your wineglass over if you don't want sangria," Ramon said.

I noticed I was the only one who turned my glass over.

Ramon noticed and gifted me with a "You're a Neanderthal" sneer.

The food made it around the table twice and I was happy it wasn't bite-sized portions. I'd just dug into my third *miga* when Davina addressed me.

"While we're *thrilled* to have you with us tonight, Walker"—no sarcasm in that—"it seems our Trinity has been keeping you her dirty little secret." She sipped her sangria. "Dish the details on how you met."

Trinity squeezed my knee beneath the table. "We met last week during happy hour and due to a . . . miscommunication didn't exchange contact information. So we were surprised to run into each other last Saturday at the Seventh Street Community Center and discover we're working together."

"Oh wow. So this is *new* new," Davina gushed. "And what are you doing for this production?" she said to me. "Are you an actor?"

I washed down the *miga* with a mouthful of beer. "I'm working on the sets."

Ramon said, "You're an artist?"

"No, I'm constructing the sets."

Davina and Ramon exchanged a look. Then Ramon added, "So you work in construction when you're not volunteering at the community center."

"You asking if I have another job? Yep."

"And what might that job be?"

Beside me I felt heat from the glare Trinity aimed at her friend. "Mostly remodeling. Some new construction. I'll add a few odd jobs occasionally if they sound interesting or challenging."

"A construction worker," Davina said. "I was mistaken to think that you were in logging."

Logging. Jesus.

"So do you own the business or do you just punch a time clock?" Ramon asked.

Snoopy little man. I had no need to impress these people so I refused to try. I was a laid-back guy—until I wasn't. "Own it." I stretched my arm across the back of Trinity's chair. "It'd be easier working for someone else, as I'm sure you're aware."

Ramon tossed his head. "I love being in charge. I'm constantly thinking of ways to expand. That's the only way to get ahead, don't you agree?"

"Actually, I don't. I'm busy enough to keep my customers from feeling like I've overextended myself. That still gives me family and free time."

"Family time? What, do you have an ex-wife and a bunch of kids to support?"

"Ramon," Trinity snapped. "That is not your business!"

I brushed my fingers down her arm. "It's okay. Your . . . *friends* should know that I'm not shirking parental responsibilities to spend time with you. No kids. Never been married."

"Sounds like you keep yourself busy," Miguel said, cutting off Ramon's interrogation. "What do you do in your free time?"

"During football season I'm at the stadium rooting for the Vikings, or if it's an away game I watch it with my family. Once hockey season starts I attend as many—"

"Minnesota Wild matchups?" Miguel inserted with a grin. "No offense, but they suck."

"I'm not a Wild fan. I'm a Blackhawks fan."

Miguel held his fist across the table for a bump. "Now you just need to support a real football team, like the Bears."

"Not in this lifetime."

"Omigod, we are *not* talking about sports at my dinner party," Davina complained.

"Amen and thank you," Ramon said. "I don't get the whole sports thing. I hear people going on and on about this player and that player and this game and that game and I want to ask them why they bother. I mean, it's not like *they're* the ones out there getting pummeled in the grass. It's not like *they're* really experiencing it, so why are they so invested?"

Several people around the table nodded in agreement.

But I couldn't let Ramon's lame argument go unchallenged.

"You're right . . . if you apply that same philosophy to the arts. Why bother attending the theater if *you're* not the one onstage? How are you really experiencing it? The same could be said for going to the opera or other concerts. Where's the personal connection if *you're* not the one belting out an aria or playing the violin?" It made me way too freakin' happy to see Ramon's mouth tighten. I'd shut him down and he knew it.

Score one for the dirty construction worker.

Miguel laughed. "Need salve for that burn, Ramon?"

Davina waved her hand distractedly. "I'm just thankful we're not sports obsessed in academia. It makes for much deeper conversations."

"Much deeper bullshit," I muttered.

I swear Miguel snorted.

Bored with toying with me, Ramon asked the dark-haired woman about one of their colleagues and the gossip fest began.

After the servers cleared the table, I excused myself.

I wandered through the house until I found a bathroom. Then I exited through the front door, cutting to the side yard where we'd first gone in, and sprawled on the stone bench facing the street. Not long afterward I heard the squeak of hinges. Glancing over at the gate, I hoped Trinity had tracked me down and we could get the hell out of there, but it was Miguel.

He crossed the yard toward me. "I'm heading out," he said. "Just wanted to say it was nice meeting you, Walker—" He frowned. "Sorry. I don't remember your last name."

I knew as soon as I told him he'd make the connections. "It's Lund."

A pause lingered.

Then Miguel snorted. "You're a Blackhawks fan because Jaxson 'Stonewall' Lund is your . . . ?"

"Cousin. And man, I really thought they had a chance at the cup this year."

"We Chicagoans had high hopes too." He groaned and lightly smacked himself in the forehead. "Of course. If you're related to Stonewall, then you're related to 'The Rocket' Lund too."

I grinned. "He's my little brother."

"Really? That is awesome. I suspected something was up when you shot Ramon's asinine comments down." He chuckled. "Why didn't Trinity point out your family connections?"

"She's not into sports."

"She doesn't know, does she?"

"Nope. And name-dropping would be meaningless here in academia anyway." I had the oddest thought about my mother. She'd probably mispronounce it "macadamia" just as an excuse to call them a bunch of nuts. I wondered if I could get away with it.

Miguel offered his hand. "I wish you luck. Trinity was looking for you. I told her if I found you I'd send you back to the party."

"Thanks."

I pushed up from the bench, more than ready to leave the dinner party from hell. I'd almost reached the end of a large row of lilac bushes when I heard my name.

"You mean Walker isn't glued to your side?" Ramon said snidely. "He seemed so insistent on that."

"He's getting some air."

"He probably snuck off with Miguel to talk sports," he retorted.

"So? He likes sports. What's wrong with that?"

"The better question is . . . what's wrong with you? You're so desperate for companionship you'll pick up any dude with a tool belt."

Ouch. Not for me—because I couldn't give a damn—but that was a harsh assessment for Trinity.

"Walker is not just a dude with a tool belt."

"Right. He's different than the last *three* construction guys you dated."

"Why do you care?"

"Because I've had to listen to you whine, cry, bitch and complain about these . . . blue-collar losers you pick up like stray dogs and then they dump you. Your work suffers; we both know it. I've tried to be supportive, but I've reached my limit."

"How ironic. I hit my limit too. So ask me why I've been avoiding your parties, Ramon."

"Because you're too busy slumming in dive bars and picking up random guys?"

That little fucker. He had no right to talk to Trinity that way. No right. I'd put an end to this shit right now.

But Trinity did not take Ramon's comments lying down.

"Did you *hear* what you just said to me? You've gotten to be so nasty and condescending that you don't even realize when you do it—because you do it all. The. Freakin'. Time."

"Oh boo hoo, I'm so mean to you. It makes me an ass to point out that I care that you're throwing your life away."

"Throwing my life away?" she repeated. "Because I'm dating Walker?"

"Maybe that seems harsh, but I have to be that way to get through to you. You've lost your ambition. Now I hear you're sunbathing at the lake instead of finishing projects that can advance your career? You're painting sets for a third-rate community theater production? I can see that you're so enamored with this Walker guy that you'll stay in a job way below your skill level just to be with him. You should be busting your ass to finish an oil painting and a watercolor to display with the textile piece to showcase your work in other mediums. Instead you're going boating. You don't deserve this chance with Kierkegaard because you'll blow it." He paused. "Tell me I'm wrong."

"You're wrong. And I'm done with you."

"You're throwing away our friendship because I take issue with the big lumber-*jock* and the fact your involvement with him means you're not focusing on what's important?"

"This so-called friendship is not ending because of him. It's ending because of you being an asshole. I'm ashamed of ever thinking you were a friend."

"Oh *no* you don't—"

I stormed around the edge of the bushes just as Ramon grabbed her arm. "Take your hand off her. Now."

Ramon released her. "Big surprise he acts all macho."

I didn't respond because my focus was on Trinity. From having a sister, I recognized she'd reached meltdown stage. I moved in front of her, blocking her from his view. "You need anything from the backyard before we go?"

She shook her head.

I pulled her in and held her for a moment. I kissed the top of her head and murmured, "Let's go."

Trinity tucked herself against my side.

The other guests had finally gotten out of their chairs and were watching us leave.

Davina had joined Ramon. Neither of them said a word as we walked past.

I situated Trinity in the passenger's side. She gently batted away my hands when I tried to buckle her seat belt.

After we pulled away from the house, she started to cry.

It ripped me up to hear her trying to mask her sobs. I parked in the first empty lot. "Trinity. Come here."

"No. I'm f-f-fine."

"Bullshit." *Don't snap at her. That's not what she needs.* "Sweetheart, you need a shoulder to cry on right now. I've got two. Pick one."

"I don't deserve for you to be nice to me . . ." She sobbed harder.

I brought her onto my lap. When she buried her face in my neck and let the tears flow, I ran my hand up and down her back.

After the storm of tears tapered off, Trinity settled into me.

Although the events that had led to this situation were less than ideal, I liked having her in my arms like this, holding her. I liked that she let me comfort her.

Neither of us spoke. I didn't track the passage of time, but after being lost in my own thoughts I realized her breathing had turned deep and she'd fallen asleep.

The warmth of her body and the teasing scent of her perfume put me into a relaxed state and I started to drift. Surely it wouldn't hurt to close my eyes for a minute or two . . .

A knee pressing into my crotch woke me. Then the numbness in my upper thigh morphed into a pins-and-needles sensation. I tried to shift sideways and Trinity's head slid toward the steering wheel, so I jerked her back.

The movement startled her. "I didn't mean to fall asleep on top of you."

"I didn't mind, since I crashed too."

Her body tensed.

I hoped it'd take her some time to come around. But one second she was sprawled on me; the next she practically launched herself back to the passenger's seat.

Okay. Not only did she have catlike reflexes, she was as jumpy as a cat.

She fumbled with her seat belt and her legs started bouncing.

"You all right?"

"I have a hideous headache. Can you please take me home?"

"Of course."

The ride to her house was silent except for her occasional mutterings. The fact she wouldn't look at me gave me a bad vibe.

After I parked next to the curb in front of her house, several long moments passed before she noticed where we were. She immediately reached over to undo her seat belt.

I stayed her hand. "Trinity. Are we going to talk about—"

"You don't understand. Ramon . . . that's just how he is. Sometimes he's not even aware he's being—"

"Such a fucking tool?" I snapped off.

Trinity talked over me. "Yes, he knew exactly where to dig into me so the barbs would do the most damage. Friends know each other's weaknesses. It really sucks that this seems to be the norm in the art world—hey, just point out those weaknesses at a damn dinner party where everyone can get a running tally of all my faults. But what gets me the most is that Ramon isn't entirely wrong and that's a hard truth to swallow."

Before I could jump in with, *It's hard to swallow because it's total bullshit*, Trinity was off on another tangent.

"I haven't been as focused as I need to be. I have to find a better way to jump-start my creative process than taking on random odd jobs and praying they'll inspire me. I know myself. I know how easily distractions become excuses. You are this larger-than-life guy who takes over my thought processes, even when I'm not with you. And you can't help that you're"—her gaze flicked over me—"all that."

Jesus. Was that a compliment or an insult?

"I can't afford to blow this chance. I need to regain my focus. Eye on the prize, right? So can we just take a step back?"

"A step back from what?"

"From this." She gestured between us. "I need to lock away the emotions you bring out in me and concentrate on my work."

My jaw might've dropped if I hadn't been clenching it so tight. "You're serious. You're cutting me loose . . . on our second date?"

"Not permanently. Just until I straighten out a few things."

"Well, that's just great, Trinity. Of course I'd love to just hang the fuck around while you 'straighten out a few things' in your life. It's not like *I* have a life or anything better to do."

She beamed at me. "See! I knew you'd understand."

Was she drunk? That's the only way she could've missed my sarcasm.

When she leaned forward to . . . pat me on the cheek, for Christsake, I noticed her eyes were expressionless. Like she'd checked out of her body somehow.

"Gotta go." She bailed out of the truck and ran—she fuck-ing *ran*—up the sidewalk and into the house without looking back.

Eight

TRINITY

Sunday morning I woke up later than usual and more refreshed than I'd expected. Ambien was good stuff. I had a momentary pang of guilt for popping a pill that allowed me to hide in sleep. It wasn't something I did often. I wondered if Walker had ever tried medication for his occasional insomnia.

Walker.

Last night as I'd drifted off I'd tried to remember specifics of our conversation after the disastrous dinner party at Ramon's. But I could only bring up silence and a few brusque words from his end. I'd chalked up the lack of recall to the Ambien.

So being bright-eyed and bushy-tailed this morning meant I should've had perfect clarity.

Nope. Why couldn't I have a normal social anxiety disorder like drinking too much? Maybe as the day wore on things would come back to me. That small sliver of hope allowed me to shove all of last night's events aside and switch into work mode.

I headed to my studio—leaving my cell phone in the house—and brewed a strong pot of tea. Then I slipped on my headphones and set my Sonos system playlist to random. I picked over the objects on the table that Esther had given me. She'd been considerate enough to label each one and rank the items in order of importance.

Yesterday I'd assembled the three separate sections into one base piece, suspending it from the ceiling with wires and connecting the bottom to hooks in the floor, allowing me mobility while it remained stationary.

The top half of the piece comprised distressed posts spaced an inch apart to resemble a fence. Each post represented a year in Mr. Stephens's youth and a significant event. In the middle section, pieces of rusted barbed wire and lengths of shiny razor wire were stretched across a camouflaged backdrop. With molds I'd reproduce the medals he'd earned during his military service in Vietnam and hang them from wires. For the bottom—the largest section of the piece—I'd clipped a chunk of chain-link fence. Each open spot would contain memorabilia from the other stages of his life—husband, father, business tycoon, grandfather, retiree. I'd had a brainstorm yesterday about using ribbons, yarn, twine and tape to connect events and people from his childhood to correlating times in his adulthood.

Right now the piece looked like a bunch of random junk the wind had bandied about and had ended up stuck to the bottom of a fence. Yet there was a pattern to the seeming randomness; it was neither indecipherable nor obvious. Art should make you think. And I thought this could be one of my best works yet.

One good thing to come out of the fight with Ramon? I'd decided to take his suggestion to showcase my skills in other art mediums on this piece. But my reasoning for the change wasn't to impress Dagmar Kierkegaard—it was to impress my client.

This piece celebrated the life of Michael Stephens. He wasn't a one-dimensional man and this commissioned art should reflect that. While Adele sang songs of rumors and redemptions in my ear, I cut out cardboard stand-ins for where I'd replace the photographs with traditional art. I'd add a small oil painting of the first house the Stephenses had purchased. In charcoal, I'd sketch images of their beloved pets over the years. With funky metallic markers, I'd craft stylistic renderings of his favorite cars. Using pen and ink, I'd re-create the picture of Esther gazing into the camera, a look of fear and pride on her face as she held their first child.

With renewed excitement for this project, I spread out on my drafting table and got to work.

Loud banging on the reinforced steel door forced me out of my inner space. I drained the last of my hot tea—gone cold hours ago—stood and stretched. Then I clicked on the live camera feed on my monitor. I'd installed a security system not because I worried about theft, but so I could see, and choose to ignore, who was interrupting my workday.

Genevieve leaned against the wall, rubber mallet in hand, glaring at the camera.

This wasn't a social call if she'd reached rubber mallet stage. She used it as a last resort when she couldn't get my attention any other way. I slapped on a smile before I opened the door. "Hey, BFF."

She stormed past me into the kitchen area. "I've been trying to get ahold of you for hours. I hate that you don't bring your phone into your studio."

I wasn't tethered to my cell phone—anyone who had grown an umbilical cord to theirs didn't understand my indifference toward mine. "What's up?"

Genevieve pulled a Coke out of the minifridge and cracked it open. "What do you want to talk about first? The fight with Ramon? Or how your Viking defender responded?"

"How did you know about Ramon?"

"He texted me. An epic text, broken into seventeen parts. I'll admit it felt deliciously bitchy not to respond to him at all." She swigged her soda. "What happened?"

"I don't want to talk about Ramon. Ever again."

"I don't care. If the fight forced Ramon to lower himself to contact me, then it was major. And I can see that you're still upset."

"Can't pull anything over on you," I grumbled, knowing she wouldn't let this go.

"So don't even try. Start talking."

I detailed the predinner convo and the interrogation of Walker during dinner. "Ramon waited until I was alone to pounce. He didn't even segue into 'What's wrong with Trinity' part eight hundred thirty-seven. He cornered me and started in, first reminding me how difficult it was to be my friend and how exasperating it was to witness my near constant stupidity. How lucky I was to have his insight about my relationships and my career." I snorted. "Lucky. Right. He'd made me sound like a bar hag, constantly trolling for new blue-collar meat. It was humiliating to listen to. But what made it worse? Walker overheard everything."

"So Ramon didn't just break normal friendship boundaries; he annihilated them."

I nodded.

"Was he drunk? Or high?"

"Does that matter?"

"No." Genevieve lost her cool. "That little prick. And the whole time he ripped you to shreds, Davina just stood beside him with that stupid, smug smile?"

"No, she was on the patio with everyone else during his diatribe. But she sort of egged him on during dinner."

"Why does Ramon feel he has the right to judge the men you date? I know you guys are more than professional peers, but it's just strange that he's so invested in your love life, T."

"I think it's because when we first became friends, outside of being professional colleagues, he considered himself a big brother and gave me advice about men. Then, after he married Davina, he started harping on me not to waste time on guys that didn't have long-term potential because hookups and breakups were distracting me from reaching the next level of success in my career."

"Whoa. Back up. Since when has Ramon wanted you to succeed as an artist?"

That stopped me. "What?"

"Are you sure Ramon hasn't been trying to sabotage your career from the start? Constantly giving you bad advice? He has always seen you as competition, Trin."

"Not true. We don't have the same types of audience."

"Because he has *no* audience. He might lord it over you that he has a prestigious fine arts degree, but the truth is he's far more successful making tacos than creating art. That eats at him. He takes it out on you because you're the only one left in your group of arty-farty friends that associates with him."

That's why I hadn't dumped him—everyone else had. I knew what that felt like and I saw how much it'd hurt him. I kept hoping Ramon would find his way back to being the guy he'd been when we first met. "I wouldn't have made it through that first year if not for him."

"Yes, he was good for you then, but he's not good for you now. Add in the drugs . . ."

"It's just pot. It's not like he's doing meth or coke."

Gen shook her finger at me. "This is the very definition of a dysfunctional friendship. You are excusing his drug use. Cut him loose. Block his number. Move on."

Or maybe publicly tearing me down was *his* way of cutting me loose. Tears pricked the backs of my eyes. I hated that it'd come to this. "Doesn't it just figure that my friendships are more of a mess than my relationships?" I looked at her. "Present company excepted."

"Speaking of relationships, what happened when the Viking got involved? Ramon said he went 'all protective caveman.'"

"That's another screwed-up situation."

"This doesn't sound good."

"It's not." I sighed. "I sucked it up and didn't shed a single tear at Ramon's—because screw him. I wouldn't give him the satisfaction. But the second I was alone with Walker, I lost it. Bad. I cried myself to sleep on his chest. I woke up in a panic, embarrassed as hell because he'd overheard Ramon's spiel about my shitty track record with men, his accusation that I was a slacker in my career, and then Walker saw me bawling like a thirteen-year-old girl."

"So?"

"So, I had the feeling Walker was about to dump the bucket of crazy train wreck that is me, so I think I sort of pre-dumped him first and told him we needed to take a break."

Genevieve's eyes widened. "You *think* you said that?"

"It's a blur, okay? I vaguely recall saying something along the lines that Ramon was right in pointing out that I needed to concentrate on knocking this Stephens piece out of the park and I couldn't do that when I was distracted by him being such a hot hunk of man flesh."

"You didn't."

"I did."

"No, I mean—dammit, I know you, Trin. Maybe in your head that's what you wanted to say, but that's *not* what came out of your mouth, is it?"

"Uh, probably not because I sort of remember Walker being sarcastic and pissed off."

A beat passed and then Gen smacked herself in the forehead.

I thought, *Better her than me*, a split second before she cuffed me in the arm. "Ow!"

"That didn't hurt." Gen inhaled a deep breath and looked me dead in the eye. "You're breaking my heart, Trinity. Honest to god, I could just curl into a ball in the corner and weep." Her chin trembled and then I saw her jaw tighten as she gritted her teeth.

"Gen—"

"Zip it. I'm not done."

"Okay. But I really really *really* will go off the rails if you're breaking up with me because you're the only friend I have."

She rolled her eyes skyward and appeared to be whispering a prayer. Then she refocused on me. "I am not breaking up with you. I love you. Straight up, no conditions. Because that's the way friendship is supposed to be. I'm here for you now and I'll be here for you in forty years when we're drinking Metamucil margaritas and bitching about our grandkids and our sciatica."

"But?"

"No buts. I just wish . . . that one day soon you'll stop focusing on what's wrong with you and celebrate all the wonderful things that are right about you." She set her hands on my shoulders. "I don't know where you got the idea that you're a train wreck—you're not. You are not a bucket of crazy. You are not a stage-three clinger."

I smiled at that one.

"I know I've told you this over and over, so how do I make you believe it?"

I took her hands in mine. "I love that you accept me unconditionally. But even you have to admit that I'm a quart low on normal."

She sighed. "Okay. But that's not a bad thing."

I raised my eyebrows at her.

"Okay, it's not *entirely* a bad thing. Your manic highs and lows could be considered aberrant behavior, but they're cyclical."

"Like the phases of the moon? Kind of like what a werewolf deals with?"

Genevieve stared at me. "A werewolf? Seriously?"

"Crap. That's my the-girl-boarded-the-crazy-train thought process showing, isn't it?"

"Uh-huh. So maybe you're a . . . quart and a *half* low on normal, but you're still not more than a smidge or two of crazy-pants."

"That's encouraging."

"Now, when you get that panicked feeling? Like you did last night with Walker and things start to go fuzzy? Take a second to close your eyes and breathe. Do not just start talking, because it morphs into a nonsensical rambling stream of consciousness."

Great.

"I suspect you react that way because that's how you create. It's a familiar switchover, but it doesn't work in translation from images to words."

When I shifted into creative mode, I had a running montage of images in my head and I could call them up with perfect clarity. But when I scrolled back to my conversation with Walker? I saw images lined up, but the inside of the frame was blank. "I never thought of it that way." I threw my arms around her and hugged her. "Thank you. You are one of the very best things in my life."

She squeezed me hard and whispered, "Samesies." Then she retreated and wiped her eyes. "There are two things I wanted to mention before you get back to work."

"Hit me." I held up my hands. "Not literally."

Gen laughed. "Connor wants me to meet his aunt and uncle this weekend."

I frowned. "Connor?"

"Sexy Irish rugby boy."

"Oh. Okay. And you're happy about that? I thought it was just hot sex with him."

"It's gotten to be more." She blushed. "He's sweet and funny and he doesn't care I'm a decade older than he is. Anyway, I have nothing to wear, so I need to go shopping. Can you take a couple of hours this week and meet me at Lane Bryant?"

"Absolutely. Call me Tuesday after you get off work. I promise I'll have my phone in the studio."

"Cool." She studied me for a moment and I got a little worried about the last thing she wanted to discuss.

"What?"

"Buck up, cupcake, and apologize to Walker. In person."

The thought of that made my stomach flip. "Really? I can't

ping him via text and let emojis express my regrets? Then if he doesn't send me the 'fuck off' emoji I can ask him out for a drink and try to explain?"

"Dude. You asked him for a 'break' on your second date. At least you *think* you did. Let that sink in for a moment."

I did. I sighed. "I suck."

She smirked. "You give him a heartfelt apology and you might just get to prove how well you do that."

"Out."

Nine

WALKER

Since Brady and Lennox were out of town until the Lund family barbeque later this afternoon, I worked out in Brady's state-of-the-art fitness center. Normally I took Sundays off, but I hoped if I pushed myself through two cycles of the excruciating, sweet agony of P90X, I could stop obsessing over Trinity.

Three hours of sweat and pain did take my mind off her.

But as soon as I hit the sauna, it all came rushing back. The sense she'd been so eager to hide away that she hadn't really listened to me. Hell, she'd barely looked at me. She'd run up the sidewalk and hadn't looked back.

I kicked myself the entire way home because I should've chased after her. I should've used the sexual heat between us to sort things out.

You are *sorted. She* is *waffling. And really, is that what you want? A woman who isn't sure if she wants to be with*

*you because her job is more important? When you could
pick up the phone right now and half a dozen other women
would be happy to get your call?*

Yet when I tried to recall the name of anyone interesting
I'd met recently, I drew a blank. The only woman in my
mind's eye was Trinity.

After exiting the shower I checked the time on my cell
and swore. Now, because of my excessive brooding, I'd be
late to the barbecue. Since Mom was hosting, my late arrival
meant a late departure—aka, assigned to cleanup duty.

My phone buzzed and I glanced at the text. Brady reminding me to bring his gear for the family basketball game. Now
I really wish I hadn't worked out for three freakin' hours. I'd
be worthless on the court.

The courtyard at my folks' house was packed with cars.
The house I'd grown up in was enormous. I'd never really
thought too much about it because it was home. While it
did take a team of domestic workers to help run a household
this size, I hadn't considered them employees. They were
part of the Lund collective. The housekeepers, the cooks, the
groundskeeper and the maintenance man had all worked for
Ward and Selka Lund for over twenty-five years.

Yet my parents hadn't hired a nanny, not even when they
had four kids under the age of seven. Since my aunts and
uncles had also raised their kids the same way, I believed it
was normal. It wasn't until I'd gotten older that I discovered
how rare that was for people of my parents' social stature.
They'd kept us as grounded as they could while providing
us with the means to do whatever we wanted. There were no
two people I respected more than my mom and dad. Somehow they'd found the balance between raising kids in a

privileged environment and not allowing us to believe we were entitled simply because our Lund ancestors had been shrewd enough to amass a fortune.

My dad opened the front door and stepped out just as I was about to go in. He smiled at me and lowered the bag of garbage he was carrying to give me a one-armed hug. "Hey. You're looking good today. Your mother will be pleased you made an effort."

I lived and worked in casual clothes—much to my mother's chagrin. This morning I'd dug through my closet for a pair of khakis, a polo shirt and my least scuffed-up pair of loafers. Yeah, I was totally sucking up to Mom for avoiding her, and Dad knew it.

"Walk with me, son."

I eyed the bag of garbage. "Mom let you waltz through the house and out the front door with that?"

"She didn't see me."

"Keep telling yourself that, Dad. She sees everything."

"Don't I know it. Be hell to pay later, I'm sure, but I like her feisty."

"More than I needed to know."

He laughed. We rounded the corner on the far side of the house and he opened the door leading to the garbage bay. "Be right back."

I leaned against the fence and gazed across the grounds. Fabian, the groundskeeper, did an amazing job keeping everything looking lush. In the last five years he'd redone the landscaping, removing large areas of manicured lawn and planting trees, shrubs and flowers in interesting configurations, significantly lowering the amount of water needed to maintain the green space. Since I couldn't hire Fabian away from my parents, I'd sent him a few apprentices to learn from the best before they came to work for me.

The gate slammed shut. "Let's cut through the garage to get to the patio."

"Don't you wanna drag me into the house so Mom can blister my ear about my selfish and rude behavior?"

"It can wait until after."

When he didn't elaborate, I said, "Until after what?"

"Lunch and . . . ah . . . stuff."

I jogged around the Mercedes coupe and planted myself in front of him. "Level with me. Did Mom set me up with someone and she's waiting out there? Is that why you're acting so weird?"

He sighed. "And I thought Annika was the dramatic one."

"She *is* the dramatic one. I'm the black sheep."

Sorrow darkened his eyes. "You know that's not true, Walker. But there was a time in my life I felt that way too."

Like me, Dad was the middle Lund son. His older brother, Archer, was the Lund Industries CEO, and his younger brother, Monte, was a former pro basketball player and now the president of the LI Board of Directors. Unlike Dad, I hadn't carved out a spot for myself in the family business between two super-successful brothers; I'd opted to forge a different path. If that decision had disappointed him, he'd managed to keep it to himself.

"Relax. There's no woman lurking outside. Your mother and I have other things on our mind today."

"That's supposed to set my mind at ease?" Now I felt guiltier yet for my self-imposed family exile. "Everything is all right health-wise with you and Mom?"

"Yes. Seriously, son, the best thing you can do is grab a beer and mellow out." He sidestepped me and exited the garage.

Mellow out. Right. He talked like that only when he was nervous about something.

I squinted in the blindingly bright sun after being in the darkness. My family members were scattered across the patio, pool and lounge areas. I ducked under the awning, reached into the steel tub filled with ice for a beer and came up with a Schell's twist-top.

I'd taken a healthy swig when I saw my sister in a heated discussion with Nolan.

Not good.

I crossed the decking to intervene, only to be stopped by a pint-sized pixie. Jaxson's daughter, Milora Michele "Mimi" resembled Tinker Bell in an acid green fairy costume she'd paired with a tiny pair of glittery rainbow wings and a tiara. I crouched down to hug her. "Princess, I didn't know you'd be here today." Jaxson's baby mama, Lucy—aka Lucifer—was a real piece of work and tried to deny Jaxson time with his daughter. The situation sucked because Jax lived in Chicago during hockey season while Mimi lived in Minneapolis with her mom.

"I've been here the last *four* times," she complained. "Where have you been?"

Hiding. "Working. Why? Did you miss me?"

"Uh-huh. I missed you a lot, Runner."

Runner. She claimed the name Walker didn't fit me since I was always in a hurry, so Little Miss Smart-as-a-Whip decided to call me Runner.

"But I forgive you." She threw her arms around my neck and squeezed.

I closed my eyes. I loved this kid. I hated that I'd missed out on spending time with her.

The hug lasted about ten seconds before Mimi struggled to free herself. "I gotta tell Daddy something." She raced off, making a beeline toward her father. Jaxson caught her one-handed and then dangled her upside down, not missing a beat in his conversation with his dad. But his big smile when she shrieked happily said it all.

"He's a great father, no?"

I dropped my arm across my mom's shoulders and kissed the top of her head. "Yes, he is. But he's learned by example. As we all have. So don't think for a moment I don't know how lucky I am to have you and Dad as parents."

She set her hand on my chest when she moved to stand in front of me.

Selka Jensen Lund was beautiful, a modern-day Scandinavian ice princess with blond hair, blue eyes and razor-sharp cheekbones. She looked a solid ten years younger than her age.

"Why the melancholy face, my boy?"

"Feeling guilty."

"You're here. That's what matters." She fiddled with the collar of my polo shirt. "I missed you. Sometimes . . . I'm pushy mama. I jump over the track."

"You mean you cross the line?"

"Yah. Whatever. The point being—"

"You're done nagging me about finding a suitable woman to settle down with?" I supplied.

"Suitable. Bah. You need woman who gives you big, messy love that makes you crazy."

Immediately I thought of Trinity.

Something on my face revealed my thought because my mother lightly chucked me under the chin. "You have girl like this and don't tell me?" Then she punctuated her displeasure by drilling her sharp fingernail into my chest with every curt word. "Talk. Walker. Gustav. Lund."

Use of my full name indicated she meant business. I clasped her hand to stop her talon from shredding my shirt. "Chill out, Mom. I met her last week. So it's . . . new."

"New is good, yah? You bring her next time."

"We'll see. I don't know if she's ready for all of this."

"All of this"—she spun her hand above her head like a sorceress casting a spell—"is what made you the man standing in front of me. If she likes that man—"

"Well, that's the complicated part."

Her blue eyes turned frosty. "I will meet this woman and *uncomplicate* for her."

Jesus. "I appreciate you pulling out your sword, Valkyrie mama, but these are dragons I have to slay myself if I want to prove myself worthy of the girl." Thank god none of my siblings or cousins were around to hear that, because they'd harass me endlessly for my romantic metaphor.

My mom patted my cheek. "You do that, my brave boy. Maybe find out she prefers . . . smooth-scaled dragon to shaggy beast, no?"

Now we were back in familiar territory. "She likes my facial hair just fine, Mom."

"Och. This too pretty a face to hide behind grizzled Adams beard."

"You mean a Grizzly Adams beard?"

"Yah. Whatever."

"Selka?" Aunt Priscilla called out.

"Be right there, sugar," she called back in a perfect imitation of her sister-in-law's Southern drawl. Then she gave me one last chest poke. "You are *not* off the hanger." She hustled away before I could correct her.

I wandered over to Annika and Nolan, noticing our cousin Ash now stood between them. "What's up?"

"Nolan is being an asshat," Annika said. "So really, nothing new here."

I looked at Ash and he rolled his eyes.

"And you're not the tiniest bit concerned about her, Ash?" Nolan asked. "You *are* her brother."

Ash shrugged. "I learned long ago that Dallas does what Dallas wants to do."

"Even if she wants to *do* a hockey player?" Nolan demanded.

"Not my business."

"It shouldn't have been her business either. But Annika—"

"Did not want to be alone with two gigantic non-English-speaking hockey brutes! I only had *your* say-so that they were decent guys."

"So as usual, immediately discount my opinion," Nolan shot back.

Annika got in Nolan's face. "It's not just you, genius. I don't take the word of *any* man that 'so-and-so' is a great guy. It's not something that men understand because they don't have to worry about it. Can you imagine how you'd feel if either of them had turned out to be creeps with ulterior motives?"

"Moot point now since *Dallas* had ulterior motives. She's with him today, isn't she?" Nolan said.

"No, she's at a mandatory cheerleading practice. Besides, how was I supposed to know they'd hit it off?"

"Who'd Dallas pick? The Russian or the Swede?" I asked.

Annika wrinkled her nose. "Igor, the Russian, of course, because Axl is an asshole. He was . . . pucking our waitress at the coat check during the dessert course."

Jaxson and Mimi joined us. "Whatcha talking about?"

"Your former teammates, particularly the Swedish"—Annika considered Mimi and curbed her tongue—"meathead."

Jaxson raised both eyebrows. "You mean Axl? He's a great guy."

"Game, set and match." Annika plucked Mimi off Jaxson's hip. "Come on, princess. Let's find an intelligent conversation."

Jax watched them walk away. "What did I say?"

"The wrong thing and let's leave it at that. So Mimi looks good."

"Because she's been with me the last six weeks. She goes back to Lucy tonight. Then I'm flying out. Training camp starts at seven a.m."

"When's the next time you'll see her?" I watched Jaxson's brooding gaze follow Annika and Mimi.

"I'll be here for her first day of school. Who knows after that?"

"We'll make sure she gets to see you," Nolan said. "And she'll be going to Mom and Dad's after school two days a week this year so we'll get to keep a better eye on her."

"Thank god for that." He scrubbed his hand over his face. "I just miss her. I'm glad that now she's old enough to miss me too."

Speaking of missing . . . I'd been so absorbed in my own stuff that I hadn't seen my youngest brother. "Where's Jensen?"

Ash pointed. "Over there."

I saw Jens pacing beside the koi pond, phone stuck to his ear. "Is he okay?"

"He's been on his cell since ten minutes after he got here."

Jensen hated talking on the phone. He'd drive across the city during rush-hour traffic to talk to me before he'd call. "I'll wander over and see what's up."

"When's Brady getting here?" Nolan asked.

"No idea."

"You guys better not be wussing out on the basketball game," Jaxson warned.

"We're not." My quads were screaming by the time I reached the top of the slope. I'd definitely overdone the work-out today.

Jensen had stopped pacing. He stood with his left hand

resting on top of his head; his phone remained pressed against his right ear. This was his "I'm about to blow" posture.

"I'm done talking about this with you, Aggie. No. I'm serious as a fucking heart attack. Last warning: Fix this or I'll fire you." He hung up and glared at his phone.

For a split second I thought he'd chuck it in the pond. But he shoved it in his back pocket, rolled his head around a few times as if he had a neckache.

Then he scowled at me. "Don't ask."

"Tough shit. I'm asking. What the hell was that?"

"A disagreement with my agent about a PR opportunity. I declined to participate. He insisted. I declined again. He insisted. Today he informed me that he'd told the PR company I'd had a change of heart and agreed to participate. And I told him exactly what I thought of that, of him and the repercussions if he didn't get my name off that fucking list."

Jens's quiet anger was far scarier than I'd remembered. It'd been a long time since I'd seen it.

"What was the PR project?"

He shook his head.

"Come on. Tell me why you said no." I crossed my arms over my chest—a clear sign I wasn't going anywhere.

His gaze snapped to mine. "It's an NFL calendar for charity. Twelve pro players, one for each month, the number of offensive players and defensive players an even split."

"And?"

"And they wanted me to be Mr. December. You know, since I'm from snowy Minnesota." He snorted. "I suspect they assigned me the last month of the year since we finished last in our division last year. Anyway, all the other months have some nudity—shirtless poses mostly—but my slot is a full nude. Not frontal obviously, but with my bare ass and bare back to the camera, looking over my shoulder, wearing a purple and gold Santa hat. A fucking *Santa* hat."

Do not laugh.

"I can't imagine why they've had a problem finding a sucker to pose for December, can you?" He sneered. "What pisses me off the most is now I'll be labeled a prude or a religious freak when I never said yes to the project in the first place. So thanks for that, Aggie. But hey, it's not like I have a shit-ton of other endorsements that decision could affect anyway."

I waited, knowing he wasn't done.

He set his hands on his hips. "What's wrong with being a modest guy? It's okay for women to be 'brave' and say no to nude photos, but I can't? Because I've worked my butt off for years to get stronger and leaner so I can do my damn job better, that means I should be proud to let everyone gawk at my body? No. *Hell* no."

"This is a serious breach of client trust, bro."

He sighed. "I know. I hate this part of the business, Walker. *Hate*. It. The head games. I am a football player. Not a model. Not a pawn."

"Nothing will get your point across faster than firing Aggie and being up front about why you did it. It's not the nudity. He put his best interests ahead of yours. That's not what you pay him for. Have you talked to Jax about his agent?"

"Not yet. But I will."

"Good." I clapped him on the back. "Enough for today. Let's hang out with the cousins and taunt them about how badly we're going to kick their asses on the court today."

"Deal."

As far as finding distractions to keep me from obsessing over Trinity, there'd been plenty at the Lund barbecue.

Jens, Annika and I were gathered at the bar when our parents strode hand in hand to the center of the patio and called for attention.

"What the hell is this?" Jensen asked Annika.

"No clue. But I hope it's not an announcement for another mandatory Lund family enrichment course."

I snickered. "What, you don't want to learn to salsa again?"

Annika shoved me. "Piss off. Who lets Mom make these decisions? She *had* to know that making salsa and salsa *dancing* were two different things."

"Yes, Roberto and Selena were rightfully confused when Mom shut off their music and banished them to the kitchen to start chopping tomatoes."

"Hey, maybe this time she'll mix up merengue and meringue," Jensen said.

Annika shoved him too.

"Making their first appearance as husband and wife, we'd like to present . . . Mr. and Mrs. Brady Lund."

Brady and Lennox came around the corner, waving awkwardly as the Lund collective started clapping.

"No. Freakin'. Way." Annika beat both Jensen and me to be the first in line to congratulate them.

"Did you know about this?" Jensen demanded.

"No, but Dad was acting weird earlier, so he and Mom knew."

Just as we walked up, I heard Brady say, "It was a spur-of-the-moment thing. We were having a great time on vacation and I realized I already felt married to her. So we made it official."

"But no wedding, Lennox?" Annika said with near horror. "No wedding dress or bridesmaids, or bachelorette party?"

"His spontaneous proposal and the surprise wedding ceremony were very romantic." She reached for Brady's hand. "I had everything I needed for the perfect wedding when I found the perfect man."

I glanced over to see my mother crying. Annika was leaking too. I let the women hug it out. When it was my turn, I high-fived my brother. "Smart move, man. Congrats."

"Thanks."

That was the extent of it for us. Didn't mean I wasn't happy for him—I was. I just wasn't gonna cry about it.

After the big announcement, none of us felt like playing basketball.

Annika, Mom, the aunts and Mimi gathered in the gazebo to grill Lennox. Dad, the uncles and Jax played horseshoes. Nolan and Ash had left together, mumbling about a golf game, but I suspected they'd gone back to the office for whatever mysterious project they were working on.

Brady kept an eye on Lennox as we lounged at the bar.

When he fiddled with his wedding ring for the tenth time, I said, "Think you'll get used to wearing that?"

"I'm already used to it."

Our youngest brother made a whip-cracking sound.

"You know what I find interesting? That for being a 'spontaneous' wedding, that big rock fits her finger perfectly." I sipped my beer. "Almost like it'd been sized to fit."

"They have jewelry stores on the island, numb-nuts."

Jens caught my train of thought and ran with it. "But I heard you have to apply for a marriage license at least a month in advance."

"Yeah? Who'd you hear that from?" I volleyed back.

"Guy on the team. He and his girlfriend took a vacay there, decided to get hitched and were told they'd have to wait something like two weeks."

I shrugged. "Maybe Brady has connections."

"Or maybe our big bro lied about the impulsive nature of his nuptials," Jensen added.

"Fine, you nosy bastards. I planned it, okay?"

Jens and I exchanged a fist bump and a grin.

"Spill the deets, bro," he said.

Brady sighed. "It seemed prudent to have Lennox pick out her own engagement ring since it'll be on her hand for the rest of her life."

I mouthed, *Prudent*, at Jens and he snickered.

"Piss off. Seriously."

"Sorry. Continue."

He took a swig of beer. "After I picked up our matching rings, I started to panic about coming up with a perfect surprise proposal. Being a practical man, I decided to skip the proposal entirely and go straight to the main event. We'd already booked the vacation, so I scrambled to get the license. I asked Lennox's old roommate Kiley to find a dress for her to wear, since she knew Lennox's style, and I had it shipped to the hotel along with my suit. I ordered her favorite flowers, booked the honeymoon suite, hired a judge, found a spot on the beach and"—he smiled—"totally knocked her off her feet."

"Cool. That's the way to do it. Keeps it private and personal."

"Thanks. Neither of us wanted a wedding spectacle."

I raised my bottle to him. "I'll say thanks for letting me skip wearing a tux."

"You're welcome. Enough about that. What's going on with you and the mystery chick?"

"What mystery chick?" Jensen repeated.

"Walker didn't tell you that he had a kiss-and-run incident in a dive bar with a hot brunette who lied about her name and gave him a fake phone number?" Brady said innocently.

Asswipe. I glared at him.

"No, it's the first I've heard of it." Jensen cuffed me in the back of the head. "Where's the damn love for me? I oughta know this shit, bro."

"I'll show you the love, jackass." I took a swing at him, but he could move lightning fast and dodged me.

"Knock it off, you two," Brady warned. "So you found her?"

"Yeah."

"How?"

"Total coincidence."

"And?"

"And . . . it's complicated."

"Thankfully I have a brain that can follow complex human social patterns," Brady said.

"Ditto for me," Jensen chimed in. Then he added, "Dubbya, it blows when you boycott the family deals and pull the turtle routine so none of us know what's shaking in your life."

"Sorry. I just—" *Didn't think you'd noticed.*

"Skip to the down-and-dirty parts and all will be forgiven." He waggled his eyebrows. "Please tell me she wore a mask or something kinky when you found out her true identity."

"There is no down and dirty. Or kinky."

"Dude." Jensen slumped in his chair. "I thought I was the only one who wasn't getting laid regularly."

"Funny, football star." I drank my beer. "You get laid more often than anyone I know except Nolan."

"Wrong. I haven't had my goalpost polished for weeks. I'm done with sideline bunnies. This year I'm one hundred thousand percent focused on my game."

Brady leaned in. "Can we get back on track? Mystery chick story?"

"Notice how the newlywed isn't lamenting *his* sorry sex life," I grumbled.

"Because it's not sorry. It's spectacular." He smirked. "It's good to be me. Now on with it."

"Fine." I filled in the blanks for Jens and relayed the week's events, including the crap night at Ramon's party and Trinity's bizarre behavior afterward. "I haven't decided what I'll do about it."

Jensen said, "Forget about her," at the same time Brady said, "Fight for her."

"Helpful advice, guys. Thanks."

"Describe your lady's weird behavior."

"She babbled a bunch of stuff that made no sense and then when I responded? It was like she hadn't heard anything I'd said. Why?"

"Every time Lennox and I crossed paths before we started dating, she blurted out rude things to me."

I frowned. "Lennox? Really?"

"Hard to believe because she's never that way now. She confessed it was a nervous reaction to me then." He paused. "Maybe her embarrassment level increased after she woke up in your truck and she said whatever she needed to to get away. Classic flight response."

I hadn't considered that.

"Or maybe she's just a damn head case," Jensen said.

Brady scowled at him.

"What? It's a possibility. Especially given his track record with women." Jensen squinted at me. "Dude. You are a magnet for crazy. You remember Firebug Fiorina?"

"She's a little hard to forget since she torched my golf cart." Not that I could prove it.

"Who was the girl who bawled about everything?"

"Wailing Whitney." The last straw was when she sobbed hysterically in Perkins when they buttered the toast she'd ordered dry.

Jensen snapped his fingers. "Which one put her cat in therapy because he 'seemed depressed' after being declawed?"

"Neurotic Natalie," Brady supplied.

Awesome that they remembered all of this when I'd tried so damn hard to forget.

"Neurotic Natalie at least could hold a conversation. I never heard Zoned-Out Zoë utter a word. She just cocked her head and stared at me every time I tried to talk to her."

Jens snorted. "I never saw ZZ without a blunt tucked behind her ear."

"The stoner was way better than Angry Amy. Christ. Do you remember when we went to that movie at the Uptown? And we saw her standing in the front of the theater yelling at people to stop misogynists from co-opting the female experience by turning every movie into a dick pic?"

"I'm pretty sure she's a lesbian now."

"I'd watch that porn," Jensen said. "Man. She was smoking hot."

"Vicious Vera was hot too," Brady said. "But that did not make up for that mouth of hers."

Jensen scratched his chin. "She's the one who made Annika cry?"

"Yep." But Vera had been no match for one pissed-off Mama Lund. That's probably why she was the last woman I'd brought to any Lund gathering.

"Who are we forgetting?"

"I wish you'd forget about them all."

"Have you talked to Annika about this thing with Trinity?"

I shook my head. "She's on an 'All men are dogs' tear."

"I noticed. What's up with that?" Jens asked.

"Hockey players."

He snorted. "Enough said."

Brady stood. "Good gossiping with you girls, but I'm going to fetch my wife."

The party broke up soon after.

I was putting the leftover beer in the bar fridge in the family room when Mom sauntered in and parked herself on a barstool.

"I hear that heavy sigh. Is it so . . . weary making that I wish to speak with you?"

"Of course not."

"You done avoiding Brady and Lennox now that they're bored married couple?"

"They've been married a few days. I'd hope they're not bored already."

"You know what I mean."

"I've told you; I wasn't avoiding Brady and Lennox."

"Yah? You came to the last barbecue that they did not. Time before that—you leave right after they arrive. Brady does everything first, no? He's oldest, you expect it. But not with this. Not with him getting what you want most. It's hard pill to chew. Of all my children, Walker, you are most like me. You're in this family, a happy family you love, but you want a family of your own. That was the way of your grandmother. That is the way of me. You are the same."

"Mom—"

"Listen to me. Why did you, young man of twenty-four, buy such grand house? Because you saw it as family home. And why, as the owner of company that renovates houses, have you not renovated yours? I tell you why. Because you are waiting to renovate when you find the woman who will live with you there for good."

And . . . once again, she'd completely blown me away. I'd never told anyone about the first time I'd entered my house and knew I'd found where I belonged. I imagined the echo of feet running up and down the long oak staircase. I heard dogs barking, cartoons blaring, the sounds of a family gathered in the kitchen to share a meal. I felt the happy vibe of the families who'd lived and loved and fought and laughed and cried together in the space and I wanted that for myself.

"There is no shame in wanting that," she said gently.

"What if I don't get it?" I don't remember ever voicing that fear aloud.

"You will. You may have to work for it. Or you may have to be patient. But that crazy, messy love is worth it."

That's when I knew, without a doubt, that Trinity was the one for me. I hadn't been actively searching for a place to live when I'd found my home. I hadn't been looking for a relationship when Trinity knocked me for a loop with the kiss of a lifetime.

She wrapped her arms around my waist and pressed her cheek into my back. "It's been rough year. Brady focused on Lennox leaves less time for you. Nolan working more at LI with Ash means they both have less time for you. Annika is . . ." She sighed. "Unaware unless she needs something. As is Dallas. Jensen picks his teammates over you. Jaxson is only about pucks and Mimi. So I understand you avoiding family time wasn't only about jealousy. I watched and hated for you that none of them realized you are lonely and forgotten in this big family."

I wasn't surprised she'd caught on to that either. I'd been adrift for more than a year and I'd yet to see a familiar hand out to pull me back in.

And here it was. I grabbed on. "Thanks."

"It is what I do."

She started to leave and I said, "Mom?"

"Yah?"

"I'll bring her to the next family thing."

Ten

TRINITY

'd had a vicious headache since my conversation with Genevieve—*because you know she's right.*

I'd managed to finish one section on the Stephens piece—*slow and steady ain't an option on this commission.*

I'd eaten nothing—*you need to lose weight anyway.*

I'd had enough of being in my own head. It was mighty crowded in there with doubt, self-flagellation and anxiety chiming in.

I locked the studio, noticing the sunny day had turned gray and windy, the air thick with impending moisture. Yeah. That fit my mood.

In my house, when I checked the messages on my cell, I had four voice mails from Ramon. One from Esther Stephens. None from Walker.

Why are you surprised? You basically told him to give

you space. You really thought a man like that would wait around for you to get it together?

"Stop. Dammit. Just stop it right now! I do not need this."

My voice echoed in the silent space as the words reverberated in my head.

A beat passed. Two beats. Then all was quiet.

I didn't trust it. Those sneaky doubts hid in all corners of my mind, constantly clamoring for attention. Most days I fought back against them. Some days I didn't have the mental fortitude.

Enough negativity. Focus on what's important: figuring out how to apologize to Walker.

After eating a sandwich, I left for the community center. I was earlier than normal, so Chris and Nate—deep in conversation—didn't notice when I slipped in.

Usually I left the door open, letting the sounds of creativity inspire me. But today I needed to drown out everything. With my wireless headphones in place and techno-pop music on my phone cranked to the highest volume, I got to work.

I didn't stop or even slow down until the last section of plywood was propped against the wall. After ditching the headphones, I turned in a slow circle for a quick inventory of what I'd accomplished in four hours. Damn. I wished I could be that productive every day.

Two knocks sounded and the door opened. Walker stepped in and closed the door behind him. "Hey. Got a minute?"

My heart raced. Two seconds in the presence of this hunky and formidable man and all the creative ways to grovel I'd conjured up the past few hours vanished. I probably shouldn't gawk at him, but I couldn't help it. He always looked amazing. Did he roll out of bed with his hair artfully tousled?

"Why are you staring at me like that? Because I'm such a distraction?"

Ouch. I deserved that. My eyes connected with his. "I'm wondering if you ever suffer from bedhead. I'll bet your beard even looks sexy first thing in the morning after being smashed into the pillow all night." I crossed my arms over my chest. "You probably don't have bad morning breath either."

Walker's eyes widened and then he laughed. "Of all the things you could've said, none of those were in the stadium, let alone the ballpark."

"I thought you hated sports analogies."

"If I hated them, I wouldn't use them. And it isn't like there are other options."

"Like from the art world? How about: 'Of all the things you could've said, none of them were in the same collection, let alone the whole museum.'"

He blinked at me as if I'd spoken Swahili.

I sighed. "You're right. It doesn't fit."

He turned and wandered around the room, checking out the scenery. "You're caught up. You in a hurry to finish this project and move on?"

"I'm just doing what I'm paid to do." Brr. Way to sound like the ice queen. "This is a side gig. The sooner I get it done, the faster I can return to my real work." That sounded frostier yet.

Walker's spine stiffened. "Yes, you've made your priorities very clear."

Truth time. My pulse spiked. "Have I? Maybe you can refresh my memory because I'm drawing a blank." I paused. "Not that you can actually *draw* a blank, because the act of drawing, even a single line, changes the composition from nothing into something." *Shut it, Trinity. Do not board the crazy train to Babble-onia this early.*

"Do you do that a lot?"

"Do what? Draw blanks? No. I'm so much better at drawing conclusions."

"That's not what I meant. Look, Saturday night you seemed fine until—"

"I wasn't fine, Walker. Not at all." I blew out a breath. "I'm sorry."

"For?"

"For everything. When I realized you'd overheard everything Ramon had said about me? That's when I closed down."

"So you actually thought I'd be swayed in my opinion of you by what that blowhard said about you?"

"Maybe it was an irrational fear, but that's the thing about irrational fears—they make zero sense. But I've been down this road before—too many times to count. Men run at the first sign of any kind of emotional outburst or drama and Saturday was chock-full of drama. When I woke up after I cried myself to sleep in your arms, I panicked and . . . I have this . . . thing. Where my brain disconnects but, lucky me, my mouth is free to run unchecked without that pesky thing called reason kicking in."

"I caught that."

"You did?"

"It's hard to miss, sweetheart. You weren't acting like you. Before I could figure out a way to help you, you bailed on me and took away my choice."

"I don't know how to help myself. I'm kind of a freak."

The tension in the air became thicker than the paint fumes.

"Trinity."

I prepared myself for the "It's not working out" speech

I'd heard my entire dating life, which I always translated to, *You are a weirdo and I'm gone.* "What?"

"Baby, you're not a freak."

I placed my hand on my belly as if I could stop it from churning with hope. "Really?"

"Really and truly." Walker moved closer and put his big hand over mine. His lips brushed my ear. "Breathe."

I did.

We stayed like that for several long moments.

He murmured, "Better?"

"Some."

"Just so you know, I left my running shoes at home."

I almost burst into tears. He couldn't have said anything more reassuring. I had to look away to compose myself. But I felt him watching me. Waiting for something. For what? I'd just given him my deepest, darkest secret. "Quit staring at me like you're still trying to figure me out."

"I wasn't trying to figure you out. I was waiting for this, for you to reveal yourself to me—as corny as that sounds. And I'm sort of stunned that you've actually started to open up."

"It doesn't sound corny. But I wasn't sure if you were patient enough to stick around for the big reveal."

He widened his stance as if bracing himself. "So hit me with it. I'm ready."

Confused, I gaped at him. "You assume I have *more* fainting goat behavior to explain?"

"Fainting goat?" he repeated. "You'd better explain that."

I sighed. "You know those goats that get scared and their response is to faint? Then they come to a minute or two later and they're like, *Whoa, what the hell happened?* And then they're back to normal, ready to eat a tin can? That's me."

Walker blinked at me. "You're a fainting goat, huh?"

"Yep. Sexy isn't it? Makes you wanna getcha some of

this"—I ran my hand down the outside of my body—"*baaaad*, doesn't it?"

He laughed. "You make me laugh like no one I've ever met."

"You're not laughing *at* me, which is good. And that means you're okay knowing this about me?"

"*That* was your big reveal? That your brain goes off-line when you're stressed or nervous and your mouth picks up the slack?"

"Well, yeah."

"You thought I couldn't deal with it?"

"It *is* weird," I said defensively. "I'm a thirty-one-year-old woman, so it's not something I'll outgrow. This is—"

He put his fingers over my mouth. "You thought I'd give up on you, didn't you?"

"I didn't know. I've never had a guy stick around past this point."

"What point is that?"

"The point when they decide I'm too much work."

"I knew going into this that you'd be work. It didn't scare me off then. It doesn't scare me off now."

Right then . . . I kind of loved him.

"Besides, this is new territory for me too."

"It is?"

Walker touched his nose to mine, then placed a soft kiss in front of my ear and murmured, "I've never been as crazy about a woman as I am for you. I've never stuck around this long." He angled his head so I could see his smirking half-smile. "So the question is, are we still on a 'break'?"

Crap. I deserved that. "Nope."

"Good. So you wanna go make out in my truck?"

"Ah . . . that was a little random."

"No more random than you wondering what I look like when I roll out of bed first thing in the morning."

"True. But I do think about it. A lot." I had to tilt my head back to look up at him. "Us being in bed together."

"Are we naked?"

"Of course we are. Have you *seen* your body?"

His eyes gleamed as brightly as his teeth and then his mouth overtook mine.

The kiss rocked my world, fired my blood, and I suspected the heat from it might've singed the inside of my clothes. When he released my lips and started kissing my neck, I clutched his shirt and sighed. "You are so, so good at that."

"Mmm-hmm," he rumbled against my throat. "You done here?"

"Yes."

He stepped back, snagged my messenger bag off the table and draped the strap over his shoulder. Then he clasped my hand in his. "Come on."

The backstage area was quiet.

We cut across the hallway to the side door that opened into the parking lot.

The humid day had dissipated into a balmy night. The orange glow of the sodium lights spilled across the asphalt. Only three vehicles remained in the parking lot.

When we reached his truck, a chirping sound echoed as he pointed the key fob to unlock it. He opened the passenger door for me and said, "Hop in."

"You were serious about us making out in your truck?"

"Kissing and making up is the best part."

"But—"

"Babe, you're letting the mosquitoes in." He tapped my butt. "Get in."

I stepped onto the running board and launched myself into the passenger side.

But I didn't stay on that side long. As soon as Walker shut his door, he slapped his hands on his thighs. "Sit on my lap."

"The steering wheel—"

"Will ensure you'll stay very close to me, which is exactly what I want. Now slide over here."

Somehow I scooted across the bench seat and settled on his lap without kneeing him in the groin.

He tucked me against his chest and sighed. "Much better."

"It's dangerous, us snuggled up like this. Remember what happened Saturday night? What if I fall asleep again?"

"You won't." He pressed a kiss to the top of my head. "You're wired. Just like I am."

Then he started trailing his fingers up and down my back. My skin broke out in goose bumps.

"So what do you want to talk about?"

"Seriously? I thought we were here to make out."

Walker started humming "Anticipation."

"The song that will forever be associated with ketchup, which sucks because it was a good tune."

"You're a big Carly Simon fan?" he asked.

"My grandma was. She loved all that 1970s easy-listening music. Especially Carly and JT. The original JT—James Taylor."

"Do you ever listen to it now?"

While his voice soothed me, his hands were revving me up. My heart thundered, my blood pumped hotter and faster and my thoughts were getting lost in a haze of lust. I tried to focus. "Not often. Mostly because even the classic rock stations on Sirius and Pandora play arena rock. Although one time I did try to set up a station with Carly and JT, Olivia

Newton-John, the Carpenters, Bread, Seals and Crofts. It was great for like five songs and then they shoved Simon and Garfunkel in there. I hate their music. It wrecked my happy vibe to the point I slashed through the canvas I was working on with my putty knife. And the other reason it's not the same is Grandma had a stereo—one of those big console models with the record player on one side and album storage on the other. We listened to whole albums, not just single tracks. So some of my favorite songs were ones that never got airplay and not all LPs have been digitally remastered. There's a lot of music that's not cataloged. Someday I'll take all the albums I inherited from her and have them digitized—"

Walker pulled my mouth down to his.

But what started as a "Shut it" kiss ended with warmth and sweetness that had me chasing after his mouth for more.

He laughed softly. "That's how I'll handle it from now on when you go off on a tangent."

"Okay with me."

"So I have to ask. Have you heard from Ramon?"

I rubbed my cheek against Walker's. I couldn't get enough of feeling that beard on my skin. "I haven't returned his calls or his texts. If I engage him at all, he'll think I've reached the 'forgive and forget' stage and that's not a possibility." I paused. "Do you think that's harsh?"

"Sweetheart, before we showed up at his place, you talked about friendship cycles, so I suspect you knew the end of the cycle was near with Ramon."

"It's still not easy. It's not like I have a ton of friends." I nestled my face in the crook of his neck and breathed him in, trying not to act like I'd just embarrassed myself with that admission.

After a bit, he said, "What else is on your mind?"

"What do you mean?"

"I can tell you're restless."

"How?"

"I've had my hand on your ass like three times and you haven't batted it away and told me to behave."

"Maybe I want to see how sexy you are when you misbehave."

"You sure about that?"

"Try me."

Walker slid his hands over my shoulders and up my neck. He tilted my head back so he could look at me. "Stay still."

My belly swooped at seeing the fire in his eyes. And that commanding tone . . . so hot.

He kept his left hand at the base of my throat and our eyes locked as he moved in closer.

I felt the heat of his breath as he feathered his lips across mine. Back and forth. Again and again. Soft and fleeting. I craved his kiss, wanting his tongue deep in my mouth as I threaded my fingers into his hair. But I remained still, letting him tease and torment me.

When his tongue darted out and he slowly licked the inner rim of my bottom lip, I whimpered and closed my eyes.

A sharp nip from his teeth had my eyes flying back open. "Watch me."

I was helpless to do anything else.

The buttons on my blouse were no match for his deft fingers.

His gaze roamed my face as he trailed the back of his hand down my jawline, then follow the column of my throat to the cleavage peeping out from the edges of my shirt. He teased that soft flesh with his rough-skinned knuckle, watching as I sucked in a quick breath and unconsciously bowed into his touch.

Then he adjusted the angle of his wrist and palmed my left breast. "Perfect fit for my hand," he said huskily.

"Walker."

"You want my mouth here?" He swept the pad of his thumb across my nipple, his nostrils flaring as he watched the tip harden beneath my thin shirt and bra. "With you straddling my lap this way, I could feast on these luscious tits."

"Do it," I urged.

"Soon." He lowered his face to my chest and ran that beard over every inch of my bare skin, like he was marking me. I almost had a tiny O just from that.

Our mouths met and while hunger clawed at us both we kept the kiss on simmer, but it was tempting to crank it up and see how long it'd take to boil over.

When I couldn't take the teasing anymore, I said, "You're being a serious distraction right now."

"Sorry."

"No, you're not."

"Okay. I'm not. But I do understand you have a major project to finish. I'll keep my distractions to a minimum until you tell me to do otherwise."

"Thank you for being so understanding." I allowed one more kiss before I disentangled myself from him.

He helped me out of his truck and we walked hand in hand to my car. "What's your schedule like the rest of the week?"

"Taking it day by day. But with three weeks to finish this textile piece, I'll log a lot of studio hours. What's yours like?"

"No late nights on the job site." He tugged my ponytail. "And there's this sexy artist who's offered to show me her etchings so I'll make time for that."

I laughed.

"I'll call you tomorrow."

"I just have to warn you that if my studio time is going well, it might be a while before you hear back from me."

"I'm a patient man."

"Happy to hear that, Walker. Chances are good I'll test that."

Eleven

WALKER

'd managed to be patient on Tuesday when I'd gotten a sweet but cryptic text from Trinity telling me the piece was going well and she planned an all-nighter.

I left a voice mail midafternoon on Wednesday asking about her dinner plans. I sent her a brief text message too, knowing not everyone listened to their cell phone voice messages. In fact, in the fifteen years my mother owned a cell phone, she'd never set up voice mail, deeming it "too Technicolor," and I hadn't asked again.

After no word from Trinity on Wednesday night, I woke Thursday morning to seven text messages, sent between three and five a.m., each more rambling than the last. The texts had both amused and concerned me. Especially the comment about her sucking at flirty sexts but being ready to flirt her butt off in person because she needed an activity to shrink the size of her buns.

The cracks she made about her appearance annoyed me. The "I'll insult myself first so you don't have to bother" reflex had to have come from somewhere, and if I ever got my hands on that person I'd . . .

Crack.

I glanced down to see the plastic pen in my hand had snapped under my death grip. I let it fall to the desk and leaned back in my chair.

During our conversation Monday night, Trinity had been more forthcoming than I'd expected, and yet I'd hated watching her struggle to explain herself. She hadn't been looking for sympathy; she'd just wanted me to understand that being with her would be a challenge. She hadn't tossed it out there as a dare to prove I was a man that could handle it, but I knew she wouldn't have shared her vulnerability if she suspected that I *couldn't* deal with it.

So what was it about this woman who had me digging in my heels instead of sprinting far, far away from her?

Granted, she was beautiful. But the glow that came from within called to me more than just her looks.

She had a quirky sense of humor. From the first night I recognized that it matched mine, so I understood when she confessed a lot of people didn't "get" her.

She had a brain and she used it. Her hot, curvy body was just a side benefit.

She was comfortable giving—and receiving—physical displays of affection. I couldn't be with a woman who wouldn't let me show that side of myself whenever I needed to.

She was independent. She didn't need me, but she wanted me. Me as a man, not as a Lund heir. As much as that relieved me, I wanted her to need me a little.

Are you getting what you need from her? You aren't sleeping with her, so there is no physical release. She hasn't cooked you a meal, or let you cook one for her. She hasn't even seen where you work.

Even when my subconscious compiled a breakdown of all the things she didn't do for me, I didn't feel like I was giving and she was taking. Relationships were supposed to ebb and flow; they'd never be fifty-fifty. But I also knew if we didn't specifically carve out time for each other from the start, we never would.

Three fast raps sounded on my door before Betsy opened it. "Jase wants to know if you're coming out for drinks with us."

"Thanks, but I have other plans."

Betsy considered me. "You are welcome to bring her."

"I know. Another time, okay?"

"All right. But I do have one piece of advice." She paused. "Flowers."

"Flowers. Meaning . . . ?"

"Women like to get flowers from their man when it's not a holiday, or a special occasion, or a bribe for sex, or an apology. 'Just because I was missing you' is always a welcome reason."

I raised an eyebrow. "You think I'm *that* clueless about women, Bets?"

"Walker, *all* men are clueless about women." She grinned. "Until they find the one that matters. Then they start to pay attention."

She got that right. "Why are you here so late harassing me?" I said gruffly. "Don't you have a drummer to bang or something?"

"He's a bassist," she said with a sniff. "See what I mean about men not paying attention?"

"I know he's a bassist. I just couldn't think of a better analogy. Except maybe if he was a string player and then 'fiddle around with' would work."

"Stick to sports analogies."

"'Night, Bets."

"'Night, boss."

A rmed with summer rolls and pad thai from Sawatdee— my favorite Thai place—I juggled the bunch of daisies and knocked loudly on the door to Trinity's studio. I hadn't shown up unannounced; I'd texted her I was coming over.

While I waited for Trinity to answer, I noticed a security camera in the corner.

The door opened as far as the chain; then a sliver of Trinity's face appeared in the crack. "Walker? What are you doing here?"

I held up the bags of food. "I texted that I was bringing you dinner. Didn't you get it?"

She shook her head. "I leave my phone in the house so I'm not distracted."

We stared at each other for a moment.

"Is that your way of telling me to leave?"

"No!"

I lifted a brow. "So are you going to let me in?"

She bit her lip. "Okay, here's the thing. I spilled quick-set glue all over my pants. So I . . . umm . . . took them off."

"You're not wearing pants." Christ. Was she trying to kill me?

"My shirt is long enough so it'll probably be okay," she said more to herself than to me. "Come into my lair, my sweet."

"Telling a man you're not wearing pants will lure him in every time, babe. Where should I put this stuff?"

"Take a left."

I found myself in a small closet that'd been turned into a mini-kitchen.

"There's not really room for two in here."

Not to mention it was hot as hell. I set the bags of food on the table and faced her with the flowers.

"For me?" Trinity grinned and grabbed the cellophane-wrapped bundle. "Thank you. What made you choose them?"

"I told the florist I wanted daisies—"

"But these are gerbera daisies, not just any plain old daisy. You knew that, right?"

I mumbled, "No, I didn't think there'd be a test."

She laughed. "These are my favorite because they're simple and sturdy. They have just one row of petals, see?" She ran her finger along the outer edge. "Which makes them simple. The stem is thick, and yet graceful, which makes them sturdy. They also hold their own as a lone bloom in a single vase or as part of a bouquet."

The way she described the blooms sounded a lot like how I'd describe her. No wonder I'd been drawn to the flowers.

She ducked her head. "Sorry. I'll just shut up now and put them in water."

After she'd set the vase on a catchall table by the door, she said, "Maybe we should eat outside."

"Why's it so hot in here?"

"Something's wrong with the air conditioner."

"How long hasn't it been working?"

"Since Monday. It was actually quite freeing to ditch my pants today."

My gaze dropped to her pink-tipped toenails and moved

up her shins, over her dimpled knees to the ragged hem of her shirt that started midthigh. "I'm not complaining."

"Grab the food."

I swear she put an extra wiggle in her ass just to see if I was a freakin' saint.

"This smells delicious," she said, scooping noodles onto her plate. "And it's really sweet that you brought me dinner. Thank you."

"My pleasure. How late did you work last night?"

"Until six or so. Then I got up at nine because I'm at that stage where it's eat-sleep-breathe-live the piece."

"Sounds exhausting."

"It is." She covered a yawn. "When it's not exhilarating."

We didn't talk much until we finished eating.

Trinity looked at her empty take-out carton as I started picking up garbage. "Guess I was hungry."

"I'm glad you liked it."

"I'm so full now." She slumped back in her chair and closed her eyes. "And sleepy."

I stood. "I'll take a quick look at that air conditioner."

"That would be awesome. I'll just wait here for you."

I returned inside. After a quick inspection of the window-unit air conditioner and seeing no mechanical issues, I tracked down the electrical box and saw that she'd blown a fuse. After replacing it, I turned the unit on and it immediately started putting out cold air. I poked my head outside to see that Trinity had fallen asleep.

That gave me time to kill, so I wandered through her studio. She had quite the setup, everything from an industrial sewing machine to a welder. Her tool bench would've caused envy in most men; she had more metalworking tools than I did. And her studio had more square footage than my garage.

Maybe it surprised me a little—okay, a lot—that everything was incredibly organized. Her huge cabinet full of oil-based paint was categorized by brand of paint first, then by color. Her paintbrushes were labeled by type—natural or synthetic—then by size. She had a separate section for watercolor paints and brushes. Another cabinet for her airbrushing supplies and yet another for varnishes, oils and paint thinners.

In the far corner of the room I found carving tools and lumps of raw clay covered in plastic. Next to that was an impressive set of woodworking instruments, including a lathe and a chunk of soft wood. An open storage unit at the far back of the room contained rolls of canvas and various lengths of kiln-fired wood. So in addition to creating the art on the canvas, she crafted her own canvases. She'd repurposed a filing cabinet for maps to hold paper of all sizes and finishes.

As I moved around the perimeter, I realized she'd divided up her work spaces. Easels were positioned by the windows. A large drafting table was nestled in the opposite corner, next to a cabinet filled with pens and ink, charcoal, chalk, colored pencils and the biggest array of markers I'd ever seen. Above the table were a multitude of lighting options, including adjustable umbrella lights and reflective panels I'd seen professional photographers use. That drew my gaze to the ceiling. She'd kept the entire structure open, adding pulley-and-chain systems for bigger pieces that she could stabilize with hooks and cables she'd embedded into the concrete floor.

But as I silently marveled at the amazing work space, it was nothing compared with the work itself. I lost track of time as I wandered from one area to the next, feeling as if I'd stumbled into a secret art vault of priceless treasures. No wonder Trinity couldn't focus on one medium over another; she excelled at all of them.

If her unfinished projects were this good . . . her completed projects had to be stunning.

And it hit me then how little I knew of her professional life. If she had pieces hanging in galleries, or sculptures in parks, or commissioned works in office buildings. Or why someone with her talent would waste her time painting sets for a community theater production.

Maybe part of the reason Trinity had gotten so upset with Ramon—besides the fact he'd been a total dickhead to her—was she'd known there was a ring of truth to his accusation that she'd sold her skills to the lowest bidder.

Who are you to judge? Just because you can afford to volunteer doesn't mean everyone else can.

The door to the patio squeaked and Trinity called out, "Walker?"

"I'm here."

"Oh wow. It's cooler. You got the air conditioner working again."

I faced her. "You just blew a fuse. Not a big deal to fix."

"I appreciate you doing it."

A few strands of her hair were sticking straight up. I reached out and smoothed them down.

"Sorry I fell asleep."

"Don't be. You needed it. And it gave me a chance to wander through your studio."

Her face shuttered and she crossed her arms over her chest. "Yeah, well, nothing in here is finished, so it's not much to look at."

"I disagree. I'm blown away. I—" I took a moment to come up with something better. But my mind emptied. "Dammit, I suck at trying to put it into words, but you are so freakin' talented that they should devote an entire wing in some fancy art gallery to you just to show the world all that you can do."

She blinked those big green eyes at me. "Uh, that didn't suck. At all. Thank you."

"C'mere." I wrapped her in my arms. I kissed the top of her head and breathed in her scent, a mix of the sweetness of apples and cedar. A scent that made me hard and urged me to seek out all the places on her body where that scent was the strongest. A scent that begged me to answer the question of whether she tasted like apples and cedar too.

My hands coasted down her lower back and over the globes of her ass. If I inched the fabric of her shirt up, I could grab a handful of her bare skin.

"Walker."

"Mmm-hmm." I angled my head to rub my lips over the top of her ear.

"I just remembered something."

"What's that?"

"You didn't kiss me hello."

I shifted my stance to gaze into her eyes as my hands lightly caressed her ass. "Well, sweetheart, hello kisses are your thing, remember?"

"Shoot. I dropped the ball." A startled look entered her eyes. "Dammit, since when do I make sports analogies?"

"Since you started hanging around with me. It's cute. At least you don't mix them up the way my mother does."

"How can you mix them up?"

"No idea. She always says she 'popped the ball.'"

"It's sort of the same meaning, right? Dropped, popped. The ball is out of play."

I pressed the pads of my fingers into the curve where her butt cheek flowed into her thigh.

"Why can I feel your fingers on my bare skin?"

"Because you're not wearing pants and I'm taking advantage of that happy circumstance."

She thunked her head into my chest. Twice. "And you've trapped my arms."

"In my defense, you're not trying very hard to get away."

"True."

Squeezing her soft flesh in my hands, I put my mouth on her ear. "I know you have work to do and I promised I wouldn't be a distraction, so I'll go."

"You're the best kind of distraction."

"Good." I grabbed onto her hips. "Hop up on the table and I'll give you a good-bye kiss."

"I'll stand." She rested her palms on the table behind her, tilting her head back to gaze at me.

I stroked her hip bones with my thumbs. "Close your eyes."

"I love it when your voice goes all deep and sexy."

As I pressed openmouthed kisses to the side of her neck, I slipped my hands up the length of her body and back down. Up and down. When she started to squirm, I moved my hands lower, onto the tops of her thighs.

Trinity shifted restlessly, offering me the other side of her throat. "I like when you make that rumbling growl like you want to eat me alive."

Oh, I want to eat you all right. I licked and nibbled and teased until her skin was damp and her pulse pounded beneath my tongue. The heat from her body released the apple and cedar scent and I couldn't wait another second to taste it.

I dropped to my knees.

I pressed my face into the soft cushion of her belly, and my fingers undid the two buttons on the bottom of her shirt.

She went motionless. "Walker. What are you doing?"

Looking up at her, I hooked my fingers in the sides of her panties, slowly tugging them down past her knees. "Giving you a good-bye kiss."

"But . . . I . . . that's not . . ."

"If you don't want my mouth on you, say so now."

She didn't utter a peep.

I brushed my beard up the inside of her thigh, across the rise of her mound and down the other side. Over and over.

Her body jerked but my grip on the outside of her legs kept her in place.

And the sweet, hot scent of her filled my lungs and lured me in.

As I kissed my way back up to where my mouth watered to be, I noticed she had a mole on the inside of her left thigh.

A small mark that might go unnoticed. Maybe even she wasn't aware it was there.

But I saw it. I wanted to claim ownership of that spot. Bite it. Suck on it. So every time she looked down at it, she'd think of me. Remember me kissing it and using my tongue on it as I glided my mouth up to do the same to her warm, wet center.

I had good intentions, planning to take my time and savor every inch of that sweet pink flesh. But from the first taste, I lost my head. I was obsessed with hearing how she sounded when I made her cry out in pleasure. Obsessed with feeling her climax against my tongue.

And was my babbling girl shy and polite when I was on my knees worshipping this intimate part of her? Hell no. Trinity made the sexiest sex noises I'd ever heard. She grabbed my head and pulled my hair hard to position me exactly where she wanted my mouth.

I freakin' loved that.

Her thighs tightened and she arched up. Her panting gasps

were a precursor to her shout of "Yes. Like that. Don't stop. Please."

Boom. Two more suctioning kisses on her hot button and she unraveled.

I almost got off just watching her.

While she caught her breath, I ran the rough tips of my fingers up the backs of her calves. The feel of her skin beneath my hands, the taste of her on my tongue and her heady scent . . . potent stuff.

"Walker?"

"Mmm-hmm?"

"Can you check the fuse box and reset the fuse that blew in my head just now?"

I smiled and kissed my way down to her knee.

Then her hands were on my face, one petting my beard, the other rifling through my hair, keeping me there and prolonging this connection.

We stayed like that until my knees protested and I had to move.

As soon as I was upright, Trinity fisted her hands in my shirt and pulled me in. "That was a helluva good-bye kiss."

"But?"

"But are you really leaving?"

I nuzzled her neck, sliding my mouth across her skin for one last taste. "Yes."

She shivered and murmured, "Stay. Please. My bed isn't very far and I'm so wired—"

"Put that energy toward your work, so then next time I want to be all up in you, all night long. I won't have to be chivalrous and leave." I rested my forehead to hers. "I won't be a distraction, Trinity, but I won't be forgotten either. We'll have to find these little pockets of time and make the most of them."

"Do you have any pockets open tomorrow? Like the one to your fly?"

I grinned. "I'm working in the office doing bullshit paperwork I can't put off. Tomorrow night Jensen has a preseason scrimmage thing."

"So . . . you're telling me . . . ?"

"I'm telling you if I'm trying to be fluid with this, you need to be too." I lifted my head and kissed her pouting mouth. "Lock up after I go."

I made it four steps from her when she said, "Walker."

"Don't say anything that'll convince me to stay, because my willpower where you're concerned is just about gone. Get back to work. I'll talk to you tomorrow."

Twelve

TRINITY

We'll have to find these little pockets of time and make the most of them.

Walker's words had been ringing in my head all morning.

So far he'd made the effort. Happy as I'd been to be on the receiving end of his effort, I needed to show him this relationship wasn't one-sided.

Walker had happily stunned me last night, showing up with food, flowers and wicked intentions. He'd fixed my air conditioner. He'd fixed me. All day I'd been dragging ass and had felt distracted by the feeling I'd been missing something. It turned out I'd been missing him.

After he'd rocked my world—just thinking about that good-bye "kiss" I got hot and tingly all over again—I would've happily blown off work last night to blow him, or to roll around between the sheets all night. But he'd retained a clear head and sent me back to work, completely inspired.

So inspired that I'd finished two sections on the Stephens piece and started on a third, putting me ahead of schedule. With a little extra time on my hands, I decided to drop by Walker's office with lunch.

I parked in the corner of the big lot and checked my hair—already frizzy from the near constant humidity—my makeup, which, thankfully, hadn't started to run from said humidity, and made sure that I didn't have chia seeds stuck in my teeth from the smoothie I'd downed for breakfast. Good to go, I grabbed the carryout bags and the picnic basket. Then I followed the sidewalk to the front entrance.

The main brick building that housed the offices of Flint & Lund had that funky, cool vibe. It totally fit the man himself. Inside, the entryway opened into a reception area with two club chairs in vibrant red that faced a dark brown leather couch. The walls were the color of celery and the rug pulled the entire space together. I squinted at the large piece of framed art on the back wall, centered above a thin rectangular sofa table. The art wasn't . . . bad, but it was a mass-produced piece that matched the décor. While I wasn't against coordinating a room, that wall cried out for a piece that gave a better indication of what business the proprietors of this establishment were in.

A smiling redhead sauntered down the hallway. "I told the boss it was a good idea to put a buzzer on the door for when someone wanders in. How can I help you?"

"I'm looking for Walker."

She studied the bags in my hand like I was a door-to-door saleswoman. "Is Mr. Lund expecting you?"

"Ah. No. I thought I'd surprise him."

"He's not usually—"

Behind me I heard, "Trinity?"

I whirled around. Walker entered the reception area from

the hallway on the right, looking so yummy in a black T-shirt and jeans that I wanted to take a bite out of him. "Hey."

He didn't stop until the toes of his work boots were an inch from my flip-flops. That sinful mouth curled into a smile and he loomed over me. "Hey, yourself." Then he slid his hand behind my neck and brought his mouth down on mine in a decisive kiss. "Nice surprise, sweetheart," he murmured against my lips before he backed off.

"Have you had lunch?"

"No. This is perfect timing because I was about to order in." He noticed the bags in my hands and said, "Let me take those."

A throat cleared behind us.

Walker gently turned me back around and kept one hand on my shoulder. "Betsy, this is my girlfriend, Trinity. Trinity, this is Betsy, the office manager."

"I prefer the term 'ruler supreme' to office manager," Betsy said with a grin. She offered her hand. "It's great to finally meet you, Trinity."

Finally? Had Walker told his coworkers about me? "Nice to meet you too, Betsy."

"I'm having Trinity for lunch, so hold my calls."

I gaped at him.

When he realized what he'd said, the cutest blush stole across his cheeks. "I meant I'm having lunch with Trinity." He pointed at the picnic basket. "You want to eat now?"

"I can wait. I want a tour of your workplace."

That pleased him and he bestowed another glorious smile on me. "I'll put this stuff in my office first."

"Give it to me. I'll do it," Betsy said. After she'd loaded up the bags and the basket, she warned, "Don't let him take you up in the attic. It's haunted."

"Seriously?"

"Yeah, one time—"

"And we're done." He grabbed my hand and towed me down the opposite hallway.

Walker gave me the full rundown of the house's history—a single-family home turned into a fourplex and then left empty for years.

We headed up a staircase that opened onto a landing.

"During the fourplex stage, the owners added walls. So the first thing we did was tear them down, creating a conference room and Jase's office."

The conference room was large enough to hold three tables in a U-shaped formation. The colors in here were subdued—grays and tans, which allowed the stained-glass windows across the back wall to be the focal point.

"Are the windows original?"

"They're reproductions of the originals that were installed when the house was built. It was fun busting out the shitty replacements and the lath-and-plaster walls, though."

"I imagine you are a dangerous man with a sledgehammer."

Walker crowded me until the backs of my knees connected with the edge of the conference table, the way he had last night in my studio. I had a flash of him on his knees looking up at me as he scraped his beard on the insides of my thighs.

He growled something and then his mouth was on mine. Not a sweet hello peck. This kiss was chock-full of hunger and need.

My heart beat a million miles an hour when he ended the intense kiss.

Those stunning blue eyes bored into mine. "You were thinking about last night, weren't you?"

"That's pretty much all I've thought about today." I slid my hand up his chest and stopped when my thumb brushed over the pulse point in his throat. "Every time I walk past the table, I remember what you did to me on that table."

Walker smirked. "Should I apologize?"

"No, you're not sorry. And I'm not either." I brushed the tips of my fingers into the hair on his jawline. "Your impromptu visit and good-bye kiss inspired me. I got a lot accomplished after you left. Since that gave me some extra time today, I wanted to spend it with you."

"That is an excellent plan," he said gruffly.

I slipped my hand around the back of his neck and pulled his mouth to mine for a soft kiss. "Continue the tour, Mr. Lund."

He stepped back and helped me off the conference table—mostly so he could cop a feel. In the hallway, I stopped in front of an elevator. "Get out. You have an elevator?"

"It was originally a dumbwaiter, so we just expanded the size of the shaft and put in this small unit. Betsy doesn't have to walk up two flights of stairs with the boxes of job specs."

"Lucky Betsy."

"Dirty thoughts running around in that brain, Miz Carlson?"

"I've always wanted to do it in an elevator. The tight space means you have to get really close. And there's the whole getting-caught-with-your-skirt-up angle—stopping the car to go at it frantically and hope you get off before you have to . . . get off."

Walker coughed. "Jesus. Warn a guy."

"You told me in that one text you wanted to know all of my fantasies. There's a big one."

His warm mouth brushed my ear. "Next time you need to visit me after normal business hours and we'll see if we can't fulfill your fantasy and mine."

I shivered. "You have a 'Love in an Elevator' fantasy too?"

"No, although it sounds like fun."

I leaned back to look at him. "Then what's your fantasy, Mr. Lund?"

"You'll have to dig a little deeper to get me to tell you."

It hit me. "Omigod. You want to do it on a piece of heavy machinery."

That surprised him. "How'd you figure that out?"

"'Dig a little deeper' wasn't a hint?"

He laughed. "A subtle hint . . . or so I thought." He kissed my forehead. "I like that you get me, Trinity. Not everyone does."

"No other woman has volunteered to literally get down and dirty with you?"

He shook his head.

I had a hard time believing that. "Is it because you haven't asked? Or have you been turned down?"

A vulnerable look crossed his face. "I haven't asked for fear of getting shot down."

"Hmm." I wrapped my arms around his neck and got in his face. "Their loss is my gain." I lightly nipped his bottom lip and soothed the sting with a sassy flick of my tongue. "Don't you know there's nothing I want more than to get down and dirty with you? Anytime, anyplace."

He released a soft groan. "If we weren't surrounded by my coworkers and it wasn't the middle of the damn day, I'd make you prove that."

"Maybe we should sneak into the elevator for a quickie. No one will know."

Just then, two doors down, a guy popped his head out. "I thought I heard voices."

"See? Everyone will know." He released me. "Come on, let's get this over with."

We entered a large office that boasted a big desk, two

drafting tables and a sitting area. The guy I'd just seen rested his backside against the desk, nearly hiding a statuesque blonde standing behind him.

Walker kept his hand in the small of my back as we approached. "This man is my partner, Jase Flint. Jase, my girl-friend, Trinity Carlson."

Jase smiled at me. "Good to meet you. I'm sure—"

"That is not your name," the blonde bombshell said, storming up to me, staring at me as if I'd just wandered in from the circus.

"Tiffany, didn't Jase tell you—"

"Jase didn't tell me you had a new squeeze, let alone the fact she's Trinity Amelia. That's you, right?"

I nodded. How did this woman know me?

Then she squealed and hugged me. "I love love love your work! The piece in the Federal Reserve actually moved me to tears." All at once she seemed to remember her manners and she practically jumped back. "Sorry."

"It's okay . . . I'm sorry. I didn't catch your name."

"Tiffany Flint. I'm Jase's wife." She looked over her shoulder. "Honey, the pictures hanging in the dining room? This is the woman who painted them."

I felt Walker studying me, but I focused on Tiffany. "You own some of my work?"

"Yes, I bought them from you at the Minnesota State Fair. One is a watercolor of a crumbling castle set against a stormy background. The other is a three-dimensional piece in oil with an older woman hanging clothes on the line and they're flapping in the wind. You can touch a piece of denim from jeans, lace from a dress and a pristine white sheet."

"You did that?" Walker asked.

"Yes. It's an earlier piece I did as my version of Midwest-ern folk art. Harvey Dunn meets pop art."

"I just love both those pieces. Everyone always comments on them," Tiffany gushed.

"I'm really happy to hear you're still enjoying them."

"Will you be at the fair this year?"

I shook my head. "I have too many other projects going on. Plus, I've sold everything and haven't had time to replenish my stock."

"Shoot." Then her gaze flicked between Walker and me. "I can't believe you're dating!"

"Yep," Walker said. "Trinity brought me lunch. She wanted to see where I worked since I've been in her studio."

Tiffany gasped. "Really? You've been where she makes stuff?"

"Yes. And if you want to see some of what she's been working on, buy tickets to *Into the Woods* at the Seventh Street Community Center—Trinity painted all the sets."

"Sets that you crafted from plywood and Styrofoam," I said, trying to deflect attention away from me.

"We have tickets. Walker, your mom bought two sections for opening night," Betsy said behind me.

"She did?"

Betsy flapped her hand at him. "Don't act surprised. She's proud of you and the time you spend volunteering for LCCO." Then she addressed me. "Have you met the Lund collective yet?"

"Sounds ominous. But no, I haven't met any of Walker's family."

Silence.

Both Tiffany and Betsy blurted out, "We won't tell her."

"Wise move," Walker said dryly. "We're eating lunch in my office, so all of you feel free to stay the hell out."

His coworkers were amused by that, not annoyed.

I said, "It was nice meeting all of you."

Once we were on the main floor again, Walker led me down the opposite hallway and into his office.

I knew he didn't spend much time in here, but the place was bare-bones. A bookshelf anchored one wall, a big open desk sat in the center of the room, filing cabinets filled the back wall and by the door there was a bench seat jammed with mysterious construction work paraphernalia. There weren't family pictures or artwork on the shelves, or even kitschy posters adorning the plain white walls.

He seemed embarrassed. "It's not much to look at, is it?"

"I'd rather be looking at you anyway."

"Nice save."

"Now I need you to do two things. First, find us something to drink."

"All right. And the other thing?"

"Stay out of here while I set everything up." When he arched his brow, like he imagined me getting naked and spreading myself across his desk for lunch, I whapped him on the arm. "I'm not on the menu. Gimme five minutes. Now shoo."

As soon as he shut the door, I sprang into action. Thankfully, the food wasn't cold. But after I set everything up and looked at it, I wondered if he'd think this was stupid.

This is Walker we're talking about. Even if he thinks it's dumb, he will appreciate the gesture.

My nerves made no sense but my palms were sweating anyway, so I wiped them on my pants before I opened the door.

Walker paused in the doorway to take it all in.

I'd cleared his desk and covered it with a red linen tablecloth. Candlelight reflected off the white dinner plates and the wineglasses. Soft music played from my phone.

Before he said a word, I started talking. "Maybe it seems

over-the-top, but just go with it, okay? Things started out kinda weird and crazy for us, and then we've both been busy and I haven't had a chance to invite you over and cook a meal for you, which sucks because I'm actually a pretty good cook. I know that romantic candlelit dinners are a staple at the start of a relationship and we haven't even had that and I wanted to be the first one to give it to you—but in lunch form. Not because I'm competitive, but because I like that you want to feed me—it's your way of taking care of me that's so sweet and thoughtful and you probably don't know that I've never really had that in a relationship before so I wanted to do the same for you. And—"

Walker's mouth stopped the nonstop flow of words coming from me. His kiss did more than just shut me up; it calmed me and grounded me like nothing else.

He didn't pull away abruptly; he just softened the kiss until my heart and respiration rate were somewhat normal.

"Better?" he murmured in my ear.

"Yes. Thank you."

"No, thank *you*. Time to feed me and romance me, baby." He locked the door, giving me his naughty grin. "Without interruptions."

I poured soda into the wineglasses. Then I popped the lids on the carryout containers. "I wasn't sure what you liked, so I ordered a little of everything. Spaghetti carbonara, lemon and herb risotto, and my favorite, gnocchi Verdi."

He said, "This is from Broders' Pasta Bar."

"Yes. I hope that means you like their food?"

"I do. I haven't eaten there in ages."

"Dig in."

I loved watching his hands as he ate. I'd noticed it last night; his manners were impeccable. The movements of those callused hands were precise yet elegant. I'd felt his careful and tender touch on my skin. But it made my mouth go dry and my panties wet to imagine the roughness in his touch and the bruising strength of his body lost in passion.

"What are you thinking about?"

I stopped pushing the last bit of risotto around my plate. "Sex."

"The atmosphere you created does bring that to mind, sweetheart. Was that your intent? Are you here for a payback from last night?"

"I'm not a tit-for-tat chick, Walker. But that's what you expected when you saw this romantic lunch, isn't it?"

He shrugged tightly. "Tell me I'm wrong."

I leaned across the table and whispered. "You're wrong. If I wanted to get on my knees for you, then I would've waited until quitting time to show up. This"—I indicated the table— "is exactly what I said it was: my version of an indoor picnic. Give me some credit. This would've been a total cliché had I walked through your door bearing food, wine and wearing sexy lingerie. I take pride in my unconventional way of doing things."

He looked properly chastised. "You are all that. And I apologize for assuming you'd be so unoriginal."

When I started picking up, he put his hands on my shoulders and said, "Sit. I'll do this."

After he'd cleared away everything but the candles and the tablecloth, he sat across from me and reached for my hand. He stroked the outside from my wrist bone to the ball of my thumb. "You said you've never had someone look after you like this? I haven't either. So thank you for thinking of me. I didn't mean to seem ungrateful."

"My pleasure. Were you shocked to see me at your office?"

"I figured I wouldn't see you until Saturday at the community center."

"I'm lucky that I can submerge myself for hours or even days at a time. But it sucks too, because when it's going well, I'm afraid to leave my studio and lose that creative connection. I've been known to stay secluded for a week, sometimes more."

"A week?" he repeated.

"Sounds pathetic. That was one good thing about my friendship with Ramon. He'd call to check up on me every couple of days when I hit that obsessive stage because he understood it."

"Ramon is still bugging you?"

"He's texted and left a few voice mails, but I haven't responded. It's getting easier to ignore. But I kind of hate that it's getting easier. Know what I mean?"

He squeezed my hand.

That's another thing I liked about Walker—he didn't offer platitudes.

"Your coworkers gave the impression that your mom is a dragon lady. Is that true?"

"Yes. And no. She's honest—sometimes too honest. For as long as she's been in this country you'd think she'd have a better grasp on the art of the little white lie. My sister, Annika, hasn't grasped that either when it comes to family stuff."

"Is your sister like her?"

"In physical appearance? Annika is completely Mom's mini-me."

A smile played around the corners of his mouth and I practically panted from longing to press my lips there and taste his amusement.

"But Annika is driven to succeed and make her own mark. My mom met my dad at a young age, married and started having children."

"There's nothing wrong with that, if that's what makes her happy."

"She's still happiest when all her cubs are in one place." Walker paused. "I want to introduce you to my family, Trinity."

My stomach did a quick loop-di-loop.

"I know you're buried in work, so I'm not asking you to make time until you're done. But I'll warn you, the longer we wait . . . the more dragonlike she'll become."

"She knows about me?"

His gaze roamed my face. "I had a family thing Sunday. Guess what kind of mood I was in after Saturday night. She knew something was up."

"If you told her what I said to you Saturday night, she probably already hates my guts."

"I didn't tell her."

Walker ran his fingertips down the side of my face from my temple to the tip of my chin. "I wish I had your talent. The first thing I'd paint is you. With the candlelight glowing on your face and reflected in your eyes. You're breathtaking."

My breath caught when he traced my lips.

"And these lips. I'd never get them right. How perfectly lush and kissable they are. Christ, I want your mouth."

"Then take it."

"No."

"Why not?"

"Because I'm a fucking masochist." His gaze followed the path his thumb took on the inside of my lower lip.

"Walker."

"Hmm?"

"Why are you taking it slow with me? Because last night—"

That blue-eyed gaze bounced back to me. "I didn't show up expecting to get laid."

"But if it's a happy result of you stopping by? That's not okay?"

"Not last night. I brought you dinner because I wanted to see you."

"Well, you saw a lot more of me than I've seen of you."

He kept up that slow, seductive stroking on the corner of my mouth. "Why do you seem mad?"

"I'm not. But I'm also not a horse that needs to be gentled."

"A horse? Seriously?"

"No. Well, maybe. That's what it feels like sometimes. But other times . . . you look at me like you're seconds away from pushing me down to the closest horizontal surface and having your wicked way with me."

He smirked. "A vertical surface would work just as well."

"True. But you strike me as an instant gratification kind of guy. Not a guy with miles of patience to spare."

"I'm greedy as hell. I want you naked beneath me, coming so hard that you forget your own damn name."

In that moment, the heat from his words scorched a few of my brain cells.

"But I won't add the stress of us becoming lovers to your life—you have enough pressure as it is."

"I don't usually associate the words 'stress' and 'pressure' with sex, Walker."

"You think once I've had you I'll be satisfied?" He shook his head. "I'll want more. I'll want all of you, all the time. And whatever plans I had not to put pressure on you will go right out the fucking window."

I bit my lip to keep myself from blurting out that we ought to test his theory.

Walker's focus shifted from my eyes to my lips. A low-pitched noise rumbled in his chest. Then he gave in to his need for a kiss, hauling me to my feet, taking my mouth in a breath-stealing show of urgency and possession.

When he finally proved his point, my head was muzzy; my pulse pounded in my neck, my lips and my nipples and between my legs.

"This heat between us isn't going away if we don't act on it. So I can wait." He nuzzled my neck. "At least another day or two."

I could get behind that time frame. If all went well, hopefully in another day or two I'd be coasting on the project. Then my hands could be coasting all over him.

"I recognize that sound."

"What sound? The sound of lust?" I made a *rowr* in the back of my throat.

"The needy sound you made when my mouth was on you last night."

"Have I mentioned that I loved that? So, so much."

"Talking about me going down on you . . . you're not helping the 'I can wait' claim that my little head doesn't understand," he grumbled.

Do not look at the crotch of his jeans.

I looked. The frayed edges of his pockets turned my mind back to my pieces of fabric that were cut out and waiting on my workbench.

"I recognize that look," Walker said. "It's your 'I'm here but my mind is back in the studio' look."

"Sorry."

"Don't be." He picked up the picnic basket. "That's my cue to send you back to work."

He unlocked a door at the end of the hallway that led to the back of the building.

I squinted at the eight-foot-tall fence topped with razor wire at the end of the lot. "You get many trespassers?"

"Not anymore."

Walker stowed the picnic basket in the back of my car. Then he backed me against the door and tucked a strand of hair behind my ear. "Thanks for the lunch surprise."

"Your coworkers are going to grill you about me, aren't they?"

"I can handle them." He brushed his lips across mine. "I'll see you tomorrow."

Thirteen

WALKER

'd just finished putting the table saw in the back of the trailer when I saw a familiar blonde headed toward me.

She offered a finger wave.

I almost responded by waving one finger in particular but refrained when she bounded up and crushed me in an enthusiastic hug.

"Surprise!"

"Annika, what are you doing here?"

"Dropping off program samples. Lund PR does pro bono work for Seventh Street Theater Productions. I thought you knew that."

"I'm the set guy. That's it." I crossed my arms over my chest. "Since when do you have enough spare time to design a PR campaign for a community theater production?"

"I don't. But my intern does."

"Since when do you have an intern?"

"Since Dallas spearheaded the program in May. I thought you knew that."

"It's news to me."

"It shouldn't be news since we discussed it at the board meeting." She paused for effect. "In March."

Board meetings bored me. Half the time I tuned out.

"Anyway, there's a new intern every two weeks."

"So you're constantly training them?"

"No. LCCO has a permanent liaison in my department. She vets the intern candidates and coordinates everything. It's a neat concept that utilizes diverse feeder programs, from high schools to colleges to technical schools to social services—"

I held up my hand. "Say no more."

"You're not interested," she said flatly. "You're never interested in what I do at LI."

"And you're always begging me for details on what I do during my days at F&L?"

Annika rolled her eyes. "You tear stuff down and build it back up."

"It's more complex than that. We need to have all the city, county and state permits in order before we can break out the sledgehammers and—"

She held up her hand. "Say no more. Seriously. You know the other reason I'm here, Walker."

"No, honestly I don't. Didn't Mom already buy tickets to the performance?"

"Oh, don't play cute. I can't believe that *Betsy* got to meet your new girlfriend before I did. Where's the love, bro?"

My eyes narrowed. "When did you talk to my office manager?"

"Last night at Caboose. Betsy was sort of tipsy. She went on and on about how cool it is your new girl Trinity is a hot-shit artist. And she secretly caught you two making out in the conference room, which she squealed about for like five minutes because it was so freakin' *cute* and then you locked the door in your office while you had lunch. I had to pretend I knew that you'd been seeing this Trinity chick for a couple of weeks. A couple of weeks!" she repeated as if I hadn't heard her. Hell, they'd probably heard her in the auditorium.

"Maybe you oughta show *me* the love once in a while, baby sis. Because not once have you asked if I was seeing someone. Not once in the times you've called to ask for my help or to vent about hockey players or anything else in the last *year* have you asked me what's new in my life."

Her face fell. For once she didn't pull her usual argumentative crap; she threw herself into my arms and hugged me tightly. "I'm sorry. I always swear I'm nothing like Dallas and then you remind me that I am self-centered. You deserve better from me since you are such an awesome brother. I'm so freakin' sorry, Walker."

"Apology accepted. You can make it up to me next week by taking me to Ike's for lunch."

"Deal. And I won't even put it on my expense account." I laughed.

"So this Trinity . . . she makes you happy?"

I almost said, *When she's not making me crazy*, but given my past dating history? Annika would jump all over that as an opening to recite the crazies from my past—chapter and verse. "Yeah, she does."

"Good. Take me to her."

"She might be busy."

"We'll see, won't we?" Annika hooked her arm through mine. "Lead on, Dubbya."

"You promise to behave?"

"You did *not* just ask me that! I have an MBA and I'm

junior VP of an entire division at LI. Polite corporate behavior is my life."

She managed to pull off an affronted look. Color me impressed. "So why didn't you use that same corporate mind-set when dealing with the hockey players?"

"I tried—believe me. But from the very start, Santa was begging for me to rack him with his own hockey stick."

"Wait." I stopped and faced her. "Did you just say Santa?"

"The Swede's name is Klaus. So I started calling him Santa. Santa Klaus—get it?"

"But I thought his name was Axl."

"Axl is a nickname. Since his last name is Hammerquist, it'd make more sense if his nickname was Thor—not only because he makes my head . . . thor." She laughed. "Thor, sore, get it?"

I groaned.

"Maybe I oughta change my name to Rocky since I clearly had rocks in my head when I agreed to revamp his image."

"Whoa. You're working for him?"

"No, I'm working for his agent," Annika corrected.

"How'd that happen?"

"Mom butted in. She knows this agent; they're from the same fjord or something. Then Jensen signed with this agent, so I took on this PR project as a tiny 'flavor' to her."

The side door opened and people flooded in, including Brady and Lennox.

"Hey, bro."

"What are you two doing here?"

"Looking for you."

"Why?"

Brady gave me a level look. "You know why."

Defensively, Annika lifted her hands. "Hey, it wasn't me who spilled the girlfriend beans this time."

"That's because I knew about her weeks ago," Brady said. "Did you?"

Annika shoved him. "Shut it, braggart." She demanded of Lennox, "Did *you* know about her too?"

"Nope. She was news to me."

I scanned the crowd. "Is Mom here? Dad? Jensen? Nolan? Ash? How about the damn gardener?"

"Knock it off. The sooner we meet her, the sooner we can report back to everyone," Brady said.

"Walker?"

I whirled around at the sound of Trinity's voice.

"What's going on?" She kept looking between me and my siblings as I strode toward her.

"Reckoning day, sweetheart."

"Oh god. It's your family, isn't it? I'm not ready. I'm covered in paint, my hair is a mess and I'm seriously sleep deprived, so who knows what will come out of my mouth? And did I tell you the homeless woman on the corner gave my clothing a pitying look and offered to give me her shoes? Plus, I—"

I kissed her. It stopped her babbling . . . for a minute anyway. "It'll be fine. They'll like you. I promise." And even if they didn't? I didn't care. *I* liked her. I slipped my arm around her waist and steered her toward my siblings, who'd lined up in firing squad formation. Assholes.

"Everyone, this is Trinity." To her I said, "First in line is my older brother, Brady. Beside him, his bride, Lennox. Next to her is my little sister, Annika."

Trinity held up her hand, heavily spattered with green paint. "I won't offer to shake hands, but it is great to meet you all. If I'd known you were coming, I would've practiced a soft-shoe routine since I resemble a hobo."

Silence.

If her hand hadn't been covered in paint, she likely would've clapped it over her mouth. She did have a disconnect between her mouth and brain when she got flustered. It amused the hell out of me and I laughed.

So did Brady. "Popping by unannounced wasn't my idea"—he shot Annika a look—"but I'm glad we did. Nate let us wander around the stage. The sets are outstanding."

"Thank you. It was a team effort."

"It paid off. People will flip when the show opens. Word of mouth is gonna be killer," Annika said.

Silence expanded as we stood around and stared at one another.

Awesome.

Trinity mock-whispered to me, "That soft-shoe routine is sounding better and better, isn't it? On the count of three . . ."

Annika laughed. "Since it sounds as if you like to dance, I can admit our ulterior motive was to convince you guys into going out with all of us tonight."

"All of us," I repeated, "is who?"

"The five of us. Nolan. Jensen. Maybe Ash. Dallas is playing Hide the Franken-weenie with Igor, so she'll be late."

"Jesus, Annika."

"What? It's true. We're not all paired off, so if you want to invite some of your friends, Trinity, that'd be cool."

Trinity smirked at me. "I could invite Ramon since it was so fun when you met him."

"Pass. What about Genevieve? I haven't met her yet."

"Gen is riding the hobbyhorse with Connor tonight." She frowned. "Wait. Do they use horses in rugby?"

"No, that's polo."

"See!" Trinity bumped me with her hip. "I told you I'm hopeless about sports stuff. Besides, Gen isn't really riding a horse—she's riding Connor."

"I caught that, sweetheart," I said.

Trinity looked at Annika. "As you can see, my list of friends is woefully short."

"No worries. We always pick up a few strays anyway." Annika high-fived me. "Bring your girl to Flurry. Eight o'clock."

I hated Flurry. Too loud. Crappy music. Overpriced drinks. Nolan and Brady both had VIP passes, which meant we'd sit upstairs in the VIP section that overlooked—or rather looked down on—the rest of the bar. If I were the type of guy who wanted to impress a date, Flurry would be the place to take her. But I preferred to keep everything on the down low.

Brady slipped his arm around Lennox's waist. "We'll let you two get back to work. Nice meeting you—" He paused, as if he couldn't remember her name—his way of warning her that he knew she'd lied about that once—and flashed his sharklike CFO grin. "Trinity."

"Same here."

"Catch you later, bro."

Grabbing Trinity's hand, I towed her back inside the set-painting room. The space had been cleared out, so we had it to ourselves. I closed the door and faced her.

"Sorry they ambushed me today. We don't have to go out with my family tonight if you'd rather not."

"Sounds like you're the one who's on the fence."

I was selfish. I didn't want to share her on the one night I wasn't already sharing her with her project. "Have you ever been to Flurry?"

She shook her head. "I hear it's a cool place. Hard to get into. And I wouldn't mind celebrating since I'm on the down-hill stretch."

"It's gotta be a huge relief."

"It is. The client is coming to check the progress on Monday afternoon."

"When's the event?"

"Two weeks from tonight." She reached up and fiddled with the collar of my shirt. "Will you be my date? It's at some fancy private country club."

That meant I'd have to wear a damn suit. But I'd do it for her. "I wouldn't miss it."

"Thank you. I'll need someone to stop me from becoming a babbling idiot and from drinking too much free champagne because that is a dangerous combination."

I stroked her cheek. "Is that the only reason you want me to go? To kiss you when your nerves kick in and the motor starts running?"

"No. I want you to go with me because we're a couple and that means we support each other on this kind of social stuff, right?"

"Right." That's when I realized she wanted to go out with my family. I'd suck it up and show her a good time for a few hours. "I've gotta unload equipment, so I'll be between here and the warehouse the rest of the day. What time works for me to pick you up?"

"I'd love to have dinner first, but maybe we should plan on dinner afterward since I'll be working all afternoon. So how about . . . seven thirty?"

"Perfect." I kissed her and ignored the high school kids whooping and hollering outside the window.

Fourteen

TRINITY

I stood in front of my closet, staring wide-eyed like a shell-shocked toddler expecting monsters to jump out.

Don't be ridiculous. How hard can it be to pick one out-fit? Just reach in and start grabbing stuff.

Within five minutes I had half of my clothing strewn across the bed in a sea of black, but I wasn't any closer to making a decision.

Should I go with a little cocktail dress? Or a fringed mini-skirt and vest combo? Or a maxi dress? Walker was tall enough I could don stilettos, but it'd been a while since I'd worn heels. With my luck I'd trip in them, fall on my ass and give his family an indecent view of my Spanx.

Maybe I should just stick with pants.

After I applied my makeup, I straightened my hair. It'd been ages since I'd fussed with my appearance, so I hoped I'd achieved the wow factor. Walker was such a hot-looking man that I didn't want anyone to question why I was on his arm.

The doorbell rang.

I grabbed my beaded clutch and my messenger bag before I opened the door. "Hey. I'm ready."

Walker made a very slow, very thorough sweep of my body before he looked me in the eye. "I knew it."

"What?"

"That I'll spend half the night mesmerized by my gorgeous date and the other half of the night wanting to punch all the men who are lusting after my gorgeous date."

I smiled. "You get high marks for that compliment."

He angled his head and placed a kiss where my cleavage started. Then he ran a finger up my arm, from the cuff at my wrist to the ball of my shoulder. "I like that this shirt is see-through."

I glanced down at the V-neck sleeveless shell I'd worn beneath a sheer black blouse. "It's not completely see-through."

"Then how come I know that your nipples are hard?"

"Because they get hard when you touch me."

Walker's avid gaze followed the movement of the back of his hand, gliding across my breasts. "We could stay in," he said huskily. "In fact, that might be best since your skin is feeling a little hot and feverish. Maybe you oughta be in bed."

"You just don't want to go out," I said a little breathlessly.

"I just want to be in with you. All night. Is that a possibility?"

"Yes." Placing my hand over his on my breast, I slid it down so he cupped me completely. He squeezed the flesh and I opened my mouth on his to swallow his soft grunt.

That seemed to frustrate him. "Let's go."

Once we were in Walker's pickup, I said, "Are we meeting someplace first?"

"No. Annika mentioned meeting to take a car service, but I frickin' hate that. I prefer to drive so I don't get stuck somewhere." He grinned at me. "That's why I didn't have a problem when you insisted on meeting me for our first date instead of letting me pick you up."

"Can you give me the details on the family members who're coming tonight?"

"As far as cousins? My older cousin Ash. Maybe his younger sister, Dallas, who's still in college. Definitely my cousin Nolan." After he said the name a tiny scowl appeared.

"Don't you get along with him?"

"I get along with him great. Until he starts tossing out unwanted advice."

"On what?"

"His favorite thing to rag on me about is my appearance. I ignored his call earlier because I didn't want fashion tips on what to wear to the damn bar."

Walker looked great. The casual way he dressed suited him. "Why does he try to change you?"

"Exactly. I'm not the suit-and-tie-wearing type."

My panties would spontaneously combust if I saw Walker Lund in a suit. The beard, the sexy man bun . . . not even pinstripes and wing tips could conceal his raw masculinity.

"So is Nolan the cousin that co-owns the boat with you?"

"Yeah, although we keep that on the down low."

"Don't want your relatives begging you to take them to the lake?"

"Something like that."

"With that many people going, will there be a problem getting in?"

"We won't have a problem. Trust me."

"Ah. So the truth comes out. You're at the club so much there's a seat with your name on it and you're feigning disdain to throw me off the trail?" I teased.

"Hilarious. Brady and Nolan are the VIP club members, not me."

Because he couldn't afford it? I had no idea what VIP memberships cost. I assumed Walker made decent money, but maybe he wasn't in the same financial league as his relatives.

Yeah, I know how that goes.

"Ash will disappear without a word at some point," Walker continued. "Don't bother to learn Nolan's date's name because we won't see her after tonight. I've heard Brady and Lennox spend most of their time on the dance floor. Don't do shots with Annika." He spared me a quick look. "Seriously. Don't. Her metabolism for booze is unmatched. And if my brother Jensen shows up . . ." He sighed. "It'll be easier to explain if you see it with your own eyes."

"Way more detail than I expected, but good things to know nonetheless." I looked at him curiously. "What about you, Walker? What warning or insight would you give me about yourself?"

He muttered, "No pressure."

"Come on. I'll even help you out. 'Don't . . .'"

"Huge help, Trin. Thanks."

I got a funny tickle in my belly from hearing him call me Trin.

"If you drink too much, don't worry. Walker will make sure you get home safely."

That threw me. Was that how he saw himself in his family dynamic? As the brother who took care of everyone? Or had that expectation been put on him *by* his family?

"Or . . . ," Walker continued, "don't be surprised if Walker stomps on your toes because he is a shitty dancer."

I beamed at him. "Really? Me too!"

"You're a bad dancer?"

"Yep. The worst."

"Babe. Why are you so happy about that?"

"I'm happy that you admitted you're not good either. We'll be evenly matched when we dance together."

He laughed. "I can't believe I'm saying this, but I'm looking forward to that."

"Tell me something else you're bad at." When he raised his eyebrows, I added, "I'll even go first. I am a terrible singer. When I'm alone in my studio, I'll just belt out a tune like I'm Christina Aguilera at a recording session, but you'll never catch me singing in public at a karaoke joint. Never."

"I'll scratch that off the list of future date possibilities." He sent me a sideways glance. "But that's not the only reason you don't have a karaoke set list. Out with it."

How had he sensed that? "It's a sucky story."

Walker reached for my hand and kissed it. "Trust me with everything, even the ugly stuff."

"Our school had a talent show for fifth graders before we started middle school. The entire student body and most parents attended. Since I couldn't dance . . . I decided to sing. There weren't tryouts or rehearsals, so I didn't know I sounded bad until I got onstage and heard myself. Unfortunately everyone else heard me too. Seeing people laughing and whispering about me . . . I was happy that my father and the stepmonster hadn't come to the show." But my half siblings had been in the audience and they relayed every awful moment.

"Babe." He kissed my hand again. "That was sucky. I'm sorry. So a water park with a karaoke bar is your idea of hell?"

"Quit stalling and confess your ineptitude, Walker Lund."

He sighed. "Fine. I'm all fat thumbs and clumsy fingers when it comes to playing the piano. After a year of lessons, I still sucked. I begged to quit. My mom said no, I just needed to practice harder. So I . . ." He seemed embarrassed.

"What?"

"Took matters into my own hands. I found a pair of wire-cutters and snipped all the piano wires."

I gasped. "You did not."

"Yeah, I did. Bratty, huh?"

"I'd say . . . stubborn beyond reason?" He snorted. "Did you get into trouble?"

"Huge trouble. I spent the summer working in the yard to pay for it. Then, in another show of bratty behavior, I tallied up the hours I toiled, multiplied them by minimum wage and subtracted that from the piano repair bill. Turned out they owed *me* money. Instead of a refund, I demanded ownership of the piano, which they agreed to."

"So if you owned the piano, you didn't have to play it and you could keep anyone else from using it."

Walker grinned. "Exactly."

"How old were you?"

"Ten. And before you ask, my financial whiz brother, Brady, encouraged me to do the math. He never wanted to take lessons either and he was unhappy I didn't have as much free time to hang out that summer, so it was win-win for both of us."

"Too clever for your own good. Both of you."

Then Walker was focused on maneuvering his big rig into a small parking spot. Too small. I held my breath as he backed in, but of course he parallel parked perfectly.

He caught me staring at him. "Didn't think I could do it, did you?"

"No. But that's me projecting my parallel-parking inad-equacies onto you. I've never figured out how to do it."

"I'm all-pro at fitting big things in tight places."

I peered at him coyly from beneath lowered lashes and murmured, "Are you, now?"

When he realized how that sounded, he groaned. "Not what I meant."

"Sure it's not."

As I turned sideways in the seat for Walker to help me out, he pressed in, nestling his pelvis between my thighs. With unexpected roughness, he curled his hands around the back of my neck and fastened his mouth to mine.

The kiss was possessive from the first touch of his lips. I released a soft moan when he rolled his hips until we were perfectly aligned, hard to soft.

A car honked and I remembered we were right on the street. In downtown Minneapolis.

Walker released my mouth in small increments, pepper-ing my lips with soft smooches and the wet glide of his lips. He stroked my cheekbones with his thumbs as he pressed his forehead to mine.

Without a word, he helped me out of the truck.

He hadn't relaxed by the time we reached the entrance to Flurry. The line to get inside twisted around the corner. I felt eyes shooting daggers at us as Walker headed to the VIP side.

A guy in a suit wearing a headset offered Walker his hand. "Good to have you back at Flurry."

"Thanks." He placed his hand in the small of my back and nudged me forward. "This is my girlfriend, Trinity."

"Welcome to Flurry, Trinity."

"Thank you."

The man spoke into his headset. "Two more for the

Lund party." Then he smiled at Walker. "You're cleared. Go on up."

The VIP entrance didn't intersect with the main entrance at all, from what I could see. The tunnel-like walkway opened into a reception area. I noticed a coat check, but no surprise it wasn't open in August. A guard manned the glass door between the spaces. As soon as he opened it, a wall of sound hit me.

Walker scowled.

"How often does your family guilt you into hanging out with them?" I shouted.

"Hardly ever anymore."

Keeping a tight grip on my hand, he dodged and weaved through the crowd until we reached the far end of the mirrored U-shaped bar where there was standing room along the wall. He backed me into the space, using his sizable frame to keep me from getting jostled.

"What can I get you to drink?" he said in my ear.

I flattened my palm to his chest. "Think a low-rent place such as this knows how to make a decent margarita?"

He chuckled. "No guarantees. But we'll give 'em a chance. If it sucks, I'll get you a beer."

When he moved, I held on to his shirt. "I thought we were meeting your family up here?"

"We are. I just need a minute to . . . acclimate to this atmosphere."

"In other words, you need a drink to chill out so they don't accuse you of being a grumpy ass because you're not into clubs like this."

"You noticed that, huh?"

"You're just happy that I confessed I'm a crap dancer so we can avoid the dance floor."

Walker nuzzled my neck, sending a tremor of desire

through me. "We'll dance to the slow songs, Trinity. Having your body plastered to mine as I put my hands all over you will be the highlight of the night."

I wanted that with a near desperate ache. To be twined around this gorgeous man as our bodies learned to move together. "Okay."

"Stay here."

He cut through the crowd with grace that belied his size and people scooted out of his way, except for a few women who put themselves directly in his path. He sidestepped them in a way that indicated he wasn't interested.

The bartenders were slammed; clubbers stood two deep waiting to get their orders taken. A few guys held up folded bills, as if that would get them immediate service. As soon as the buxom blond bartender noticed Walker, she ignored everyone else and took his order.

A tiny bit of jealousy surfaced and I felt ridiculous for it. Walker Lund defined rugged and sexy. Any woman would want a piece of him. I counted myself lucky that he wanted me, given my various traumas and dramas that caused any man to think twice about getting mixed up with me.

Was he frustrated with this slow pace? After three weeks we hadn't gone beyond kissing and heavy petting—with that one very unexpected, incredibly hot exception. Through our conversations, I determined that Walker preferred hooking up between his brief relationships, so he likely wasn't used to waiting this long to hit the sheets. Then again, he hadn't gone the "Baby, get naked with me or we're done" route either. Truthfully, I wasn't used to waiting this long. I'd never put sex on a pedestal; it wasn't a sacred act that had to follow certain parameters before it could happen. I opted for the "no harm, no foul, if it feels good do it" philosophy.

As Walker headed toward me with that purposeful stride, I let my eyes devour him.

He handed me the drink.

"Thank you. Where's yours?"

"Wasn't feeling it."

"Lucky for you, I share." I stirred the ice and raised the glass to lick the salt off the rim. Then I pursed my lips around the straw and sucked. "Want a taste?"

His eyes went molten. He leaned in, resting his forearm on the brick wall above my head. "No. I'm thinking I'll get a little lust drunk just watching you."

"Watching me what?"

"Lick. Suck. And swallow."

That husky growl zipped straight to my core. My mouth had gone dry, requiring another sip.

Walker angled closer. "Maybe just a small taste of you to tide me over."

His lips were so warm against the coolness of mine. His beard so downy soft brushing my chin. I'd parted my lips, wanting him to dive in and suck the salt off my tongue.

The buzzing from inside his shirt pocket broke the moment.

I gave him props for trying to ignore his phone.

He expelled an annoyed sigh. "Sorry."

Maybe it was evil, but I took a long lick of salt from the rim of my glass, enjoying the heat flaring in his eyes as he answered the call.

"This had better be fucking good," he barked into the phone. Then he froze. "Whoa, Betsy. Slow down. Say it again."

Betsy. Why was his office manager calling him on a Saturday night?

"I don't know. We haven't had rain that would back up the sewage system." A pause. "Which one? Yeah. There is a reset on it." He looked at me. "No, I'm not coming over. Because I'm not a damn plumber. But I will look at it, okay? I'll get to a quieter place where I can hear and I'll FaceTime you." He hung up.

I immediately asked, "What's going on?"

"Betsy's parents are out of town and when she checked their house she found water in the basement. The sump pump isn't working. Since I have the same kind of pump, I might see a quick fix that'll save her an emergency service call on the weekend."

"Is this what you do, Walker Lund? Save women in distress? Your sister? Your cousin? And now your employee? Does everyone call you when they have a mechanical problem?"

"I'm the Lund with the practical experience and dirty hands. They call me when something breaks. I call them—" He scowled. "It doesn't matter." He ran the backs of his knuckles down the side of my face. "Give me five minutes and we'll pick up where we left off?"

"What about your family? Aren't they waiting for us?"

"They probably haven't noticed I'm not there yet."

He hadn't said it in a self-pitying way, but it caused a sharp pang near my heart to think this vibrant, thoughtful man wouldn't be missed by the people who mattered most to him.

"Don't go anywhere." He kissed me quickly. "I'll be right back."

After he disappeared, I dug out my phone. Better to appear antisocial than look like I felt: totally out of place.

Less than two minutes passed before I heard, "Trinity?"

I jumped and met Annika's gaze. "Hey. How's it going?"

"Terrible. Where's Walker?"

"He's on the phone someplace dealing with some crisis Betsy called about."

"You don't have to wait for him here. Our table is just around the corner."

"He asked me to hang tight for a bit, which is fine. It'll give me a moment to prepare myself to meet more members of the Lund collective."

"At least you didn't call us the Notorious Lunds."

"Why would I do that?"

"Everyone else does." Annika scanned the bar patrons. "You don't seem the type to believe everything you hear or read about us."

What? "I don't—"

"Good. I'm in PR, so I know everything can be spun. Everything." Her entire body went rigid beside mine. "Stupid man, just had to test me, didn't you? Now you'll see how fast I'll have you by your twig and lingonberries for disobeying me."

Confused, I said, "Who are you talking about?"

"Santa."

"Santa? As in . . . Claus?" Now I started scanning the crowd too.

"No, as in Klaus 'Call Me Axl' Hammerquist, who I've nicknamed Santa because it pisses him off."

She'd pronounced his name Ka-louse. "I'm sorry. I don't know who that is."

"The Swedish hockey pucker I'd like to whap upside the dick with his stick."

"What's the story with him?"

"He got traded to the Wild from the Blackhawks because he performed like a Tier 3 amateur last year. A large part of his crappy rink skills was due to his inability to keep his tiny Swedish meatballs in his pants when he's off the ice."

I blinked. Had she even been speaking English?

"And because I'm cursed with the ability to communicate

in his native tongue, I've been tasked with revamping his image from a brawling, vodka-swilling manwhore to . . . yeah, I'm still working on what'll erase that impression."

"Couldn't you say no?"

Annika sighed. "Not to my mother."

A dark-haired woman, compact in size and yet boasting an impressively muscled physique, stormed up, the fringe on her belly shirt bouncing angrily against her skintight sequined miniskirt. "What the hell, Annika? You told me I couldn't bring Igor tonight but I see Axl is here."

"First off, Axl is not supposed to be here and I haven't had nearly enough to drink to deal with him. Secondly, this is why we're here. This is Walker's girlfriend. Trinity, this is our cousin Dallas."

She scrutinized me thoroughly. Up and down, side to side. Then she announced, "Your aura is lavender."

"Excuse me?"

"Your aura. It's lavender." She held up her hand. "No, it's not an illusion from the neon lights. You're highly creative, almost as if you function on another plane, which is totes awesome because this family needs diversity in the next generation's bloodline. So I'm very happy to meet you, Trinity—totally rockin' name BT-dubs. And no, I'm not the whack-a-doodle cousin. I just have an active vola."

Did she say she had an active Volvo? Or an active vulva? God. What was I supposed to say to that? "Ah. Lucky you?"

Annika laughed. "Freaks people out when you do that, D." Her smile dried. "Dammit. He followed you."

"Of course he followed me to get a gander at you, because you're smokin' hot tonight." Dallas held out her hand. "Ten bucks says Axl marches straight up to you with an ax to grind."

"Huh-uh. Ten bucks says he ignores me, but he makes

sure I see him breaking the rules and letting two chicks grind on him on the dance floor."

They shook hands and leaned against the wall.

What was taking Walker so long?

"Shit. Here he comes."

"You are so screwed. His aura is dark red. I am out of here." Dallas hustled off.

An enormous guy, at least six foot six, with shoulders as wide as a pool table, planted himself in front of Annika and snarled, "Attila."

"Santa."

This magnificent creature was the guy Annika had been complaining about? I could totally see why he was a player. Golden blond hair that brushed the top of his shoulders. Cheekbones so sharply defined they cast the lower part of his face in shadow. A thin blade of a nose gave him an air of superiority. A wide-set jaw was marked by a divot in his chin. Even in the dark bar I noticed his eyes glowed the same pale silvery blue of a Siberian husky's and were spiked with thick black eyelashes.

Then he ground out a spate of words that were indecipherable.

Annika ignored him.

I didn't have to understand Swedish to figure out these two were oil and water.

Then Hot Swede's voice turned silky and taunting. He invaded Annika's space completely.

She seemed flustered for a moment; then her retort wiped the smug smile right off his remarkable face.

He stormed away.

"I have to deal with dick-for-brains. Tell Walker I'll be back."

I'd finished my drink and started to wonder if Walker was

coming back when I saw him striding toward me, looking as agitated as his sister.

He said, "Don't ask. Let's get this over with." He snagged my hand and towed me behind him until we reached the even more exclusive VIP section, a raised platform with a premium view of all sections of the club, blocked off by velvet ropes. Even before I saw the private security guard standing like a sentry, I felt that ripple of power coming from the four men sitting at the table.

I'd spent my life around powerful men, so I knew the difference between wannabe power brokers and the real deal.

These guys were the real deal.

Who the hell was the Lund family? More important, why didn't I know who they were?

I tugged Walker off to the side before anyone saw us.

"You change your mind about being here? Because we can go—"

"No. What don't I know about your family, Walker?"

Uneasiness passed over his face. "The Lund name is pretty well known around here."

Then I remembered I'd seen Annika talking to Chris and Nate. The aloof director and his assistant had treated Annika with reverence—I'd assumed because she was a beautiful woman. But now I realized I'd misread the situation.

"Why didn't I know that?"

He shrugged tightly. "It's public knowledge. It's not like I kept it a secret."

It's not like you asked was implied. "Okay. Let's assume I don't get out much—"

"No, if you want the truth, then at least be honest about why you don't know what's common knowledge among the three million other people who live in the Twin Cities."

I didn't have time to respond before he jumped back in.

"You do your own thing with your art and your group of artist friends. You don't give much thought to the world outside your bubble—unless it directly affects you. But even when things do directly benefit you, you don't pay attention to details. Painting sets for the community theater is a paying gig for you. What company name is on the front of the check?"

"I don't see the relevance—"

"I'll give you a hint. LCCO."

I'd heard that name and was vaguely aware it was the charitable organization that funded several programs at the community center.

"Those initials stand for Lund Cares Community Outreach."

"Lund? As in . . . ?" Holy shit. "That's your family?"

"Yep." Walker scrubbed his hands over his beard. "Christ. It's so fucking loud in here I feel like I'm shouting at you. That's not my intent. I just . . . should've explained before now."

"I still don't understand."

"And I'm way too wound up to explain." He pointed to my phone. "It'd be easiest if you did a Google search. While you're doing that, I'll get that drink because I sure could use it now."

Unnerved by Walker's uncharacteristically terse responses, I typed "Lund Minneapolis" into the search engine, my fingers shaking.

387,492 results popped up. The top one was a wiki page about Lund Industries.

The more I read, the more my stomach churned. Lund Industries was a multibillion-dollar company. Billion. For the last hundred years they'd had a hand in everything from flour mills to lumber to fishing to agriculture to real estate development. Over the course of its history the Lund family businesses had evolved and diversified, but Lund Industries was a big business that employed a lot of people. Not just in the Twin Cities, but all over Minnesota.

When I reached the list of corporate officers, I saw Lund names I recognized: Brady as CFO. Ash as COO. Nolan and Annika were listed as department heads. The only place Walker's name appeared was on the board of directors. But that made sense since he'd told me he didn't work for the family business.

I returned to the initial search and clicked on photos. The second picture that popped up was of a big blond guy wearing a white and purple jersey. I enlarged it. The caption read: *Jensen "The Rocket" Lund, Minneapolis native, is picked up in the third round of the NFL draft by the Minnesota Vikings.*

Walker's younger brother was a big-deal football player. No wonder he'd gotten so defensive at the party when Ramon started ripping on sports.

But why hadn't he told everyone—or at least me—about his personal family connection?

Because artists and academics are so smug and proud about not being part of the madding crowd that follows violent athletic contests where brawn is prized over brains. And would you have understood even if he had told you?

No.

Walker's accusation, *You don't give much thought to the world outside your bubble,* taunted me. Because it was embarrassingly true.

Two pictures down from Jensen's was an image of a guy in a different sports uniform. The caption read: *Jaxson*

"Stonewall" Lund, Chicago Blackhawks center, scores a hat trick to shut out the Pittsburgh Penguins, keeping the 'hawks' play-off hopes alive.

After that, I couldn't stop thumbing through pictures. Pages and pages of images were devoted to Jensen and Jaxson. Finally I reached other pictures of the Lund family at numerous charity events in the Twin Cities. Pages of fundraisers and galas to bring awareness to various causes. It didn't look to me like any generation of Lund heirs was exempt from volunteering time to LCCO and other family-run charities. In many of the photos the Lund heirs had banded together for group recognition instead of being singled out for individual achievement. I also noticed that there were less than a dozen pictures—total—of the eight Lund kids during their growing-up years. So the parents had ensured their children had some privacy—or the private schools they'd attended had added that extra layer of security.

While it appeared Brady and Walker stayed out of the limelight as much as possible, that wasn't the case with Annika and Dallas. There were hundreds of pictures of each of them at college parties, at football and hockey games, at black-tie events. Although I hadn't met Ash or Nolan, when I did meet them I'd recognize them because their handsome mugs were everywhere. When did they have time to work?

Maybe they're just corporate figureheads like your father and the real work is left to their staff.

Maybe you shouldn't assume anything. Because, as Walker pointed out, you're oblivious to anything going on around you that doesn't have to do with you.

I'd screwed up. And what sucked was I didn't even know I'd screwed up until Walker had pointed it out.

I closed my eyes, trying to keep my head from spinning. I couldn't believe that a man like Walker had been interested in me in the first place. I couldn't fathom why he'd stuck around through all the drama. And now, when I proved how self-absorbed I am—

"Trinity."

I slowly opened my eyes. My heart clenched at seeing Walker's wariness.

"You do the search?"

"Yes. It's been enlightening and humiliating that I didn't know your family is an institution in this town. I'm sorry. I've screwed this up every step of the way." I swallowed the lump in my throat. "Why are you even with me? I always knew you were out of my league, but this proves it. I'm a"—*mess*— ". . . and you're . . . I mean, you should . . ." Very eloquent. *Get it together.* I opened my purse and slipped my phone inside. "Go be with your family. I'll just—"

"Whoa." Walker caged me against the wall. "Why does it sound like you're leaving?"

I blinked at him. "You don't want me to?"

"No." He curled his hands around my face. "That's the furthest thing from my mind."

"But . . . aren't you upset that I've been clueless about your family and who you really are from the start?"

"You're the first woman in a really long time who didn't see dollar signs when she looked at me. You know who I really am, because you saw me. Just me. Not my name. Not my family connections."

I didn't know what to say to that.

"At first I wasn't sure if—"

"I was faking not knowing your family connections so I could get close to you and pretend to be completely shocked you were one of 'those' Lunds after you'd fallen for my abundance of quirky charms? Or I'd convince you that I liked you and then I'd flirt my ass off with your football star brother or your hockey star cousin? Or maybe I was pretending to be oblivious to your family's generosity in funding the arts while scheming—"

Walker covered my lips with his thumbs. "You're getting a full head of steam, babe. So how about I talk and you listen?"

I nodded.

"You're always pointing out that I get you. I know how much that means to you. I don't want the fact that my family has money to change what we have going on with us. Because you and I are damn good together. It's real. I don't know if I've ever had that with any woman." He moved his hands and pressed his forehead to mine. "Please don't make a big deal out of it."

It was a big deal and he knew it. But he hadn't said anything that didn't ring true. What we had was real—I didn't doubt that. We'd already made it through a couple of bumpy spots and neither of us had given up. That said a lot to me.

His gaze collided with mine. I hated seeing the turmoil in his eyes. I preferred fiery passion. "If you can forgive me for the mix-up with my first name, surely you can forgive me again for me not being properly awed by your last name."

He smiled and the clouds lifted from his eyes. Man. Those dimples were just killer.

"Yeah, sweetheart. I can do that."

I stood on my toes and buried my face in his neck. An almost primal need blasted through me with teeth so sharp I had the panicked feeling if I didn't get this man's hands and body all over me as soon as possible I'd be ripped apart by regret. "Walker. I have a really great idea."

"What's that?"

"Let's get naked and go at it so hard we forget we even have names."

He nearly knocked over a dozen people in his haste to get us out of there.

I stumbled behind him but couldn't get him to stop until we'd exited the VIP section. "Walker. Wait."

He whirled around. Desire had turned his eyes a deep smoky gray. "Done waiting."

I loved seeing this caveman side of him. I fantasized he'd throw me over his shoulder once we got outside because that would be seriously hot. *Focus, Trin.* "What about your family? They are waiting for us." As I reminded him, I wondered why his family hadn't sought us out.

Walker removed his phone from his pocket. Without looking away from me, he tapped on the screen. Then the sound of another phone ringing echoed on his speakerphone. A male voice boomed, "Where the hell are you?"

"Sorry, bro. We're not gonna make it tonight."

"But . . . Annika said you were already here."

"We were. And now we're not. Later." He ended the call and slipped the phone back into his pocket. "Done." He started to crowd me, his intent clear. "What else?"

Good lord, we wouldn't even make it to his pickup if he kept blasting me with those "I'm going to ruin you for other men" looks. "Do you have condoms? Because I didn't grab any from home—"

Turning the opposite direction, he pulled me along behind him at breakneck speed.

As he closed in on the door to the men's bathroom, I tried digging my heels in. But I was no match for him strength- or determination-wise; a man who thinks he might get laid will do anything to ensure that happens. When we burst through the swinging door, I slammed my eyes shut against images of guys standing at the urinals, leering over their shoulder at me as Walker . . .

I heard plastic crinkling and chanced opening my eyes.

Walker was stuffing complimentary condoms into the pocket of his jeans as fast as he could manage. I would've been laughing my butt off, if not for the men's room attendant gaping at him.

"Is there something I can help you with, sir?"

"Nah. I'm good. Thanks."

"You sure you've got enough of those?" the attendant said testily.

I started to respond, but Walker beat me to it.

"Good point. Trin, baby, open your purse."

"Walker!"

He grinned. "Just kidding. We're set."

As we sailed past the attendant, I didn't hear what he said—something raunchy, I'd bet—but I didn't care because things were about to get raunchy for me.

Finally.

Fifteen

WALKER

My brain was bombarded with images of the ten million ways I wanted to intimately acquaint myself with every inch of Trinity's body.

First option: both of us half dressed, with Trinity's legs wrapped around me as I pinned her against the closest vertical surface and plunged into her.

Second option: holding off until we got into the house. We'd start undressing in the kitchen, slowly taking our time to touch and taste each other. Our hands and mouths would be reverent, not greedy—at least not at first. And since Trinity wore less clothing, she'd be naked before me. But if I saw her bare ass sashaying up the stairs, I'd hike her hips into the air and slam into her right there. Her back would arch, her fingers would dig into the carpet, trying to find balance as I lost myself in her sweet body.

So both scenarios ended with us going at it fast and hard. Might as well go with option one, then.

"Walker?"

I blinked and looked around. I'd already parked in the garage? Shit. I didn't even remember driving home from the club. My last clear thought before lust took over was pulling Trinity behind me as we left Flurry, the packs of condoms crackling in my pocket and the loud *tap-tap* of her heels on the concrete as we raced to my truck.

"You okay?" she asked softly. "You haven't said a word."

I turned my head to face her. "No."

Her eyes were sharp with concern. "What's wrong?"

"I'm—" *Scared that I'll fuck this up.* Not that I'd confess that pussy bullshit to her.

She said, "Don't overthink this."

Too late.

Trinity climbed out of my truck. She scaled the steps leading into my house and faced me, holding her hand to her forehead to cut the blindingly bright headlights.

Then everything went dark.

That prompted me to move. The interior lights clicked on long enough for me to see her waiting in an unfamiliar place and get my head in the game.

For some reason the sports analogy reset my focus.

When I reached her, I took her hand, opened the door to my house, tossed my keys on the table and led her up the stairs straight into my bedroom.

I closed the door and pressed her against it. I found her sweet mouth with mine. Immediately her lips parted and I dove in.

The kiss was unhurried. But the hunger was there with every stroke of our tongues, with every soft groan, with every pause for breath. My hands began their own quest, roaming freely but never stopping in one place for long. Until my fingers bumped against the button at the top of her blouse. Then my hands had a singular purpose: to get to her bare skin.

After I divested her of the sheer blouse, she kept one hand pressed against my chest and the other alternated between sifting through my hair and stroking my beard. We broke the kiss long enough for me to pull her shirt over her head and for her to yank mine off. Then our mouths were back in motion, taking little sips, nips and tastes. Sharing breath and letting our need expand at a slower pace.

But my impatience to explore had my fingers seeking her softness. I traced the straps of her bra, from the inside edge and then down the curve of lace to the clasp beneath her breasts. I teased her with the rough-tipped ends of my knuckles, repeating the same path until she arched into me with her whole body, begging for a more complete touch.

One twist and the clasp of her bra gave way; one tug and her bra hit the floor.

Then slow and steady didn't compute at all as the weight of her breasts was in my hands, the hard tips stabbing into my palms. I heard a soft thud when her head fell back against the door as my mouth engulfed her nipple.

I groaned, going back and forth between the pink crests, gauging by her soft pants and tiny whimpers whether she liked my tongue better than the brush of my beard across the wet tips. She really went crazy, thrashing against the door, bumping her hips into mine when I sucked slowly on them. When her rocking hips actually started to smash my hard-on, I forced myself to step back.

She blinked at me, her eyes glazed, her lips full and pink from kissing me.

I wanted to see that look as I buried myself inside her. I

wrapped my fingers beneath her jaw and traced her bottom lip with my thumb. "Bed. Now."

At that point I was so far gone with getting to the goal that I didn't pay attention to how either of us got naked the rest of the way—I just know we did.

Then Trinity was spread out in the middle of my bed, her skin flushed, her eyes drowsy with desire, waiting for me to put on the damn condom. As soon as I had it in place, she parted her legs as I braced myself above her. Then she wrapped her fingers around me and guided me to where she was wet.

I didn't hesitate to push in because we were both ready. We both wanted this so badly we were shaking with the need for it.

Once I'd bottomed out, I rested my forehead to hers, taking a moment to savor this. Because once I started moving, this connection would be something else entirely. Hot and hard and passionate—which would fill another part of me. But this stillness filled my head with the muted whisper that this was what I'd been waiting for. I murmured her name before I fit my mouth over hers.

I eased out and paused at her entrance, swallowing her gasp when I thrust back in. I kept up the steady pace until our bodies were damp with sweat.

She sank her teeth into my shoulder and came undone.

That love bite nearly set me off. But I slowed things down. Using my mouth on her neck and her nipples, building her back up and up again, then letting her take us both over the edge.

After we'd caught our breath and kissed and nuzzled, I dealt with the condom. I wasn't sure which Trinity I'd encounter when I returned. Given her tendency to chatter out of nervousness, the fact we hadn't talked at all seemed unusual. I hoped she hadn't panicked, gotten dressed and called a cab, because that wasn't out of the realm of possibilities with her. But if that'd happened, I'd go after her. Because nothing was going to stand in the way of us building something permanent together now that we'd smoothed out the rocky ground.

I oughta remember that wording for the next time she freaked out as proof that I could use something besides a sports analogy.

I walked into the bedroom to see she'd turned on the lamps on the nightstands. She'd propped herself against the headboard among the pillows and greeted me with a satisfied smile. Her eyes tracked my every movement—which made me want to strut and flex. But when I reached the end of the mattress, she held up her hand like a traffic cop.

"Before you get into this bed and put your skilled mitts all over me and utilize that magical mouth in all sorts of dirty and delicious ways and use that"—her gaze dropped to my crotch—"Swedish longboat to render me a quivering mass of postorgasmic goodness . . ." She paused and looked me in the eyes. "I want to say thank you. Not just for the best sex of my life—which it totally was—but for being patient through all my dramas and general weirdness so we actually got to the naked and sweaty portion of our relationship."

I waited. "That's it?"

"Yes. Why?"

"Because you usually keep going. And, sweetheart, I wanted to see what you'd come up with after 'Swedish longboat,' because that description will be hard to top."

She threw a pillow at me. "Smart-ass."

I pounced on her.

She shrieked and tried to get away.

But I trapped her against me in a wrestler's hold, her back to my front with my arms and legs wrapped around her.

She retaliated by wiggling her ass into my groin. "I didn't know you were into kinky stuff, Viking, but I'm game for anything."

I rolled her over until she was under me again. "Good to know."

Trinity brought her hands up and caressed my face. My eyebrows and forehead, cheeks and mouth, jaw and beard. She didn't bother to mask the longing in her eyes.

"What, sweetheart?"

"I . . . I really dig you, Walker Lund."

Jesus. She just planted a flag in my heart with her name on it.

"You make me happy. Do you think . . . ?"

Somehow I knew what she was getting at. "You make me happy too. And I was hard-core digging on you even before we rocked the bedframe." I brushed my lips across her smiling mouth. "But I think we'd better rock it again just to make sure."

"You have the best ideas."

woke up in a really fantastic mood.

Not just because I finally had Trinity in my bed—but I ain't gonna lie; that was a huge part of the reason I felt so content.

As was my habit—even on weekends—I hopped out of bed early. I brewed a pot of coffee, assuming that would rouse my bedmate.

No such luck.

When I attempted to coax her out of bed, she mumbled something about the eight o'clock rule and yanked the covers over her head. She was so freakin' cute I let her be for another hour. When eight twenty rolled around, I brought her a mug of coffee and she damn near purred.

Since she hadn't packed anything but art supplies in her messenger bag, she raided my closet for loungewear, picking a Flint & Lund T-shirt and a baggy pair of sweatpants.

Once she was coherent, I gave her a brief tour of the upstairs. Four bedrooms, two bathrooms, plus my master bedroom and bath. She wandered into the large alcove at the top of the stairs but didn't comment on the utter lack of furniture.

Trinity's focus bounced between the top of the window and the blank wall across from it.

"What's going on in that creative head of yours?"

"This cool old window . . . they don't make them like this anymore. The upper section should be stained glass. It'd throw colors and patterns across the opposite wall, creating its own art."

"Do you work in stained glass?"

She shrugged. "I've blown glass." She smirked at me over the rim of her coffee cup. "Let's pretend both your big and little heads didn't get stuck on the word 'blown.' I love shaping molten sections of glass into objects. But soldering cut pieces of glass together is more tedious than putting together a jigsaw puzzle."

"So I couldn't commission you to make a stained-glass window for me?"

"I'll think about it." She walked past the last bedroom door I'd left open a crack and peeked inside. "This room looks occupied."

"It's my grandpa Jensen's room when he comes over from Sweden."

"He stays with you and not with his daughter?"

"Grandpa likes to tag along with me to job sites. He'd

be bored sitting at Mom and Dad's. I'm happy to have him with me because he's a great troubleshooter. I wish I could clone him."

"How old is he?"

"In his eighties."

"It's sweet you're close to him." Smiling, Trinity stood on tiptoe and kissed me. "You're lucky to still have him. I only had my grandma Minnie until I was ten."

"He's slowed down a lot."

"So will I if I don't get more coffee."

TRINITY

After I downed my third cup of coffee, I said, "I need to get my bag out of your truck."

"You take that purse with you everywhere?"

"It's not a purse. And yes, I always have art supplies with me. I never know when I'll—"

"Get the urge to whip up a graphic novel?" he supplied with a grin. "That seems to be the only medium you haven't worked in."

I whistled and looked at the ceiling.

"Of course you've done a graphic novel. Can I see it?"

"I did it three years ago, and no, you can't see it. I'm not even credited as the artist." I held my hand up when he growled. "Stop acting like you want to pound on someone because a big bad publishing house took advantage of a na-ive Minnesota artist. That's not what happened."

"Fill in the blanks when I get back, baby, or I'm going to find my brass knuckles. Nobody better mess with my woman." He cut around the corner and disappeared into the garage.

His woman? I loved to hear him call me that.

After he dropped my bag on the counter, he stole a kiss. I loved that about him too.

"So, Stan Lee, spill the ink."

And I really loved that he could be such a dork. "I dabbled in graphic novels in college. I had a few offers to make that my career, but—" I gave him a sheepish smile. "I knew I'd get bored. My prof contacted me when this well-known graphic artist had some health emergency and couldn't work for two months. The project had already been delayed six months, so they needed a 'ghost' artist. Meaning they paid me a lot of money to keep my mouth shut and do the work, which was outlined to the tiniest detail. End of story."

"But did it sell really well and get rave reviews?"

I shrugged. "I didn't check. Seriously, I couldn't tell any-one even if it *had* hit the top of the bestseller lists. I'm better off not knowing." I pushed my coffee cup toward him and pulled out my sketch pad. "Now flex those drool-worthy muscles while you're slaving over a hot stove, and I'll see if I can't earn my breakfast this morning."

Walker's big hand reached out to hold me firmly by the back of the neck and tipped my face up to press a hot kiss to my lips. "Sweetheart, you more than earned this breakfast last night."

We stayed like that—his hand on me in a possessive way it hadn't been before, studying each other because there was no denying things had changed for us in a big way last night.

In the past, if my friends had waxed poetic about sex, claiming it had changed everything for them, I'd secretly sneered at them. Sex was sex. Kissing led to touching; touch-ing led to part A into slot B; friction of A and B led to tingly, pulsing release.

But last night with Walker? I had become a true believer.

We'd reached a level of intimacy I hadn't known existed. Our bodies were in perfect sync—from the rapid thundering of our hearts to our ragged breath to the wet heat my body created to welcome his.

Not that it hadn't been urgent and fun, thrilling and maddening as we teased and taught and learned each other. But that first go-around, face-to-face, in his bed, I'd felt the change start. Not in my head. Not between my legs. In my chest. A click of the last tumbler that finally unlocked the vault to my heart. When Walker looked at me and said my name, I realized he'd felt that same click too.

Even now, it didn't feel like it'd been a fanciful moment we could laugh off in the light of day. Yet I didn't know what to say.

"Christ, Trin. You're so pretty first thing in the morning."

I raised both eyebrows. "I am?"

"With your sex hair and the pink tinge to your cheeks and your mouth looking well used. It's about all I can do not to haul your luscious ass back up to my bed."

"Sex hair?" I repeated. "Dude. You oughta talk. I seriously did a number on your hair last night."

"Babe, you did a number on *me* last night."

Of course Mr. I Suck at Words proved he didn't suck yet again, by saying the perfect thing.

I smiled. "Back atcha, babe."

That satisfied him. He kissed me and released me.

Walker started chopping mushrooms, onions and peppers.

I sketched quickly, opting to draw his entire torso and not just the appendages attached.

"I do have one way you can help me."

My gaze flicked between the paper and the subject. "Hit me."

"This room—hell, all the rooms—needs color on the walls."

"I agree." I scrutinized the space. As the color wheels in my head spun, I walked to the refrigerator, pulling out bottles of ketchup, mustard, barbecue sauce and mayonnaise. I squirted all four condiments onto one plate. Then I dug through my bag until I found a paintbrush.

Using a butter knife, I cut the piles into quarter sections and began to mix them.

Walker seemed intrigued with my experimentation . . . until I painted a swath of barbecue sauce down the center wall in the kitchen.

"What the hell are you doing?"

"Giving you paint options." Next I painted a thick line of mustard. Lastly a mix of barbecue and mayonnaise that ended up pink. "If it were me? I'd go with this bolder hue of barbecue sauce." I pointed to it with the tip of the paintbrush. "This large space can sustain a vivid color. And the light in here will wash everything down a tone. Plus, barbecue against the pickled wood cabinets will really make them pop."

"She's serious," he said to my back as I ducked around the corner into the living room.

Immediately I had a pang of sympathy for the empty space.

Walker moved in behind me and set his chin on my shoulder. "Why the big sigh, sweetheart?"

"Because this is such a cool room. You could do so much with it, but you've done nothing. This is the poor little room that could be great. Decorator magazine worthy. And the room knows it. That makes it so sad. Can't you see how even the floor sags with desolation?"

"Funny. How would you fix it?"

Maybe I went into too much detail about painting opaque pearlescent glaze over lemon-colored walls. Adding two oversized slouchy sofas covered in khaki fabric facing each other with a square wooden coffee table between them, situated on a cream, yellow and khaki patterned rug. I described the shapes and colors of the throw pillows and the blankets. I added a bookcase and a sofa table and one fussy damask chair with a zebra stripe. I started to conceptualize the art, but that was abstract and this place needed realism.

He was so quiet after I finished, I held my breath. Did he hate my ideas? Or had he realized I'd been decorating this room for me and it freaked him out? "You didn't stop my ramblings with a kiss this time."

"You weren't rambling. I got sucked in when you began describing everything. I could see it for the first time since I moved into this house six years ago."

"Why didn't you hire a professional designer? Don't take this the wrong way, but it's not like money is an issue for you."

"The designers I've worked with have been nutjobs. I'd rather have nothing in here than the wrong thing."

"I disagree."

He turned me around to face him. "Maybe I should put you in charge. I don't know if anyone has ever told you this, but you have an eye for color."

His ability to go from serious to funny was one of my favorite things about him.

As was his ability to go from funny to intense when that lust-filled look darkened his eyes.

I had a two-second warning and then his mouth collided with mine.

Walker's hands were on my ass and his teeth had started the journey down my throat when the doorbell rang.

I froze.

"Ignore it. Christ, I want this shirt gone. I want my mouth on you."

His aggression increased and the doorbell chimed again. Four times in a row.

"Let's go upstairs," he murmured against my breast.

"Walker. They can see us sneaking up the stairs!"

"No, they—" He raised his head and peered over my shoulder. "Yeah, I guess they can."

"Who is it?"

"My parents."

"What!"

He tugged me toward the door and I dug in my heels—my bare heels—and I almost landed on my ass. "I cannot meet your parents looking like this."

"Why not? You look hot as hell with sex-mussed hair and my beard marks on your throat." His gaze roved over me as thoroughly as a caress. "And, babe, at least you're wearing clothes. If they'd shown up just five minutes from now . . ." He smirked and tapped my butt.

Dear Mr. and Mrs. Lund,

I didn't mean to kill your son. It all started when he . . .

The doorbell pealed again.

Walker sighed. He sidestepped me and answered the door. "Mom. Dad. What a surprise."

Where was a big potted plant when I needed one?

The beautiful blonde, dressed to the nines in gray-and-pink-striped suit pants and a gray silk blouse, strolled in and put her hands on Walker's cheeks. "Smile at me, precious boy. Pretend happiness that we are here."

He bared his teeth and even then his dimples popped out. "See? Not so hard."

A tall, extremely good-looking man with dark hair and an easy smile approached me.

Walker returned to my side to make introductions. "Dad. Mom. This is Trinity. My girlfriend."

Mr. Lund offered his hand. "Good to meet you, Trinity. I'm Ward. This is Selka, my better half."

"So nice to meet you both." *Now please let me run up-stairs and hide until you leave.*

"There's coffee. And I was about to make breakfast, if you're hungry."

Selka's right eyebrow went up. "It's late for breakfast, no?"

Walker shrugged. "We had a late night and didn't feel like getting out of bed."

He might as well have shouted, BECAUSE WE HAD SEX ALL NIGHT LONG AND ONCE THIS MORNING AND WE WERE ABOUT TO GET OUR NAKED GROOVE ON WHEN YOU SHOWED UP.

"Coffee would be great," his dad said.

"We will *fika*. I make Swedish cake," his mother announced.

"No, Mom, that's okay. You don't—"

"Walker, if your mother wants to make a cake, let her. I, for one, would love cake."

She looked at me skeptically. "You like *mandelkaka med björnbär*?"

Crap. What if this was a test? To see if I liked herring cake or something? Wait. Was lutefisk considered cake?

Ward came to my rescue. "It's an almond and berry cake. Quite delicious actually. And it doesn't take hours to prepare like some of her *fika* specialties," he said to Walker.

"My grandma used to let me help her make no-bake

chocolate balls that were so good. She told me it was a traditional Swedish recipe, but I don't remember the name."

"*Chokladbollar?*" Walker said.

I looked at him with shock. "Yes! That's it. How do you know about them?"

"We used to make those all the time growing up."

"Me too! We should make them together sometime."

We exchanged a silly grin.

Selka watched us very carefully. To Walker she said, "You will put on shirt." Then she said to me, "You will help me."

Seeing her designer outfit, I translated that into, *I will make you do all the work and judge every move you make.* I kept a smile in place as I said, "Sure. It'll be fun."

S elka surprised me. She whipped up the batter in no time and didn't get a speck of flour on herself.

But as soon as she put the cake in the oven, she switched from baking to grilling.

She pointed to the wall behind us. "You have food fight with my son?"

"No. We discussed paint colors for the kitchen and living room. He needed an example so I used what he had on hand. It'll be interesting to see what color he ends up with."

Selka sauntered to the counter and picked up the drawing I'd started of Walker's oh-so-fine, oh-so-naked chest. "You are artist? You do this?"

"Yeah." *Excellent verbal skills, Trin.*

She sighed. "My boys. Big men, like their father. Handsome men, like their father. Smart men, like their father. I see these . . . cheesecake muscles and admit those? They did not get from their father."

Cheesecake muscles? That didn't make sense. "Oh, you mean beefcake muscles."

"Yah. That."

"There are another couple of pictures that I started." I didn't add *of his face*, because that implied I'd done other pictures . . . *not* of his face.

Selka flipped through the pages until she reached one of the ones I'd mentioned. She squinted at it, then at me. "Did he pose for this?"

"We were hanging out together and Walker dozed off. The light was perfect so I sketched him. He couldn't sit still for long after he woke up, so that's all I finished."

"It is good."

I almost said she could have it, but I didn't want her to think I was bribing her to like me, even though I totally would if I thought it'd work.

She spun on the stool and faced me. "We play twenty questions. I start. You have ex-husband?"

"No."

"Current husband?"

Was she for real? "I've never been married."

"Children?"

"None."

"Family?"

"My mother died when I was nine."

"So young." She *tsk-tsk*ed and patted my hand. "My mother died after I turn eighteen. Twice your age. I still miss her. Her dying . . . that is why I left Sweden for U.S. I wanted new life. One not filled with sadness."

"Walker speaks highly of your father."

"My father is good man. Good father. For that I am grateful." She leaned closer. "But he make terrible husband."

I made a sad sound that I hoped passed for a response.

"Back to questions. You have pet?"

"A cat. But she's kind of a jerk. She only tolerates me because I feed her."

"Cats and kids can be much alike."

I laughed.

"Happy laugh like that is good."

Selka's smile reminded me of Walker's. Where had he disappeared to?

"Trinity."

My gaze returned to Selka's. "Yes?"

"I make you jumpy like bean?"

"Of course you do. You're Walker's mother. I want to make a good impression."

She sipped her coffee but I could still see her smirk. "How you think you're doing?"

"Above average, which is really good for me because I tend to talk uncontrollably in situations like this. See? I'm doing it right now, chattering like a monkey."

"My son . . . knows this monkey chatter about you?"

I sighed. "Yeah. And he likes me anyway." At least he did until I completely blew it with his mother.

I swore I could hear myself sweating in the silence.

Then she declared, "I like you also."

Do not fist pump.

"So I tell you secret."

My head started shouting, *Oh no. No no no no no no no. Not the secret test!* But my mouth said, "Sure."

"Lund family, big art patrons. We attend art openings. As young wife I use them as excuse to buy nice new dress, pretty shoes, to see my husband . . . slobber over me."

I assumed she meant drool but I didn't correct her.

She poured more coffee. "As young mother with one son, I was tired and not seeing point of buying pretty things or going to art gala. My sister Edie, she takes me to dress shop, shoe shop and lingerie shop. I feel hot like mama, not tired mama. My husband, he like hot mama so very much that he . . . *persuades* me to go into empty coat check room with him to show him lingerie."

I snickered.

"I am easily persuaded. I'm also easily pregnant. Our second son was convinced that night."

"You mean conceived?"

"Yah, that, whatever. The art gallery where persuading happened? The Walker. That's how his name is Walker."

I wasn't sure if I should laugh or high-five her.

"I cannot believe you told her that story, Mom."

How long had Walker been leaning against the wall listening?

Selka shrugged. "Just keeping it real, homey."

Then I did laugh because she pulled off gangsta.

Ward moved in behind her and set his hand on her shoulder. "She's still a hot mama."

Seeing that connection, built over the years that had formed the family that meant so much to Walker, caused equal pangs of longing and loss in me. I feared I'd never have it as much as I worried that, if I did find it, somehow I'd screw it up and lose it anyway.

Walker's lips brushed my temple. Then my cheek. Then he whispered, "Breathe," into my ear. It calmed me, but I still glanced across the counter to see if Ward and Selka noticed my melancholy. But they were taking the cake out of the oven.

So just Walker had caught that.

I knew I should be happy that he could read me so well. And it wouldn't be a crime to hope that I might have found what I'd always wanted. Still, it was a bit unnerving. I hadn't known him that long. And there were things he didn't know about me.

Ward and Selka didn't stay long after we finished the cake. As Walker and his dad were talking, Selka took me aside.

"There's second part to story that is secret part. From time Walker was born I knew in my gut that he would find his heart with an artist." She gifted me with that same glorious smile her son had inherited from her. "You may be monkey-chatter girl, but he is boy who cuts off what frustrates him. Don't be piano wire. Be piano repairer."

I had no idea what that meant, but I nodded like she'd given me sage advice.

After Walker closed the door behind them, he said, "See? I told you my family would love you."

"I don't know if I'd use the word 'love.'"

Confusion distorted his face for a moment, as if I'd just said I didn't love him.

I didn't love him. I liked him a lot. A whole lot. More than I'd ever liked any guy in any relationship. And just because I couldn't imagine not seeing his smiling face every day, or laughing with him about stupid stuff, or because, now that I'd had sex with him—three times!—I felt a hard pang at the thought of never being skin to skin with him again, none of that meant I loved him.

But it does mean you're falling in love with him, dumbass.

"Stop it."

My gaze collided with his.

"Whatever rambling thoughts are racing though your head, put a lid on them, put them on the back burner and leave them to stew for another day."

"Hey. That wasn't a sports analogy—points for switching it up with food."

Walker started to stalk me. "I'm cashing in my points. Right now."

I couldn't see behind me, but there wasn't furniture to trip over, so I kept moving backward. "You don't have enough points to buy anything."

"Oh, sweetheart, I beg to differ. My point system is different than yours. Every time I kiss you and you make that needy little sigh? I get ten points. So by my calculations, with the amount of time we've spent with our lips locked in the last month? I have at least 20,000 points."

I laughed. "Creative math, Viking."

"I can be very creative with figures." His gaze traveled over me as hot as a lick of fire. "Let's start with yours. Strip out of those clothes."

I'd cleared the entryway to the kitchen and remembered a pair of French doors on the far right. If I could make a break for it and sprint outside . . .

Sprint? You're not even a jogger.

I told the snarky voice to shut up, turned and ran.

Walker wasn't expecting that and I had a decent head start.

The patio door wasn't locked and I burst into the sunshine, the concrete warm beneath my bare feet, and I came to a complete halt.

Hands landed on my hips and my back met Walker's solid chest. "We playing tag?" He leaned in to press an open-mouthed kiss on the side of my neck and my knees went weak. He held me up and emitted an evil little chuckle.

But my focus was on the sparkling water in front of me. "You have a pool?"

He stilled. "You didn't know that?"

"How would I know it? This is the first time I've been here." I surveyed the backyard. "Geez, Walker. You think you have enough space? You could put a whole other house back here."

"I like room to move and it's fairly private. Nothing like my folks' place, but the second I saw this place, I bought it."

"Was the pool here?"

"Nope. Seems crazy to have an outdoor pool in Minnesota when there's about two months of summer, but we had a pool growing up. Some of my best memories are from summers hanging out there with my family."

"And you wanted that for when you have a family of your own." My heart warmed. Walker had such a sentimental streak. Every time I got a glimpse of that sweet part of him, I wanted to twine myself around him, hold on and let it seep into me.

Soft lips landed on my temple. "Let's swim."

"I don't have a suit."

"Sure you do, babe. Your birthday suit."

"I'm not stripping down outdoors in the middle of the day. I'll fry to a crisp in this heat."

Walker turned me around. "So swim in your underwear. We won't stay in the pool all day. I'll make sure you don't burn."

I had worn my nicest bra and panty set last night for our date. It could pass for a swimsuit. Feeling daring, just to counter Walker's expectation that I'd say no, I stepped back and yanked the T-shirt over my head. Then I shimmied the sweatpants down my legs.

Once again I was bowled over by the pure lust on my man's face.

"Don't. Move," he growled. "I'll be right back."

As soon as he disappeared inside the house, I wandered around the pool. While the design was unique—a lagoon shape with a waterfall surrounded by concrete pavers finished to resemble stone—the furnishings on the big pool deck were as scant as in the house. This space needed planters with flowers. Seating areas with pockets of shade to escape the sun. A fire pit. My beloved fire pit would look killer in the corner, surrounded by funky mismatched chairs.

Walker strolled out wearing board shorts in a horrendous shade of orange. He grinned at me. "Next time we're out on the boat, I'll wear these and you wear your hat. We'll match."

I laughed. "Or we could just burn them both."

"Aww. Now you've hurt my feelings." He held out his hand. "Let's get wet and slippery together."

That's when I saw the wicked glimmer in his eye and knew this wouldn't be us innocently splashing around in the water like a couple of kids.

He said, "You the jump-in type? Or would you rather ease in?"

I turned as if headed for the steps at the shallow end of the pool but ducked around him and launched myself into the deep end.

Ouch ouch ouch. I'd done a spectacular belly flop and my skin stung. But the water temp was perfect and I floated to the surface.

Walker was grinning at me. "Just when I think I've got you pegged, sweetheart, you surprise me." He hopped in, with barely a splash, and then he popped up in the water next to me.

The sunlight glinted off his hair and his beard. I could stare at him all damn day.

"Let's hit the shallow end that's in the shade." He cut through the water effortlessly, those muscled arms leading the way.

He stopped in the shade by the four-feet depth marker. As soon as I was close enough to grab, he had me plastered to his chest.

The warm, floaty feeling that flowed through me had nothing to do with the pool water. I wreathed my arms around his neck and closed my eyes, giving myself over to him completely.

Walker's hands were busy as his mouth reacquainted itself with my skin. The press of his fingertips as he skimmed my spine. His thumbs lazily caressing my hip bones. Then he grabbed my ass in both hands and rocked against me.

Yes. I needed that pressure to relieve the ache he was creating.

But when I slipped my hand down his rigid pecs and the six-pack above his happy trail, he returned my hand to his neck, swallowing my inarticulate protest with a soft, seductive kiss that made me feel like I was sinking deeper into him.

My butt bumped against the side of the pool and my eyes flew open. Evidently the floating sensation had been somewhat real; we'd moved a few feet closer to the shallow end.

While Walker was licking, lapping and nipping at my skin, I felt a quick tug as he unhooked my bra. He slipped the straps down my shoulders and tossed the bra behind us, where it landed with a wet splat.

"Walker—" My protest died when he enclosed his hot mouth around my water-cooled nipple. His growl of pleasure seemed to vibrate through my skin, tightening the back of my neck, my belly and between my legs. I loved his silent show of passion. No need to tell me how much he loved my breasts or how hot and hard it made him. I knew that at the most basic level with every nip of his teeth, every suctioning pull of his mouth, every plundering kiss and his every labored breath skating across my skin.

Then his mouth was on my ear. "I want you like this. Wet and pliant in my arms." He sucked the skin below my ear and I squirmed. "Are you wet for me?"

"Yes."

"Turn around."

I did. Almost blindly. But then I remembered. "Condom?"

His fingers were pulling my underwear down my legs. "Already covered."

I looked at him over my shoulder. "What? When did you—?"

"When I went inside to change." He slipped a finger inside me. "Saw you half naked and went hard as a fucking brick. I knew there was no way I was letting you go home without having you at least once more."

The fabric of his board shorts fluttered against the backs of my legs like tiny soft fingers. And even with my body shaking with need and my hips moving to drive his finger in deeper, he asked, "You want this, right?"

"God yes."

He canted my hips and drove inside me.

I braced myself against the side of the pool, absorbing his powerful thrusts. He had one hand kneading my breast and the other hand on my lower abdomen holding me in place. When his finger moved down and stroked me in time with his panting breaths in my ear, I splintered into a million pieces like a glass dropped on concrete.

Walker wasn't far behind me. After another minute his entire body went rigid and he pressed his face against the nape of my neck, releasing a drawn-out groan.

Even when I noticed my fingertips resembled prunes, I didn't want to move. I'd happily stay right there, with his heavy weight pressing against me, those big hands touching me tenderly, the heat of this breath warm on my neck and his contentment surrounding me as thoroughly as the water.

"Trinity."

I loved that whiskey-rough way he said my name. "Yeah?"

"I wish you could stay with me today." He kissed the slope of my shoulder. "But I know you've gotta work."

"You kicking me out?"

"Yes. I won't be a distraction until you want me to be. I'd rather have you missing me than resenting me."

Right then, I fell just a little more. "Thank you for . . ."

"Getting you. Yeah, babe. I do get you. And now"—he scraped his teeth down the nape of my neck, sending a shiver through me—"I get you this way too. I'm a happy man."

Mr. I'm Not Smooth always knew exactly what to say.

Sixteen

WALKER

Normally after a bad day on the job, or on all the job sites like today, I'd go to the gym to relieve my frustration on the treadmill, in the weight room or in a CrossFit session. If that didn't appeal to me, I'd see if my brothers or cousins wanted to spar and grapple. Then again, it'd been almost a year since any of them had time to do a little ground and pound. If I dwelled on that, it was liable to make me pissier yet.

I knew what would fix my mood. Trinity. One look into those guileless green eyes, one glimpse of her mouth curved into a smile, one whiff of her skin and everything else would fade away.

Don't use her as a crutch.

I didn't know where that thought had come from. I'd never dated a woman long enough to become dependent on her. For once in my life I'd like to have that. I'd like to knock on Trinity's door and be confident that when she looked at me she'd know what I needed. It wasn't just sex that'd soothe my ragged edges. But how was she supposed to possess this innate knowledge if I didn't let her know when I needed it?

That train of thought had me turning around and heading to her house.

But it wasn't a serene, smiling, helpful woman that greeted me at her studio door. She had her phone to her ear, vehemently arguing with someone. I grabbed a bottle of water, noticing her mini-kitchen was piled with garbage and odds and ends. The flowers I'd given her were dead in the vase. The heat in here indicated her air conditioner had blown a fuse again.

The damn woman needed a keeper.

It could be you.

I snorted. Miss Independent would take offense at that, even if it was true.

When her phone call kept going, I bagged her trash and tossed it in the garbage bins in the alley. I wandered up the sidewalk and noticed her scraggly lawn was a few weeks past needing a trim. No surprise with her schedule that she hadn't gotten around to it. At loose ends, I cooled my heels for another minute before I searched out her lawn mower.

The thing was a cheap piece of crap, but it worked. I started out in front of her house and blanked my mind to everything except the grinding whir of the lawn mower motor, the pace of my steps and the loamy scent of fresh-cut grass.

By the time I reached the backyard, my mood had improved drastically. Strange to consider I hadn't mowed my own lawn for a few years. I didn't have the time. So why when I did have free time was I cutting her grass?

Because you're a nice guy?

It went deeper than that. In some bizarre way, finishing the tasks Trinity didn't have time for gave me a sense of accomplishment.

After I parked the mower in the shed, my mood perked up even more as Trinity meandered down the sidewalk toward me, the light from the late-afternoon sun backlighting her hair.

With a ferocity I'd never experienced, I realized I wanted this—her greeting me after a long day of work. It didn't seem like a pipe dream; it felt like a premonition when I saw Trinity carrying two bottles of beer—my *favorite* kind of beer.

"As much as I need a hug, sweetheart, my clothes are dirty and I don't—"

"You think I care about that? Wrong." Then she hooked her arm around my neck and pulled me down so she could fasten her mouth to mine in a kiss that hit the mark between passionate and calming. She backed away and gave me a shy smile. "Hello, my dirty, hardworking man. I'm happy to see you and I'm sorry that phone call took me so long. Could I interest you in a frosty beverage?"

God, I love you.

"What?"

I froze. I hadn't blurted it out to her before I'd come to terms with it myself?

"Walker? What's wrong? Don't you want a beer?"

"Of course I want a beer. I was just surprised that you have my favorite."

"I've been in your refrigerator. I figured you'd be over here sometimes, so I should have it on hand."

Her thoughtfulness threw me more than her quirkiness. I could handle quirky. Seeing firsthand that she had been thinking about me and went the extra mile to make me comfortable in her home? I might as well just propose to her right now.

"I do admit surprise that a billionaire heir prefers the cheap stuff."

"It's cheap and it's good. Besides, Grain Belt beer won the medal of excellence for their lager several years running."

She tapped my cheek. "Just giving you crap, Viking. Thank you for mowing my lawn. You didn't have to do that."

I shrugged. "It needed done."

"Still, I'm happy and grateful you did it. So you want to sit by my fire pit and enjoy our beer? Or would you rather go inside?"

"You know . . . I've never been inside your house."

"Really? Huh. Well, it's kind of a dump—especially compared to your fancy-schmancy Lake District digs."

I lifted my beer to my lips. "Do you have furniture in your living room?"

"Of course."

"That shows me up because I have none in my fancy-schmancy house."

She laughed and the familiar sound soothed my last ragged edge. "Come on."

"Give me two minutes and I'll change that fuse first."

The way she shifted back and forth I knew she warred between telling me I didn't have to do that and relief it'd get fixed. She exhaled. "Thank you. That would be great."

She hung back as I dinked around with the fuse box. When she said, "I like watching you work, Walker. Promise you'll let me come to a job site sometime so I can see you in action?" I knew that she wasn't just paying lip service to accepting all parts of me; she meant it. I'd never had that before. And no way was I giving it up.

"Done."

After Trinity set the alarm, we strolled hand in hand up the sidewalk to the front door.

I followed her inside. The small entryway opened up into the living room. Her furniture was white. Her walls were white. Her carpet was white. Even her end tables and coffee table were covered with white paint.

Given her vibrant personality, I'd expected her private space to reflect it. But this place was a void. I looked over at her and saw she'd been watching me.

"It's intentional. The all-white space."

"Why?"

"Working with colors and textures and images all day, my eyes and my brain need blank space to recharge."

"I guess that makes sense."

One of the puffy white pillows jumped and so did I. "Jesus. What was that?"

"My cat."

"You have a cat?"

"Yes. Didn't your mother tell you?"

I frowned. "How the hell does my mom know you have a cat and I don't?"

She tiptoed over to it, offering reassuring words that she only wanted to pet it, but the white fur stood on end as it arched its back and hissed at her.

I refrained from voicing my opinion that cats were assholes. "What's your cat's name?"

"Buttons."

"Buttons," I repeated, studying the pure white fluff ball. "Babe. Buttons doesn't have marks anywhere on that lily white fur."

"I know. When I found her out by my studio, she had three black circles in a line down her chest. When I cleaned her up, the black spots were gone. But I'd already named her."

"Dogs are better than cats."

She sighed. "But I can't just cut her loose. She has been my cat for two years."

"I wasn't suggesting you eighty-six her. I was just saying if I had to choose, I'd pick dogs."

"You could have dogs," she pointed out. "You have room for them."

But I wanted family dogs and that wasn't something I'd ever admit out loud. "Someday."

"Are you hungry? I could make clam linguine."

That sounded awful. "I wouldn't want you to go to any trouble."

Her eyes narrowed. "Mastered the art of the little white lie, have you?"

"Fine. I don't like clams. Not crazy about linguine either. Why don't we just order a pizza?"

She wrinkled her nose. "I ate enough pizza in college that if I never have it again it'll be too soon."

"That sucks. I love pizza."

"You're a bachelor. You probably only like pizza because someone makes it, drops it off at your door and all you have to do is open the box."

Partially true. I wasn't about to argue with a woman who didn't like chicken wings or bar food either. I sipped my beer.

She sipped hers.

Fuck it. I'd just go there, since it's where we'd end up anyway. "So is your bedroom all black?"

That startled her. "Why would you ask that?"

"It seems if you need blank space here, then you'd want a different atmosphere in the place where you sleep. The exact opposite. Light and dark."

Trinity blinked at me.

"Am I wrong?"

"No. My bedroom is completely black. But no one understands why. They just think I'm morose."

"No one meaning . . . other men who've been in your bed?"

Her eyes narrowed again until she was nearly cross-eyed. "Are we doing the jealousy thing? Because I can give it right back to you by asking how many women have swum in your pool."

I loved that she didn't back down. And hated that she had a point. "I fucking hate thinking about other guys having their hands on you, Trinity. I know it's in the past and it won't be a thing between us, but you oughta know that I'll probably act like a caveman when I see guys eyeballing you. And if one touches you? He'll be picking his broken teeth up off the floor."

She said nothing. But her cheeks were flushed. With anger?

"What?"

"That makes me hot, imagining you going all primal and possessive over me."

"It does?"

"Crazy hot." She drained her beer. "Want to see my bedroom?"

"Like you wouldn't believe."

Trinity rushed past me; I chased her.

I slammed the door shut and we fell into a dark void where we were nothing but sighs and moans, heated skin and frantic movements.

It was exactly what we both needed—and way better than clam linguine or pizza.

———————

Afterward, we settled with her head on my chest, our bodies twisted together between her satiny sheets, still completely in the dark. I finally felt completely reset and heaved a huge sigh.

She said, "Bad day?"

"Might say that."

"Can you talk about it without getting all tensed up again?"

"You sure you wanna hear it?"

"I love lying on your chest and listening to you talk. And with the added bonus that I get to smell you, it's like a drug."

Shit. I hadn't showered after a long day spent outside in the dirt. Was she hinting that I reeked?

"I love all the different scents that make up Walker Lund. Earth and spice and mint and that yummy cologne, and some citrusy one I can't place. You're intoxicating."

I smiled even though she couldn't see my face in the dark.

"Talk to me. This is what couples do after the lovin'."

So I told her about my frustration with the Smith Brothers' project and how I was ready to cut them loose and Jase wasn't, which put us at odds. Then we had supply delays, and employees with Monday-itis, leaving us shorthanded. I hated when Mondays were a shitshow because it usually meant the rest of the week would follow along those lines.

Trinity just listened. I didn't know how much I'd needed that. I kissed the top of her head. "Who were you yelling at on the phone?"

"It's a long story."

"I've got time."

"Esther came to look at the piece today and suggested minor changes, which is no big deal. She's telling me about the country club where she's having the party and I ask specifics about how the piece will be displayed because it's heavy. She had no idea about display costs or temporary and permanent installation costs. So I'm imagining this work crumpled up on the floor of a garage someplace. We get a plan figured out and I call my usual display and installation guy—who incidentally is a good friend of Ramon's—and he declines to help me."

"Jesus. He's taking sides?"

"I should've expected that. I call another guy. Same answer. I'm thinking I have this gorgeous piece and no way to transport it to the event, so I call my friend Nicolai, who I haven't talked to in over a year. He and Ramon had a crash-and-burn moment, so Nicolai can't wait to share the gossip that Ramon went into rehab this weekend."

I stopped my hand in the middle of her back. "What?"

"Remember I told you about Ramon having a personality change? And Gen always making cracks about him being high? I guess it'd gotten really bad. He was pulled over in his food truck for driving under the influence. There's some snag with quantifiable limits when you're stoned, but after he was released on bond, he checked into Hazelden."

I tilted her head back, but in the pitch black I couldn't see her eyes. "Don't feel guilty, sweetheart. He made his choices. The breakdown of your friendship didn't send him down the path to self-destruction; he was already on it."

"I still feel bad for him, though. And I do feel guilty that maybe if I'd been a better friend—"

My mouth found hers in the dark. The sweet taste of her was my drug. I fed off her until we both needed to break apart to breathe.

She snuggled into me, burying her nose in my chest with a contented sigh.

"After Nicolai finished gossiping, did he get you the names of installation guys?"

"Nope. That's why I was yelling and pacing. But I'm not thinking about it tonight."

"I'll be your installation guy."

She lifted her head. "What?"

"You need a strong guy, I'm your man. You need a strong guy who knows other strong guys, I'm your man. If you need equipment to load the piece, I'm your man. If you need transportation, I'm your man. Get where I'm going with this?"

"You're sure? Because I'm a completely different person when I'm coordinating an installation."

"I've watched you kill yourself during this process and if I can take some of the burden off, let me help you."

When she kissed me, I felt her smile on my lips. "Okay. But you can't forget I'm in charge. You can't second-guess me or argue with me—"

I flipped her on her back. "I get it. I'm still the man for the job. But there is one thing."

"What?"

"I won't hide the fact I'm sleeping with the boss."

"I'm good with that. Now be a little worker bee and get busy."

Something awakened me and I opened my eyes, but in the pitch black of Trinity's room, they may as well have been shut. I blinked a few times and lifted my head, trying not to wake the snoring woman sprawled across my chest. I let my hand follow the outline of her body. I liked sleeping with her and I didn't remember ever feeling so comfortable with a woman beside me in bed. Trinity curled into me and conked out immediately. Like she trusted me to keep her safe even in sleep.

I saw movement across the room.

A white lump sat on the dresser, staring at me.

Buttons, you spooky bastard. How did you get in here?

The only thing that moved was the long white tail, twitching back and forth with irritation.

I leveled my meanest look on Buttons because I knew she could see me perfectly well in the dark. I swear she chuffed out a noise that sounded like a cat sneer.

"Watch it," I whispered. "Or when she moves in with me I'll replace you with a dog."

Trinity shifted and muttered, "We *can* have a cat *and* a dog."

I wasn't sure she was awake, so I said, "A cat and *two* dogs."

"Okay. But a guard dog for safety and a fluffy little one for the kids to drag around and dress up." She sighed. "I always wanted that. And a bunch of kids."

Talking about pets and living together and kids . . . when we'd been together just a few weeks? My balls should've been sweating. At the very least I should've been staring at the ceiling unable to sleep for the rest of the night.

But I couldn't stop smiling as I drifted off.

Seventeen

TRINITY

t was six days until I'd deliver the Stephens commission.

I'd taken the day off to laze around with my man. But lying in the sun without purpose always sent my brain into overdrive.

"What are the odds?"

He sighed. "I don't know. I'm not exactly a statistician."

I adjusted my sunglasses. "Or maybe it's just a rich-person thing?"

"Meaning what?"

"Meaning all you rich people hang out at the same places."

No comment from Richie Rich. He took my ribbing about our financial disparities in stride.

Once again, I tried to empty my mind and listen to the trill of different birds in the maple trees, or the steady buzz of the cicadas, but my brain was wound up. "Does this happen often?"

"What? You chattering away while I'm trying to take a nap? It's happening more than I'd like it to, babe."

"I'm the one who deserves a nap." I'd finished the Stephens piece with time to spare—only a few days, but ahead of deadline was ahead of deadline. But ever since I'd deemed it done, I hadn't allowed myself to relax. My brain started asking me what was next. And I didn't have a clue.

Like that's new.

Walker snagged my hand and kissed my knuckles. "I'm sorry. I'm just wiped out. Keeping up with your sexual demands could be a full-time job."

I smirked. "First you complain we don't see each other enough. Now you complain it's too much."

"I will never complain about that. I should've taken a rain check last night when you wanted to play grab-ass because I'm dragging ass after my early morning."

Walker invoked the eight o'clock rule whenever we stayed the night together; I had to be up and ready to spend time with him by eight a.m. That meant he couldn't use our limited hours together to work out, so he hauled his fine ass out of bed at six a.m. to be done by eight. And last night, we'd messed around until two a.m. I kept waiting for the need between us to cool, but it hadn't. "Who did you work out with this morning?"

"Myself. Why? You wanna come tomorrow?"

I snorted. Like that'd happen. "I thought you had a work-out schedule with your brothers and cousins?"

"We used to. They're busy doing their own things, so I do mine."

I'd heard that excuse a lot. It hurt my heart to think the close connection Walker felt with his family wasn't reciprocated.

"Since you're determined to keep me up and involved in

your circular thought processes, let me remind you that the client who commissioned you to do the project has money. And yes, money people stick together. So the fact your client is hosting her husband's surprise birthday party at the Minneapolis Club isn't unusual. Club members have to spend X number of dollars there every month, so the private rooms are almost always booked."

"Does Lund Industries have events at the Minneapolis Club frequently?"

"Often enough. Especially for the smaller stuff."

"So the party they're holding the same night as the Stephens party? It's not a major corporate thing that every Lund board member has to attend?"

A shadow loomed over me. My sunglasses disappeared. Then I was gazing into the beautiful face of the man who rocked my world and filled my soul with happiness.

"Trinity. I'll be there with you. I promise. No one at LI will miss me. But you. You . . ." He waited for me to fill in the blanks.

"I need you."

"In case something goes wrong with the installation?" he pressed.

I touched his face. "In case something goes wrong with me."

"Not." Kiss. "Gonna." Kiss. "Happen." Kiss. "Everything will go perfectly; you'll have people lined up with their checkbooks out to commission an original Trinity Amelia piece of art. And curator dude will demand a piece for all the galleries he reps."

"How can you be so confident?"

"How can you look at all the beautiful stuff you create and not be cocky about it?"

"Because I'm neurotic."

Walker kissed me again. "I know. I don't get it, but it's part of what makes you . . . you, so I figured it'd be easier to accept it than to question it. Kind of like how I accept that Buttons is an asshole, but she's your asshole cat and part of the package."

I grinned. "She's growing on you."

"Yeah. The scratches on my calves are signs of her affection." He smirked. "I guess that could be true since the scratches down my back are signs of yours."

He scooted away before I swatted him.

"You want something to drink?" he called from the patio.

"No. I'm good."

I watched as Walker raised the bottle of water to his mouth. His T-shirt rode up, exposing the blond happy trail vanishing into the waistband of his board shorts. I knew that section of his abdomen would be warm from him sitting in the sun. I knew how hard his muscles and how soft that strip of hair would feel against my lips. I knew he'd taste of salt and sweat and man.

It still shocked me, that immediate rush of need when I caught his musky, masculine scent. The knowledge that I could have this man anytime I wanted just made me greedier.

He crouched beside me. "You wanna stop staring at my junk and licking your lips so we can finish this conversation?"

"Not really." I reached out and pushed his sunglasses on top of his head. The heat in his eyes wasn't solely from the scorching temperatures on the patio. "You were complaining about me talking. So I assumed you'd rather I used my mouth for something else."

"Jesus, Trin."

I set my hand on his cheek, tracing the bow of his bottom lip with my thumb. "We both know if you got it in your head that you wanted a taste of me as we're lazing in the sun, you'd just do it and wouldn't ask permission."

His nostrils flared.

"So I'm not asking, Walker. Stretch out on this blanket with me."

He stood, stripped off his shirt and sat behind me. Snugging his groin to my backside, he bent his knees so I could rest my back to his chest as he braced his hands behind him. His lips brushed the top of my ear. "Happy now?"

"Very." My heart sighed. *You make me happier than anyone I've ever met. When I'm with you, for the first time in my life I know I'm exactly where I'm supposed to be.*

As much as my heart wanted to whisper that confession to see how his heart responded, my mouth remained uncooperative for a change.

I felt the tension in every inch of Walker's body. He was such a complicated man, used to being in charge in his work, so I suspected that sometimes he wanted me to take control. He needed my focus one hundred percent on him.

Setting my palms on his knees, I ran my hands down the outside of his legs. For being so fair-haired everywhere else, the darker hair on his calves and thighs intrigued me. My fingertips mapped the bulging muscles of his calves and the delineated lines of his quads. They quivered at my touch. He took great care of his body. Not in an obsessive way, but I assumed competition with his family played a big part in why he remained fit.

I rolled forward onto my knees and turned around to face him. "Look at you. All stretched out like some kind of Norse god ready to be worshipped."

He didn't speak. He just watched me and waited with coiled energy.

His body was so much longer and broader than mine that

we were mismatched when I tried to hang above him. He started to shift to accommodate me, but I shook my head. "Let me."

As much as I wanted to slowly lick the beads of sweat from his skin, starting at the top and working my way down his magnificent body, teasing him until he moaned and begged, we were outside on a Sunday afternoon in a neighborhood teeming with kids. I didn't want to leave it to chance I'd only get the job half done.

I paused at his nipples, taking one thorough swipe with my tongue and a tiny nip with my teeth on each side.

His only response was a quick hiss of a breath.

I tapped his butt and said, "Lift." I eased his baggy board shorts down past his erection.

A few loose tendrils of my hair teased his skin as I started my southward journey. His belly bunched and flexed as I zigzagged my lips down the golden trail bisecting his abdomen. When I reached his hips, I ran my tongue down the ridge of his flexor muscle. And back up the matching one on the other side.

I looked up at him as I lowered my head and licked the plump tip.

"Trinity."

"Let go and let me make you feel good." I wrapped my fingers around his shaft at the base and moved my hand up as I slid my mouth down.

He pretty much went incoherent after that.

I let myself go too, staying focused on his pleasure and nothing else.

Once he hit the point of no return, I stayed with him through every hot pulse and every jerk of his hips. I thought maybe the aftermath would be weird, because face it—sometimes sex was awkward even when it wasn't new. But he just reached down, pulled up his board shorts and hauled me into his arms, nestling me against his body.

Walker didn't say "Thank you" or "Baby, that was great." He just sighed like the weight of the world had been lifted off his shoulders and muttered, "Fuck yeah," almost to himself.

Even snuggled together like this, I couldn't not touch him. I nuzzled his beard. "Does this ever get too hot in the summer and you think about shaving it off?"

"I've had it so long that I don't notice."

"I can't imagine what you'd look like without a beard, but with this gorgeous bone structure . . ." I nuzzled him again. "Maybe I'll ask Selka to show me a pic of her baby boy before his beautiful beard." I laughed. "I get points for alliteration."

"She'd like it if I had no beard," he half grumbled. "What will you do with all these mysterious points you're awarding yourself?"

"It's a thing I did as a kid. My mom used a point system for rewards. If I picked up my room without her nagging me, I'd get points. Or if I did my homework right after school, or if she saw me helping someone, she'd add those to the tally. When I reached a certain amount of points, I could cash them in."

"Cash them in for what?"

"She offered me options. If I wanted to see a movie, it'd 'cost' points. If I wanted a new toy or jewelry, those cost more. I don't know if that was supposed to teach me not to be materialistic, but it worked."

"How?"

"I almost always spent my points to do things with her.

As I've gotten older some of those memories started to fade, prompting me to write them down, because that's all I had left of her."

Walker kissed the top of my head. "I can't imagine not having my folks." He paused. "How did she die?"

"Hit-and-run. She was changing a tire late at night. They think the person that hit her lost control on the ice and plowed into her. The cops never found out who did it."

"Baby."

His sorrow for me brought all those memories rushing back. "For a while in my teen years I had this big conspiracy theory that my dad had her taken out." Before he asked the obvious question of whether my father had the connections to do that, I said, "Guess I'd been reading too many thrillers. The theory faded when I realized after my mom died, he'd had to take on the daily responsibility of me. I'm pretty sure he would've done anything to prevent that, not cause it." I changed the focus. "Have you lost anyone close to you?"

"Not really. Maria, our first cook, died when I was sixteen and the house seemed empty after school without her. She and my mom were so funny together. It was hard on Mom too."

"What about the Lund family patriarch?"

Walker's body tensed beneath me. He said, "I've gotta move. I'm getting a crick in my neck." He sat up and grabbed a bottle of water out of the cooler. After draining it, he crushed the plastic in his powerful hands. "It's been a long time since I've thought about him." He blew out a breath. "Probably because he was an asshole. He didn't have much time for me anyway, which I am thankful for now."

I turned onto my side and propped my head on my hand. "But you weren't thankful back then?"

Walker shrugged. "I was a kid. It seemed I always ran

into him when I'd been rolling in the dirt or something. Nolan could be just as filthy as me but Grandpa would praise him for the artistic placement of mud or some crap like that. Where I was just dirty."

"He played favorites?"

"Oh yeah. I was maybe twelve when the almighty Jackson Lund informed me that I had an inferior intellect to my siblings and my cousins—including my four-year-old cousin Dallas. He suggested I run off to the woods and learn to carve clogs with Sven because working with my hands was all an oaf like me would ever be good at." He snorted. "My grandpa Jensen's name wasn't Sven, but that's a perfect example of how dismissive he was."

"What a miserable jackass." I touched him, just a brush of my hand across his skin. "You didn't . . . I mean, it wasn't because of his nastiness—"

"That I moved to Sweden when I turned eighteen and became a carpenter?" he supplied. "Nope. I figured his cut-downs were supposed to inspire me to try harder to be like him."

"What did your parents say when you told them?" When Walker didn't respond right away, my heart clenched. "You didn't tell them."

"I've never told anyone." He looked at me over his shoulder. "I can't believe I told you."

"I'm glad you did."

"I didn't see any point in telling them. It'd just hurt and anger them—and they'd already dealt with that enough. It's a testament to my grandmother's influence—a woman I never met—that my dad and his brothers didn't turn out to be entitled pricks, cruel fathers, heartless men and conscienceless business tycoons. They are the exact opposites in all ways."

The next thing I knew, Walker had rolled me beneath him. "How'd we get on that shitty topic anyway? When I should be entirely focused on the fact you're strutting around in a swimsuit."

"Strutting?"

"If you're not, you should be." He buried his face in my cleavage with a happy sigh.

"Can we talk about the installation?"

A petulant look darkened his eyes. "*Now?*"

"Do you have everything on the list I gave you?"

"Yep." He started nibbling on my jaw.

"Who's helping you?"

"Thought I'd hang around the railroad tracks on Saturday morning. See if any vagrants need work."

"Walker. I'm serious."

"I am too. It's six days away. You'll add twenty things to the list by then. So can we please focus on what's important right now?"

"Us having sex in the yard?"

"Us having sex in the yard and then you making me lunch."

He deserved it when I pushed him in the pool.

Eighteen

WALKER

I pulled up to Trinity's house in my '57 Chevy Bel Air. She'd made an offhand comment earlier during the installation about cleaning my truck out so she wouldn't get her dress dirty. For an event like this I had no intention of driving my work truck. I had *some* class.

Cars hadn't been a topic in any of our conversations. Most women's eyes glazed over when talk turned to engine size and speed-to-horsepower ratios. We Lund boys had been born with a love for cars. Brady preferred vehicles on the high end. Jensen's requirement was the car went fast. Ash chose unique and rare models. Jaxson had traded in his Corvette for "the safest family car on the road" since he had Mimi. Nolan and I preferred muscle cars. In our pre-driving days, we spent hours compiling lists of our must-haves when we could finally purchase the classics of our dreams.

This baby was the first thing I'd bought after I'd returned

from Sweden. Just because I hadn't rebuilt the motor myself or lovingly sanded down each panel prior to painting didn't mean I wasn't in love with this car. Not that it was the only one in my collection, but it was my favorite.

The tie was choking me and I loosened it as I walked up the sidewalk. I'd dropped Trinity off four hours ago after we'd finished the installation. She'd insisted on being home to get ready, which I'd understood meant she needed to get in the right mind-set more than figuring out what she was going to wear.

Today I'd witnessed a different side of her. Over the past few weeks I'd seen her in many scenarios—some good, some bad—but I'd never seen her in professional mode. She'd been clear that she expected her instructions to be followed to the letter. Any deviations were to be cleared with her first. I'd had no problem taking orders from her. In this case, she was the expert. Just because I had more muscles didn't put me in charge by default, as so many men I knew assumed. I'd made sure the guys I'd asked to help weren't of that boneheaded mentality.

Trinity flung the door open before I knocked. As I stood on the step trying to roll my tongue back in my mouth— because she looked like a freakin' goddess—her mouth ran at full speed.

"You're late—not really late, but late enough. I didn't realize until I had this dress on that I can't even zip it up by myself. Now I don't know whatever possessed me to buy it. To be honest, I don't remember when I bought it. I probably should've gotten something new, but I just don't have the shopping gene and if I can't get it online and have it dropped at my door then I don't need it." She grabbed my sleeve and tugged. "Come in. I can't stand here half undressed. And we were supposed to leave like five minutes ago."

Once I was in the entryway with the door shut, she gave me her back and lifted her hair up. She peered at me over her shoulder and said, "Zip."

I'd zip her up. But first I wanted to trail my fingers down that slice of exposed skin. I loved her softness, her scent and the way she shivered at my touch.

"Walker, please hurry up. We're running behind."

I pulled the zipper up slowly, letting my lips brush the back of her neck. Then I wrapped my arms around her middle and nuzzled her ear. "Breathe."

"Walker—"

"Come on, sweetheart. You're all wound up and we haven't left the house yet. Take a moment and just breathe."

She rested her body against mine, raising her left arm to twine behind my neck, allowing her to rifle her fingers through my hair. Turning her head so the bridge of her nose bumped the bottom of my jaw, she slowly and steadily breathed me in.

I couldn't wait to take her this way, with her on her knees as I pushed into her from behind, freeing my hands to be all over her.

"You're thinking about sex, aren't you?"

"It's always the first place my mind goes when we're body-to-body like this." I kissed her temple. "You'd rather I was thinking about golf?"

"You golf?"

"Not well. Nolan always whips my ass."

Sighing, she lowered her arm. "I'd say something funny about a 'hole in one,' but I'm trying to cut down on sports analogies."

I laughed. I kissed her again and murmured, "Turn around, babe, so I can get a good look at you."

Trinity took three steps forward and faced me.

She'd worn a lace dress the color of ripe peaches. It was more modest than I'd typically seen from her, high necked, with a heart-shaped cutout above her breasts that was covered with sheer fabric the same color as the lace. The material molded to her ribs, her hips, her belly and her ass, showcasing those mouthwatering curves, the hem ending just above the knee. Her shoes weren't strappy stilettos, but closed-toe platforms, sexy in an understated way. My gaze zigzagged back up her body to her face. She'd chosen dramatic makeup, giving her a more polished flair, but it wasn't overly done. Her glossy hair was tamed, sleek with the ends in a soft curl.

I touched her cheek. "You are stunning. People will be looking at you as much as your incredible art."

She smiled. "Thanks."

"You're ready?"

"Yep. But first I want to gawk at you since I've never witnessed the glory of you in a suit." She gestured for me to turn around.

I felt ridiculous but I did it anyway. Then the heat in her eyes as I slowly spun around to face her was worth it.

"I think I just had a mini O. Damn, Walker Lund. You can wear a suit. A custom suit, no less."

"Brady, Nolan and Ash have the same tailor, so he's my tailor by default, the poor SOB."

Trinity's hand skimmed my shoulder and across my chest. Her fingers started at the knot in my tie. She slipped the silk between her thumb and index finger in a loose fist, stroking the fabric the way she stroked my shaft.

I groaned and snatched her hand away. "Have mercy, sweetheart. I can only take so much with you looking hot and sexy and touching me that way."

Rising on her toes, she kissed me. "I can't wait to peel these clothes off you later."

"Same goes." I stepped back and heard a hiss. "Jesus." I glanced down and Buttons glared at me. "You need a bell for that damn cat. She's always sneaking up on me."

"I think that's her way of showing she likes you." Trinity draped a purse on a thin gold chain over her shoulder. "Ready."

When Trinity noticed the car parked at the curb, she grinned at me. "Keeping secrets, Mr. Lund? Why didn't I know you had a bright red hot rod?"

"You didn't ask." I opened the door for her and she slid in.

Once we were on the way, she said, "This goes fast?"

"Very. But I won't demonstrate tonight." I picked up her hand. "We'll take it to the racetrack sometime and I'll let you drive."

"Cool. I've never driven a performance car. I've always been focused on gas mileage and reliability."

"Nothing wrong with that."

She was quiet for several miles. She kept twisting the chain of her purse around her fingers, unwrapping them and doing it again.

"What's going on in that head of yours?"

"This should be the moment I enjoy the most. The hard work is done, I'm satisfied with how the piece turned out, my client is thrilled and she gets to spring a surprise on the man she's loved for almost fifty years."

"But?"

"But thinking about the guests at the party judging me gives me anxiety. Esther wants me to give a speech. If there's anything I hate worse than defending what I do, it's *explaining* what I do. And no, they're not the same thing, but I will be doing both tonight and that makes my lungs seize up."

I stroked her hand to let her know I was listening.

"When you say 'art,' most people think of oil paintings,

watercolors, charcoal, pen and ink. They see mixed-media pieces like mine and don't consider them art. They consider me a hack. Because if I was a real artist, I'd be creating still life paintings like the masters. They either admit they don't 'get' my kind of art and mention the time they saw the Jackson Pollock exhibit at MoMA or Maurizio Cattelan's catastrophic mobile at the Guggenheim, neither of which is anything like my art. Or they nod at me, grim set to their mouths. It's apparent they're silently judging me. Silently judging the Stephenses too, thinking they have too much money if they choose to spend it on trashy artwork. And it's not my paranoia talking. I've seen this time and time again."

I didn't respond because I'd been that sneering guy—and I'd grown up in a family that regularly attended art events. I'd silently scoffed at anything that didn't fit into the little box I'd been taught in school had the right to be called art. I couldn't even admit that, up until a few weeks ago when we'd started dating, I'd been stuck in that same mind-set.

"And to top it all off tonight, I'm a cliché. Falling into the brooding stereotype and swearing no one understands me because I'm a sensitive artist." She sighed. "So tell me about this Lund party that's going on at the same time."

No surprise she'd deflected back to me. "It's to celebrate an acquisition."

"Will all the LI board members be there?"

Except for you? went unsaid.

"It doesn't matter if they are because I'm with you tonight. Period."

"But if you have to step away—"

"I'll do it when you're surrounded by a throng of admirers."

"Okay. That makes me feel better."

I pulled up to the members-only valet parking stand. Immediately a valet appeared as I climbed out. "Keys are in the ignition. Be warned, I'll know if you hot-rod this. Any rubber that's off those tires? I'll take the same amount off your skin. Understand?"

"Yes, sir, Mr. Lund."

I skirted the back end of the car and took Trinity's elbow, leading her up the limestone walkway. As we passed groups of people, I wasn't surprised I didn't recognize anyone. I only showed up here when I had no other choice. The admiring looks some of the guys bestowed on Trinity earned them a back-the-fuck-off glare from me.

"You always so possessive with your car?" she asked.

"Yes. Some assholes want what other men have and I will fuck them up if they don't stop eyeballing you."

"I thought we were talking about the car."

"We're talking about what belongs to me."

Trinity stopped just inside the door to the club. "Walker. Take it down a notch."

"Nope." I curled my hand beneath her jaw and tilted her head back for a kiss.

She wiggled out of my grip. "Can we leave this for another night?"

"Leave what?"

"Talking about these feelings and crap."

"Crap?"

She kept her focus behind me. "You know what I mean. How would you like it if I just announced that you belonged to me?"

"I'd consider myself the luckiest man in the world."

"Oh."

"Trinity. Look at me."

I watched her inhale a deep breath before she tipped her face up.

What I saw in those green depths staggered me. She loved me. If I hadn't known it in the way she touched me, listened to me and gave me importance in her world, it was right there. But fear also lurked on the edges. And it almost eclipsed the look of love.

Holy shit. Was she scared of me? Of this? Why?

"I can't do this right now. I have to see where they are with the party." She sidestepped me and hustled down the wide hallway teeming with people.

I followed her at as discreet a distance as I could manage. Instead of focusing on trying to place her fear, I focused on the pair of dudes who'd turned around to leer at her ass. Felt good to knock into each of them with a hard shoulder. The next group of guys giving her a head-to-toe once-over earned a scowl. And the men my father's age—those perverts deserved my low-pitched warning growl.

Trinity stopped outside the banquet room. A long glass panel ran down the side of the door, allowing her to peer in.

"Can you see anything?" I said, covering her body with mine.

"It looks like it's still cocktail hour. He just started opening his presents. There's a pile of them."

"What's that mean for your time frame?"

"We're out here until Esther gives me the signal." She glanced at me over her shoulder. "If you want to go say hi to your family—"

"Trin, are you trying to get rid of me?"

"Well. You are hovering."

"You asked me to hover, remember? Social anxiety and free champagne not a good mix?"

She sighed. "I could use a shot of something to loosen me up."

"The LI party has an open bar. I could get us both a drink."

"One drink. But if your relatives catch you?" She patted my cheek and ruffled my beard. "You're on your own. I'm booking it back here."

"Deal." I took her hand and weaved through the crowd until we reached the last banquet room.

"This is a crappy location."

"Actually, it's the preferred location since it has great soundproofing." I spun her around and pushed her against the wall. "What shot, sweetheart?"

"Tequila."

"Coming up."

I didn't go in the main door. I ducked around to the employee entrance and cut to the prep room. Maxwell, the head of catering, rolled his eyes when he saw me. "What you up to now, Walker?"

"I need two shots of tequila. My girlfriend and I are splitting our time between this and the Stephens party. If I go in there . . . you know my family won't let me leave. And we have to get back."

"It is a brotherly trait tonight. Jensen said hello and vanished to the club bar."

Jens didn't like these corporate events either. But I was surprised he was here.

Maxwell spoke in Spanish to a server and she hustled away. With as many people as I'd seen milling around, Maxwell had to be slammed so I didn't expect he'd talk to me.

But he said, "Stephens party, eh? That one's not as fancy as the Lund party or the bigwig party next door."

"Who are the bigwigs?"

"Political guys. Campaigning for funds."

"That's why there are so many people here?"

"Partially. There's a big wedding in the ballroom too."

I withheld a shudder. Brady had tied the knot the right way.

The server returned with two shot glasses and limes. I said, "*Gracias*," and returned to my date.

Trinity grinned when she saw the shots. "Impressive. Under two minutes."

I handed her one and proposed a toast. "Let's celebrate your finishing another amazing piece of artwork."

We touched glasses and knocked back the booze. Then I placed a lime between my teeth and leaned closer.

"You think of everything." She pressed her mouth to mine and sucked, licking my lips and sinking her teeth into the pulp. "Much better."

This time she led us back. As we passed the room with the bigwigs, I saw two guys standing outside the door watching us. Trinity hadn't noticed; her focus was getting back to her post. The one guy seemed familiar. A friend of my parents' maybe, since he was around their age.

The door to the Stephens party had been opened. A silver-haired woman in a black and silver pantsuit reached for Trinity's hand. "It's time."

Trinity squared her shoulders and sauntered in.

I lurked in the doorway so she could see me when she had to start her dreaded speech.

The big reveal of the work was so touching to see. Both Stephenses holding hands and looking at it together; then he bent to kiss her cheek.

My girl didn't bother to hide her tears and that brought a lump to my throat. I loved seeing all aspects of this woman. I wanted what the Stephenses had—a love that had stood the test of time. And seeing how my woman had killed herself to make this happen, I knew there was a romantic streak in her that wanted this too.

Trinity kept her speech short. She tensed up when the party guests left their seats to take a closer look at the piece.

"Am I too late for the food?"

I looked at the guy who had approached. He reminded me of the ruddy-faced men I'd met in Sweden who'd lived a life on the sea and couldn't wait to share their fish tales. "They haven't served the food yet, as far as I know."

Then the guy did exactly what I'd expected. He launched into a diatribe about how long he'd spent in traffic getting here, blaming it on the bumbling fools in charge of urban planning. And the idiot sports enthusiasts. I nodded and made the appropriate noises while keeping my eye on Trinity. So far she seemed to be holding her own.

"Are you here as security?" the man demanded.

"No, I'm a guest." Pride wanted me to brag on my woman and her talent, but I refrained. I doubted I could be polite if someone made disparaging remarks about either one.

After bending my ear for what seemed an hour, he said, "Where's the closest bar?"

I pointed to the back of the room across from where Trinity stood. "On that side. I haven't seen what they're offering, but if they don't have what you want there's a club bar on the main floor."

He offered his hand. "I appreciate your help. I'd rather pay for one decent top-shelf drink than drink two or three freebies that are subpar."

I quickly dropped the guy's hand when I saw Trinity gesture to the door with her chin and hustle out of the room.

There weren't as many people roaming around in the hallway. "You did great." I pulled her in and kissed her forehead, despite her standoffish vibe. "What now? Do you have to stay around?"

"I think so. But I don't have to stay right in the room."

"Aren't you hungry?"

She placed her hand on her stomach. "I feel sick if I think about food."

"Maybe we should just—"

"Trinity?"

A man wearing a three-piece suit approached us. One of the men I'd seen watching us earlier. He was several inches shorter than me, with dark hair. He had the slick demeanor of a lawyer or a salesman. I shot Trinity a quick glance to see she'd gone motionless.

Jesus. This was not another asshole friend of hers like Ramon? Maybe he was an agent or an art dealer. Maybe this was the acquisitions guy who'd been invited to the Stephenses' party.

But as I looked him over, I had the feeling I should know him.

"Paul said he saw you."

"Good for eagle-eyed Paul," she said coolly.

"I'm surprised to see you. Are you here for a party?"

"Why are you here? Oh, let me guess. Glad-handing. It's that time of year again."

"I do what I can to help out." Then his gaze landed on me, checking out my long hair—I'd forgone the man bun tonight—my beard and my suit. "Aren't you going to introduce me to your friend?"

"Walker Lund, meet Robert Carlson." She paused. "My father."

Good thing I had an excellent poker face. I thrust out my hand and he shook it. "Sir."

"Lund. Related to the Lund Industries bunch?"

"Yes. Ward is my father. Do you know him?"

"I've been acquainted with your dad and your uncles for a long time." His eyebrows drew together. "I thought I saw

Monte earlier. Some kind of Lund Industries shindig going on you're here for?"

"Actually, we're here because Trinity revealed a commissioned art piece tonight."

Why did I feel her glaring at me?

"I can assume things are going well?" Robert said to her.

She shrugged. "I'm not starving or living in a homeless shelter, so yeah, everything is great."

I couldn't wrap my head around the fact this was the kind of relationship they had.

"Do you work in the family business?" Robert asked me. "I have a hard time keeping this next generation of Lunds straight, since there are so many of you."

"I'm not in business with my family. I own half of a construction company."

As soon as he heard "not in business with my family," he dismissed me and addressed Trinity. "Tell me about this artwork commission."

Trinity snorted. "Don't pretend to be interested for Walker's sake—or for mine."

"I *am* interested. A commissioned work is a big step."

"Yes, I'm aware of that. But it doesn't seem as if you're aware this isn't my first commission."

His look broadcast that he hadn't been aware.

"Is your family here stumping too?" Trinity asked with an icy coldness I'd never heard from her.

"Laura is."

"Of course she is."

"Bobby had a previous commitment. Kathryn spends most of her time in Boston with her fiancé, Meyer. You met him at the engagement party."

"I wasn't at the engagement party because I wasn't invited. As a matter of fact, I haven't seen Kathryn for ten years.

Bobby either. It's a lucky thing," she said with scorn, "that you had trusty Paul to pick me out of the crowd so you wouldn't be embarrassed after harassing some unsuspecting woman who isn't your daughter."

Stunned silence.

Enough. Trinity didn't need this on a night that was supposed to be a celebration.

Another suit approached the group. His beady-eyed gaze zoomed from Trinity to me, back to her. "Trinity. Nice to see you."

"Paul," was all she said.

Then Paul addressed his boss. "Sorry to interrupt, Senator, but they're ready for you."

He flashed me a smile and offered his hand again. "Duty calls. Been a pleasure to meet you, Walker. I hope to get a chance to say hello to your folks at some point tonight."

I could just nod. Now I knew why he'd seemed so familiar. I'd seen him on TV for years. I'd seen him glad-handing in person. I'd fucking *voted* for him.

After he disappeared into the "bigwig" banquet room, I looked at Trinity.

"What?" she said defensively.

"Why didn't you tell me that your father was Senator Robert Carlson?"

Nineteen

TRINITY

"*Former* Senator Carlson," I retorted. "He's been out of Congress for several years."

"That doesn't change the fact that not only is your father a two-term senator, he's CEO of Carlson Technologies. Which is in the top five of Minnesota's most successful family-run companies."

"So?"

"So?" His eyebrows went clear up his forehead. "You didn't think that was worth mentioning?"

"Nope."

"When you said you moved to the East Coast, you meant to Washington, D.C."

"Last time I checked, D.C. was on the East Coast, Walker."

"You know what I'm saying."

Being around my father brought out my combative side. "I told you I moved. I told you I was sent to boarding school.

I told you about going to college and finding my art groove. I told you all about me, which is what you wanted to know. But now you're giving me grief because I didn't award Senator Robert Carlson a starring role in the recap of my life. You want to know why? Because he wasn't in it." Something else occurred to me. "Since when do you have a mental dossier on Carlson Technologies?"

Walker bristled up, as if I'd insulted him. "I *am* on the LI board. Last year a division of Carlson Technologies tried to acquire a start-up tech company we'd been grooming. It turned ugly before Carlson finally backed off."

"Why are you looking at me like that? I have nothing to do with my father's business. I don't even know what Carlson Technologies does. I don't get dividends from it. I don't have a trust fund. I walked away one hundred percent when I turned eighteen. The only reason I could afford to go to college was because my grandma had set up a college fund. He paid for *nothing*. I owe him *nothing*. And I don't get why this is such a big deal to you. Weren't you the one who told me not to judge you by your family's name? Well, apply that here times about a thousand."

I hated the discord between us. We weren't speaking loud enough for anyone to hear us, but the hallway was not the place to have this discussion.

"Is this a private party? Or can anyone join in?"

A dark-haired guy in a custom-made suit and a leggy blonde stopped in front of us.

I recognized the guy from the pictures I'd seen online and he'd been at Flurry.

"I've been looking forward to meeting you." He offered his hand. "Nolan Lund. And this is—"

"Paris," she said haughtily.

I shook his hand but not hers. "Trinity Carlson."

Nolan's eyes narrowed. "Any relation to Senator Robert Carlson, who we saw walking through here a bit ago?"

"He's my father."

"You don't say."

"So, Paris, this is the third time I've seen you with Nolan. That's got to be some kind of record for both of you," Walker said in an effort to deflect.

But his comment annoyed her. "I hope Nolan is starting to realize I enjoy spending time with him." She cocked her head at me and then at Walker. "Is she another one of your projects?"

I said, "Excuse me?"

She deigned to look at me. "Evidently the Lund family gives Walker a hard time about always picking women who need fixing. A hazard of his job spilling into his personal life. He doesn't have a great track record—or so I've heard. But at least his failures make funny stories. Nolan had me rolling earlier with some of them."

It pained me to give credence to her claim, but Walker wore such a guilty expression my stomach bottomed out. All the stress from tonight—the unveiling, seeing my father, being at odds with the man I loved—wasn't enough of a burden. The universe decided to see how I toughed it out upon discovering I was the latest in a long line of fixer-upper girlfriends everyone in the Lund family joked about. That's what my brain homed in on.

Vaguely I heard Walker snap at Nolan, but it was just noise.

Nolan took off so fast Paris had to run to keep up.

Walker invaded my space and bracketed my jaw to tip my face up. "Don't listen to her. She's—"

"Right, isn't she? For whatever reason you've been drawn to train wrecks. Maybe you can't help yourself—you're used to fixing things for your family, so what's the difference if you end up doing the same thing for the women you sleep with?"

"Stop it."

"No. Please get your hand off me."

He retreated immediately, frustration evident in the stiffness of his posture.

Even though we were standing less than five feet apart, I felt the distance between us growing. When I turned away, I saw Ward and Selka closing in on us. I welcomed the distraction. It was easier to focus on Selka's attire and spectacular style rather than being mired in the spectacular crash and burn going on between Walker and me. Selka's cocktail dress, the color of twilight smoke, was made of asymmetrical layers of chiffon dotted with sequins. Her normally golden blond hair had taken on an ashier tone, which reinforced the unattainable Nordic goddess vibe. Her silver stilettos clicked on the marble as they approached.

Selka hugged me. "Congratulations. How thrilling for you, no?" Then her gaze flicked up and down my outfit. "Pretty. And not black like so many *arteests*."

"You look outstanding, Selka." I winked at Ward and he winked back. I'd forgotten how easy it was to slip into this polite social mask even when I was screaming inside.

"Thank you. It is fun, this slinky dress." Then she moved in to hug Walker. "I love seeing you in sharp suit—shows you as such handsome man. Why the dark face?"

"He's upset with me. I didn't know my father would be here tonight."

"Your father is here to support your art?" Ward asked.

I shook my head. "He's here glad-handing, which is what he does best."

Ward's gaze turned shrewd.

Before he spoke, Walker jumped in. "I see you put two and two together, Dad, and realized that Senator Robert Carlson is Trinity's father."

"I did not know this," Selka said.

Walker gave me a dark look. "Neither did I."

I pointed at his phone. "You have Google. That seems to be the way we discover new things about each other's families." Bitchy? Yes, but he deserved it.

"I didn't realize Robert and Laura had a daughter older than their son, Bobby," Ward said.

"Laura is not my mother. She married my father when I was three. After my mom died I went to live with them until I started college."

"We've dealt with Robert on and off for years . . ." Ward exchanged a look with Selka and aimed a strained smile at me. "I'm sorry we didn't make the connection."

"No one does. I'm used it. And being here when he's here . . . just reminds me how much I don't miss the 'How are you related to the senator?' bullshit I dealt with for years." I sent Walker a pleading look. "Now that you've met him, can you really blame me for exorcising him from my life and not wanting to talk about him?"

Walker opened his mouth. Closed it. I swear I heard him grinding his teeth. But he said nothing.

I needed to escape before something else happened—like a meteor hitting the building.

And karma laughed in my face when I heard, "Amelia?"

I didn't turn around. She'd come to me, if for no other reason than to see if I'd chatted up anyone important or if I'd lost the twenty-five pounds that she'd always professed would make me "such a pretty girl."

Laura glided up, wearing her standard uniform of a non-descript beige dress, allowing her to slip into the background so her husband could shine. She flashed me a quick smile, then checked everyone else out. "Your father said you were here. How are you?"

"Oh, you know. Keeping a stiff upper lip."

Selka moved in closer and demanded, "Who is Amelia?"

That startled Laura. "That's what we called Trinity when she was growing up."

"Why?" Selka asked.

Laura sent me a "Did you put her up to this?" look.

I could do nothing but watch as things deteriorated further.

"Did she ask for name change?" Selka demanded.

"No, but—"

"You are not her mother, yah?"

"I'm her stepmother."

Selka harrumphed. "You admire evil stepmother character in child's fairy tales? You think, 'I want to be that cruel woman,' and that's what you do?"

"No! Why on earth—?"

"Then explain to me this. You are *not* her mother. You did not get to choose what to name her at day of birth. So after her mother died, you just . . . decide to change her name? The one thing that her mother chose just for her? Poor child, grieving for her mama and you take her name from her too?"

Laura looked absolutely horrified.

"Congratulations for achieving goal of such coldness."

Selka faced me with tears in her eyes—not crocodile tears; she was genuinely distressed. She clasped my hands in hers. "I hate this for you, Trinity. I hurt with a mother's heart to witness such behavior to a grief-stricken little girl and see that cruelty continued for years without a thought or a care. You have kinder heart than I. You should've changed *last* name. You should've cut ties forever and become the orphan they made you feel." She pressed her cheek to mine and whispered something in Swedish. Then she blindly took the hand Ward offered and he led her away.

When Laura started to speak, Walker said, "Don't. Just go."

After she slunk away, he reached for me. And for the first time in our relationship, I recoiled.

"Trinity—"

"I . . . need some air."

"I'll come with you."

I looked at him. "No. I need a break from you too."

"Fuck that."

"Back off, Walker."

He held up his hands, surprised that I'd snapped at him.

I wheeled around and strode down the hallway with no idea where I was going, desperate to find someplace where I could breathe.

Spying a side exit, I pushed through the glass doors and ended up on a patio. With a bar.

Thank god.

As I waited in line, the night's events played on a continuous loop. Why couldn't I spiral into the blackout zone at will? Because I'd gladly let that vortex suck me up right now.

I told the bartender, "I'll have a shot of tequila. No. Make it two."

When I reached for my purse to pay, I realized I didn't have it. "Sorry. I don't have any cash."

Then I heard, "Put those on my tab, Bill."

I waited for the bartender to move so I could see my benefactor. When I realized who it was, I almost walked off without the tequila. "Did he have you follow me?"

"Nope. Been in here a while avoiding the Lund party."

I ducked around a couple and stood in front of him. He was a giant. And not one of those troll-like giants, but a titan.

A gorgeous titan. The pictures online didn't do him justice. When he smiled at me, I might've swooned if I hadn't seen Walker's smile first.

"You're Trinity."

"You're Jensen."

"Good to meet you."

"Same."

Jensen held up his lowball glass. I touched my shot glass to his. He said, "*Skål.*"

Oh, sweet fire. I needed that.

"Why'd you think I followed you? Are you paranoid or something?"

Strange response. "I thought maybe Walker sent you after me."

"Did you have a fight?"

"Sort of."

"That's why you're hiding from him?"

"I'm not hiding. I'm taking a breather from everyone."

"You do that a lot?"

I rolled my eyes. "What? Breathe? Why, yes, I do."

"Smart-ass sense of humor. No wonder Walker likes you."

Something was off with him. Was he drunk? "I get the feeling that you're reserving judgment on whether it's a good thing or bad that Walker likes me."

His handsome face remained blank. "What makes you say that?"

"I know Walker is close to his family, and I've already met Brady and Lennox, Annika, your mom and dad, Dallas and Nolan. And yet this is the first time you and I have met. So either you don't give a damn about your brother's life because you're so invested in your own, or you consider me a"—I refused to call myself a fixer-upper or broken— "drive-by."

"Have you ever been involved in one?" he said sharply.

"One what?"

"Drive-by shooting."

"Omigod, no!"

"Do you own a gun?"

"No."

"Do you enjoy setting things on fire?"

What the hell? "Of course not."

"Ever been arrested for trespassing at an ex-boyfriend's house?"

"No. I've never been arrested for anything."

"Not even speeding?" he said skeptically.

I shook my head.

"Do you drive a car?"

"No, I drive a damn donkey," I snapped.

But Jensen wasn't done. "Do you have anger management issues?"

"I'm starting to."

"How many cats do you have? And ones hidden in the attic because they're on Prozac *do* count."

Okay, he had to be drunk. Or high. "One."

"Have you ever been involved with a motorcycle club?"

"Yeah. Me and Jax Teller go way back. What is this, Jensen?" That's when I threw back the second shot. I waited for the burn to fade before I spoke. "Are you an asshole to all of Walker's girlfriends?"

He granted me an evil smile. "Just the crazy ones. But that describes all of them since he's magnetic north for chicks toting a whole bucket of crazy."

And he assumed I was like all the rest?

Aren't you?

I shot a paranoid glance over my shoulder to see if my stepmonster lurked behind me, whispering doubts into my ear.

Just then it hit me that I had plenty of those doubts these days even without her influence.

"So what's your damage? Daddy issues? That'd be new." Enough was enough.

"You don't have much faith in your brother. And that sucks. He's a good man, the most genuinely decent guy I've ever met, and I'm crazy about him. And if that makes me crazy, so be it."

I walked away. I wasn't going to take on the "Are you another crazy one?" burden because I shouldn't have heard any of the stuff Jensen had shared tonight. That was Walker's personal business and not fodder for casual conversation.

The Stephens party was still going strong. Two hours remained and then security would boot everyone out and lock the doors, so the piece would be covered up and safe until the teardown crew returned Monday to take it to the Stephens home.

I'd stashed my purse beneath a banquet table during my mini-speech and bent down to retrieve it. That's when I noticed the guy lingering by the first table. The same guy Walker had spoken to at length earlier.

He approached me, so I waited with a polite smile affixed to my face.

"You're the artist?"

"Yes, sir. You're a friend of the Stephenses'?"

He stared at the piece. "Mixed media is your preferred medium?"

"One of them. I'm eclectic."

"Meaning you haven't settled on a style. You're just throwing things up to see if any will stick."

"Maybe I work in a variety of styles because I'm good at all of them," I retorted.

"Touché. Where else do you have installations?"

Mediums? Installations? This had to be Dagmar Kierke-gaard. My nerves went haywire. My palms started to sweat. My chest got tight. I tried to act normal.

"You have no other installations?" he asked.

"I have a piece at the Federal Reserve."

"What's the theme?"

"War and the aftereffects, victims and violence."

"War," he scoffed. "Those pieces will be a dime a dozen in twenty years. Anything else?"

"A metal sculpture in the Marquette Hotel lobby. A lime-stone carving on the twentieth floor of the Wells Fargo building."

"Paintings?"

As Kierkegaard went down his list, I answered by rote. I could tell he thought my answers—my work—were sadly lacking.

"I'll be honest, Miss Carlson. You have talent. But it hasn't been honed, or maybe I should say *harnessed*, as it needs to be. One piece does not a career make . . ." He smirked. "Un-less it does."

Art school joke I'd heard a thousand times.

"You're not ready to have a piece in a gallery's permanent collection. And something like this"—he gestured to the piece—"would have limited potential even as part of a trav-eling exhibit."

"It's a commissioned piece, so the only place it's traveling to is the Stephens home."

"Well, we all have to eat, I suppose."

"Yes, elitism isn't accepted currency for art supplies, rent, health care and food. But wouldn't it be grand if selling one piece of art could sustain me all of my days? Then I would have plenty of time to brag about my singular accomplish-ment in whichever gallery deigned to hang it and I'd never have to lower myself to take another commission again. Oh, right. One piece does not a bank account make. Ever."

He looked me in the eyes for the first time and I saw annoyance. "Here's a professional tip. I don't care who you are or how much money you have or what your last name is. You cannot buy your way into respectability. With one piece or twenty."

"What are you talking about?"

"I was approached tonight and asked the going rate for a 'donation' in exchange for hanging some of your work."

No. No no no no. "I'd never condone that. I had nothing to do with that! I understand protocol, Mr. Kierkegaard."

"You should educate them on it, especially now that you know what it's cost you."

"Cost me?" I repeated.

"I don't like being bullied. Chances are very close to zero that I'll ever hang one of your pieces in any of the many galleries I represent. I'd say that your attitude toward artists who strive to make a difference with one piece was the final straw in my decision, but I'd made up my mind before you shared your opinion. I'll admit it was refreshing. Few are ever so brutally honest with me for fear of . . ."

Being blackballed.

He didn't have to say it. It wasn't a secret that if you ended up on Kierkegaard's bad side, you were screwed. It wasn't verbal bile that rose in my throat but actual bile. I was three seconds from adding insult to injury and barfing on this man's shoes.

I raced out into the hallway, but I didn't make it to the bathroom; I vomited in front of the door. Well-dressed people scattered. But plenty of them saw me leaning against the wall and apologizing to the janitor about the mess before I fled to the bathroom.

I hid in the stall, my mind in as much tumult as my stomach.

After I was relatively sure I wasn't about to hurl again, I left the stall and headed to the sink to rinse my mouth and wash my hands. I glanced up and saw myself in the mirror. I looked like a train wreck. And tonight the analogy fit because in one stupid, reckless moment someone had derailed my career.

Who? Walker? My dad? The stepmonster? One of the Lund family members? Something occurred to me—maybe Ramon had slipped in with the sole purpose of torpedoing my career.

You're reaching, Trinity. He's in rehab, remember?

With the way my thoughts were ping-ponging, I managed to focus on one thing: I wanted to go home. Immediately. But I didn't have a car. Dammit. I was stuck here. I hated being stuck places.

Talk to Walker. He'll take you.

My stomach churned at the very idea of talking to anyone. My mental shields were fried and I couldn't deal with even one more thing. I needed to go home and regroup. Tomorrow I'd ferret out the truth. Tonight was a wash and the last thing I needed was to stay and end up saying more of the wrong things.

Mind made up, I did the logical thing and called a cab.

In a daze, I wandered toward the front exit, praying no one saw me. I'd text Walker once I was in the cab.

But karma must've put a neon "Kick Me" sign over my head. The first person I saw was Walker.

He said, "Trinity?"

I kept walking.

Of course Walker followed me. "Where are you going?"

I whirled around and managed to keep my balance as his

soulful eyes searched mine. "I'm escaping what has become my own personal version of hell."

"What can I do?"

"Haven't you done enough?" I took a breath and back-tracked. "Did you do it? Throw your money and your family's name around? Offer to pay to have my work shown?"

"Sweetheart, you've lost me. Are you feeling okay?"

"Besides the humiliation of vomiting in public?"

"When did you get sick?" he demanded.

"It doesn't matter. I'm going home."

"Trinity—"

Jensen approached us and said, "What's going on?"

"I've had enough of tonight. Oh, and thank you for giving me the spiel about all the crazy women Walker has dated. I'm sure he appreciates you talking behind his back just like Nolan did."

Walker instinctively tried to step in front of me. "What is she talking about?"

"She had a couple shots and made a remark that tripped my warning bells. So I asked her a bunch of questions—"

"You grilled me like I was under arrest!"

"How would you know what that's like if you've never been arrested?" Jensen shot back.

"Why would you say that to her?"

"Because we both know she's no different than the rest of them except now she's got you acting crazy too."

Walker shoved him.

"Whoa. See what I mean? Don't deny—"

"Shut up. You know nothing about her, or about me, for that matter."

"Walker," Jensen said carefully. "That is crazy talk. Of course I know you, man. You're my brother."

Nolan stepped between them. "Take it outside."

Walker turned on him. "And you. Using my life as a punch line to make yourself look cool? Bravo. It fucking worked." His furious gaze flicked between them. "You've humiliated me. But worse, you've humiliated the woman I love and you're acting like it's nothing."

"Walker. Come on. We didn't know that you were serious about her," Nolan said.

"Yeah. I'm all too aware of the fact my life isn't worth keeping up on. None of you"—he pointed to Nolan, Jensen and another guy I assumed was Ash—"know dick-all about me anymore."

My stomach lurched at the raw emotion in Walker's voice.

Then he stood in front of me, blocking me entirely from their view, as angry and riled up as I'd ever seen him. His gaze tracked the tears on my face and the vomit on my shoes. "I love you and it's killing me you're dealing with all this crap on a night that's supposed to be a celebration for you."

"If you loved me, you wouldn't have hand-grenaded my career."

His head snapped up. "Why do you keep saying that?"

"I saw you talking to Kierkegaard. You offering to pay whatever it cost . . . well, that cost me everything. I've been blackballed from the galleries he reps."

"What? I would never . . . You know me. You know I wouldn't do that."

My phone buzzed, indicating my cab had arrived. "I don't know anything right now except my cab is here and I'm going home."

"Trinity. Don't go. Not like this. You're not thinking clearly—you're upset—"

"I'm beyond upset. I'm wrecked," I whispered.

"Let me take you home and we'll talk—"

I shook my head. "Not tonight. Can you please just let me go quietly without making an even bigger scene?"

Something in my eyes triggered his retreat. He said, "This is the only time I'll let you walk away from me, Trinity. Once your thoughts clear, you'll remember I'd never do anything to jeopardize your career. You'll remember this look on my face and know in your heart that it's fucking *killing* me to watch you go. You'll know I'm only doing this so you'll find your way back to me. To us."

Everything after that was a blur—mostly because I couldn't see anything through my tears.

WALKER

I kept my composure until Trinity disappeared out the front doors.

Then I geared up for the confrontation with her father—no way was that fucker getting away with this. No way. I wasn't without power of my own to throw around. I decided my fist in his face would be a good place to start.

I turned and stormed toward the door I'd seen Robert Carlson coming out of earlier.

A hand on my shoulder stopped me. Then Ash, Nolan and Jensen fanned out in front of me like gunslingers.

"Where are you going?"

"Not your concern," I said to Nolan.

"It is my concern if you're about to do something stupid."

"Move. Now."

Jensen said, "Dubbya, let's talk about this—"

"Don't you think you've said enough? And since when do you have time to talk? You haven't had time for the last goddamned year." My angry gaze encompassed Nolan and Ash. "None of you have. So I don't need this fake show of concern. This is my life and I'm dealing with this my way. Now move." I bumped both Nolan and Ash with my shoulders and I charged through their blockade; I knew better than to try to knock Jens down.

I pushed the door so hard it smacked into the wall when I entered the banquet room.

Everyone turned and looked at me. But I had eyes for one man.

Robert Carlson didn't meet me halfway. He waited like a king granting an audience to his subjects. The guy who'd pulled him away earlier remained at his side. But he was no real threat to me and he knew it. Still, he tried.

"Senator Carlson—"

"Former Senator Carlson," I corrected, as Trinity had done. "A word, please." I looked at his lackey and said, "Alone."

He started to sputter but Robert said, "It's fine, Paul. I assume Mr. Lund and I can have this . . . word right here?"

"Whatever."

Paul slunk off.

"So, son, what's on your mind?"

"I am not your son. And I'd like to know why you decided tonight, of all nights, to meddle in Trinity's career."

"I don't understand what you're getting at, Lund."

"I saw you go into the Stephens party. At some point you attempted to bribe the curator into hanging some of Trinity's work at the Walker. I know that you don't give a damn about art or you would've known that is not done." I stepped closer. "So was that your intent? To prove what a big man you are that you can destroy your daughter's career?"

"Destroy? That's a little dramatic. I merely informed the

man it would be financially beneficial to everyone. The visibility for Trinity—"

"Isn't as important as the visibility it would bring you, right? You get to pretend you're supportive of the arts because, hey, look—my daughter's an artist and I support her."

"I fail to—"

"Yes, you've failed her over and over again. Going behind her back? Total dick move, *Senator*."

"And you're so sure of that?"

"One hundred thousand percent sure. All the years she's struggled and accomplished everything on her own merit and talent doesn't matter because you suddenly decide Trinity has value to you? She hasn't needed you and hasn't wanted anything to do with you for *years*, which should be clear from the obvious slam of not using your last name in any professional capacity. That's when you stroll in and fuck up her career?"

He sighed wearily. "Fine. I'll contact the man and withdraw my offer."

I laughed. "Withdraw your offer. It was too late as soon as you made it. There are some things you cannot buy, and your attempt to do so put a black mark on Trinity's name for every gallery in the region."

"You have no idea the power my name wields, do you? I can have things back to the way they were with a few phone calls."

"I doubt it."

"But if not—" He shrugged. "Maybe she should see this as an opportunity to do something more substantial with her life."

"Substantial," I repeated.

"Did she tell you her IQ is 185? She could've attended any college and earned a degree worth something. Instead she chose . . . art." He shook his head. "What a waste. Just like her mother."

One punch, dead center on his smug mouth—that's all it would take.

"But perhaps . . . now that she's involved with you . . . she won't have to work at all. You have the means to support her since this 'art' phase likely won't pan out."

A red haze filled my vision. My hands were on his chest, pushing him back before my actions registered.

People surrounded us. Things were shouted.

But I heard only one voice. My father's.

He curled his hand over my shoulder and said, "Easy, son."

Robert straightened the collar of his shirt and smoothed his tie. "Ward. I'd suggest you keep a better eye on your son, but I understand he isn't under your purview at LI. So I appreciate you stepping in to stop him from making a big mistake."

My father gave Robert the nastiest look I'd ever seen from him. "That's where you're wrong. If he wants to take a swing at you, I won't stop him. I'm just here to hold his coat."

Robert's mouth fell open, but he recovered quickly. "Encouraging violence isn't something I'd expect from you, Ward."

"I've spent my life not giving a damn about anyone's expectations. If you ever fuck with my family again, I will bury you. And you know that is not an idle threat coming from a Lund. Understand?" He turned away and waited for me to do the same.

We'd almost made it to the door when I saw the stepmonster lurking by the buffet table. I said, "Hold on one second," and strode over to her to say my piece.

I expected Dad would try to lure me back to the Lund

party to decompress. My feet felt encased in cement. Ash, Nolan and Jensen were loitering by the door. Upon seeing us, they started to approach, but Dad shook his head.

Then he led me outside to the valet stand. "You driving that hot rod tonight?"

"Yeah."

"Not anymore. I've been itching to get behind the wheel of that baby."

"You want to tell me what's going on?"

Dad faced me and scrubbed his hand over his face. "You may think you need to track Trinity down and have it out with her tonight, but you need to let it go."

"Fuck that. I'm not letting her go."

"I didn't say let *her* go, son. I said let it go. Neither of you are in a place to have a rational discussion tonight."

"But I'm too damn restless to just go home."

He studied me. "How much have you had to drink?"

"One shot of tequila two hours ago." Had it only been two hours since my life had imploded?

"I'm sober too, so we're good to go."

"Go where?"

"The best places for man therapy. Let's hit the racetrack, then the gun range, and if we're still angry and restless after that, we'll spend time in the batting cage."

"It's ten o'clock at night. Are any of these places open?"

He smirked. "They will be for us."

"Dad. You don't have to do this for me."

"Who said I'm doing it for you?" He loosened his tie. "You're not the only one who gets pissed off at your brothers."

"But you never fight with Monte or Archer."

He laughed. "Wrong. Guess you'll learn some new things about your old man tonight."

I lifted a brow. "Mom is okay with this?"

Dad lifted a brow right back. "I don't need permission from my wife to spend time with my son. Especially when she understands I need this more than you do."

Not expecting that. Nor was I expecting the valet to hand my dad the keys to my car.

Dad grinned at me from behind the steering wheel. "Better buckle up, son."

Twenty

TRINITY

Monday morning when I showed up at the country club, I half expected Walker to be there.

I hadn't spoken to him since Saturday night. He hadn't tried to get in touch with me yesterday. If he'd called, I would've talked to him. If he'd shown up at my house, I would've let him in. In retrospect, I shouldn't have run away like I did. Every time I thought about the ferocity in his eyes and what he'd said right before I'd bailed, my chest ached, my throat got tight and I called myself ten kinds of fool.

In the banquet room, I scrutinized the guys Esther had hired as the takedown crew. Although this piece had been crafted on a chunk of fence, it was delicate. Earlier in my career I would've trusted the workers knew what they were doing and not interfered. But after a near disaster with another piece, I no longer assumed anything. I insisted on being on-site to ensure my instructions were followed.

What I was seeing didn't make me happy. "Whoa," I called out as I crossed the room. "Do *not* attach that chain there. You'll pull the wire too taut and the frame on the front side will pop out."

The guy holding the chain looked at me. "Who are you?"

"The artist. There's a hook on the back side. In fact, if you'd bothered to look, you'd have seen all of the hooks for stabilizing it are back there. Use them."

He said, "Yes. Ma'am," tersely.

Esther spoke to him before she approached me. "I'm glad you're here. I really wish I could've had the crew that installed it take it down."

"Me too." Thinking about how diligent Walker had been caused that pang of guilt. "So you've cleared a place in your home to display this?"

"Michael spent all day yesterday rearranging his home office. Then he decided to display it in one of the main living areas of the house. Our construction expert is coming over to figure out if structural changes are needed. He's used to our unusual requirements. We commissioned an Uhlman piece two years ago carved out of Minnesota limestone that weighs 12,000 pounds."

"I can't wait to see that. I love Uhlman's work."

"So that means you'll supervise final installation?"

I squeezed her arm. "Of course. I'm relieved Michael is so thrilled with the piece."

"We both are, Trinity. It's incredible. And easily the most personal piece we own. Thank you."

"Truly my pleasure."

Esther put her hand on her hip. Her gaze was on the workers, but that wasn't where her focus was.

Crap. Had these guys already broken something and she

was figuring out a way to break the news to me? "Esther? Is everything all right?"

"No. But I need to tell you something that might upset you."

My stomach tightened. "Okay."

"We've been friends with Dagmar Kierkegaard for years. Our love of art is a common interest, although we disagree frequently on style. I booked this venue for Michael's birthday as soon as I knew the piece would be ready. I didn't consider there'd be other events going on at the same time and I should have. This place was a zoo Saturday night."

"I thought security did a good job keeping looky-loos out of the room."

"Not all of them." She watched me closely. "You must've been out in the hallway when your father came in."

The knot in my stomach tightened. "My father?"

Esther set her hand on my arm. "Sweetheart, I know you don't broadcast the fact that Senator Robert Carlson is your father. In fact, I find it interesting that you don't use the Carlson name at all professionally. Anyway, Michael and Robert are acquainted, and when he ran into Robert, he invited him to the room for a drink. Evidently Michael was showing Robert the piece when Dagmar approached them. After making introductions Michael got called away . . ."

Leaving my father alone with Dagmar Kierkegaard.

"When Michael returned, he noticed Dagmar's agitation when Robert kept trying to get his attention, which Michael found odd. So I think something might've been said that had to do with you."

Guilt stopped my mouth from opening and spewing my tale of woe regarding Kierkegaard essentially blackballing me. I cringed, remembering how I'd believed, even for a moment, that Walker would've had any part in Saturday night's fiasco. Of all people, Walker understood what it meant to make it on your own, in your own time frame, on your own terms. Even if he had somehow mentioned me to Kierkegaard? It would've been out of love and pride, not for his own gain.

That's the only explanation for why my father had done something so stupid. I didn't for a minute believe he'd had an epiphany and decided to prove he supported—and acknowledged—me. Nor did I believe he'd done it out of spite; he'd simply never cared enough about me one way or the other to be bothered. No, former Senator Robert Carlson had seen an opportunity to make himself look like a patron of the arts—what better proof than to help showcase his daughter's work?

"Trinity? Are you all right?"

No. I needed to call the love of my life and apologize for being an idiot and pray that he'd forgive me. Again.

I shook my head. "I knew someone had spoken to Kierkegaard. He made sure I knew bribery didn't work and he added a black mark by my name." I swallowed hard. "I was upset and sort of . . . accused my boyfriend of doing it. Then we had a big fight."

"I imagine you did. But you are talking about the Lund boy who accompanied you?"

Lund boy. Except there wasn't a boyish thing about him; he was all man. "Yes."

Esther ran an agitated hand through her hair. "That pompous little prick."

Immediately I bristled. She had no right to say that about Walker. She didn't know the first thing about him.

She touched my arm. "I'm not referring to Walker."

"Oh."

"I've tolerated Dagmar because of Michael's friendship with him. But the man doesn't have a clue about what real art is or what it means." She looked at me, her eyes fierce. "You create because it drives you, but there has to be a balance between conceptualizing in private and commerce. Your work has to be *out there* in order for it to be noticed. If you're good, art lovers will buy your work and support you. Taking commissions allows you to make a living, which in turn might spur you to create a unique piece that appeals to curators like Dagmar. He's wrong. Take pride in the fact he's wrong a lot. Men like him are dinosaurs. The only reason he still wields any power is because people let him. He has no power over you. Remember that."

I hugged her and whispered, "Thank you." Then I stepped back and wiped my eyes. "After I had time to mull it over, I came to that same conclusion. It stung that Kierkegaard summarily dismissed the 'type' of art I love creating. While it'd be an ego boost to tell people I have a piece hanging in a prestigious gallery, I'm more proud of this creation since it's art that has personal meaning." I paused to admit something I'd been reluctant to give voice to. "I got sucked into the mind-set that only art in galleries and museums has value and the little projects I do are just filler. Not all art has to have the same value. I'd like to believe the person who buys one of my funky folk art pieces for a hundred bucks at the state fair loves it just as much as you do this piece."

I heard a grinding metal sound and turned to face the crew. Dammit, had they even listened? "Not like that! Even on the dolly all the weight has to be spread evenly across the back—nothing on the front."

An hour later the piece was on a truck headed to the Stephenses' house on Wayzata Bay. I supervised the unloading process and spoke to the structural carpenter about ceiling suspension versus wall attachment. So by the time I left, it was two thirty in the afternoon.

I checked my phone. No new messages or missed calls. My heart raced and my mouth went bone dry as I called Walker.

The call went to voice mail.

It went to voice mail fifty-four times over the next two days.

Part of me didn't blame him for ignoring me. Part of me was worried about him.

The worried part won out.

Thanks to Walker's insistence I pay attention to who signed my checks, I knew where to start looking to track him down.

Twenty-one

WALKER

'd just started to drift off for my second nap of the day when I heard two blasts of an air horn. It wasn't the lake patrol guys. They'd already been here once this morning to make sure I wasn't passed out drunk on the boat or I hadn't fallen overboard and they'd have to drag the lake for my body.

Cheery thought.

Four more annoyingly loud blasts sounded and the noise was getting closer.

Go the fuck away.

When the air horn didn't get my attention, the next thing I heard was a bullhorn.

"Prepare to be boarded. You will be assimilated. Resistance is futile."

Why'd they give the bullhorn to smart-ass Trekkie-like Brady?

A motor cut off. Something bumped the boat. Then it

pitched and swayed as several pairs of feet landed on the deck.

I opened my eyes and shifted in my chair.

Brady, Jensen, Nolan, Ash and Jaxson were on board, with a cooler.

"Little early for a social call. Especially since I'm not speaking to any of you ass-monkeys, so go the fuck away."

"It's not an early social call for you," Nolan said, ignoring the last part of my statement, "now that every day is one big partay since you're living the life of a boat bum."

Living. Right.

"Do you know how long you've been out here?" This from Brady.

"Without a word to any of us?" Jensen added. "Jase said you haven't been at work all week."

I raised a brow. "What do you care? I didn't see any of you assholes filing an itinerary with me when you went on vacation. But then again, you would've only let me know if you wanted me to water your plants." I sipped my water and tilted my head back, dismissing them all. "And yes, that *was* a shot at all of you. Now you know I'm still pissed, so get the hell off my boat."

"*Your* boat?" Nolan said. "It's joint ownership, so I can be on my half anytime I want."

Without lifting my head, I pointed to the front. "That's your half. This"—I made a box in the air, denoting the back half of the boat—"is mine. Respect my space. And try to keep it down."

My declaration was met with silence.

I heard chairs scraping and the hiss and pop of cans being opened.

"What should we address first? What happened with her?"

Don't you even say her name or I will lose my shit.

Jensen belched. I didn't have to look to know it was him. From the age of eight he'd made it a personal goal to belch the alphabet—a feat he'd accomplished by age ten. Funny that the Vikings PR department did not list that factoid on his stats sheet.

"At least he's not drunk," Brady said.

"How can you tell?" Nolan asked. "With the beard and the hair and his clothing he always looks like he's been on a bender."

Tempting to flip him off. I opted to ignore him.

"What's he been eating? The guy at the marina said he hadn't docked for two days," Nolan said.

"Maybe he brought a jar of peanut butter and a loaf of bread," Jaxson said.

"Think he's been catching fish and eating it raw? Do-it-yourself Minnesota sushi?" Brady suggested.

"I think he's totally lovesick," Jensen said, "and he's not eating anything—just drinking his own bitter tears."

"Nah. That'd be love-*starved*," Ash corrected. "And since I can see empty chip bags and beef jerky wrappers in the garbage . . . the boy ain't starving."

Then I heard someone rustling through the trash. "Jesus. There are candy wrappers everywhere," Nolan said. "He should have chocolate poisoning after eating all of this."

Jaxson said, "Check for empty ice cream cartons."

"Yep. Two. Fudge ripple and rocky road."

"Where the hell is he getting all this food?"

Let them try to figure that one out. I hoped my young fishing buddies were late with today's delivery.

"For Christsake, this is worse than we thought," Brady snapped. "Someone grab his phone and see if he's been watching sappy Lifetime movies."

Jensen sighed. "I'll do it."

"My phone is at the bottom of the lake." Not intentional. I dove into the water with it in my pocket and it slipped out. "But feel free to tie a rock around your leg, jump in and see if you can find it."

Silence.

"Walker—"

"Is this why you tracked me down? You get a huge laugh out of seeing how goddamn miserable I am?"

"We are not those guys."

"Yeah, you are."

"You think we enjoy seeing you like this?"

I let out a slow breath. "I don't care. So for the last time, get the hell off my boat. I've got nothing to say. To any of you." I plugged the earbuds hanging around my neck into my ears and flicked on my iPod.

I'd just started bobbing my head to "Lose Yourself" by Eminem when my arms, legs and torso were immobilized. My eyes flew open as someone removed my sunglasses and ripped my earbuds out. Then Jaxson and Jensen picked me up—in my chair—and set me down at the front of the boat in the blazing hot sun.

All five of them lined up in front of me like the Scandinavian inquisition.

"What the—?"

"Shut it or we will gag you too, you ornery jackass," Brady said in his "Don't argue with me" CFO tone.

I looked down and saw my arms and legs were tied to the chair with blue nylon rope. I didn't have a freakin' prayer of loosening the knots. "Which one of you is the kinkster with the rope fetish?"

Ash squatted down. "That'd be me. And I was an Eagle Scout, remember?"

"I don't give a damn. Untie me. Now."

"Nope," Nolan said with far too much cheer.

"Welcome to your intervention, bro," Jensen said.

I laughed. "*I* need an intervention? Why? I'm the most well adjusted of all of us."

"True. We all sort of laughed about the fact we'd probably never have to do an intervention on you because you have your shit together."

"So why am I here, trussed up and roasting in the sun like some B-movie plotline of mistaken identity?"

"Because this intervention is for us. We failed you," Brady said.

I looked from one face to another, shocked by their hang-dog expressions.

"So you need to listen to us."

"Like I have a choice? And is this really coming from you guys? Or from Mom?" Loved my mom, but dammit, I didn't want her pulling that "No fighting in this house—you apologize now" discipline like during our childhood, forcing us to say sorry when we didn't mean it.

"Actually, our dad approached us about it," Jaxson said.

Ash nodded. "Same with mine. Evidently Uncle Ward had words with his brothers Monday morning, how he was being ignored by them much like we'd been ignoring you."

The one good thing about Saturday night had been the time I'd spent with my dad. We'd been able to talk without interruptions and reconnect one on one. The cool thing was, it hadn't been one-sided—a father passing down advice to his son. He'd opened up to me about his struggles with his brothers and the family business. We'd parted ways at dawn with a better understanding of each other and a reminder that all relationships need tending—especially those taken for granted.

"That's why we're here. No more ignoring this or letting it fester." Brady gestured to Nolan. "You're up first."

"I've had my head up my ass for a while," Nolan admitted. "Last year after Brady's intervention, it didn't occur to me right away that if Brady was working less, someone else had to pick up the slack at LI. It was . . . embarrassing to approach Ash and admit I'd been screwing around. For the last eight months I've worked to become the executive I'd been pretending to be. My social life was sacrificed. Somehow you ended up getting sacrificed too, cuz, and I'm sorry."

Ash said, "I'm guilty of having a corporate mentality—letting others handle the small things and I step in only as a last resort. I applied that to family stuff too and that's pretty cold. I'm making a conscious effort to change that." His eyes narrowed. "As far as my little sister? You've gotta stop rescuing her. I won't apologize on her behalf, but I'll apologize for being so damn oblivious this last year to the shit she was pulling."

I hated this pouring-out-feelings-and-spilling-your-guts crap. If they hadn't tied me up, I would've already jumped overboard.

That's probably why they tied you up.

But they weren't done.

Brady ran his hand through his hair. "I went through major life changes last year. I wouldn't have found the love of my life if not for you all kicking my ass. But finding Lennox didn't mean I had to lose what I already had. I pretty much blew all you guys off all the time to be with her. I won't lie; my wife is my priority now. I just have to remind myself it doesn't have to be all or nothing." He smirked at me. "So fair warning, prepare to get your ass handed to you, little bro, since I'm reinstating our workout schedule."

I flashed my teeth at him. "Bring it."

"Jens, you're up," Brady said.

Jensen looked at me and then aimed his focus across the lake. "I'd rather take a beating from the entire Broncos defensive line for three hours than talk about this stuff. But here goes. No surprise I'm gonna make this about me. In the last few years I've resented the expectations of being present at every Lund family gathering. Didn't anyone realize I have a life, friends, women, teammates that are way more important than these stupid family things? So I figured if I did my time at the Lund compound, none of you had the right to expect anything more from me outside of that." He snorted. "Talk about self-absorbed. But since we're doing this, I'll say the last year has been the loneliest of my life. None of my great new buddies know me like you guys do. Being with them is all about the partying, usually with me picking up the check. I realized during training camp that I was looking for something with these guys that I already had and I oughta be thankful for what I've always taken for granted." His gaze met mine. "Sorry, Dubbya. You've been there for me without fail and I'm gonna figure out how to give it back to you." A gleam entered his eyes. "Let's hug it out now, bro."

"You touch me and I'm—"

"It's not like you can get away." Then the smart-ass hugged me, while Brady, Nolan and Ash argued about who got to be the next to hug the "man of the hour."

Assholes.

I'd really freakin' missed them.

"And last but not least . . . Jaxson?" Brady prompted.

"At first I was feeling cocky, thinking I'm the least guilty in this situation," Jaxson said. "But then it hit me that I'm probably the worst of the lot because I don't know what's been going on with you in the last two years. What really made me feel like crap was when Mimi asked me why you were so quiet and I gave her some lame-ass answer because I didn't know. But she said it's probably because no one listens to you anyway."

There was a punch in the gut.

"We've all got our dramas and traumas. But through it all? We had this." He gestured to the six of us. "Our folks had a lot to do with forcing that to start with, but we formed this family bond out of choice. We've always had each other's backs. And even if one person is flailing, there are seven other members of this family to offer a hand and pull you back in. It sucks balls that we all assumed someone else was taking care of it with you, Walker. I'm speaking for all of us that we won't make assumptions about that again."

Silence stretched as they all stared at me, waiting for me to say something.

"Guess it's my turn, huh? I'm glad you all pulled your heads out of your asses. If this happens again, I won't wait so long to call you out on it. Fair?"

"That's fair."

"Now untie me. I can't feel my damn arms."

That prompted Jensen to break out into a chorus of "Can't Feel My Face."

Brady told him to shut it. Jaxson started singing along.

Ash started to untie me, but Nolan said, "Wait. He might go ballistic when we bring up the Trinity thing."

My head snapped his direction. "What about her?"

Nolan said, "I tracked her down and tried to apologize to her."

"You *tried* to apologize?"

"She said that you were the one I owed the apology to, not her, for violating your trust and being a first-class douche canoe—whatever the hell that is. And she's right. I don't know what possessed me to make cracks about your dating history to a chick like Paris. But I promise you it was just that one time. It wasn't like I've always been talking trash behind your back. Seriously, sorry. Total dick move."

"Put me in the 'tried to apologize' category too," Jensen said. "She went off on this tangent about me not having a right to judge crazy because everyone has some craziness in them. Then she talked about never painting a person or a situation with a wide brush or you'll just end up painting yourself into a corner. Does that make sense?"

An artist's analogy? That made my heart twist. I missed her so damn much. It'd been hard as hell staying away from her—that's why I'd spent the last three days on my boat. She needed to come to some realizations on her own or this would never work between us.

"So, uh, yeah," Jensen started. "I said some stupid shit to her that she did let me apologize for. I thought I was looking out for you the way you do for me, but I botched it. No surprise. Sorry."

"I did a dumbass thing last year, talking out of turn to that woman Lennox used to be friends with. I have a different perspective seeing it from the other side." I looked at Brady and he nodded. "Now we all squared away? So you can untie me?"

Ash undid the knots fairly quickly. As I tried to get the circulation going again, they loaded the cooler onto their boat and prepared to leave.

"We would stay and shoot the shit with you for the rest of the day," Brady said, "but I figured you wouldn't be sticking around after I relayed this last bit of information from Mom."

"What?"

"She decided to have your piano delivered this morning."

"Jesus. Why? That thing has been in storage for years."

"No idea, but when she was leaving, Trinity showed up at your house. And—" He and Jens exchanged a look.

"And what?" I demanded.

"Not *and* what. You should be asking *with* what. Evidently she had a sledgehammer. And a cat."

"You're joking, right?"

"Nope."

I had no idea what Trinity was up to, but I needed to find out ASAP.

Jensen said, "Dude, word of advice from someone who's recently hugged you? You need a shower before you race off to deal with your not-crazy girlfriend and her pussy."

Nolan high-fived him.

I flipped him off and pulled anchor.

Twenty-two

TRINITY

I was in the living room of Walker's house when the door blew open and he stormed inside.

Finally.

"Trinity! Where are you?"

"I'm right here."

Walker stopped five feet from me. His hair was wild. He was sunburned.

He was the best thing I'd ever seen in my life.

"What are you doing here?" he demanded.

"Waiting for you."

"Why?"

This time, my rambling stream of consciousness wasn't random words I'd struggle to remember. I had had days to plan out exactly what to say to him. "To apologize for running out on you. To grovel for being an idiot and believing for one second you had anything to do with trying to buy off

Kierkegaard. As soon as I got home I realized the situation had my father's handprints all over it."

Walker didn't move. He waited, patiently, like he always did.

"I'm here to tell you that you are the most amazing man I've ever met. You get all the weirdness and neurosis that is me and yet you prove time and time again that you like me anyway." Now that I'd reached the hardest part, I swallowed with difficulty. "And yes, I knew it killed you to let me walk away. But you did it anyway. You are the strongest, most self-assured man I've ever known. You believed in this—in us—from the start even as I kept unintentionally trying to derail this with my actions and my words. You knew earlier Saturday night before the storm hit that I loved you, but I was too afraid to say it. You let it go when you should've demanded the truth from me. I regret that so much. It wrecked me when you snapped at Nolan about how he'd humiliated me, the woman you're in love with, because I could see that it gutted you for me to find out that way. And yet I never doubted that you meant it. But even knowing that? Saturday night as I stared at the ceiling, miserable and alone, I told myself I didn't deserve you." I stomped over to him and got right in his face. "But you know what? Fuck that. I deserve you and you deserve me, a woman who loves you with everything she has, who will always give you her all. I love you, Walker Lund, more than you can ever possibly comprehend, so I will spend the rest of my life proving it to you. You will know every minute of every hour of every day how much I love showing you how completely you belong to me. And—"

Walker's hands cradled my face, his mouth landed on mine, not to stop the flow of chatter but to show me how profoundly my declaration had affected him.

He shook so hard I clutched him tightly to quell his tremors, proving I was strong enough to be the one who anchored *him* for a change.

The kiss slowed from full-flown passion into tenderness. Sweetness. With maybe a little relief thrown in. When he released me, I burrowed my face into the crook of his neck, grateful the warmth and scent of his skin filled my soul.

"Trinity."

"Let me just stay like this for a minute."

When the minute was up, he shifted back to look at me. "I love you."

"Yay me!"

He laughed. "Not the reaction I expected, but oddly enough I have come to expect that from you."

I gave his smiling mouth a smacking kiss. "What else is on your mind? Because the smile doesn't hide the clouds in your eyes, babe."

"Your father is an asshole."

"Uh, *yeah*. I told you that." I poked him in the chest. "You should listen to me about that kind of stuff. Wait. Did you talk to him again?"

"I wanted to let my fists do the talking, but I refrained. He tried to play off bribing Kierkegaard as an honest mistake that his 'name' could fix." Walker splayed his fingers around the back of my neck and followed the arc of my jawline. "I hate that he did this to you."

"I'm not being flip when I say I'm used to it. It's a perfect example of why he's out of my life, Walker."

"I get that now. And I'm sorry for being a jerk about you not telling me, even though you should have. From here on out, we share all family stuff, okay?"

"Okay. Speaking of . . . Annika the PR whiz might've

created a silver lining out of the Kierkegaard situation. When your mother told her what happened, she was outraged, mostly because she hadn't been there."

He frowned. "Now that you mention it, I never asked why Brady, Lennox and Annika weren't at the LI shindig."

"Because Annika was at the hospital with them. Evidently Lennox got really sick and Brady freaked out. He hauled her to the ER and called Annika, who immediately showed up and jumped to the conclusion that Lennox was pregnant. Which pissed Lennox off, because she's not pregnant; she just had food poisoning. But thankfully Annika didn't call Selka with the news she might be a grandma because can you imagine how mad your mom would be if that was yanked away from her?"

Walker stared at me with the oddest expression.

"What?"

"You're in the Lund family gossip loop now."

I grinned. "Isn't it great?"

His slow-blooming smile was a thing of beauty. "Yeah, babe, it is."

"Anyway, Annika has created this whole PR campaign for me. 'Trinity Amelia's artwork is deemed too edgy and controversial for local art galleries' or something along those lines. She claims my work will be even more in demand. Isn't that crazy?"

"Very." Walker lowered his mouth to mine, kissing me with the seductiveness I'd grown to crave. As much as I wanted to surrender to him, I also knew that once we were in his bed we wouldn't leave it the rest of the day.

I forced myself to break the kiss.

He growled. "Come back here."

"You're distracting me."

"That's the plan. I plan on distracting you to the point you don't know your own name."

Gulp.

Walker whispered, "It's time to fuck and make up."

"Umm . . . don't you mean 'kiss and make up'?"

"Nope. We're starting a new tradition."

My mind blanked.

And the sexy man kept it blank for the next three hours as he proved just what an awesome tradition it was . . . four times.

I kissed Walker's damp pectoral and attempted to roll to my side of the bed.

He clamped a big hand on my ass and said, "Where are you going?"

"To the neutral zone. We need to finish talking."

He sighed.

I disentangled from him. "I need at least five feet between me and your lips during this discussion."

"You get five minutes to say what you need to. Then my lips are gonna be back where they belong."

"Where's that?"

His wicked smile caused my heart to trip. "All over you."

Swoon.

He sat up and glanced at the clock on the nightstand. "Meter is running, babe."

"All right."

"Hold up. First, you want to tell me why you showed up at my house with a sledgehammer and your cat?"

And about twenty cans of paint. But he hadn't seen that yet. "How'd you know about that?"

"Mom told my intervention crew—my brothers and cousins—that showed up at the lake today."

"That's where you've been the past few days? Chilling at the lake?" I kicked myself for not thinking of that.

"We do our soul-searching in different places. On the water is mine."

"Since I couldn't get ahold of you, I brought everything with me, including Buttons. You know, as a sign I was here to stay."

"That cat is in *my* house?"

"Ah. I think so. I haven't seen her since the piano delivery guys were here. Anyway, I didn't bring a sledgehammer. It's a rubber mallet for the paint can lids because I found my next project."

"Which is . . . ?"

"You."

That blue-eyed gaze hooked mine.

"I mean, your house. I'm painting the living room and then we'll buy real furniture. After that, I'm working on the kitchen. Since you own a restoration company, I assume you can get the staircase updated and redo the big window and alcove up on the landing before I start up there."

"How long will that take?"

"Years, probably. So you'd better get used to—*eep*!" Walker plucked me up and settled me on his lap so we were face-to-face.

"Is this your way of moving in with me?"

"This is my way of telling you I love you and I want this to be *our* home. So let me do that for you. For us."

He rested his forehead to mine. "That sounds like heaven, having you here with me, in my life, in my bed every day for the rest of our lives."

"Well, I will have to go back to my place to work since

that's where my studio is, but I'm sure most nights I'll make it back here—"

"No. You will be with me *all* nights. I'll build you a brand-new studio on the back corner with all the bells and whistles and whatever you want in it."

"But that'll take time and I can't not have a studio for a few months."

"Fine. We'll move into your house while the renovations are being done and your studio is being built. Then, as soon as it's finished, we'll move back in here and sell your place." He kissed me twice. "Because now that I have you, sweetheart, I ain't ever letting you go. I've been waiting for you . . . for what seems like forever."

"Same goes. You don't think . . . this happened too fast?"

"What? Falling in love? Or us moving in together?"

"Both, I guess."

"No, baby. It happened when it was supposed to happen. When we both needed it to happen."

There was my sweet, sweet man. "So no regrets about me kissing you in the bar that night?"

"None."

"I was thinking it'll be a great story we can tell our kids someday."

"Babe. I love the way you think."

SEE HOW THE NEED YOU SERIES BEGAN
WITH LENNOX AND BRADY'S STORY IN

What You Need

AVAILABLE NOW FROM SIGNET.
CONTINUE READING FOR A PREVIEW.

One

—

LENNOX

"What's *he* doing in our department?"

I glanced up from my computer, knowing even before I saw the suit at the end of the hallway who garnered the reverent tone from my coworker Sydney. I had the same reverence for the man; however, I did a much better job of masking it.

"Oh hell, here he comes. How do I look?" she whispered.

"You know the only thing that matters to him is if you look busy."

Sydney smoothed her hair. "Lennox, lighten up. And ignore me while I busily and silently compose sonnets to that man's everything, because he is the total package."

I laughed—longer than I usually did. "Go for it, Syd. I'll just be over here, you know, doing my *job* while you're waxing poetic about him." I returned my focus to spell-checking my notes from this morning's meeting. I knew I had a misspelled or misused word, but I couldn't find the damn thing.

"Wait. He's stopping to talk to Penny," Sydney informed me.

I felt a slight sneer form on my lips. Of *course* he's stopping to talk to Perky Penny—she hadn't earned that nickname from her disposition. Even I couldn't keep my eyes off her pert parts—which she kept properly covered in deference to the dress code at Lund Industries. But I knew that given the chance, she'd proudly display them as if she worked at Hooters.

Wouldn't you?

Nope. Been there, done that.

Sydney muttered and I ignored her, hell-bent on finding the mistake. I leaned closer to the computer monitor, as if that would help. *Ah, there it is.* I highlighted the word in question. Had he meant to say disperse? Or disburse? And was there enough difference in the definitions to warrant a call for clarification?

Without checking the dictionary app on my computer, I said, "Sydney. You were an English major. What's the difference between *disperse* and *disburse*?"

"*Disburse* means to pay out money. *Disperse* means to go in different directions," a deep male voice answered.

I lifted my gaze to see none other than Brady Lund himself, the CFO of Lund Industries, looming over my desk.

Outwardly I maintained my cool even as I felt my neck heating beneath the lace blouse I wore. I picked up a pen and ignored the urge to give the man a once-over, because I already knew what I'd find: Mr. Freakin' Perfect. Brady Lund was always impeccably dressed, showcasing his long, lean body in an insanely expensive suit. He was always immaculately coiffed—his angular face smoothly shaven, his thick dark hair artfully tousled, giving the appearance of boyish charm.

As if a shark could be charming.

My coworkers and I had speculated endlessly about whether the CFO plucked his dark eyebrows to give his piercing blue eyes a more visceral punch. And whether he practiced raising his left eyebrow so mockingly. For that reason alone I avoided meeting his gaze.

Okay, that was not the only reason. I didn't make eye contact because the man defined hot, smart and sexy.

But he also defined smug—half the time. I wanted to ask if he job-shared with an evil twin, but I doubted he'd laugh since he had no sense of humor, from what I'd heard.

Aware that he awaited my response, I said, "Thank you for the clarification, Mr. Lund."

"I shouldn't have to clarify that since you've worked here for—what, ten months? Financial terms should be familiar to you by now."

He was chastising me? First thing? My mouth opened before my brain screamed, *STOP*. "I've been employed here for almost a year, actually. And, sir, I'll remind you that just because the office temps department is located on the sixth floor—one of the five floors that are the province of the financial department—we floaters don't specifically work *only* for the Finance department at Lund Industries. We also float between Human Resources, Marketing, Development and Acquisitions, as well as Legal."

"Explain what you mean by *floaters*."

"You had absolutely no idea that our small department exists, let alone what we do, did you?" I said tartly.

I heard Sydney suck in a sharp breath next to me. "What she means is that since as CFO you have an executive assistant and don't normally utilize the services of the office temps—also known as *floaters*—you wouldn't personally be aware of the breadth of our responsibilities," Sydney inserted diplomatically. "Our department is supervised by Personnel."

"Indeed. Then, please, enlighten me on which department you're transcribing that document for?"

"Marketing."

"Mind if I take a look?" Then he sidestepped my desk and sidled in behind me.

My body went rigid as he literally looked over my shoulder. I wasn't as disturbed by the thought he might see something I had done wrong as I was by his close proximity. His *very close* proximity, since I could feel the heat of his body and was treated to a whiff of his subtle cologne.

He put his hand over mine on the mouse and murmured, "Pardon," as he completely invaded my space. I didn't move because it'd be my luck if I shifted my arm and elbowed the CFO in the groin.

Three clicks and two huffed breaths later, he retreated. "I apologize. I understand your confusion. Marcus in Marketing misused the word. It should be *disburse*. Nice catch."

"That's my job."

"Since it's a formal request, Marcus will have to correct it before you can pass it on to Legal. If you'll give me the original paperwork, I'd be happy to drop it off in Marcus's office on my way to my meeting."

"Thank you, sir, for the offer. But company protocol requires me to deliver the paperwork directly to Marcus— Mr. Benito."

His shoes were so silent I didn't hear him move. One second he was behind me; the next he stood in front of me. "A real stickler for the rules, aren't you?"

"Yes, sir." I finally met his gaze. "With all due respect, how do I know this isn't some sort of performance review pretest?"

His lack of a smile indicated he wasn't amused.

But I didn't back down; I needed this job. It was the first job I'd ever had where I wasn't slinging drinks or scrubbing toilets. Besides, the CFO—of all people—should be aware of the rules.

"Bravo, Miss Greene—sorry, that's an assumption on my part. Or is it Mrs. Greene?"

"No, sir. Ms. Greene is fine. But I prefer to be called Lennox."

Then Mr. Freakishly Perfect bestowed the mother lode of smiles; his lush lips curved up, his dimples popped out and the lines by his eyes crinkled. "Well, Lennox, please see that Marcus—Mr. Benito—is aware of his error before day's end, because I *will* follow up on this."

"Yes, sir."

He nodded and started down the hallway.

I clenched my teeth to keep my jaw from dropping. Not just from the weird interlude, but because the man looked as good from the back as he did from the front.

"Holy shit," Sydney breathed after she was sure he'd gone. "What was that?"

"No idea."

"Lennox. He knows your name."

"Of course he knows my name. It's right here on my desk." Working as a floater meant my nameplate went everywhere with me, but on the days I was at my desk I usually didn't bother putting it out.

Aren't you glad you bothered today?

"Come on. He was fishing for information on whether you were single."

I groaned, hating that Sydney wouldn't let this go. "So, now he knows . . ."

"Maybe he'll ask you out," she said with a drawn-out sigh.

"Maybe you should put some of that creative thinking into your report," I retorted, and got back to work.

BRADY

"Jenna. Could you come in when you have a free moment?" I didn't wait for my admin to answer. I just poked the intercom button off and spun around in my chair. Not even the forty-fourth-floor view of downtown Minneapolis held my interest.

Restlessness had dogged me the past several months. I kept waiting for it to abate, for something to occur that required my full focus. But nothing had happened either professionally or personally. I just continued to drift along, waiting for . . . what, exactly?

Your life to begin?

Jenna knocked twice and walked in. Why she bothered to knock escaped me; there was no pause between the knock and her entrance. One time when I asked her why she knocked first, she said her Midwestern upbringing was too ingrained to just barge in. I warned her that someday she might barge in and find me in a delicate situation. She'd retorted that if I actually took the time to do something bad, raunchy or out of character, she deserved to be the first person to witness it.

"You rang, sir?"

Sir. Jenna refused to call me Brady. It was "sir," or "boss" or "Mr. Lund." She'd been my admin for two years and I spent more time with her than with anyone else in my life.

When I was newly minted in my position as CFO, I'd equated her using my first name as a sign of our professional intimacy, whereas she saw using it as a sign of disrespect since she had fifteen years on me agewise.

"Yes. Forgive my ignorance, but how closely do you work with the office temps—the floaters?"

She sat in the high-back leather chair across from my desk. "Not often. If you've got a large presentation that requires assembling reams of paperwork, I'll ask for assistance. But they're usually spread so thin down there it's just easier to get Patrice to help out."

Patrice. She was my admin's secretary, which gave Patrice the false impression that she was somehow *my* undersecretary. And Patrice had made no bones about how much she'd like to be under me.

"Why do you ask?"

Because there's this prim blonde I'm hot for who intrigues the hell out of me. "I ended up down on the sixth floor and publicly showed my ignorance about what the term *floater* means as well as what the office temp job entails."

Jenna's eyes widened. "I imagine that went over well with their department."

"Not so much."

"What were you doing down by Personnel? Are you looking for a new secretary, boss?"

"I'll get you any secretary you want if you'll send Patrice packing," I said dryly.

"No deal. She's still afraid of me. Once she loses that fear, she'll slack off and I'll replace her."

"So that's how it works with you and your minion. I wondered."

"Back to the floaters. Did you find them lazing about or something?"

"No. And can't someone come up with a better term for their department than *floaters*?"

"If you want to be technical, sir, in the past that group of employees used to be called the 'secretarial pool.' They're permanent office workers who temporarily float to any department where additional help is needed, hence the term *floaters*."

"I still don't like it. Anyway . . . am I really that out of touch with this company that I didn't know about the existence of an entire group of employees?"

"First of all, boss, the number of employees working for Lund Industries in the Twin Cities is over five thousand—fifteen hundred employees work in this building alone. You don't know the minutiae of the dockworkers' jobs any more than you do the floaters in the office temp department. That doesn't make you out of touch. It makes the managers in those departments effective, because they're not coming to you with personnel problems."

"You should've gone into diplomacy."

"It's my job to remind you of yours—you cannot do it all and know it all, sir, though you are determined to try." She smirked. "There are some people in this company who claim the floating crew of office workers concept is outdated and they're proposing Lund do away with that department altogether and outsource temporary help when needed."

"From your tone, I take it you don't agree?"

Jenna pointed at my computer. "We have an IT department. They go to whatever department they're needed in. I don't see how the office temps are any different. Like with IT, it's important to keep hiring new secretarial workers because they're trained with the most recent technology."

"You've given this more than just a passing thought."

She shrugged. "My executive assistant title means 'secretary with more responsibilities at a higher wage,' so the office workers, floaters, secretaries—whatever you prefer to call them—are my sisters in arms. I get defensive when their abilities or importance is questioned."

Usually Jenna was so even-keeled. Her brittle attitude alarmed me, so I needed to keep a closer eye on the situation with her *sisters in arms*, regardless of whether it was my job. "Where'd you hear these rumors about disbanding the temp workers?" I held up my hand. "Forget I asked. I know you won't reveal your source. But I would ask, if you do hear anything else, that you let me know so I can make sure Personnel handles it fairly." I disliked Anita Mohr, the head of Personnel. Human Resources fielded more issues involving her than all other employees in this building. But she was my uncle Archer's pet, so she had a weird immunity.

"Will do." Jenna stood. "That was all you needed to talk to me about, sir?"

"Yes."

"Then I'll remind you there's a meeting at three in the boardroom." She paused after opening the door. "And Maggie seemed really excited that your father has some kind of big opportunity for you."

I gave Jenna an arch look. "As my admin, the least you could do—"

"Huh-uh, boss. You're on your own with the craziness that is the Lund Board of Directors. Buzz me if you need anything else."

I glanced at my watch. Even for a Friday, it was too early to start drinking.

ALSO FROM *NEW YORK TIMES*
BESTSELLING AUTHOR

LORELEI JAMES

What You Need
A Need You Novel

As the CFO of Lund Industries, Brady Lund is the poster
child for responsibility. But eighty-hour workweeks leave
him little time for a life. His brothers stage an intervention
and drag him to a seedy nightclub . . . where he sees her:
the buttoned-up blonde from the office who's starred in
his fantasies for months.

Lennox Greene is a woman with a rebellious past, which
she conceals beneath her conservative clothes. She knows
flirting with her boss during working hours is a bad idea.
So when Brady shows up at her favorite dive bar and
catches her cutting loose, she throws caution aside and
dares him to do the same.

After sparks fly, Brady finds that keeping his hands off
Lennox during office hours is harder than expected.
Though she makes him feel alive for the first time in years,
a part of him wonders if she's just using him to get ahead.
And Lennox must figure out whether Brady wants her for
the accomplished woman she is—or the bad girl she was.

Available wherever books are sold or at
penguin.com

facebook.com/LoveAlwaysBooks

31901059830382

S0651